Acclaim for the Debut
of Richard VINE!

"Suspenseful...sets the intrigue of pulp fiction against the decadence of New York's downtown art scene."
— *The New Yorker*

"A taut, impeccably plotted debut."
— *Monocle*

"A labyrinth of deceit and greed...in the tradition of the best of pulp fiction, at once thrilling and disturbing... *SoHo Sins* is Richard Vine's entry into crime fiction. The debut marks him out for classic status."
— *The Daily Mail (UK)*

"*Soho Sins* is the perfect emblem of the excellence of its publisher, Hard Case Crime, which has carved out a leading place in the recent hardboiled revival."
— *USA Today*

"A terrific addition to the pulp tradition...a wonderful blend of high art and low-down deeds."
— *The Millions*

"Built masterfully...[a] powerhouse debut."
— *Criminal Element*

"Plumbs the depths of the human heart...Truly impressive."
— *Maxim Jakubowski*

"Rarely has a first novel shown such confidence in its prose and such insight into its characters and setting. You'd swear it was the work of a seasoned novelist with national renown."
— *Bookgasm*

SOHO SINS

by Richard Vine

A HARD CASE CRIME NOVEL

A HARD CASE CRIME BOOK
(HCC-124)
First Hard Case Crime edition: July 2016

Published by

Titan Books
A division of Titan Publishing Group Ltd
144 Southwark Street
London SE1 0UP

in collaboration with Winterfall LLC

Trade paperback edition ISBN 978-1-78565-573-9
E-book ISBN 978-1-78329-929-4

Design direction by Max Phillips
www.maxphillips.net

Typeset by Swordsmith Productions

Printed in the United States of America

Visit us on the web at www.HardCaseCrime.com

To my own true Melissa —Wong Kit Yi

Every work of art is an uncommitted crime.
—THEODOR ADORNO

SOHO SINS

I

I slept rather badly the first few nights after Amanda's murder. Once I heard the story of how her body was found, twenty-four hours following the shooting, I walked alone from the Odeon to my Wooster Street loft, chilled through by the dampness. For warmth, I stood at the sink and drank a shot of Glenfiddich before going to bed. The whiskey helped me to nod off quickly, but my mind came alert again just before three AM, chanted awake by the refrain of "Philip and Amanda Oliver." That was how the art world had celebrated my friends for years, their names run together like the scientific term for a rare, vanishing species: the SoHo conjugal pair. On the donor lists of countless arts organizations, among the lender credits for major exhibitions, embossed on museum-opening invitations, sparkling from the lips of Park Avenue hostesses: Philip and Amanda Oliver— Phil and Mandy, or sometimes just "P and M" to their close friends and would-be intimates.

For all their glitz, the two had taken good care of me, in their nonchalant way, after my own wife died in Paris. They talked casually about Nathalie, as if she were still waiting for me back in the twelfth arrondissement, while the three of us traveled relentlessly around Europe together, dropped in at the couple's various residences to recoup briefly, and later attended a ludicrous number of exhibition openings in New York. I don't know if it was a proper form of mourning; we didn't have much practice with death in those days. Mandy's style was to lunge ahead. She and I would often leave Philip behind—stuck with his intercontinental calls and glowing computer screen, making the high-tech money that made everything possible—while we went off to the latest cultural site or soirée. Maybe things got a little stickier between us all than they should have, a bit too Bloomsbury for this aging American lad, but the couple gave me back my manhood—or whatever is left of it. For that I was deeply grateful, a fact that only added to the damned annoyance of thinking about Philip's mental ruin, his betrayal of their marriage, and now Amanda's wretched death.

To prepare for the blank hours ahead, I took two 10-milligram Ambiens and chased them with another scotch. When I tried to go over our shared life chronologically, nothing would stay in order. Anyway, it would be hard to say exactly when Philip decided to dump his second wife. "Eight years with one woman, Jackson," he said to me once. "You have no idea."

Actually, he was wrong about that. Even though I had not confined myself to anything so quaint as "one woman" during my own term of marriage, I recalled that the motives for domestic rupture are minutely cumulative, a Chinese torture of minor irritants and small, exasperating quirks—a bill left unpaid, a pillow moved to the wrong side of the bed, a black hair coiled on the bathtub soap. Every spouse keeps a running catalogue of capital offenses, a book of poisonous hours. And what does anyone, to say nothing of a man with Philip's appetites and financial means, do about the temptations? Mandy—rich and free and lithesome, his "Upper East Side gypsy"—had spirited him away from his first wife, sweet Angela, just a year after the young Brit gave birth to their daughter. Then, six years later, Mandy in her turn became an encumbrance.

The trouble began with an image. Philip's first sight of Claudia Silva (or, rather, of her sleek, ample anatomy) was via a photograph in *Flâneur* magazine. Taken from behind, it showed the young painter in pink vinyl pants, her hips cocked, as she— with the viewer—surveyed a canvas at her second solo show at

Patricia Knowles Gallery in Chelsea. The painting was a tangle of quasi-pornographic S-curves afloat in a limbo of monochrome white. The photo's accompanying paragraph reported that the artist, a recent School of Visual Arts graduate, was the daughter of a well-known Italian museum director. As a champion of figuration and juicy brushwork, she considered herself—at 26, with pictures selling at $35,000 apiece—an embattled outsider, suffering critical and financial neglect from an art establishment preoccupied, for the moment, with video experiments, lame digital imaging, and installations of household detritus. Her life, meanwhile, consisted largely of all-night parties in Williamsburg and "self-educational" trips to biennials in Venice, Havana, and São Paulo. "I need to know what's happening globally," she said—a sentiment no doubt shared by the sophisticated readers of *Flâneur*.

For Philip, flipping through the high-gloss pages of the magazine on his way to JFK, the first challenge—something that always roused his virility—was simply to see Claudia's features. From the backseat of his town car, he called me at the gallery, using my private number.

"Save me from torment, compadre. Do you know this new SVA comer named Claudia Silva?"

"I do. Since she was on her papa's knee."

"Well, she's not a kid anymore, in case you hadn't noticed. What's the scoop—is her art as good as her ass?"

"You won't know which to grab first."

"Don't be too sure." He seemed to weigh the options for a long moment. "Can you arrange a studio visit?"

I laughed. "Have you forgotten who you are? Just name the date. It's a poor artist's dream."

"Let's keep it low-key, shall we?" He broke into a phony daytime talk show voice. "I just want to be loved for myself."

"Great, Philip. Isn't that why you have a wife?"

There was quiet at the other end for a moment. "You figure that one out, old chum, you let me know."

I waited, not wanting to let him off that easily. "There must be something you like about matrimony," I said. "You keep getting into it."

"I do, don't I?" He sounded sad and amazed. "From Angela to Amanda, nineteen years spent with the two of them."

"You could do worse."

"I could," he admitted, "and I probably will. But right now, I just want to do different. My life is half over, Jackson. There's a whole lexicon of women out there, and I've barely made it through the A's."

He'd been talking that way for months now, ever since the modern and contemporary auction at Sotheby's, where Mandy, in a rush of subtle excitement, had waved her bid paddle once too often. The couple had agreed to stick to contemporary work and not to exceed $500,000 for the evening, or $100,000 on any individual lot. But with choice pieces from the Steinberg collection hitting the block one after the other, Mandy got carried away by the twirl of the turntable, revealing delights in succession like coffee-shop cakes in a rotating pastry case. A Robert Longo drawing, turn, an Alice Neal portrait, turn, a collage by Ray Johnson. Finally, a prime example from Ian Helmsley's "Bad Blood" series did her in. She'd drunk three glasses of champagne at the private viewing, and now was gaily amused by the play of auctioneer Todd Simon's blue eyes, and by the clandestine thrill of coming up against an unnamed bidder on one of the three onstage telephones. (Philip, for his part, suspected the caller was a shill for Helmsley's own dealer, upping the ante to keep the reputation—and unstable prices— of the AIDS-stricken artist at an acceptable market level.) The bid hovered at $98,000 for a moment, already an auction record for the 36-year-old painter, then went to the caller at $102,000, before Mandy signaled yes at $106,000 and Simon announced it going once, twice, and sold, with the crack of his palm-sized rapper, to the astute Mrs. Oliver, number forty-three.

Afterward, Philip threatened to call his good friend Walter Heinz and ask him, as chairman of the international firm, to void the sale on some technicality. Mandy, however, was having none of it. She reminded Philip, loudly, in front of several friends gathered for a last drink downstairs at the Bid, that she bought art with her own goddamn money—funds that her father had released to her when she turned twenty-one, long before she ever laid eyes on Philip; wealth that her grandfather had wrung out of the coal fields (and obdurate coal miners) of Western Pennsylvania. Philip accepted the put-down with a modest shrug, saying to his friends, "Amanda, last of the Wingate dynasty," in much the same way that Mandy once sighed and laughed and passed off his mounting affairs with a sharp, falsely light "men are animals."

Every marriage is a mystery, especially to its victims, yet this much I knew: Philip would never truly have left Mandy while she lived. All their repeated separations and reconciliations, all their legal maneuverings, were a kind of sport. In reality, Amanda was life itself to him. Once Melissa was born, an overwrought Angela, no longer so sweet, harped on Philip's familial responsibilities; Mandy just laughed, and taught him to play. Later, when she and Philip were both burned out from openings and benefit dinners and parties, she would wave the back of her hand in the air and say, "We'll sleep in another life." So they plunged on, transported fluidly by their driver, to the next radiant event. The booze helped, as did Mandy's yellow-and-white pills, but mostly the Olivers seemed to subsist on pure money; it affected them like nuclear fuel. Even when Mandy had her bout with cancer, the pace never slackened. They threw themselves, together, into her treatment regimen—chemo, diet supplements, positive imaging, cardiovascular exercise—as though it were all a street carnival in Trinidad.

"You can find beauty in anything, Jack, if you look at it intelligently enough," Mandy said one night. She had just been freed from her hospital regime, and we were all sitting, very drunk, in a corner booth at Jean Georges. She quickly raised her blouse, revealing a stitched slash, a raw and puckered absence over her heart. "How smart are you?"

After three years, Amanda recovered, and seemed perpetually on the verge of going off to wade in a fountain somewhere. But no one much wants to see a woman with one breast and a thickening midsection, her dress soaked, frolic drunkenly in the Trevi waters. Age was the one enemy Mandy couldn't laugh into submission, not after Philip's eyes began to follow every coltish waitress who strode past with a cocktail tray. Indeed, her best-friend-and-husband made Claudia his public lover soon after Mandy's cancer went into remission. While she rested near Edgartown, Philip romanced the girl in private Manhattan dining clubs, at European art fairs, and in the fields and hot evening bedrooms of the Dutchess County enclave where his nonprofit trust housed its artist residency program. It was not one of his prettier episodes.

2

Once I sobered up the next morning, a question kept coming into my head. What is the normal way to react to the violent death of your spouse? Maybe there is no proper answer, really. Only the stunned queer things we do automatically, because they seem expected—or, if not expected, inescapable—when the pain is new. Philip, as soon as he discovered his partner's body jumbled and blood-soaked in a living-room chair, walked into the local police station and offered a benumbed self-indictment: "My name is Philip Oliver, and I believe I murdered my wife."

That expression of grief might have seemed a little strange in other parts of town, but all this occurred south of Houston Street, back when SoHo was the new-art capital of the world. Though I am sure of few things in life, I am willing to bet that a dozen far more peculiar events took place in the neighborhood that day. They just weren't tied to any official crimes.

In my gallery a few days later, I got a call from Hogan, who was already at work on the case.

"You're good buds with this Philip Oliver, right? The husband?"

"Sadly, yes."

"How well do you know him?"

"Well enough to sell him second-rate paintings at first-rate prices. We're like brothers."

There was a brief and indefinable noise at the other end. "Are you trying to be a hard-ass about this?"

"Maybe, I've had some pretty good lessons, thanks to you." Then my tone changed. "Philip and I have been close for half my life. How would you like me to behave?"

"You could deal with it straight. Meanwhile, just remind me to stay out of your old-pal category."

"Too late, Hogan. But don't worry. You won't be buying any Lucio Fontana monochromes on your lousy pay."

"No, not if my luck holds out." The line crackled for a moment. "Screw you, Jack. And screw your money, too."

As you can probably tell, Hogan and I go back a long way. We were restless boys together, bumbling through adolescence in a small town upstate. Eventually, a few years after hitting the city at eighteen, we went very different ways—myself to the Institute of Fine Arts and the gallery business; Hogan to the Marines and, after the war, to the New York Police Department. Now he works as a private investigator.

"So do you think this crazy-man act of Oliver's is for real?" he asked.

"It's been going on for two years."

"Sure, but is the guy clever enough to fake it that long in order to throw us off him as a suspect?"

"I thought he confessed."

"That's right. Marched into the First Precinct out of the rain, went straight up to the intake counter and started blathering. McGuinn led him inside, and the rich fool signed a statement. Thing is, his story rambles all over the place, and half the details don't match what the cops found at the crime scene."

"What did they find?"

"This Amanda, his wife—she was a friend of yours, too?"

"Of course."

"A good-looking woman?"

"For her age."

"Then you don't want to know."

I waited. Silence, I learned long ago, is Hogan's principal form of mercy. In his line of work, he has a lot to keep mum about.

"She was shot in the back of the head with a couple of soft-nosed slugs," he said finally.

"Twice?"

"At a slight downward angle. The bullets flattened and blew out through her forehead and left cheek."

"All right, I get the picture."

"I could show you the photos, but I don't think you'd enjoy them."

Something inside me seemed to falter and drop. Against my own wishes, I thought about Mandy on the warm fall night I watched her, her sharp bones flashing as she danced with the white-haired raconteur Victor Borge, after a dinner party at the Danish consul's apartment on Fifth Avenue. The lights had been lowered, and we could see the dark treetops of Central Park beyond the stone rim of the balcony. Windows in the far high-rises glowed yellow, like heirloom gold, above the thick black branches. I pictured Mandy again in that ivory silk dress, laughing at the old man's jokes as she danced, her green eyes welling with tears—and then I tried not to think about her delicate face anymore.

"What do you say?" Hogan asked. "Is her husband slick enough to plan something like this two years in advance? Could he be pulling a stunt like 'the Chin'?"

I'd almost forgotten about Vincent Gigante. When I first moved to SoHo, the aging mob boss used to shuffle through the downtown streets in a bathrobe and slippers, mumbling nonsense to a "caretaker." The big idiot charade, intended to throw off the feds, cast Gigante as mentally incompetent, too crazy to command the highly profitable Genovese syndicate he was actually running from a social club in the Village.

"Philip is extremely vital," I told Hogan.

"Meaning?"

"He built his company from nothing, from an old warehouse

in Queens, in twenty-five years. Now he's got his own little fiefdom, O-Tech, a new-media spinoff of his father's rust-belt enterprise, Oliver Industries."

"So he had a head start."

"It wasn't that easy. The old man was self-made, a nobody, and as tight as a virgin. Philip took his MBA from Wharton, where he learned a bit—very painfully—about social privilege. Afterwards, he played possum at Sunrise Components for five years, until the morning he breezed in, holding a majority of stock proxies, and took over the business."

"Sounds like a man who makes plans," Hogan said.

"Guile is part of his charm. When he wanted to beat out Palo Alto Consolidated, he spent three years buying their top execs away one by one, then fired the lot of them on the same June day, once he'd picked their brains clean."

"Right. I got a lot of tales like that in my chat with Bernstein yesterday. So, tell me something I don't know."

"Philip is a terrific art customer, a truly generous man—and capable of just about any degree of cunning you care to imagine."

"Or maybe he's genuinely loony," Hogan said. "He's got a medical file a yard deep that says so."

"But medical opinions can be bought?"

"With his dough, he could buy the whole New York hospital system."

"You want me to talk to him?"

"Just tell me how he seems to you now. Lots of people put on a good act, until the bodies start to bleed. Then sometimes they get antsy, maybe fall out of character. It takes someone who knows them well to spot the crack."

"Anything else?"

"Yeah. I want you to go over to the Prince Street apartment with me. Don't worry; Mrs. Oliver's body is long gone. I need you to tell me if anything seems to be missing, if the physical setup looks off. You know the place pretty well, don't you?"

"I leased it to Philip and Mandy eight years ago. I've been there countless times since."

"Good. See you in half an hour."

Occasionally, I wonder why I let myself get pulled into helping Hogan. But if it weren't this complication in my life it would be something else, probably less respectable. That's the tradeoff. Keep yourself occupied, or you might end up examining your own acts and desires—a decidedly unappealing prospect.

Then there's the equity thing. To tell the truth, Hogan didn't have such a brilliant career as a cop. His old Homicide Department partner, Tommy McGuinn, was a drunk who spent most of his workday hours "gathering background" in bars. Hogan, whose tolerance for orders and rules had gone haywire after two years of Marine combat, was stuck with the street duty, the paperwork, and the covering up for McGuinn. It all soured him, understandably. Hogan still tries, in his way, to follow orders and rules—those of the Catholic Church at least—but no longer the regulations of the NYPD. One night in an alley, he had to shoot a drug-addled Honduran teenager to save McGuinn's life. He quit the force the next morning. These days, as an independent investigator, Hogan is far from prosperous but at least he answers to no one but his clients and himself. It's a professional condition we share.

"How come they don't have Philip in custody?" I asked.

"One word. Bernstein."

That must have shaken up the day room. I myself had come up against Joel Bernstein, Philip's personal lawyer, back when we were thrashing out the terms of the Oliver lease—or rather when Bernstein was thrashing me like a wheat stalk in a twenty-foot combine. His firm was famous among my real-estate pals and art clients for beating taxes, fleecing ex-spouses, merging companies that didn't particularly want to be merged, and even providing counsel before government subcommittees. Bernstein didn't ordinarily handle criminal cases, but Philip Oliver was no ordinary client. Over the years, with his vast entrepreneurial dealings, he had become Bernstein's golden retirement fund.

"This Oliver guy may or may not be nuts," Hogan said, "but he sure had one lucid moment when he called Bernstein from the precinct. The big gun himself was down there in about five minutes and practically bitch-slapped McGuinn. Holding a distraught husband without a shred of physical evidence, just because the poor, shocked spouse—a man with a certified brain disorder—had babbled some nonsense after coming home to find his wife with her face blown away. Brutal, outrageous— and maybe grounds for a full-bore harassment suit."

"I can just hear him."

"Anyway," Hogan said, "thanks for turning the lawyer-king on to me."

"You can thank Philip, really. He had Bernstein call me, asking if I knew an investigator who could make his way around SoHo. I lied and said you were an old hand."

"Well, I do know you. It's like having a second brain."

"Yes, such as it is."

Linking him up with Bernstein was one of the many small favors I had traded with Hogan. Given my means of livelihood, I feel the need for a little virtuous activity now and then. Tommy McGuinn, out of guilt and gratitude, does the same. But there was more to it this time. This time I was personally involved. Amanda was my friend; Philip was my friend; even Philip's long-deserted ex-wife, Angela, was my friend. I resented that crime had contaminated one of my buildings, that death had intruded on my private domain.

I had already heard a lot about the murder in a general way, of course. The art world buzzed with it all weekend after the Olivers' cleaning lady came in that Thursday afternoon and found Mandy's body askew in an armchair. One glance at the corpse up close and the old Polish lady ran out, all a-jabber, to wave down strangers in the rain-smeared street. By then Philip, still wet from a muttering walk, was making his incoherent confession at the police station a few blocks away.

Within hours, rumors were going around the galleries and museums. Not since Ana Mendieta went smash out a Mercer Street window and Carl Andre became suspect number one had there been such division. Back then, the debate was whether the up-and-coming Latina's death was a drunken accident or an act of jealous rage by her big-name Minimalist husband. With the new case, there was no doubt about the nature of the event, only about who squeezed the trigger and who most wanted Amanda Oliver dead. The story hit the evening news broadcasts, of course, and got major play in the Friday papers. Heiress art collector murdered. Wayward husband has microchip empire, progressive brain disorder, 28-year-old Italian girlfriend.

Ironically, Philip also had a solid alibi, which everyone was paying attention to except him. At openings and dinner parties the talk was all about how he couldn't have killed Mandy in New York while he was away on a business trip in L.A.—a scenario that several associates were willing to swear to and that, presumably, airline and hotel records could confirm. Even returning on the early-bird flight, as his travel voucher specified, he wouldn't have gotten home until about twenty-four hours after the killing.

Hogan, as usual, had his own take on things. He didn't especially care if Philip was guilty or innocent. As a private eye, he simply owed Bernstein solid information; the lawyer could do with it what he pleased, even ignore it if it didn't help his case. The most useful findings, though, were clearly those that could counter the police theory of the crime. If the cops were going to go after Philip—questioning his actual whereabouts, delving into his private life and his potential motives—Hogan wanted to be there first, doubting the client now in order to save his ass later.

3

I asked Hogan about the L.A. business trip story when he picked me up at the gallery and we started to walk north on Greene Street.

"Might mean something," he said. "Might mean nothing."

"Like the medical records?"

"You got to figure that an operator like Philip Oliver could get just about anything he wants, just by asking. Or even easier. This guy, he's paying big salaries to a bunch of corporate suck-ups who like nothing better than to please the boss. Now for a long time, maybe, old Phil has been in the dumps. He's got a new girl, sure, but he can't really be with her the way he wants, because the old lady would take him to court for half of everything he's worth. So maybe Philip slips one day and says to some flunky, 'God, I wish that damned bitch would just disappear.' Maybe he doesn't even have to be that specific. Maybe he just complains a little too often, a little too loud, about how Amanda is a giant goddamn drag on his life. About how, sometimes when she really pisses him off, he dreams of walking into the apartment one day to find her gone for good."

"But he did love her, in his way," I said. "I've known the two of them since they met at Bernar Venet's loft here in SoHo years ago. Sure, I was with Philip a few times when he played around—at the last FIAC in Paris, or whatever. But that doesn't mean he'd have Mandy killed."

"You'd be surprised, Jack. People do some pretty awful things to get rid of partners who hold them too close, too long. You ought to know."

The May afternoon rain had turned to a fine, whispering mist. "I suppose so," I said, "if I let myself think about it."

We walked in awkward silence for a moment.

"SoHo," Hogan said. "You'd think with all the art deals being done down here they could get some decent asphalt on the streets."

My friend is not particularly sentimental about 19th-century cobblestone roadways and cast-iron facades.

"Relax, Hogan, you'd never be happy in this neighborhood."

"Is anyone?"

I turned up the collar of my raincoat. "A lot of people seem to like it. Historic shells, long open floors, thin interior columns. Great for lofts, galleries, fashion boutiques."

"Spare me your real estate pitch."

"Anyhow, it's moody in its way, don't you think?"

Hogan grunted his response. "Sure. Most of these buildings were sweatshops, weren't they?"

"You could put it that way. Some of the galleries still are."

"Your buddy Philip has his own sweatshops in Asia. Kids with thin, nimble fingers cutting silicon circuits for pennies an hour. And he deals with a lot of tough freight haulers to get his products shipped cheap. For some of his dad's old-school cronies, a fat contract with Oliver Industries could be worth a courtesy hit, a little lethal favor among friends. Maybe that's what the O-Tech ads mean when they brag about 'global reach.'"

I did my best not to hear him. You can't deal successfully in art if you dwell on where the money comes from and how it gets made. I concern myself with my clients' tastes and credit ratings, not their ethics.

We turned onto Prince Street and made our way past the sidewalk vendors selling jewelry, stolen art books, incense, and fake designer handbags. Their tables, piled with goods, were wrapped in sheets of plastic as they waited in vans or doorways for the soft rain to pass. At the corner of West Broadway, I waved Hogan into the stainless-steel elevator and keyed the top floor.

"Look," he said as we rode quietly up the eight floors, "it wouldn't even have to be that complicated. Who actually saw Philip in L.A.? Some hotel flunkies who wouldn't know him from Adam—just the name on the credit card. And the business meeting? One plant manager with stock options, who depends on Philip for every knee-sock his kid wears to soccer practice and every hope he's got of paying someday for UC Berkeley. The plane ticket could have been used by any dutiful yes-man with a passing resemblance to the boss. And frankly, to my eye, these corporate types all look alike. That leaves your pal Philip completely covered, if he decided to stay here and take care of some messy business at home."

The elevator opened directly onto the Oliver apartment, where spare, angular furniture caught the light from two walls of windows. Ahead, we could see the long slash of West Broadway and the trees below Canal and then, rising beyond a smattering of Tribeca buildings, the white, immensely tall Trade Towers partially lost in the clouds of a low sloppy sky. On our right, the apartment's west bank of glass, dulled by its anti-UV glaze, looked out over rooftops thick with wooden water tanks, clustered halfway to the Hudson.

I didn't care for the feel of the Oliver place in this rain-gray light. Still, everything inside was the way I remembered it: a Corbusier pony-skin chaise longue, a Bendtsen sofa, a Mies coffee table, four Breuer "Wassily" sling chairs in chrome and black leather, a tall Noguchi floor lamp made of white paper.

I went over to the switch panel. "OK?"

"Sure," Hogan said.

I twisted two knobs and the track lights came up, throwing the paintings—a Kline, a Pollock, two Rauschenbergs, a Johns, a Warhol "celebrity" portrait of Mandy—into vivid, irreverent color. Hogan stared briefly at a Giacometti sculpture by the zinc-and-lacquer bar.

"And I thought *you* were thin," he said.

"It's a piece personally selected by Mrs. Oliver," I told him. "Poor Mandy never saw a modernist cliché she didn't love."

It must have given her some comfort, when everything else in her life was disrupted and marred, to surround herself with the safest forms of radical art. Once the split came and Philip turned up in public for the first time—flagrantly—with Claudia on his arm, Amanda went immediately to her lawyer and laid claim to the SoHo loft and its blue-chip contents, saying Philip could take his collection of works by "emerging" talents and his little Wop artist-cunt (if I recall her words correctly) and haul them all to some unheated walk-up in Brooklyn for all she cared.

Of course, none of that kept Amanda from taking her man back every time he stumbled home or from putting on a good act for the family court judge, so that they could continue to have visits from Philip's preteen daughter, Melissa, beloved by them both.

"Cruise around," Hogan said. "Tell me if anything seems strange."

I went first into the kitchen area, a 20-foot-deep alcove of pearwood cabinets and sweeping granite counters anchored by a Viking stove and a chrome refrigerator that could have serviced a five-star restaurant. The appliances were spotless from lack of regular use, since Mandy and Philip did not keep a full-time cook in the SoHo pied-à-terre. This was their "bohemian" get-away, after all, where Mandy could play at art patroness while Philip was at his midtown office, knitting the world together with fiber-optic cable and piling up his millions. On the far side of the wall was the exercise room, stocked like an upscale spa with resistance machines, a treadmill, and a StairMaster on which Mandy was forever striving, Sisyphus-fashion, to climb her way back to a lost youthful figure.

"Try this," Hogan called. He was standing by the Eames lounger and ottoman, rotating the chair slightly from side to side. "This is where she took it, you know." I glanced down at the assemblage of bent cherrywood and black leather that itself resembled a semi-reclining body. There was a blood smear on the headrest and, below, a much larger stain on the kilim.

"No, I didn't know."

"Sit in it. Go on. Everything's dry now, and the police techs have been all over the place for two days."

I eased myself into the shallow leather pocket, Mandy's favorite resting place. Here she would read art books by herself in the afternoon, or lean back, hooting, waving a vodka gimlet, when someone amused her at one of the couple's parties. From that perspective, I saw the whole stretch of living space gradually merge, through the west windows, with the troubled sky over the rooftops. Behind me, I knew, was the corridor to the home office and the two matching bedrooms.

It was all strange, from my point of view. The deep stillness, the emptiness of the place, Mandy bleeding and dead. Meanwhile, Hogan moved through the white-cube spaces, among the sleek furnishings, like a bird dog in corn shocks, his bald pate glinting under the track lights. His shoulders were hunched with the old compelling intensity. I could feel his mind working from across the room.

"She was sitting like you are now," he said, "with her back to the hallway. Whoever shot her came from behind and leveled a nine-millimeter at the center of her skull. You see what that means, don't you?"

Yes, it was clear. Either she didn't realize the person was there at all—a sneak intruder—or else it was someone she knew well and trusted, maybe someone she expected to come and lay a hand on the nape of her neck and massage all the day's tension away.

"Which reminds me," Hogan said. "How come, with all this premium merchandise on the premises, there's no doorman, no security camera?"

"That's the way the tenants want it. Casualness is part of what we're selling here. The hip downtown lifestyle, you know. SoHo cool."

I didn't bother telling Hogan that Philip, acting through Bernstein, was a relentless negotiator, even with me. By my calculation, there was no sense wasting money on a door staff and closed-circuit video for an eight-flat where rent from the best apartment was locked in for a decade, with small biannual increments, at ten percent below market rate.

"Besides, when evidence crews don't leave the floor open, it takes three separate keys to get in here—one for the outer door, one for the elevator, one for the loft. Nobody enters by chance. As for street-level security, I'm sure stores on the block have cameras. Maybe some of the bars too."

"A lot of good that did Mrs. Oliver." Hogan glared around at the empty apartment. "All right, Jack. Take a stroll through the rest of the place. See if it speaks to you."

4

I knew what to expect in the back of the Oliver apartment. The first bedroom was Mandy's, a low, wide room with two walls of walk-in closets and a platform bed flanked by cube-shaped tables, one still stacked with monographs on Matisse, de Chirico, Miró. A door, standing open, gave onto the mirror-lined bathroom with a sunken marble tub. I went through, glancing at the racks and shelves of scented unguents, and opened the opposite door into Philip's bedroom. There was nothing much to see, just an extra-wide bed under a black coverlet, two recent issues of *Artforum*, and the thin plasma screen of a wall-mounted TV.

The far door, I confirmed, connected with Philip's office, a dim room aglow with computer monitors that Philip had left behind and Amanda had never turned off, flickering their bright, ever-changing Oliver Industries screensavers. Beyond that was a small room, stuffed with posters and randomly strewn CD cases, where Philip's daughter stayed sometimes on weekends.

I took the corridor back, passing the suite of Kandinsky prints that were Mandy's first proud purchase of high-modernist art. Ahead of me, Hogan's thick shoulders and sleek head, perfectly illuminated, floated above the chair back as he reclined in the Eames lounger. I slowed down and treaded softly, stepping as the killer might have stepped, while I watched Hogan survey the living room. Soon I would be close enough to pat his bare dome.

"Tell me what you think," he said, swiveling the chair unhurriedly around to face me.

"I think you make a pretty good target. Although, I have to admit, it would be a lot easier to shoot you from the back."

"Why do you suppose Mrs. Oliver didn't hear her assailant the way I heard you?"

"Well, it might be because of this." I went to the east wall and pushed a button on the Bang & Olufsen unit. A Philip Glass choral piece filled the room with insistent violin strokes and bleating voices.

Hogan listened for a while, looking a bit like a human version of the RCA Victor Dalmatian.

"If she played that very often," he said, "I might shoot her myself."

"Maybe Mandy did hear someone, but had no reason to worry, no reason to turn."

"Nothing's been disturbed in the place?"

"No, nothing. Just me."

"You'll get used to it."

That seemed unlikely somehow. It was more than just a matter of imagining, too vividly, what had happened at that juncture of corridor and open space. Something was off in the apartment itself. There were no signs of ransacking or theft, not so much as a broken wineglass. Yet the very normalcy of the environment felt bogus, as though the rooms were sworn to unwilling secrecy, the designer objects longing to reveal some rude, unspeakable truth.

"Tell me about Philip's mistress," Hogan said.

"That's an awfully prim term for a girl like Claudia Silva."

"Yeah, I'm an old-fashioned guy. Do you know her?"

I walked over to one of the Wassily chairs and sat down facing Hogan. His expression told me he was ready to take all the time necessary.

"Philip asked me to make an introduction. So I did."

"You set him up with a babe who's older than his daughter but way younger than either of his wives?"

"That's right. Then you know about Melissa, the little girl from his first marriage?"

Hogan gave me a pitying look. "Did this Claudia Silva ever come here?"

There was a chord shift in the Glass composition, a major alteration in the flat aural horizon.

"Sure," I said. "In those days, Phil and I used to tomcat around together a bit. Sometimes we'd hang out here, when Mandy was away in Europe. You can guess how it went."

"No, not exactly. But I get the general drift." Hogan put his feet up on the ottoman. "So Claudia would know the layout. Like where the bedrooms are and how the hallway opens onto the living room. She'd even know the position of Mrs. Oliver's favorite chair."

"I suppose."

"You suppose?"

"All right, yes," I said. "She'd know the whole place. Intimately."

Hogan's eyes focused on his cheap brown shoes, then on me. "Good times here while the wife was away?"

"Some girls, some drinks, some coke. The usual."

My friend regarded me without any change of expression. "I guess it depends where you live."

I was beginning to understand, firsthand, the vaunted Hogan interrogation technique. It was like talking to a therapist with a pipeline to the cops.

"I swore off all that stuff a couple of years ago."

"Great, Jack, you're forgiven. Anyway, it's not your damned social life, or lack of it, that interests me now."

"It's a pretty dull story these days."

"At least you've got your memories." Hogan's face shifted, becoming utterly serious. "Which is more than we can say for

Philip, if the doctors are on the level." He paused, allowing himself a half-smile. "Quite a change for you, Jack. Don't tell me you got religion."

"No, just a bad conscience. Does that count?"

"It's a start."

Hogan stood and walked over to the windows. The sky had darkened into evening, and the rain had stopped. The street lights were weak.

"Let's get out of here," Hogan said. "This place is like a crypt." He turned to me. "You know you have to keep all this to yourself, right? Like always."

I made my way to the light panel.

"Are you sure, Hogan?" I said. "I thought maybe the idea was for me to go share details over canapés at the Whitney Museum. Or maybe leak your pet theories to the *Post*, so you could blow the case and lose McGuinn his job. Sort of an early retirement plan."

"You're a laugh riot, buddy. Just set me up with some meetings—one with Philip at his office, one with Claudia Silva."

"Since when do you need me for that? Just call them up."

"Yeah, like I know crap about these art types and their little world. I need to talk to Philip's contacts in their own surroundings, get an idea of the context. It helps to have a buffer, somebody they trust to put them a little more at ease. People tend to get uncomfortable talking to a detective."

"Really? I can't imagine why."

"Just set it up."

I doused the lights and we rode down without saying any more. On the sidewalk, we stood shuffling for a moment.

"Got time for a drink?" I asked.

"Not tonight. I'm bushed, and Dorothy expects me home. It's Salisbury steak night."

I nodded and we started south down West Broadway, past a knot of people gathered in front of the four bulky black doormen at Tessa's. In the distance, the Trade Towers imprinted themselves massively on the night. The galleries around us were dark and only a few lights remained in the boutique windows, shining on long phantasmal dresses and overpriced shoes. At Grand Street, all the Eurotrash places were full. The cafe tables spilled out onto the sidewalk and flickered with candles and cigarettes. Everyone was talking over the live music at Novecento.

I stopped, and Hogan asked me if I was all right.

"Sure, OK," I said. "Just kind of pissed."

"Murder will do that to you."

"You're used to it. I'm still an amateur."

He nodded, his face set. "Somebody killed a lady you liked. What are you going to do—blame the cosmos? Don't be a putz."

"It's hard to know what to think," I said. My voice had a hollowness I had not heard there before. "Little things throw me. You know, like using the past tense with Mandy's name. Like the silence inside the apartment."

I didn't tell him the rest. Living in the art world, I had many acquaintances but very few friends—almost none who mattered once a check was written or the latest show came down. Now, at midlife, I was starting to lose my best companions to craziness, deception, and death. It felt like a mean prank. My complaint, however futile, came out in stark terms.

"I don't much care to find dead friends in my buildings," I said.

"Terrific," Hogan responded. "So go to work. It's your only chance to feel halfway right again."

"I don't know. Revenge might help."

"Don't waste my time." Hogan shifted his weight from one

foot to the other, impatient to be on his way. "Believe me, Jack, spite never solved a case. It just warps your thinking."

"All right," I said. "I haven't got any better idea."

With that, we said a quick so long and Hogan headed down the block to Canal Street, where the porno shops mixed into the outskirts of Chinatown and the traffic thickened in and out of the Holland Tunnel. I watched him cross over into the small cobbled park on the north edge of Tribeca, passing under the wet trees toward his dumpy office in Lower Manhattan.

5

When I tried to sleep that night, the picture of a crazed Angela Oliver came into my head, and I had to lie for a long time without stirring, for fear of coming fully awake. I clung to the sight of a small distraught woman in a sleeveless white blouse, standing on a porch with a pistol in her hand. Her brown hair was pulled back from her face with two silver clips.

Despite all its defects, you see, my mind works best in the dark. It is there, in silence, that I have tried many times to understand my past life with Nathalie. How could a thing so simple—the infatuation of a visiting American graduate student with his French classmate at the Sorbonne—turn so mercurial and wrenching in the course of a marriage?

Our plan seemed reasonable enough: a courtship among the cafés of the boulevard Saint Michel, followed by a transatlantic life as Nathalie pursued her assignments for *Libération* and I attended to my buildings and art gallery in SoHo. How did it lead to the howling nights, the mutual threats, the sex that was more like vengeance than love?

Angela would understand, the Angela who trembled and threatened. I pictured her standoff with a rival as Philip had described it more than once—his slender first wife, with a revolver held level, cursing out the "other woman," one of many, in front of a tract house in Bronxville. Yes, Angela got it.

Nathalie and I were supposed to be too smart for jealousy, but in fact nobody is. Not for long, anyhow. Not all my wife's fey Left Bank entourage and not all of SoHo put together. Not Mandy or Claudia—not Philip himself, for that matter. Not even Hogan. That's why I didn't for a moment think of Angela as a killer. I thought of her as a woman driven to an act of high drama—a bit of British theater on an American front porch in the suburbs.

I had first heard about the incident a couple years earlier, the night I met up with my Icelandic sculptor friend, the Viking, at an opening at Rush Gallery on Fourteenth Street. The beefy Scandinavian, who makes his work with steel beams and dynamite, wasn't too impressed with the show's photographs of skateboarders in the concrete apartment blocks of Frankfurt.

Needing a change, we headed over to the Stockyard. The short walk led past a few shuttered meat-loading stalls, some of them still active during the day, and onward to a desolate corner near a barbeque shed. A red glow of neon led us like a beacon through the fog. When we arrived at the bar, we saw half a dozen Harleys leaning under the bare lights of the old metal canopy. A black stretch limo waited at the curb. It was that kind of mixed-up place, one where the Viking would feel at home. He was constantly on the road, jetting from one country to another, setting off explosions in various landscapes and picking up girls here and there. His hair was blond and bright; his arms erupted thick and bare from a black canvas vest.

We entered to a blast of heat carrying Charlie Daniels music from the jukebox and made our way through the crowd of bikers in leather and lawyers in Polo shirts and art world slackers wearing Goodwill castoffs from the '70s. The Viking bulldozed our way to the far end of the bar, near the pool table in back.

The barmaids, both in straw cowboy hats, wore halter tops and low-slung jeans. When the Viking ordered beers, one of them immediately upped the ante on him.

"A honcho like you should drink like a man," she said. "What are you guys, wimps?"

"No," the Viking said, without inflection—the way you state a plain fact.

She laughed, smacked four shot glasses down on the bar, and grabbed a bottle of Wild Turkey. "You up for it?"

"Surely. If the sweet American ladies will join us."

The other barmaid came over and glanced the Viking up and down. "Too bad the rodeo left town," she said. "They need a few more bulls to wrestle."

Before the sculptor could answer, the girls clinked glasses with us and slammed back the Wild Turkey in unison.

"Shit," the first one said, "I hope you ain't this goddamn slow when you lick pussy."

The Viking and I quickly downed the whiskey, and the first barmaid slid two Budweisers toward us. "Thirty-six dollars."

"I have it," a voice said quickly behind us.

One of the cowgirls actually allowed herself a fast smile. "Well, if it isn't Prince Charming, dressed for the ball."

I turned to find Philip standing three feet away in a tuxedo. Behind him was Claudia, oozing halfway out of a low-cut sheath. She had stopped to talk to a biker with a gray beard pulled into two points over the crest of his belly.

"We were just at some excruciating reception at the UN," Philip explained. "Hell on earth."

"And well deserved," I said. "So what brings you here?"

"Claudia's friends in Williamsburg told her about it. She thought it would be amusing." Half-turning, he called back to her, "What would you like, sweetheart?"

"White wine. *Grazie, carino.*"

Before I could warn him, Philip called his order to the barmaid over the din.

"What?" she asked, making him shout even louder.

"Two white wines, please. Do you have a decent chablis?"

At that precise moment, the cowgirl reached under the bar and turned down the jukebox. Philip's words suddenly sang out, bringing jeers of laughter from every corner of the room. The second barmaid snatched a red-and-white bullhorn from beside the cash register.

"Did you hear that?" she scoffed to the crowd. "Sir Prissy over here thinks he's in the goddamned Sonoma Valley. Don't worry, hoss, she looks like she can swallow more than chablis."

More laughter, and a foul name or two.

"Who wants a beer?" the barmaid shouted.

The music came swelling back up, but not before I heard Claudia's biker friend start to hassle the barmaid.

"Hey, you scag," he said, "that's no way to talk about a real lady." He stepped toward the bar.

Philip, who probably couldn't guess how close we were to disaster, nevertheless showed the right instincts. "No harm done," he said, heading off the biker with a smile. "My mistake, really. Let's all have something more respectable. Whiskey, is it?"

Philip turned and flagged down the first barmaid. "All right then, beer and whiskey all around for my friends here. For everyone."

That got him a cheer.

The girls lined shots and bottles from one end of the bar to the other. The crowd came up in waves, downing the booze and laughing. Meanwhile, touching her bare arm, the biker resumed talking intently to Claudia. His voice was low as he hovered protectively, his eyes darting repeatedly to her luscious half-exposed bust. Claudia, in contrast, seemed oblivious to the whole situation. She was rather accustomed to causing a stir in public places just by arriving.

"All in good fun," Philip said. He handed more brimming shot glasses around. "Cheers, one and all."

The good times escalated when the barmaids ordered all drinks off the counter. Someone cranked up the jukebox with a fast Dwight Yoakam number, and the two girls climbed up on the bar.

They whooped, the crowd whooped back, and the girl on the right poured a cold beer over her shoulders and halter top. Sweat trickling on their bare bellies, the cowgirls began a lurid, clogging stomp up and down the bar, making the wood bend and the bikers holler.

"I can't hear you," the taller one said through her bullhorn. "What? Not goddamn hot enough for you?"

"No," yelled our bearded outlaw biker. He had an arm around Claudia.

"All right, then, you hog jockeys. Step back." The girl handed her drenched friend the bullhorn and took a swig from an un-marked green bottle. Pulling a cigarette lighter from her jeans pocket, she flicked it in front of her mouth and blew a stream of flame halfway along the length of the bar.

"Hot damn," her accomplice shouted into the bullhorn. "Ladies, don't leave us up here alone."

The two started pointing at women in the crowd—"you, you, up here."

They reached out to haul the candidates—some reluctant, some quite eager—up onto the creaking bar.

"If you're bitchin', you dance. If you're chicken, you sing. Two choices. Otherwise, haul your ass outside. Come on, you sluts, don't be shy."

The barmaid's persuasion, if that's the right term, proved unnecessary. Dancers were already lining up on the bar—a Jersey girl with volcanic hair, a woman in her twenties who could have been a corporate secretary or maybe a junior PR flack, another whose tan slacks and demeanor signaled depart-ment store clerk, and even a female attorney I knew. All that was missing was an art babe, and then suddenly Claudia was being hoisted past me with a heaving assist from the biker. She popped up and turned with a smile and blew Philip a kiss.

"Well, this is novel," he said to no one in particular.

Claudia was the only girl in a dress, a garment the bikers seemed to appreciate—loudly. It wasn't hard to see why.

The next song kicked in, a live Farm Aid recording of Willie Nelson's "Whiskey River." The room sang along with each chorus as the girls shook and flaunted their stuff. The Viking, keeping time with his beer bottle, wailed away with the rest.

Philip nodded his head and did his best to get into the spirit.

"You know, it's bizarre," he shouted into my ear. "I mean, look at Claudia up there. Don't you think she's superb?"

"You don't want to know what I think right now, Phil."

"Yes, well, there you have it. Claudia's enough to drive any man crazy. I couldn't be happier."

"You're a lucky man."

"Oh, I am. Truly blessed." He took an elegant pull from his beer bottle. "But do you know, the oddest thing happened tonight. After the UN, we stopped first at some fashion shop just over there across from the meat stalls."

"Jeffrey."

"That's it. And while Claudia was in the changing room trying on skirts, I found myself flirting with the sales clerk. A girl from Mumbai, not even particularly pretty. Dark and done up with rings and piercings, you know. Exotic, if you go for that look. Nothing like my Claudia. It was the damnedest thing, though. I couldn't stay away from her. Even took her phone number. How peculiar is that?"

"Pretty normal, I'd say."

"Is it? Something similar happened when Angela was in the hospital giving birth to Melissa. I ended up having an affair with her OB/GYN nurse. I mean, what the hell, Jack?"

"Forget it. You're all right," I shouted back over the clamor. "Just like the rest of us, only a little meaner."

"Am I?"

"You're rich. You can afford to be."

Philip nodded, not hearing or understanding really, just trying to look as though he enjoyed the music. "Sometimes I wonder what ever became of that poor nurse," he said.

"Why?"

"Angela found her name in my address book."

"How'd she react?"

"Went to the girl's place and gave her quite a scare. I'm sorry I can't remember the young lady's name."

As the music grew louder, a terrible kind of relief welled up in me. At least Nathalie's death had brought an end to certain grueling battles. I had no one to answer to now, and no one to care what I did. No one to welcome me, or to threaten me either.

"Did Angela do that kind of thing often?" I asked.

"Often enough to keep me on my toes."

"Pretty effective, I suppose."

"I never heard from the nurse again. She wouldn't even answer my calls."

"Maybe she needed some time."

Philip shook his head. "I went back to the hospital to look for her once. No dice, as they say. It was as though she'd fallen off the edge of the earth."

"What would make her do that?"

"Angela on her porch with a gun."

"A gun?"

"Oh, yes, Angela used to belong to a shooting club in Westchester. Something to fill the long days up there, I suppose."

In its odd way, it was typical. Philip, a dedicated sportsman, liked his wives to share his hobbies, if not his soul.

"Later, after I left, she even took Melissa with her sometimes. Signed her up for some youth affiliate. National Organization of Girls United for Feminine Firepower—NOGUFF. A lovely group, though the young things got a bit touchy at times. The acronym is more or less the agenda."

"They shared their mission with you?"

"Oh, yes, insistently. It seems there are all sorts of awful female problems that we men are responsible for. Who knew?"

"I've heard some talk."

"Are you aware, for example, that there's such a thing as mental rape? Quite a traumatic experience, I gather."

"Did Angela ever forgive you—for the nurse and such?"

"I never asked."

Silent, I contemplated my beer for a moment. "It's been a while, Philip. A decade or so. Maybe you should."

"Oh, I wouldn't know where to begin. For me women are a foreign country, Jack. Exciting to visit, useful to colonize, but that's about it. You can't let yourself go native. If you do, you're doomed. Pussy-whipped and all that."

Just then the noise level went higher, and I glanced up to see several girls unhooking their bras under their tops and tossing the loosened lingerie in the general direction of the stuffed moose head behind the bar. A couple of the bolder ones, smiling, flashed their breasts. At that, Claudia looked at once delighted and perplexed—the artist in her, stirred by her comrades' audacity, craving to invent some bold variation on the Stockyard ritual.

Her solution was to hike her dress high and extend one leg, exposing a swath of pale flesh above patterned hose slung from an old-fashioned garter belt. At her beckoning, the fat biker stepped forward to unfasten the clasps for her, and that's when things got truly rowdy.

A whistle started blowing, and the music stopped. The bar-maids, who enforced a strict no-touch policy, were not about to exempt an overdressed foreigner and her fat Harley Davidson swain. One of them trained a long-handled flashlight straight on the biker's face, turning his beard a more ghostly gray. Two enormous bouncers moved swiftly toward him through the crowd.

Acting quickly, I pulled Claudia from the bar and told the Viking to block for us, and somehow—thanks to his blond bulk—the four of us got through the crush and out to the night air, ducking swiftly into Philip's limousine.

"What happened to Mr. Pete?" Claudia asked. Curled in the far corner of the rear seat, she tried to peer out through the tinted glass.

Philip covered her shoulders with his jacket. "I'm sure he explained it was all quite harmless."

The car pulled away smoothly, circling up to Fourteenth Street and cruising east toward the Village, where Philip knew a quieter membership bar.

"Mr. Pete is a very nice man. Did you know his left leg is wooden?"

"You don't say."

"Oh, we do have a good time together, don't we, *amore*?"

"The best."

6

With the full light of morning, the drive upstate—a very leisurely counter-commute—was a pleasant enough affair. I laid the dead weight of my left hand on the wheel and shifted with my right. The expressway curved gently from time to time, first through exurban clutter, then among spring green trees. Once out in the true country, cruising among the hillocks and new growth, I called the gallery to let my director know I would be coming in late.

"What are you doing?" Laura asked.

"I'm on my way to Westchester to see Angela Oliver."

"As a friend or as a dealer?"

"Can't it be both?"

"Jack, don't do anything stupid."

"She's actually quite a good sculptor."

"So what? She's old."

"She's a little younger than I am."

No answer came back for several seconds. "Just please don't commit us to anything," Laura said finally.

"I thought I should give her new work a look, that's all."

"This is getting worse."

"Why?"

"I didn't sign on to run a charity here."

"Angela doesn't need money."

"No, but she needs shows and magazine ads and catalogues and collectors."

"I thought that was our job."

"Don't be so last century, Jack. If she doesn't have her own buyers to bring us, what's the point?"

"Do you think I'm such an easy touch?"

Laura paused. "Just be careful, all right?"

"Angela's harmless."

"Not to you."

About twenty minutes later, just before my exit, I phoned Don to check on the buildings. There was a gas leak at the place on Thompson Street and low water pressure in the Sullivan Street brownstone. Meanwhile, our answering service was getting jammed with inquiries on the Oliver apartment, all from people who had read about Amanda's murder and so surmised that the loft might be coming onto the market soon, at a bargain price.

"Tell them it's still a crime scene."

"I did, but they don't seem to care. One guy even offered to re-do all the floors at his own expense."

After that, I was glad for the sunlight on the fields and the fresh breeze rippling the trees. Real estate affects people in peculiar ways. During my Institute of Fine Arts days, I used to work in the summers for a freelance carpenter who specialized in downtown rehab jobs that were too small and too cheap for most regular contractors. The cash-only deals weren't exactly legal anyhow. No one was supposed to be living in the SoHo spaces back then, since the old commercial structures had been zoned for daytime business use only. The squatters had to develop a system of whistles to warn each other when the building inspectors came around. Beds would become couches, and stoves would disappear behind false cabinets. In fact, the officials didn't care very much what we did. The city had been ready to condemn the whole area just a few years before, and the housing authority considered artists a small step up from the winos and hoodlums who usually hung out on the SoHo sidewalks.

We were a happy little community, in a way—young men

and women working in studios all day, trooping twenty blocks
to the nearest grocery store, then partying with beer and weed
in somebody's loft before going out to the Mudd Club or the
Tunnel for darker late-hour amusements.

Ralph and I didn't always get paid, or sometimes our compensation came in the form of recreational substances or works
of art—the latter worthless mostly, except for the three or four
that are now cultural icons and as pricey as a truckload of stur-
geon roe. A few of our customers got famous, and they all got
decent places to live.

Ralph's profits went up his nose, but I used the tax-free cash
for grad school. Until, one day during Easter break, I took
advantage of the price spike on a young artist's paintings—two
of which I'd recently obtained in trade for my skilled labor—to
purchase a raw, disused, 3,000-square-foot space in one of the
rat traps on Mercer Street. After doing a quick fix-up, I sold it
for enough to buy an entire derelict building a few blocks away.

So it went. Twelve years later, when my accident payment
came through and I had a new gallery enterprise to divert funds
into, I already owned seven up-to-code buildings in SoHo. And
then the real estate frenzy hit.

Once I exited the throughway, the land around me began to
roll and I would catch occasional glimpses of grandly under-
stated houses flashing white among the old trees and hedges.
The county road passed through a little village with several
antique shops, a bagel café, and a Lexus dealership. Half a mile
farther on appeared the black mailbox that marked Angela's
driveway. Only with the last twist of the drive did I see the
house whole—a broad, two-story, green-shuttered Victorian
with a three-quarter porch.

Angela, still puzzled by my morning call, stepped out to
greet me. As soon as I glimpsed her—short and brown-haired,
lilting down the walkway in designer jeans and a cambric blouse

knotted at her half-exposed waist—I knew I had miscalculated. Apparently, without quite realizing it, I had been expecting to encounter, here on her own turf, the woman wronged, the freshly ditched housewife I remembered from a decade before. I should have known better.

"Hello, Jack. I thought you might come round soon." Angela kissed my cheeks when I got out of the car. "Did Philip send you?"

"No, I came on my own. It's been too long."

Over the years, we had kept in touch. Usually I saw her, once a season or so, for a multi-course lunch somewhere outside SoHo, with her young daughter in tow. I chose the restaurants carefully, knowing that Angela wanted, as a condition of our friendship, to avoid crossing paths with Amanda, the thief of her husband and life.

"What brings you all the way up here? Besides checking to see if I have powder burns on my fingers, that is."

"You might say I'm looking for Philip."

"What on earth are you talking about? He's not here."

"He doesn't seem to be anywhere lately."

"That's true, poor soul."

I had driven too far to be overly tactful. "You know him, Angie—better than anyone else alive. Do you think he could be faking?"

She met my eyes evenly. "I think Philip could say absolutely anything, do absolutely anything, fake absolutely anything, if it would help him get what he wants."

"Even now?"

"People don't change that much."

It seemed an odd thing to say, given what she'd been through and done. I laughed. "Well, we're all in a hopeless fix then, aren't we?"

We went into the house, passing through several carpeted

rooms to the kitchen, where a sliding glass door looked out on the pool. Melissa, on the diving board, was being watched by a middle-aged nanny. Her mother waved vigorously, and the girl replied with a quick, convoluted dive. When Angela turned to me, she had a faint smile on her face.

"So, how are you in the romance department these days?" she inquired.

"All right, I suppose. Why do you ask?"

"I rather thought sex might be the goal of your visit."

I must have looked perplexed.

"Don't you want to sleep with me, Jack? It seems everyone wants to have one off with me lately, now that I've started spending time in the city again."

"I hadn't given it any thought."

"Really? Rude chap, you're the exception."

I should have known. After Philip left, Angela told me in confidence long ago, she felt as though half her body had gone. She had to get it back bit by bit, wherever she could. Evidently, that covered a lot of territory—and a great many lovers.

"It's phenomenal really," she said. "Chaps I scarcely know are ringing me up left and right. They all offer dinner, then maybe Tibetan throat singers at BAM or whatever, but what they're really saying is 'Let's go for a drink and a quick shag, shall we, dear?' "

"Sounds annoying."

"I don't mind. It's all in good fun, mostly."

"Thanks, Angie, I've had my fun."

"Haven't you though?"

"Enough for now."

"So what do you want, Jack? Now that the fun is over?"

"Oh, just one pure and loving heart."

She laughed, then caught herself. "My God," she said. "You're serious, aren't you?"

"So I've been told."

Melissa came in through the sliding door, shivering and wrapped in a towel.

"Hi, Uncle Jack. Did you see me do the full gainer?"

"I was mesmerized."

"Missy, please don't drip." Angela scowled at the droplets that splattered onto the kitchen tiles from the bottom of Melissa's white one-piece.

The girl blinked her eyes at me once and headed off, teeth chattering, to her room.

"Cute kid," I said. "How's her French coming? Does she still order *crème brûlée comme dessert*?"

"Don't be fooled. She's a little hellion, that one, in her own quiet way."

I hadn't come to discuss childcare issues. "Tell me, what brings you into the city more often now?" I asked as casually as I could. "Besides your dating schedule, I mean."

"I'm having a show in the fall."

I tried hard not to reveal my surprise. "Good for you, Angela. Where?"

"At Michael Loomis's gallery in Chelsea. Do you know it?"

"Second-floor space on Twenty-fifth Street? Sure."

"Obviously, it's not the best. But it's what I could get."

We both realized she'd done fairly well. At her age, having spent a decade as a small-town socialite, she was lucky to find anyone to take her art seriously at all. Even Michael Loomis.

"I'd love a preview," I said.

"Would you really? My pleasure."

7

Angela led me across the lawn to the white clapboard studio, a former carriage house. When she slid the door aside, a shaft of sunlight cut into the darkness, illuminating scores of humanoid forms in the interior gloom. Some life-size, some smaller, many cast in fiberglass or resin or metal, a few carved in wood, the figures hung from the walls, held twisted postures in corners, crouched half-dismembered on platforms, spilling polyurethane entrails.

"Best behavior, ladies," Angela said into the dimness. "We have a gentleman caller."

"Your work has changed a lot."

"Yes, it had to."

"Just be careful with some of those materials you're using. Polymers, resins, hot glue—they can be terribly noxious."

"Don't worry, I know. Wouldn't want to end up with a brain tumor like Eva Hesse. Or mad as a London hatter."

She flipped on an array of overhead lights, and the sculptures turned pale. We walked among them as Angela explained how her new process reflected the mental transformation—from self-abasement to mute pride to anger—that came over her after her fortieth birthday.

"I've been working some things out," she said.

"So I see. How did it happen?"

"It's hard to say. You can't control the things you create really. Motherhood taught me that."

"But you can manage your career at least."

"I've hired a publicist. She wants me to call the show 'Asylum.'"

"At last, a title we can all relate to."

"I know you don't think much of publicists, Jack. But I have to make up for lost time. Playing coy doesn't cut it at this stage."

She was right, in a way. The art world, like Moloch, consumes its young. Eager kids fresh out of grad school, ready to throw themselves into the searing arms of dealers like me. The younger the better, for our name-driven market, with the promise of a fresh vision now and rising prices for years to come.

Angela's artistic metamorphosis, a more self-motivated act, had begun with some transitional maquettes made from Melissa's broken doll parts.

"She was always managing to pull something off her Barbies or plastic baby dolls," my hostess explained. "An arm, hair, legs, even a head now and then."

"No mercy, that girl."

"Once the dolls were damaged, Missy lost interest in them. So I started putting the odd bits together. I found that I quite admired the little freaks I'd created. Even more so once I set about using grittier materials and scaling the bodies up. Do you like them, Jack?"

"I do indeed. Though I'm not sure 'like' is the proper word. They're rather fierce."

"Good. I've been much too nice in my life. It's time for something tougher."

"Actually, Angie, I never thought of you as particularly meek. Rigorously polite, maybe."

"Yes, I was schooled in good appearances. It was the only way to live with Philip as long as I did."

No one could fault Angela's performance as a wife, or her absolute fidelity during the marriage. I should know. But after Philip dropped her for Amanda Wingate, Angela did the one thing that her ex-husband had not expected and could not abide. The little Brit immediately found other men—attractive, intelligent, successful men—and bedded them in quick succession, with energy and delight, almost with abandon.

The once blasé Philip was shocked. Even though he had betrayed his wife, leaving her for his own well-to-do lover, he was devastated by Angela's new appetite. When I pointed out the inconsistencies, he waved them aside.

"All I've ever wanted in my life," he said, "is a woman who's wise enough to accept a double standard."

"What would be so wise about that?" I asked.

"It just might work, and nothing else does."

Philip made his complaint almost sadly—as though Angela owed him an indulgence. After all, she was small and plain, while he was enormously wealthy and, as Angela's mother said, "quite posh for a Yank."

"Is that so much to ask?" Philip said. "Of all the things that people do for love, is it really the oddest or most difficult?"

He seemed genuinely baffled, oblivious to the fact that the same brash manner and sleek, eager body that once drew him repeatedly across the ocean to Angela, "that little English minx," now made her equally alluring to other men.

"You've had your hands full," I conceded to Angela as we walked among her twisted figures. "First with Philip, now with your daughter."

"Yes, sometimes I do worry awfully about Melissa and her dolls." Angela paused for a moment to close up the studio. "Why on earth would a child do such a beastly thing?"

"I have no idea. I'm not very familiar with dolls."

"But you know something about girls."

"A little, but the ones I deal with are older. They prefer dismantling men."

Angela gave me a wry look. "Oh, poor old Jack," she said. "We're not all French, you know."

8

We strolled back to the house and settled into a small sitting room. With a bit of embarrassment, Angela asked if I could help her find a decent apartment downtown, a loft preferably. She wanted to be back in the SoHo mix. Melissa, fortunate girl, had already been accepted at the Bradford School on the Upper East Side.

"It'll be hard for her to leave her friends here in Westchester, of course," Angela conceded. "But she's a trouper, and it's Bradford after all. Her life will be made."

There was an odd noise in the hallway, and then Melissa appeared, in a short sundress, carrying a large silver tray laden with teacups, a white pot, Melba toast, and three small jars of jam.

"Such a lady," I said.

"I do try to teach her not to be a total barbarian."

Melissa wrinkled her nose. "Mom, you're being a prig again."

Keeping her back very straight, the young lady set the tea service down and poured out a steaming cup.

"Serve your mother first, sweetheart."

"No, you're the guest."

Angela accepted the second cup. "I think she's got a crush on you, Jack."

"*Mom*, don't be gross."

"All right. Help your Uncle Jack with the marmalade lid."

Melissa made a face. "I know."

Taking the jar from me, she freed the top with a single firm twist—one of the little things my withered left arm will not permit me to do.

"Would you like to see me ride my horse later?" she asked.

"I certainly would. But business first, Missy. I have to help your mother get famous."

There was a measure of truth to the thought. Somebody would have to do something to save Angela from the ruinous effect of a hired flack.

But for the moment, I had other preoccupations. Once Melissa left, I pressed Angela to tell me exactly what she knew about Mandy's death.

"Just what I've read in the papers, and heard through the rumor mill," she said. "I assume she was killed by that new tart of Philip's. The pneumatic Italian."

"Why?"

"Who else would want Mandy dead?"

"I hate to say it, but there are other candidates. Philip, for one. You, for another."

"Philip was in California."

"Did you read that in the papers?"

"No, he told me he was going. I called him there on Tuesday night—at the Beverly Wilshire."

"Why?"

"He has to co-sign the papers for Bradford."

"When they check the phone records, the police might wonder if it was some other message you gave him. Maybe an 'everything's set for tomorrow.' "

"Oh, please. My only task last Wednesday was for the membership committee at the Katonah Museum. I chaired the annual benefit that evening, a gala attended by seven hundred people."

"And you were here all day before the party? The cops are sure to ask."

"They already have. Yes, I was home with Melissa. We did yoga together and made gingerbread cookies."

"Of course the nanny can verify that?"

"And the gardener. Would you like me call them in?"

"No. I'm no sleuth. But my friend Hogan is."

"The one who walks like a bantam rooster?"

"He's been hired by Joel Bernstein."

"That damn shyster. If Philip had listened to Joel when we split, I'd be homeless."

"That's the Bernstein we all know and loathe."

"He screwed me out of every share of O-Tech stock, but Philip—dear man that he can be sometimes—drew the line at the house. 'She has to have a roof over her head,' he said. 'She and my little Melissa.' "

"Quite a heart."

Angela smiled faintly and shrugged. "With Philip, you learn to take what you can get."

"Just make that clear to Hogan, if he comes around."

"I don't hide things in my life, Jack. It's a big difference between you and me. One of the reasons we get on so well."

Before I left, we stopped out by the barn so I could say goodbye to Melissa. Wearing jodhpurs and an English riding hat, she held the chestnut gelding in a disciplined trot. As she rose and dropped successively in the stirrups, the buds of her breasts pushed briefly against the white cotton of her shirt. She halted the big animal in front of us.

"Are you leaving already?" she asked.

"For now," I said. "Be good. Have your mom bring you to town for a visit sometime."

"I will, but I won't be good. It's too boring."

I glanced at Angela. "Another artist in the family, I see."

"Not if I can bloody well help it."

Melissa adjusted the reins. "I like your car," she said judi-
ciously. "But it's kind of old."

I looked back at the silver Porsche 911, gleaming under the
trees along the driveway.

"It's vintage," I said. "Like its owner."

"There's no room for kids."

"No, that's right."

"Who do you play with then?"

"Oh, Uncle Jack plays lots of games," Angela assured her
daughter. "He plays the art game and the real estate game, and
sometimes the girlfriend game."

"Mostly I play with my pal Hogan."

"What do you guys do?"

"We pretend to be grown up and solve mysteries. Hogan's
better at it than I am."

"I'll bet I can pretend better than either of you."

"Maybe so, honey." I kissed Angela's cheek and lifted my good
arm in farewell to the girl. "When you're a little older, Missy,
we'll see."

9

I arrived at the gallery in the early afternoon, nodding to two staff members as I passed through the outer office. In the private back room, my Diego Giacometti desk waited in monastic quietude. Laura, ever thoughtful, held off until I was at ease with my coffee before bringing in the first routine items.

"You look like crap," she said. "Sign these checks."

"Thanks for your concern. What am I buying?"

"Mostly you're paying me and keeping the lights on. Then you're giving Harold Baxter his stipend, settling with the printer for the Denton catalogue, and purchasing a 1951 de Kooning pastel."

"Do I like the de Kooning?"

"You're going to love it, once it resells to the Whitney next month at a ten percent gain."

"Is that going to happen?"

Her eyes rolled almost imperceptibly. "Don't start with me, Jack."

As you can see, I have an ideal relationship with my gallery director. Like most people in her position, Laura Cunningham, her mind as sharp as her style, once dreamed of walking away with half my clients and opening a shop of her own. Instead, I bought her full loyalty by granting her an outrageous commission rate and letting her make key managerial decisions without running any of the high risks of ownership.

Fortunately, Laura is a natural. Her skill, backed by the intangible asset of beauty, relieves me of the daily headaches of administering the business. As sole proprietor, however, I retain the right to full write-offs for virtually everything I do—from dining with a museum director at Aquagrill to buying a distressed-silk jacket at Yoshi's. Plus it's remarkably easy to lose money through an art gallery. The income that underwrites a year of high living can be negated, on paper, by a fourth-quarter purchase of one blue-chip painting—a system that provides me both a sumptuous daily life and a healthy offset, at tax time, for the embarrassing profits from my real estate holdings.

Laura stood waiting.

"Something else?" I asked.

"How's Angela Oliver?"

"Good, progressing quite nicely. She's going to have a show in the fall."

"A show, Jack?"

Rigid, with one hand on her hip, Laura looked like the world's most exacting schoolmarm—dressed out of the best SoHo boutiques.

"With Michael Loomis in Chelsea."

"Thank God," she said. "That seems about right."

When I turned to my private messages, I found a dozen voicemails, sixty-three e-mails, and a six-inch stack of paper invitations and charity appeals. Using my left arm as a paper-weight and working with my one good hand, I spent an hour or more sorting through artist pitches and curator queries before I got around to scanning my e-mails.

Suddenly I was stopped by an unopened entry from "arthag@aol.com." Amanda Oliver—ever wry, even in death. I checked the "sent" date carefully, then clicked the message with a faint dread, half expecting some grim record of fore-boding or terror—only to encounter Mandy's bright, insouciant voice one last time:

Jack Dearest,

Erich Tennenbaum just called to offer me $7.5 million for my '63 Rauschenberg. What do you think? I'm tired of the thing and it clashes with the Miró, so I wouldn't mind selling, but the price seems awfully low, don't you think? These dealers are all such snakes. Except you, of course, darling. Do you suppose I could do better at Christie's? Oh probably, but that's so public and dirty. People writing in newspapers about how much you get and whether it's higher than estimated or sets some new auction record. As if that were anyone's business. Isn't it enough that I give a few pieces away to museums each year? Now I have Philip's lawyers to contend with. And the house in St. Bart's needs to be completely reshingled, whatever that means. It's terribly costly, I hear. Life is just one trial after another, isn't it? Do tell me what you advise. I suppose I should hold out for $8 million even.

Many kisses,

A

After a few minutes, I called Hogan's home number in Bayside, hoping to catch him before he started the long commute into Manhattan. My friend does most of his legwork in the late afternoons and evenings, when the criminal element tends to emerge. His wife picked up the phone.

"Hello, Dorothy. Ready to run away with me yet?"

"Nearly, Jack dear. Are you eating enough?"

"I'm OK."

"You looked so thin the last time I saw you."

"Hogan worries, too. About other aspects of my well-being."

"Three years is a long time."

"It certainly is. I'll get over it."

"You must. You really must."

"I promise. Just for you."

"You should come visit sometime. I'll make pierogi."

"You seductress, you."

It was an old joke—until you went back too far, to the time when no one laughed.

"Nathalie was a lovely, lovely girl, Jack. But you've got to take hold. Life is for the living."

"So they say, Dot. It's strange. Everyone tells me life must go on. Nobody tells me why."

After a moment, Dorothy said quietly, "Please, just don't dwell. I miss the old devilish Jack, you know. We both do."

"I'm better than I was."

"Really? I'm glad. But don't get too, too good, dear. It doesn't suit you. Would you like to speak to Ed?"

"He's not as sexy as you, but he'll do."

"That's much better now. You see what I mean? Hold on."

The phone gave a dull hiss for a few seconds, and then Hogan came on the line. "What's up, Flash?"

Same old Hogan. Whenever he wants to prod me a little, he uses that nickname from younger, faster days, when we were both more interested in stroked-and-bored '57 Chevys than in spousal homicides or secondary-market prices for Henry Moore bronzes.

"I just got a message from Amanda Oliver."

"Don't tell me you're going mystical on us. What did that woman do to men's heads?"

"It wasn't just her personality, it was her bank accounts."

"Since when can you tell them apart?"

"I'm learning. Mandy's e-mail helps. She sent it on the day she was killed."

"Great. Does it say anything like 'Philip is off in the study loading his automatic'?"

"No such luck. By the way, what did you think of the Oliver apartment?"

"Spiffy joint."

"Of course, but did you notice a laptop anywhere?"

"Nope. One room loaded with computer stuff, but no laptop in sight."

"Well, Mandy always kept one by her bed. Philip used to complain about it all the time. Every morning, she'd wake up and fire off a string of e-mails before she even washed her face. Said it kept her in touch, and she didn't have to hear anyone else talk. She just sat propped up on pillows, clattering away at the keyboard for an hour or so. The thoughts went straight to her fingertips."

"E-mails can be tough to track down."

"Not Mandy's. She had things rigged so all her messages fed automatically into a desktop file. Preserving her correspondence for the Archives of American Art. Or maybe for her memoirs, who knows?"

"Which means we've got the electronic equivalent of a diary."

"We would if we had the laptop, but someone beat us to it."

"Now, who would want to do a thing like that?" Hogan laughed glumly. "If we recover that computer, we'll have the text of every e-mail message she sent in the last three months."

"More like three years. It will be a tome."

"Something for you to read through at your leisure."

"Thanks. What did I ever do to you?"

"Don't ask."

Hogan didn't say any more. He and I have known each other too long, too well, to be without a few reciprocal injuries. We joke about the small wounds; the others are pointless to discuss.

"Do you think," he asked, "that Philip's girlfriend might do his dirty work for him?"

"She loves him," I said, "so I suppose anything's possible."

"Does she have a set of keys?"

"I don't know. Philip doesn't share all his domestic arrangements with me."

"But you never saw Claudia use keys at the building?"

"When I saw her, she was always with Philip."

"How touching. No hanky-panky between you and the Italian wench, on the side?"

"No."

"I'm impressed. Honor among philanderers?"

"Maybe. Caution anyhow."

"I think I better talk to her right away."

"Tomorrow? I can call her now and see if she's free."

"The sooner the better."

10

The next afternoon, we drove over to Williamsburg and parked Hogan's dinged-up Torino near the Bedford Avenue subway stop.

"So this is where Philip Oliver wanted to hang out for fun?" Hogan asked.

Through the windshield, we watched small bands of twenty-somethings, in faded black jeans and scuzzy sneakers, drifting in May sunlight among bookstores, music shops, delis, low-end boutiques, and slacker-chic restaurants.

"You haven't met Claudia yet," I said.

We got out and walked down a side street toward the river, passing one low, boarded-up industrial building after another, until we came to a steel door bearing a partially peeled-away poster for Johnny Bubonic and the Pestilence. Claudia's buzzer dangled at the end of two wires.

"I hope the doorman finds the *signorina* at home," Hogan said.

There was no intercom. After a minute or two, we heard sounds behind the door and Claudia leaned out to swing it open.

"Jesus," Hogan said under his breath.

Claudia was wearing a scooped-neck black top and tight jeans. Her skin was startlingly white, her face accented by long, midnight-black hair.

She smiled. "*Ciao*, Jack," she said, kissing my cheeks. "What is the name of your friend?"

"This is Hogan. He's kind of a cop."

"Yes, of course. Philip told me. You want to know if I maybe killed his old wife. A very reasonable question. I think she wished, naturally, to murder me if she could. So why not wonder the other?" She put her hand out to Hogan.

"You have a gorgeous smile," he told her, and pressed the back of her hand to his lips.

"*Grazie*. Please come up. I am sorry for the such long climb."

We followed her four flights up the steep concrete stairs. I had the feeling that Hogan, who kept glancing up at Claudia's fluid hips as we ascended, would have gladly done any number of floors.

At the top landing a corridor led past stacks of scrap lumber and discarded machine parts to a paint-splattered door scrawled with a flamboyant gold "Claudia." The whole building smelled faintly of turpentine.

Claudia pushed the door back and motioned us through. Just inside was an L-shaped kitchen with a service island. Two bottles of red wine sat on a wooden table improvised out of sawhorses and a length of plywood covered with an ivory-hued bed sheet. A vase of fresh flowers stood between the bottles.

"Sit, sit," Claudia said, waving us toward several folding chairs by the table. "Be comfortable."

Hogan and I eased into the unstable seats.

"Jack, please, would you open for me?"

I clamped one of the wine bottles under my limp left arm and uncorked it, while Claudia went to a cupboard and brought out black olives, two cheeses, and a round loaf of bread.

"Fresh baked," she said. "From two blocks, very near."

I poured wine into three straight-sided glasses.

"To all our friends," Claudia toasted, "living and dead." Strangely, it was a salute I had heard Hogan use.

"You understand, Claudia," I told her, "we're not here just for a visit. Hogan has some unpleasant work to do. He might have to ask you rude questions."

"But why?" She looked Hogan in the eye. "I did not kill

Amanda. I liked her a great much. And I did not ask to Philip that he kill her."

"What did you ask him to do?" Hogan said.

"Just to leave her."

"To Mrs. Oliver," he said, "it might have amounted to much the same thing."

"It was not so easy for Philip also."

Hogan nodded, with an expression that looked almost like sympathy. "All right, let me guess. He told you he would walk out on her, once a few important matters got settled—with his company, and between him and Mandy."

"Yes."

"But every time one thing got settled, something new came up."

"Yes."

"The art collection, the houses, the investments."

"Many such things."

"Until finally you got fed up and said you couldn't take it anymore."

"I told him I would not be his little art whore."

Hogan studied his wine for a moment. "When was that?"

"Last week, before he left for California."

Hogan slugged down my short pour of wine. Claudia, perfectly calm, slowly sliced two pieces of cheese onto a wedge of warm bread and handed it to him. She refilled his glass. All the while, Hogan's eyes followed her skilled hands, darting away just once, when her head turned, to take in her swelling form.

"My friend wants to learn a bit more about you," I said. "Can we look at your work?"

"With pleasure. Whatever you like."

I topped off Claudia's glass and mine, and we all walked into the studio. Paintings leaned in stacks against three of the walls. Pinned on the fourth wall was a loose canvas, its surface dense with the stylized carnal tanglings that had gained Claudia her nascent celebrity. The oversized studio had north light from a row of windows set high up under the fifteen-foot ceiling.

"I work on a new series," Claudia said. We paused before the unstretched canvas, and she tilted her head from side to side as she studied it. "Do you think it's alive, Jack?"

"Definitely."

"Yes, it's the only thing that matters in art."

"Or in people," Hogan added.

Claudia turned to face him. "No, some people are much better dead. In Italy we have much history, and we know the value of killing."

"Anyone you'd care to nominate?"

"More than one. The men around Philip. Those *consiglieri* at his office."

"What's wrong with the men at his office?"

"They hate me, they're evil. They try to make him—how do you say?—a hostage, a caged *padrone*."

I stepped away from the interview scene, passing a cart loaded with paint tubes, brushes, rags, a coffee can jammed full of stir sticks, and several paint-thinner tins. Here and there, metal columns sprouted braces that triangulated up to the ceiling beams. As I made my way back to the kitchen, I caught sight of a mattress on a low pallet, facing a small TV with a rabbit-ear antenna. Bricks showed under the corners of the bed platform, and I tried to imagine Philip Oliver stretched out there, fidgeting as he waited for Claudia to come out of the shower with her skin moist and her black hair dripping. I wondered if he hung his hand-tailored English shirts in the same closet with her vintage bellbottoms and Chloé tops. Then I remembered, per-versely, that he had told me once, in meticulous detail, about her penchant for La Perla lingerie.

At the table, I opened the second bottle. I could see Claudia and Hogan, vivid as miniatures, perfectly framed by the high steel-frame archway.

"You wish to question me, no doubt. I feel pleased to tell you whatever I know."

"How often did you get together with Philip?"

"At first, once every two of weeks. Soon, twice the each week. Now almost all days."

"A smart man, your Philip."

"You are very kind, Mr. Hogan."

I followed their conversation distantly, absently, as I slowly sampled Claudia's cheap wine. Only a few words eluded me.

Had she ever seen Philip become violently angry?

No, he was a dear, sweet man—especially now that his mind was falling to pieces.

Wasn't that just an act?

Not at all. Philip never pretended with her; he came to her bed in order to be true to himself, for the first time in his life.

Had she ever actually met his wife, Amanda Oliver?

Only once, yes, when for some reason Mandy turned up, trailed by a video cameraman, at the opening of a group show that Claudia was in at Roebling Hall. It was not a place one expected to see the great lady, who seemed shocked to find herself confronting the *something something* of her *something* husband.

How did the meeting go?

She had called Claudia a "minor media slut" (as Claudia repeated, not for the first time evidently) and left quickly with her handsome *something* friend still running the video camera.

As the wine began its subtle work on my brain, I forced myself to listen more closely.

"Have you visited the Oliver loft in SoHo?" Hogan said.

"Why would you ask this when Jack is right here? Would I lie? Even if I had done the worst, I would not be the foolish girl enough to fall into an ignorant trap."

"So the police might find your fingerprints in the apartment? That wouldn't be a surprise."

"I am not so proud of how Philip and I met, or the things we had to do to be together. But love must find its way. It must."

"And you loved Philip enough to take chances together?"

"Think what you like. Have you not felt some great awful passion, Mr. Hogan?"

"Once or twice."

"And did feeling it mean you would kill?"

"A fair question. If they ever find Jack here dead, you'll know the answer."

Claudia tossed her hair slightly, puzzled but not backing down. "You tease me," she said.

"That makes us even, Miss Silva."

She turned slightly toward Hogan. The two, holding each other's eyes, exchanged minute smiles.

11

Alone at Claudia's makeshift table, I was watching it happen again, the old inexplicable business between Hogan and women.

What is it with this guy? To me, he's just an average-looking man, of middling height, with so-so charm. But for a great many women of various classes and ages, Edward Hogan is an unexpected lothario, capable of exerting a gravitational pull. Maybe it's the equation of baldness with sexual vigor; maybe his ladies are slightly awed to meet a man of such calm, polite demeanor, who, as he leans close to peer into their eyes, reveals a handgun strapped to his rib cage.

In any case, Hogan never lacked for confidence. Once, and once only, I asked him about his technique. All he could say was: "Hey, I know how to listen. It counts for a lot." No doubt. But once he gets his answers, I've noticed, his attention quickly shifts elsewhere.

Right now, though, the full force of Hogan's mind was focused unwaveringly on Claudia. He was sorry to have to ask, but he needed to know where she was last Wednesday, the day of the murder.

"I was here. Working in the studio."

"Alone?"

"Completely. That is the only way to work."

As Hogan shifted minutely toward her, his voice lowered and slowed. "A woman with your looks," he said, "is alone only by choice."

"Thank you, yes. But I choose solitude often."

"A pity."

"No. I have, of course, many admirers—always. But not so many are kind gentlemen like you. Or like Philip."

"So tell me why you want this lonely life."

"It is not so lonely, since Philip. For the work, yes, it's necessary to be alone. This is what I do, who I am."

Hogan dipped his head an inch or two. "At least you know what you need," he said. "And how to get it."

With that, they seemed suddenly to remember themselves—and me. Hogan nodded and Claudia led him back through the archway. By the time they returned to the kitchen, I half expected the two of them to be bathed in love sweat. Hogan slid Claudia's chair from the table and stood waiting. As soon as she settled into her seat, he took his place across from her. She refilled his glass. They looked at each other and drank without speaking.

In the midst of this flirty rigmarole, they both turned to me. I had to say something.

"You must have some idea," I said to Claudia. "Some idea who would want Mandy dead."

"Oh, yes, I have thought. Philip's ex-wife, for one—the mother. She hated Amanda always. Or those awful men around him—the company liars—they could perhaps wish it, so they get more control."

"Why his first wife?"

"Because, with Amanda dead, half of everything Philip owns goes back to his child. To a thrust, for when the girl turns twenty-one."

"The word is 'trust.'"

"Is it? Good, I learn: a trust."

"And if Philip died, too?" I asked.

"Then everything. It is one of the many things we discussed. One of the plans he had to make before he could divorce again."

"You talked about his death? Philip looks awfully healthy to me."

"You are not a doctor. The special ones, at the big ugly hospital, they say his head will kill his body very soon."

"Would anything change if the two of you got married?"

"Then the young girl, Melissa, would get only a half."

"That's still a fortune."

"Still, yes. Philip felt much badness about how he once treated Angela and the baby—when he left to go to Amanda years ago."

"And what about other girlfriends?" Hogan asked. "Any around who might resent Philip's new plans with you?"

"You don't know Philip. He is not the kind of man to cheat on his lover."

"Just his wife."

"This is normal."

I ate an olive and placed the pit in a little saucer by the empty wine bottle. "Claudia, my dear, you should write a lonely hearts column," I said.

She tilted the second bottle in the direction of my glass. I covered the top with my hand.

"*Prego*," she said. "Take, enjoy."

I gave in and accepted another half-glass. As Claudia poured, I worked hard to keep my concentration. Her abundant, self-proclaiming body demanded full notice, and usually got it. Everything about her was bountiful, generous, flowing. No matter what she did, no matter how she moved, you were aware first of her breasts, her white skin, her thighs. You could easily see how a man of Philip's age, or any age, would be intensely drawn to her scented flesh and tender care, to long slow hours in these casually welcoming rooms. There was about her a sense of arrival, of journey's end. Fortunately, I was no longer susceptible to such treacherous myths.

"But Amanda, for one," I reminded our hostess, "might not have agreed with your view."

"No, she did not. She said she was going to take away the one thing Philip loved truly. His company."

"Did he tell his top brass about the threat?" Hogan asked.

"Top brass? What is 'top brass'?"

"Those men around him—his false *consiglieri*, as you call them."

"Of course. They had to prepare, to protect. Like a war. They were making ready a big lawyer fight."

"You seem to know a lot about Philip's business."

"No, nothing. I am too much like my father."

She laughed bitterly, but the humor was clearly lost on Hogan. He didn't know what it meant for an old-fashioned museum director, especially a European intellectual like Enrico Silva, to face the transition to market-driven arts management.

"My father calls himself a 'displaced person,' " Claudia told Hogan. "You know what this means? Like a refugee. A man without a home or a future."

"Because he's lousy at business?"

"It is too cruel. When he was my age, Papa wrote a book on Fra Angelico. Three hundred pages. Such beautiful pictures, such beautiful words."

"And now?"

"He only raises money. Without rest."

"Like most people, one way or another."

"He is not like most people. He should spend his time to think, to write, to make fine shows of the very best works—to be a man of culture. Isn't that why they hired him?"

I shook my head. "No, Claudia, they hired him for the semblance of those things. In order to attract trustees and big-money sponsors to the museum."

"It's not fair. They want him to make a new building, to think a budget for ten years ahead, to be a 'pro-active manager.' You know what this is, this 'pro-active manager'?"

"Yes," I said. "It's something Enrico will never be."

Hogan leaned forward, his elbows on the table. "If you married Philip Oliver, it would make your father's life a lot easier," he suggested. "He could be a man of culture again."

Claudia drew back slightly. "What do you say by this?"

"How much longer until Papa is due to retire?" Hogan asked.

"Seven years."

"A quick answer. You must have given his situation some thought."

"Now you talk like a stranger, like a policeman," she replied. "It's a pity."

Hogan laughed to himself. "I'm not suspicious by nature," he said. "Just by experience."

"There, you see, Hogan is more European than he knows," I joked awkwardly. I had that anxiety you get when you're caught, a third party, in the middle of an old lovers' spat. "Let's just finish the wine," I said, and poured all around.

Claudia looked hard at Hogan. "You can 'check me out' all you want," she offered. "Come back here whenever you like. Talk to everyone who knows me. In the end, you will decide I tell truths. I love my father, and I love Philip Oliver. Those are my crimes. Of everything else I am not guilty."

"I'm glad," he answered.

"Are you? Somehow I doubt."

"No, it's true. It's my fondest wish to find you, to find anyone, truly innocent." Hogan forced a mild laugh. "At least it would break the monotony." He raised his glass, waiting for us to join him. *"Buono, salute.* To the health of our friends."

"And the death of our enemies," Claudia added.

"I like this girl," Hogan said, turning toward me. "She reminds me of my Marine drill instructor."

We drank down the last of the wine.

12

A couple days later, Hogan and I went to see Philip at his office on 55th Street. The building lobby was two stories high and clad in green marble. A girl at the solid mahogany reception desk sent us up the express elevator to the forty-fifth floor. The doors opened onto another counter and another sleek business-suited woman. She smiled up at us from beneath an enormous Oliver Technologies wall logo, its stylized "OT" glistening in hand-polished brass.

The greeter, her brown hair pulled smartly back, told us we were expected, and to please follow her into a conference room. She made it a pleasure to comply.

"Coffee, gentlemen?"

"Black," Hogan said. "A guy could get drowsy in the hush of this place."

The girl smiled. "No danger of that once Mr. Andrews arrives." She went to the head of the room's long wooden table and pushed a button. "You'll be meeting with the executive staff."

"We don't want to bother anyone," Hogan said. "We just came to talk to Mr. Oliver for a few minutes in private."

"I'm sure Mr. Andrews will take your wishes into account."

A cart appeared at the door, maneuvered by a young man in a gray smock and dress slacks. He drew coffee for us from a towering silver urn perched on the white-skirted cart. Without a single word, without eye contact, he left.

A moment later, a man wearing steel-rimmed spectacles and a dark pinstripe suit walked swiftly into the room and seized first my hand and then Hogan's.

"Bob Andrews," he said. "Comptroller and deputy chief executive officer. How are you?"

His hair, thin and black, was gelled straight back close to his skull, pushing his blunt features into prominence. The severe style seemed to emphasize the swell of his oversized forehead. Whenever he turned his face, the light glinted sharply off his lenses and frames.

"Mr. Wyeth, Mr. Hogan, thank you for coming." He motioned us to two facing seats at the end of the table. He sat down between us, at the head. "I'm aware, of course, of the reason for your visit. An awful turn of events. Mrs. Oliver was well-known to us all here, and universally liked."

"So I hear," Hogan said.

"That's why I want to assure you that you'll have the full cooperation of Oliver Technologies in your investigation."

"A smart decision."

"We expect, of course, nothing less than a full exoneration of Philip."

"I'll see what we can do. But there is the small problem of his confession."

"Phil is not a well man," Andrews countered quickly. "Trauma, fatigue, self-blame have all, understandably, disoriented him."

"It happens a lot in this town."

Andrews nodded gravely, his lenses flashing like semaphore lamps. "And as you know, Philip has been suffering from Wolfsheim's Syndrome for the past several years."

"How exactly does that work again?" I asked.

"Insidiously. Phil retains his analytic and decision-making functions, but his memory is deteriorating rapidly. He tends to remember only those parts of his experience that he enjoyed at the time. The doctors sometimes describe it as 'obliteration by bliss.'"

"That must cut down on his bar bills," Hogan said.

Andrews looked at him blankly, as though he had just spoken in Chinese.

"At the same time," the comptroller continued, "Phil is consumed by guilt over his wife's death—and unable to censor his own conversations."

"But he still runs the company?"

"No one here, or anywhere in the world, has noticed any decline in Philip's business acumen."

"So the stockholders are happy?"

"Oliver Technologies has increased its global revenues at a rate of eighteen percent annually for the last five years. The stockholders are very pleased. Glowing."

"I imagine that Phil, you, and the other top staff members here all have a healthy portion of those shares."

"The portion set by the board's compensation committee. In line with industry norms. It's how we hire and retain a talented staff."

We all nodded amiably to each other.

"The thing is," Hogan said, "we're actually here to see Mr. Oliver. We have an appointment for eleven o'clock."

"Of course," Andrews replied. "Phil will be joining us shortly for lunch."

"It was a personal appointment. You know, for some reason folks tend to clam up with an investigator when their coworkers and friends are around. Maybe it's a group-dynamics thing."

Andrews—a squash player, I'd wager—returned the shot deftly. "Surely you don't expect someone like Phil, a grieving spouse with a brain disease, to submit to your questions without his lawyer present?"

"I work for his lawyer," Hogan said. "Which means I work for Philip, indirectly. So you guys and me, we're all colleagues, in a way. And we've got a big problem to solve. Philip, our boss, waltzed into a police station a few days ago, dripping wet, and indicted himself for murder. Bernstein pulled him out of the fire that night. But if we can't do a proper follow-up now, the cops are going to take Philip at his word. I guess you've heard how his statement begins."

Andrews grew rigid in his seat. "I really don't think, as deputy CEO, that I can allow our company's founder, chief stockholder, and managerial head to be interrogated alone."

"It's an interesting point, Philip's position here and all," Hogan said, "especially since his father died. When was it—four years ago? That left Philip suddenly in charge of everything, didn't it? Not just O-Tech but all of Oliver Industries."

"That's correct."

"Could be pretty overwhelming, don't you think? A lone guy, under so much new stress. He'd probably want to reach out to his most trusted advisers."

Distractedly, Hogan was toying with a sugar cube on the table.

"You see," he said, "right now I'm just thinking of this as a nice simple homicide case. Woman gets shot in her apartment. She had some marital problems—who doesn't?—but she was also in line for a very big inheritance from Philip, her mysteriously sick husband."

Without looking down, Hogan crushed the cube slowly between his thumb and index finger.

"Now, with Amanda dead, that huge stash goes somewhere else—at least half to Philip's daughter. All of it, if Philip dies soon. So there's his first wife to think about. A woman scorned and all that—one who might like to secure her child's future, along with her own. Also, closer at hand, we have Philip's impatient young girlfriend, a struggling artist who could certainly use some cash."

"Yes, she certainly could."

"Then there's always the chance that the lady was killed by an intruder who just wanted to rip off some very valuable art."

"An abundance of leads, as you call them," Andrews said.

"Not leads yet exactly. Just banal, everyday facts. The kind that make my job almost dull. But eventually, put together the right way, they might result in a break."

"What can we do to help you?" Andrews asked.

"You can tell me what you think of Claudia Silva."

The executive's big gleaming head turned away. "I try not to think about her at all."

"Easier said than done."

"Not for those of us at O-Tech. She has no relationship with the firm."

"Unless, now that Mandy's dead, she becomes the new Mrs. Philip Oliver."

"That won't happen."

"Says who?"

Something—a wince, perhaps—darted across Andrews's face. "Just a surmise," he said.

"Yeah? You seemed awfully sure a second ago."

"Phil is much too sensible, where business is concerned, to allow a little *peccadillo* to endanger his fortune."

"I thought he was losing his mind," Hogan said. Shifting slowly in his seat, he finished his coffee. "Seems to me that if a man is crazy enough to want to get married for a third time— especially to some hot number half his age—he's probably crazy enough to kill for the chance."

"You can't possibly regard Phil as a suspect."

"Right now I regard him as a guy with mental problems— a rich player who just suddenly got a whole lot richer, and more romantically available, than he already was. So the quickest way to eliminate him as a 'person of interest' to the police is to pick his crazy confession apart."

"Of course," Andrews said.

"Horror, panic, overreaction," Hogan continued, "that's all

regular stuff. The cops are not about to arrest a man, sane or otherwise, for freaking out at the sight of his wife's corpse."

Absently, he dusted the sugar off the table.

"Where the situation could get sticky is if I'm suddenly denied access to Philip. Then I'd have to ask myself what might motivate the people who are keeping him penned up. What do they stand to gain from his confession? Or what do they have to hide that Philip, upset as he is, might blurt out to me face-to-face? Those are both very annoying questions because they get me into all kinds of things I know nothing about."

Hogan glanced quickly over at me before he went on.

"I mean, we'd have to start looking at the effect that Phil's gaining clear title to his wife's fortune would have on Oliver Technologies. Like if he started buying up the company's shares, the ones he doesn't already own. And that involves looking at ownership structures and profit distributions and offshore operations and IRS regulations—all crap I don't begin to understand. So then I'd have to bring in outside help, some sharpie like Charlie Mullens over at the D.A.'s office." Hogan bent toward me. "What's that place Charlie used to work before? STC? CES?"

"SEC," I said. "The Securities and Exchange Commission."

"Right. It's all Greek to me, but I suppose you fellows here know what they do. Real fussy stuff, I hear. All those subpoenas for files and records, all those sworn depositions, all those plea bargains where people start double-crossing each other left and right."

Andrew's voice was flat when he answered. "We have some idea."

The executive fixed Hogan with his gaze, as if calculating the odds on a high-risk investment.

"If you don't mind," he said, "I'd like to confer with my staff down the hall for a few minutes. Phil should be available shortly."

Andrews rose in one quick motion and was gone.

In the sudden silence, I turned to Hogan. "Who the hell is Charlie Mullens?" I asked quietly.

"The bartender at Puffy's Tavern."

A few minutes later, the attractive young businesswoman reappeared.

"Mr. Oliver will see you now."

She smiled at Hogan as we made our way out to the long corridor.

"You must have been very firm with Mr. Andrews," she said.

"I just told him what he needed to hear. It's my version of the Dale Carnegie method."

"I wish I could learn your technique."

"You can," Hogan grinned slyly. "I give lessons."

He slipped a business card from his jacket and handed it to the woman. "Might help you get your next raise."

"Thank you, Edward."

"My friends call me Hogan."

"Do they? You must get around."

"Sometimes. If I'm invited."

The girl reddened faintly, laughing at her own forwardness and palming the card as we approached the end of the hall.

"I just try to help out where I can," Hogan told her.

"In this place," she answered, "a woman needs all the help she can get."

13

We had come to the most privileged corner of the O-Tech layout. In a large outer office, the entire senior staff was gathered in a tight knot around the slim, wan-faced Philip. He stood very straight, his slight frame impeccably turned out in a bespoke English suit, the sort that Angela had long ago taught him to require. With his salt-and-pepper hair slightly ruffled, he had the air of a crown prince fallen among pool-hall hustlers. The management staff—men in their thirties and forties, all in expensive shirtsleeves—introduced themselves in a flurry of handshakes and single-syllable, all-American names: Chuck, Dick, Tim, Steve, Mike.

Hogan and I nodded, and proceeded to ignore them.

"Philip," I said, "how are you? I'm deeply sorry about Mandy. My sympathy."

He brightened suddenly. "Hello, Jack. So nice to see you here."

"Are you doing all right?"

"Fine, fine. These gentlemen have been a great help to me. Especially Mr. Andrews. Have you met?"

"I've had the pleasure."

"Coffee?"

"We're good. I'd like you to say hello to an old friend of mine, a straight-shooter named Hogan. Bernstein asked him to clear up a few things about Mandy's death."

Philip extended his hand. "Hello," he said. "My name is Philip Oliver, and I believe I murdered my wife."

"So I've heard. I'm the private eye your lawyer hired."

"Excellent. I'm all in favor of transparency, Hogan. Investigative work must be very gratifying that way. You start with a cloud of uncertainty and then, bit by bit, everything becomes wonderfully clear."

"That's the idea. Unfortunately, things don't always turn out that way."

"Ah, but the process, Hogan. The rooting things out, the dogged search. What sport!"

Philip had been using fake British phrasing so long—ever since he fell for Angela back in London years ago—that it had become natural to him now, even with his mind half gone.

"Well, you've got that part right," Hogan told him. "It is a dog's life sometimes."

"But surely that's nothing compared to the rewards," Philip insisted. "So enviable, to live in pursuit of clarity—it sounds tremendously bracing. Do you know how many people try to make things needlessly muddy and complicated?"

"Yeah, most of them I meet." Hogan glanced casually around the room. "This is some spread. You could hold the World Series in here."

"It is quite grand, isn't it? I told Andrews it was too much, but he insisted. He thinks I should be ensconced like an Arab sheik—to impress clients and scare the bejesus out of competitors. Or was it the other way around?"

"You've got it right," Andrews said.

"Good. Some people think old Philip has lost it, that my brain has turned to mush or whatnot. But we know better, don't we?" He paused, speaking next at a slightly higher volume. "We know better, don't we?"

"Yes, of course," Andrews replied. "You're completely clear, Phil."

"Thank you."

"We should have a little chat," Hogan said. "Just you, me, and Jack."

"And Carl. I always have Carl Marks with me. He tells me

exactly where Oliver Industries and I stand financially."

Andrews leaned toward us. "Carl Martes, actually," he explained. "The nickname started as a little joke among some junior staff members here."

"It's no joke," Philip insisted. "Carl Marks keeps me fully informed. Constantly. I find it most comforting."

Eyes downcast, the so-called Marks—a tall man in an anonymous navy suit—stood wordlessly at Philip's elbow, one step behind. I had met him several times before, though we never spoke. He carried a black laptop, prepared, on his employer's demand, to provide financial stats at any moment. Bristling with colorful graphs and flowcharts, the device tracked data streams from the two Oliver firms and Philip's various personal holdings—stocks, real estate, art collection, foreign currency, precious metals—then correlated them with current market values, deducted liabilities and expenses, and gave him a net asset figure updated automatically every hour. Philip thus possessed—continuously, no matter what the markets were doing in any part of the world—an answer to the vital question that plagued him: "What am I worth?"

"We won't need the kind of information Carl has right now," Hogan said. "I just want to know a little more about you and Mandy."

"She was my one true love," Philip replied. "Now she's dead."

"That's a shame," Hogan said.

Philip blinked at the two of us in turn. "What did I do?" he asked. "What? Tell me. Am I a killer?"

"We'll try to figure that out, Phil," I said, nudging him toward the door of his inner office.

Reluctantly, glaringly, Andrews and the others parted to let us pass. As Hogan closed the door behind us, I saw the execs start to deposit themselves on various anteroom chairs and couches, like buzzards perching on the edge of a safari camp.

14

Philip's inner office was the size of a three-bedroom SoHo apartment, wrapped by glass walls that made his desk seem to hover magically six hundred feet above the frenetic streets, free floating among the towers of Midtown. Nervously, he pointed out his "mascots," the sleek metal eagles on the Chrysler Building, a dozen blocks distant, gleaming in the unclouded sky like the rims of Andrews' spectacles.

"I can see nearly everything here," Philip asserted. "Apartments, offices, hotel rooms—the whole mixed-up city at a glance. And everyone, if they only look, can see me. Total mutual exposure." A chuckle escaped him. "Rather grand, wouldn't you say?" He stared out at the steel-frame buildings, sharp against the sky. "Off we go," he crooned softly, "into the wild blue yonder."

Stepping quickly away, he motioned us to a small table, far from the windows and their vertiginous view. We sat awkwardly in black leather chairs with chrome legs, arranged beneath a suite of Motherwell "Spanish Republic" prints that I had sold Phil and Angie fifteen years earlier, when O-Tech first exploded with absurd growth and profits.

"I do imagine Jack told you about my Claudia?" Philip asked Hogan.

"Better than that. We paid her a visit."

"How is she?"

"Worried about you."

"Ah, the dear girl. Why does she put up with me? I called her right after I left the police station, you know. She took care of me for days on end, every minute. Then this week I started coming back to the office for a few hours at a time—because it was too strange, just the pair of us knocking around together in a suite at the Plaza. Like newlyweds on some macabre honeymoon."

"Why there?"

"I couldn't go to Williamsburg. The studio is pure Claudia—her work, her clothes, her music. All of it, like Claudia herself, so young." He turned his face away. "She must be why I did it, don't you suppose?"

"Did what?"

"Killed Amanda."

"It's conceivable." Hogan measured his words. "Some guys would sell their mother to the Turks for a woman like Claudia. I just don't think you're one of them."

"You don't? That's not good for my theory."

"What theory?"

"That I shot Mandy to be done with her, once and for all. Done with the past, with our mutual friends, done with the stale married sex and the fights, free to have Claudia." He looked down. "The odd thing is, I don't feel very liberated right now."

"Maybe you chose the wrong approach."

"What do you mean?"

"There is such a thing as divorce."

"Yes, if I wanted to lose everything—at least half my business and property. But I don't. I love every one of my assets, my dear vulgar toys."

"That's a lot of love, from what I hear."

"It is, isn't it? A damned bloody lot, as Angela used to say."

I watched Hogan's face, remembering how he told me once that, when a truly rich man talks about "losing everything," he usually means being reduced to a standard of living that most people could only covet from afar. Keeping one beachfront manse instead of four fully staffed houses worldwide, selling the Jaguar but holding on to the Mercedes, sacrificing the 18th-century portrait collection at auction for a few million bucks. It was enough to bring tears to your eyes.

"Angela, your first wife," Hogan said, "do you still see her?"

"When she brings Melissa around. Or when we both attend events at Missy's school."

"How did Amanda feel about that?"

"Not pleased, I'm sure. I can't really recall. We were never able to have children of our own. I think something had happened to her."

"Did Mandy give you grief over all this—enough that you could have stood in the middle of your loft downtown and aimed a gun at the back of her head?"

"Well, I'm a very good shot. Very steady on target. Ask Jack."

"That's right. With a rifle and scope anyhow," I said. "In Montana last fall, I watched him drop an elk at two hundred yards."

"This is your wife, Philip, not a trophy buck. And she was shot with a handgun, from behind, at a range of six feet. Could you do that to a woman you loved once?"

Philip looked blank, then deeply uncertain.

"Do you even own a handgun?"

"No," he hesitated. "But Mandy did."

A small grimace played across Hogan's features.

"After I took up with Claudia, poor Mandy grew rather paranoid. She kept a pistol in her bedside drawer, because she was worried that someone might break in to steal her precious paintings. Or try to rape her."

Poor Mandy, indeed. Someone should have warned her that it's not strangers you need to fear so much as the people who love you.

"Now you tell us about the gun," Hogan said. "Do you know what sort it was?"

"Something quite impressive. An automatic. My wife was that kind of woman."

"Really, what kind?"

"Assertive."

Hogan shook his head and leaned forward. "Don't mess with me, Phil. I'm not one of your stooges."

Philip blinked. "Hogan," he said. "Edward Hogan. Don't you work for me somehow?"

"That's right. And take my word for it, boss, I'm doing you the biggest favor anybody ever could. Talk real to me now—no lies and no holding back—or you just might end up with a Murder One rap."

"Amanda's lawyer has the gun registration, no doubt," Philip offered.

"That isn't the question," Hogan said tightly. "You hunt, Philip; you know what a bullet does when it breaks through a skull. I want you to picture the impact of two nine-millimeter rounds, to imagine the raw exit wounds—and tell me if you could do that to the person you lived with for eight years."

"Possibly. I can't remember."

"Did you hate her that much?"

"I didn't hate her at all; I just wanted her dead. For years, every time she took a trip, I'd picture the plane dropping out of the sky. She'd be screaming and falling, and the plane would go down and down. Then it would smash, usually in the mountains, and everything would be quiet—forever. I would never hear her voice again. There would be a funeral, and chaps would come up to me and say what a good woman she was, and that I was so tragic and brave. Afterwards, beautiful women would pity me and find me eerily attractive, because—deprived of my great love, poor man—I was going through life heartsick and silent."

"Very touching," Hogan said. "But routine." He had a look of bored irritation. "Me, I usually imagine my wife getting smacked by a bus."

Hogan's voice drifted; his words were addressed to no one in particular. "Everybody thinks about the death of their spouse; everybody fantasizes a nice clean escape from the trap. There's a tricky thing about marriage, though. Once you're in it, you never really get out."

"But the things I wish for come true," Philip said.

"Here, sure. You own the company."

"Not just here. Everywhere, all my life. I wanted to be rich, and I am. I wished for Angela, then Mandy, and now Claudia. I got them all."

At that, I had to break in. "It was wishing backed up by some very intense campaigning, don't forget."

"Lots of people work hard," Philip replied. "How many actually get what they want?"

Hogan sat back abruptly, with a hint of subdued violence.

"That's right," he said. "Look at me. I wanted to solve a murder, and instead here I am listening to your bullshit. Why can't I get what I want?"

"What's that, Mr. Hogan?"

"The straight story."

"I already told you: I think I killed my wife."

"And is that your way, just maybe, of sheltering Claudia? Because you figure that, with Bernstein and his crew of associates, you can beat any rap the cops lay on you? Especially since you were in California at the time that Mandy was shot."

"I don't remember being in California; I don't like it there."

"So what do you remember, precisely?"

"Last Thursday, I came back to the SoHo loft in the early afternoon. When I got off the elevator, I saw Mandy's legs sticking out from her favorite chair. She never sat so still in her life, not like that. Then I saw blood on the carpet. I walked up and looked at her face—I mean, where her face should have been. Her head had slumped forward and her forehead was gaping open. There was something hanging over her cheeks that looked like the insides of a chicken."

"Was it what you wanted to see?" Hogan asked. "What you paid for?"

"No. No, of course not."

"But you remember it, so you must have liked it. Isn't that how your mind works these days?"

"I have no idea. Do you understand your own mind, Mr. Hogan? That would be most impressive indeed."

"Just answer my question. Did you like it?"

"It was…irresistible. Have you ever seen a wreck on the highway?"

Hogan stiffened. "I've been in combat."

"Then you know. It was ghastly, frightening. But also exciting. Terribly exciting. There's no denying the truth."

"Isn't there? People do it to me all the time."

"Did I like it?" Philip repeated. His voice had taken on a singsong cadence. "Did I like it? I dreamed about it, and it happened. Maybe I've found the power to make all wishes come true. Money is like that, quite fascinating. Look how my staff attends to me now. Claudia embraces me. And you, sir, why else are you here? A private detective in my own office. How extraordinary."

He seemed to be drifting, his mind wandering.

"Philip," I said. "Philip, are you in there somewhere?"

Hogan rose slowly to his feet. "We're finished here. I've got no time for this dog-and-pony show."

"Don't you want the truth?" Philip pleaded. "We're alike, you know. I want only the truth. The truth and nothing but the truth."

"The truth is," Hogan stated evenly, "I've got a case to settle.

You want to get yourself put on trial, so you can feel better deep down inside, or get your girlfriend off the hook, or cover your own ass with an insanity plea—fine. But for any of that you've got to come up with some solid evidence, things the D.A. can work with. If McGuinn goes traipsing in with the story that Mr. Philip Moneybags here says he's the killer, but he can't place himself within three thousand miles of SoHo on the day of the crime, the captain will toss him out of his office like a slice of stale pizza. I'm not playing that game with you."

"If only it were a game," Philip said. "If it were a game, I would win."

"Are you playing with us now, Philip?" I asked.

"No." He peered at me beseechingly, like a man long marooned. "Games don't make you feel so guilty."

15

That night, lying alone, I talked to Nathalie for a long time in the dark. There, my French was perfect, and I had not yet seen my wife lying dead on a hospital gurney. I had never been maimed; my left arm was whole.

Nathalie and I sat outside at the Café des Phares, looking across the roundabout to the Bastille column as the evening traffic thinned out. We talked about Philip. I knew our conversation was pure fantasy, even while I too clearly heard it, because many of the events we discussed lay still in the future, which is now the past.

We laughed at the way Philip had transformed himself, under Angela's sharp teasing, from an eager MBA grad with a fledgling microchip business to a would-be man of the world—complete with a taste for London tailoring and the occasional clichéd Brit inflection in his speech.

The waiter came a second time, saying *monsieur/dame?*, as he stood with one finger crooked in the pocket of his black vest. A group of young people went by, laughing on their way to the bars on the rue de Lappe.

Nathalie and I switched from Pernod to red wine and tried to guess how the first date had gone, back when Angie was an art student at Goldsmiths and Philip was a young entrepreneur visiting England in pursuit of foreign investors and corporate insurance from Lloyds.

"He acted, I think, a big baby," Nathalie said.

"A big baby with a very active brain, full of ways to make money."

"Yes, he was like that. Very fast in the head."

After a two-year courtship, Philip and Angela settled as husband and wife in the U.S., where they spent the next ten years together—though not together enough. The company absorbed Philip day and night, while Angela puttered in larger and larger studios, getting nowhere with her career, in houses farther and farther away from New York. Finally, she found herself rambling around a modest Westchester estate while Philip was on the road—or "at work" in Manhattan, being swept along to gallery openings and dinners by the svelte, athletic Amanda Wingate.

Late in the process, Angela began to plead for a baby, in the mad hope of saving her marriage and, pathetically, binding Philip to his dependents, mother and child, with a sense of paternal duty if nothing else.

She and Philip had been married for five years when he first started to stray with other women out of town, eight when he took up with Amanda, ten when he walked out on Angela and their infant daughter.

"Still, Angela is fiercely strong," Nathalie insisted. "It's the other wife—Mandy, the spoiled one—who could not bear a desertion."

"Claudia Silva would be hard for any woman to take."

"Perhaps, but one has to expect such things in time."

"With a man like Philip, yes."

Nathalie breathed a long stream of smoke. "All men are like Philip," she said. "Given the chance."

I had learned long ago not to question Nathalie's expertise on masculine failings and vices. In Philip's case, she certainly had a long bill of particulars. As his wealth increased, Philip's lovers multiplied, and the women in his life got successively better looking—a progression from cute to lovely to stunning. Remarkably, the age of his wives and lovers stayed more or less the same as his own years advanced. Angie was precisely his age, Mandy eight years younger, Claudia about a quarter of a century his junior.

Nathalie shrugged, and flipped the blue cigarette box in her fingers. "It's banal," she said. "Cruel and banal."

No doubt, yet I reminded her that Philip had paid a steep price for his pleasures. Is there anything sadder than a man who longs madly for something, and suddenly gets it, only to discover that his dreams amount to the wreck of his life?

"You think he suffers now?" Nathalie asked.

"Many would."

Her lips made a small puffing sound.

"Knowing Philip," I said, "he probably has little choice."

I saw the scene as though I had been there myself. When Philip came into the room, discovering Mandy's body and seeing how the blood had run down her face and soaked into the brocade of her hand-stitched dressing gown, something inside him gave way. The break was at the center of his being, and he could not repair it. Claudia would try, poor girl, but what could she do?

In his murdered companion, her head thrown forward as if bowed in shame, Philip saw the demise of his best self and the end of the long partnership—mixing great passions and fortunes and hopes—that he once thought would preserve him from the worst ravages of passing time. His citadel, the walls he had built to repulse the uglier aspects of, well, everything, had been fatally breached. Age, disease, and death now rushed in on him, and all he could do was name them, one mundane assault after the other, as they afflicted his malfunctioning brain.

"What else could you expect?" I asked.

"A little discretion," Nathalie said. "Philip could have kept quiet about his adventures, as politeness demands."

"There comes a time, darling, when you can't. When the whole *histoire*, even the worst, must be told."

"For what?" Nathalie, her hair as dark as the night, looked away. "You said nothing to me when it mattered. Now I can barely hear you anymore."

Her pale hand was steady as she finished her wine. "It's getting very late."

Then I knew I was coming to the end of my dream of Nathalie, because that is how all the visitations from my dead wife conclude.

16

"We just got some interesting test results from the autopsy," Hogan said on the phone the next morning.

"Such as?"

"Mandy had sex on the day of the murder, probably an hour or so before she was killed."

"Good for her."

"Apparently not. When Philip was in the police station for his big confession, he was very cooperative. The cops did a gunpowder residue test and took a mouth swab."

"Let me guess. Powder burns and the DNA match put Philip in the apartment, in Mandy's bed, shortly before the murder? Bernstein will never let them bring the findings into evidence. No court order, no Miranda warning, no proper handling safeguards—crap like that."

"Don't be so sure. Actually, there were no gunpowder traces, buddy boy, and the saliva wasn't a match. They took more samples—from Mandy's bedsheets this time. All the same, none of them Philip's."

"McGuinn let you know?"

"Just now."

"That was big of him."

"He'd better. It's the least the jack-off owes me. They'll have to disclose all the evidence to Bernstein anyhow, if they ever charge Philip."

"We can't let them."

"We won't. Even a jerk—even McGuinn—will go out of his way to help a guy who saved his hide once."

Given my history with the Olivers, this was a principle worth contemplating. "So now Philip is off the list?" I asked.

"Maybe. Unless he arranged a hit. Or unless he walked into the apartment too early and made a really nasty discovery. He wouldn't be the first guy to freak out at the sight of his wife getting porked."

"What? Then strolled her at gunpoint to the chair before killing her? While the boyfriend watched? No, my money says Mandy's stud did her in when Philip was away."

"Your loyalty is admirable. So who's the boyfriend?"

"I never knew Mandy had one."

"I'm disappointed in you. If you want to clear Philip, find out. Ask around."

He hung up.

I was at a loss. This was not the kind of information I ordinarily traded in. There were no dollar figures attached.

However, I knew the right person to ask.

That night, after work, I invited Laura for a drink at the Temple, a stylish, low-lit establishment not far from the gallery. We passed the L-shaped bar with its retro chrome stools and went to the back room, a quiet den of heavy wood-lined walls, small tables, and darkness. For years my favorite seduction lounge, the Temple always made me feel I was living inside a Sinatra song. It was a pity to waste it on Laura, but I was still deeply drawn to the place from time to time—out of nostalgia, I suppose.

You see, I was like an addict trying to go straight. Don't drink alone, don't think too much—especially about Nathalie—and don't have random sex. Hogan's moral prescription. It sounds easy, but just try it sometime—especially when your business is selling art. I live in SoHo, not Bedford Falls.

"I picked up a funny rumor today," I said to Laura.

"What's that?"

"Did you ever hear that Amanda Oliver had a boyfriend?"

Laura laughed and clinked the ice in her glass. "Of course."

"What do you mean 'of course'?"

"I mean Philip was doing her dirt for years. She was a vibrant woman with scads of money. What do you expect?"

"Not much. Just to be told who my friends are screwing. It's common courtesy, you know."

"You're Philip's sidekick. The opposing team, so to speak. Mandy wasn't about to share that little tidbit with you."

"Who did she share it with?"

"Me, for one. We used to get facials together at Arden's. There's something about lying back with all that glop on your face."

"And she gave you some details?"

"Some? Have you ever heard women talk, Jack?"

"Don't remind me." I swirled my drink. "I just can't believe I didn't sense anything."

"Look, Philip is all right in his man-on-the-make way. Nice manners, good hair. I might do him myself, if he asked politely enough."

Philip's executive playboy crap." Laura smirked. "The lady was bored. She went shopping for something new, something hotter."

"How did I manage to miss this?"

"It's genetic. Most men just aren't very bright that way. They don't realize what's going on with women until something hits them head-on like a garbage truck. Really, it's a wonder you guys can find your way to the bathroom."

"All men or just your ex-lovers?"

Laura signaled the waitress for another round. "That's a pretty broad sample."

You had to admire Laura's self-knowledge. It was a shame to use that phony "rumor" tactic on her. I don't customarily mislead my friends and colleagues. Lying is just an old habit I slip into in bars.

"So, this love interest of Mandy's," I said. "Anybody I know?"

"Take a guess."

"Young or old?"

"Mandy had some decent looks left. Young."

"Money or talent?"

"Neither."

"I guess we know what that leaves."

"It leaves Paul Morse."

I hesitated. The name was vaguely familiar, but I hear about two hundred new names a day in the art business. Then something came to me.

"Not the performance artist with the video hang-up?" I asked. "The one who sports a cowlick?"

"You're so out of it, Jack. It's not called a cowlick when it's in front and done on purpose. Then it's a statement."

My gallery director is a genuine bargain. Sure, I pay her exceptionally well, but the fashion tips—and the psychological abuse—come gratis.

"You do mean *that* Paul Morse then?" I said.

"The one and only, according to Mandy."

I couldn't believe it. The guy was hunky enough, I suppose. Smooth-faced and blue-eyed, an art scene regular. Who knows what women are going to like, anyway? But this particular boy-toy had the measly income of a poet and the conversation of a video-store clerk. One of those pretty, brutish male-model types who look like they've just been smacked between the eyes with a brick.

When I got home to Wooster Street, I gave Hogan a ring.

"Now we're cooking," he said.

"So it seems. The O-Tech crew, Claudia, this Morse kid—we're not short on suspects."

"I still want to hear what Philip's first wife has to say for herself."

"That's a dead end. Angela had nothing to gain from Mandy's death."

"Except piles of Philip's loot for their underage daughter," Hogan said. "Half the estate for sure. And if his brain disease does him in now, with no wife, Melissa gets the whole enchilada."

"That's Melissa's money."

"But the two are thick as thieves. What's Angela's is Missy's now—and vice versa once the girl turns twenty-one, I bet. That setup might prod anybody into action."

"Angela's an artist," I said. "She likes money, but not enough to kill for it. Unless it would buy her a retrospective at Tate Modern."

"We're not talking money alone," Hogan noted. "Maybe she also wants peace of mind."

"From the barrel of a nine-millimeter?"

"Look, Philip dumped her for Mandy, right? Certain people, if they're too proud or too weak, can't get over that at any price."

"It was years ago."

"So what? Some pain never ends, Jack. It's a funny thing. To a guy like me, a mansion in Westchester seems like a pretty nice settlement for any insult. But I never lived the big-money life, Oliver-style. And I don't know what it's like to see the bitch who bumped me aside take three times my haul."

"You've got Angela wrong. She's no murderer."

"No one is—until the first time."

"It's not in her. She's just not the type."

"We're all the type, Jack."

17

Hogan and I got to see Paul Morse in action a few days later. In fine spring weather, a large portion of the New York art world gathered at the Whitney Museum for Amanda Oliver's memorial service. Her funeral proper, a very Wingate affair in an Episcopal chapel on the Upper East Side, had transpired in privacy a few days before.

To her downtown friends, the museum seemed the closest thing our Mandy had, when still alive, to a genuine church. The little auditorium on the second floor, customarily used for panel discussions and video programs, was lined that afternoon with dozens of ornate sympathy bouquets. Music—actual music for once, with harmonics and melody—emanated softly from an audio system usually given over to art-film dialogue or tuneless sound-art installations. A temporary stage had been set up and a podium stood sentinel-like at the center, caught in the numinous glare of a pin-spot.

"Not my usual crowd," Hogan said, clearly puzzled by the way people greeted each other without really touching.

"It's the art world," I explained. "Everybody sleeps around. Nobody shakes hands."

We sat far back, watching the collectors, museum staffers, dealers, critics, and star artists file quietly in and distribute themselves among the padded seats in an unpredictable mix. I had invited Hogan along on the assumption that some chance remark uttered in grief or an odd lack thereof, some emotional tension between mourners, some recollection by one of the

speakers, might give a clue to the crime that brought us all together in this minimalist cavern, away from the fragrant spring
light.

"You won't see this often," I told Hogan. "Some of the artists
even wore jackets."

For a while, I had tried to feed him all the famous names as
the attendees entered and nodded or bumped cheeks with each
other. But the list started to sound like a textbook, and from
Hogan's lack of reaction I could tell that none of it registered.
The paragons of postwar American art, it seems, meant nothing
outside our little confraternity.

Then I nudged him. "There's Paul Morse."

Mandy's boyfriend was not one of the glitterati. Rather,
he stood off to the left side near the back of the auditorium,
adjusting a video camera on an eye-level tripod. He was there
to record the ceremony, to be excerpted later on his cable
access TV program, *PM Videos*. It was his way of showing
respect for a deceased paramour. He'd put on a clean white
shirt, which he wore hanging out over black Hugo Boss jeans.

"So what's the lowdown on this pretty-boy?" Hogan asked.

"He's a performance artist."

"What's that, some kind of hustler?"

"Only sometimes. Basically, he videotapes himself doing
weird things in front of small audiences."

"What kind of weird things?"

"Once he had the words 'sex victim' branded on his ass."

"You mean tattooed?"

"No, I mean branded."

"And that's art?"

"So the PhDs tell me."

Just as all the whispered exchanges died down in anticipation
of director James Aubersson's welcome, a small commotion,

originating at the rear doorway, moved along the main aisle to the front row of seats.

Philip had entered the auditorium with a stone-faced Carl Marks gliding behind like a ghostly caddy.

The rumpus at the door was about getting Carl to close his glaring laptop for the duration of the service. His employer finally agreed, but nothing could completely stifle a second, even more appalled reaction when the mourners saw that Philip was also accompanied by Claudia Silva.

At once demure and voluptuous in a high-necked black dress, Claudia kept her hand on Philip's elbow—just as she had two years previously at the opening of the ARCO art fair in Madrid, their first public acknowledgment of betrayal and lust.

Ignoring a mental chorus of "how could he?" the trio—a dazed Philip, flanked by Carl and Claudia—walked down the center aisle and sat in the front row near the steps to the podium.

As the music faded to silence, the gray-templed Aubersson, tall and straight in a double-breasted charcoal suit, mounted the stage to deliver an impeccable statement on behalf of the museum. He would remember forever, with great fondness, this most generous of patrons. Amanda Wingate Oliver had gifted the institution with substantial financial support, with artworks of major historical significance, and with countless hours of her own overtaxed time. She had been a board member for six years, providing leadership on numerous committees and projects. On and on the canned testimonial went for ten minutes, elegant and hollow as the man who delivered it.

The string of artists and fellow collectors who followed told similar tales of open-handedness and cynicism, issued in equal, often simultaneous measure.

Jim Jameson, the celebrated abstract painter and perpetual drunk, recalled Mandy grilling hamburgers at a fundraising party on the beach near East Hampton, then "vending" them insistently to museum trustees at $10,000 each, mustard extra.

Art and Language maven Reginald Shaw, leaning into the microphone, recited samples of what he called Mandy's Maxims: "Never trust anyone who uses 'old' and 'beautiful' in the same sentence. They're obviously either deluded or lying."

A wave of stray titters went through the audience. We all missed the head-back "ha!" that always accompanied Mandy's sardonic pronouncements.

No doubt she would have also laughed, cuttingly, at what came next—having as her final eulogist the man who had wronged her for years and who was, in the view of the NYPD, still the most likely suspect behind her killing.

"Hello. My name is Philip Oliver, and I believe I murdered my wife," he said quietly upon arriving at the lectern.

My bereaved friend was at it again—sincerely or with great calculation, I couldn't be sure.

"People tell me that my memory is not what it used to be." As he spoke, Philip gripped the podium firmly on each side to still the tremor in his long, pale hands. "Perhaps so. Sometimes it's a mercy to forget."

He stopped. For what seemed like ages he looked out at us, over us, through us.

"I just want to know if I killed Amanda," he said at last. "Can anyone tell me?"

The silence deepened as Philip peered watchfully out at the audience. "My lawyer says no, but I'm not so certain."

In the front row, Aubersson stirred, clearly intending to rise and save Philip—and all of us—from further emotional distress. But Claudia grasped the director's wrist and held him gently in place.

Philip was trembling in his Savile Row suit.

"For ten years," he said, "Mandy and I laughed and argued,

bored each other and fell into passion. She was my companion and adversary, the other half of my life. Now they tell me she's gone, that she doesn't exist anymore…Does anyone really believe it's that simple?…No, I tell you, she's in here." His fingertips touched his head, then his solar plexus.

"She talks to me," he rasped, "but when I look around to find her, she isn't there, or she won't answer. She's hiding. It's a spiteful ruse. She wants to punish me for running after girls too often—as if that made any real difference. Tell me, men out there, where does cheating lead you?…Where?…Home, eventually—unless the woman there turns against you."

A glassy shine had come over Philip's eyes. "Where does your wife live? In your house, of course, but also in your brain and your bones and your guts. Always. But I can't find Mandy anywhere now. Does anyone here know what I mean?"

He fell silent, and a subtle disquiet rippled through the crowd as they realized he was waiting for a response. Even Hogan stirred.

"What a crock," he said.

I whispered an answer that was only half in jest. "Maybe it's what murder does to your brain."

Hogan tilted his head, a sign he didn't entirely dismiss the idea.

"Can I get a witness?" Philip called out.

In the front row, Claudia rose smoothly. She walked to the stairs and slowly began to mount one step after the other, her mute, swaying figure making it difficult to focus on Philip. And that was certainly a relief.

"I tell you," he said, "Mandy should be here. She was at home in this place, with you art people. Not me. I don't belong—here or anywhere."

Claudia, having crossed the space in three unhurried steps, stopped next to Philip and, nodding, touched his shoulder. He seemed to recoil minutely.

"What have I done?...Mandy, what have I done?" He sounded determined to go on. But as he looked at Claudia, the panic suddenly passed out of his body. His head dropped to his chest. He shivered and appeared to shrink before our eyes.

"You, my life." Philip's eyes were on Claudia, yet it was hard to know exactly who, or what, he addressed. His words had a miserable air of defeat.

Claudia took his arm. Firmly, like an attendant in some ancient Greek procession, his young lover led him away from the podium, off the stage.

18

As we filed out of the auditorium, I saw Angela hovering in the back, furtively watching while Philip was escorted away.

"Hello again," I said. "This is…"

"We've met." She gave her hand to Hogan. "Ed paid me a visit the other day."

"I'm surprised to see you here," Hogan said to her.

"Really, why?"

"Not everyone cares to attend a memorial. Especially one honoring the woman who made off with her husband. You must still care a lot for Philip."

"Apart from the fact he was the love of my life, you mean? Or that we had a daughter together?"

"Does that really matter," Hogan prodded, "when it comes to Amanda?"

"Yes, believe it or not. Those big dumb things—marriage, parenthood, love—actually make a difference. They get you to behave a tad better, for a time anyhow."

"None of it seemed to work on Philip," I said. "He treated you pretty shabbily."

"He's the father of my only child, Jack. I can't begin to explain."

For an instant, I thought Angela's cool demeanor might crack.

"How's Melissa doing?" I asked. "It can't be easy for her."

"It's not. She's very close to her father. Extremely."

"Kids hear things. And her schoolmates must ask her some very hurtful questions."

"No, frankly, that seems to be the role of my best friends." Angela did not blink as she spoke. "Melissa knows her father is innocent. And so do I."

"And what does the girl know about Claudia?" Hogan asked.

"Claudia? What is there to know? That she's one more slut in Philip's long roster. One that he's happened to stick with for a time, that's all."

I glanced pointedly at Hogan, and he took the hint to excuse himself for a smoke.

"Sorry," I said to Angela. "Hogan can be a little tactless sometimes."

"We all do what we have to, don't we?"

"I suppose. Even Philip—with that speech."

Angela's face hardened. "Yes, isn't it ironic how nicely the dead are remembered, while the living are forgotten?"

"Like who?"

"Like me for one." She glanced over at the doorway. "Like Philip for another. That little fool, Claudia, didn't even protect him from himself up there. She'll never make a bloody wife."

I couldn't decide whether Angela's words sounded more like a lament or a veiled threat. They kept replaying ambiguously in my head in the wide, echoing stairwell we walked down. Angela chose to avoid Claudia and Aubersson and the others, all nodding and murmuring and shaking hands as they waited in a knot by the elevator. She wanted no sympathy from this crowd, no rote condolences about "our dear Philip."

Once we reached the ground floor, I asked her if she had ever gotten to know Mandy.

"No, I think she felt too guilty to try to be friends with me. We talked now and then when it was unavoidable, that's all. I can't recall the last time I saw her."

Unfortunately, I could remember all too well my last encounter with the deceased. Philip and I had come back to their Prince Street loft, a little tight, after the reception for a Chuck Close show. We were all supposed to go out to dinner together—

Mandy, Philip, myself, and a leggy Brazilian curator I had met the week before at an opening on 57th Street.

Amanda, however, was far from ready. Instead of dressing, she had been pacing back and forth in the apartment. Vainly, Philip was now trying to speed her preparations along.

"Come here, Jack," he called from her bedroom. "Mandy's in a snit."

When I entered the room, he gestured toward his wife and said, "She's going to make us all late, just because I have no idea how to help her pick a proper outfit."

Mandy was standing—quaking, really—in front of her wide vanity table, clutching a comb in one hand and a silver-backed mirror in the other. She wore a white bathrobe and her hair had been teased out, forming a ratty aura around her no-longer-young face.

"You want me to behave better, Philip?" she said. "You want me to be less hysterical?" Amanda turned to him with the mirror in her hand, useless as her makeup cracked and smeared, her tears running crookedly, steadily. "You're screwing another woman. Again. Can you make that any less true? Well, can you?"

Philip fiddled with some jewelry in a tray. "Come, please, Mandy, get hold of yourself. Don't make a scene."

It was all he would say.

With my eyes, I signaled Philip to leave, to let me talk to Amanda—or, rather, listen to her—alone in the room.

As soon as he left, she sank to the bed.

"It's hopeless," she said. "An aging woman has no chance."

"Why not just let Philip be Philip?" I said, straining for some form of comfort. "He will anyhow, and this way he always comes back."

"Yes, he comes back, all right. And I take him in—knowing this affair means nothing, and knowing it will happen all over again." Her lids lowered, and she seemed to speak only to herself. "What more can a wife hope for these days?"

Looking at Angela now in the Whitney lobby, I knew she must have experienced that marital bitterness, too, and for longer. The difference was that she had never publicly broken down. Long deserted, stuck in a sprawling house up in Westchester, enduring years of despair in those useless rooms, she persevered without outward complaint. She revealed her resentment—if at all—only behind closed doors, by some secret means, to the attentive, quick-witted little Melissa, with no outsiders present.

Before we parted, I asked Angela about her apartment search. The answer was pretty much what I expected, given her desire for enough space to live comfortably, raise a child, and work on her sculpture. Affluent but no longer fabulously wealthy, she was trying to economize because of the new Bradford School expenses. Her budget was not going to buy a Westchester lifestyle in Manhattan. I told her I had a space that might work for her, if she didn't mind taking a floor-through in my oldest building, the one I lived in.

"In the belly of the art world beast? By all means, as long as the place is safe for Melissa."

"I'll be right upstairs, if that helps. Do you think she'd like being a SoHo girl?"

"Oh, in most ways she already is."

I offered Angela some very attractive terms.

"God, yes," she said. "I have to tell Missy right away."

Smiling, she squeezed my left arm, air-kissed me, and headed over toward Lexington to hail a cab.

Walking outside, I spotted Hogan easily in the covey of mourners on Madison Avenue. With a slight tension in his shoulders, he was leaning against the museum's retaining wall, talking to a cute little intern from, I think, Metro Pictures. His paunch was discreetly sucked in.

I found a spot on the sidewalk, well away from the traffic, and called Don on my cell, telling him to reserve the fourth floor of the Wooster Street building when it came vacant in August.

"Are you sure?" he said. "I've got a dozen brokers interested already."

"Never mind. I've found a tenant for it."

"What's the rate?"

"Five thousand a month."

"Very funny. How much?"

"I'm serious. Don't worry; you're not on commission."

"Jack, come on, we're talking twenty-four hundred square feet."

"She's a friend—an artist with a kid."

"You've got more friends than money right now."

"That's my problem, not yours."

Once Hogan saw that I was off the phone, he finished his chat with the girl and sauntered over. Before he spoke, he wiped the sides of his head with a handkerchief.

"It's a great world you live in," he said.

"It has its attractions."

"I mean, basically, it's hordes of young art babes, some fairies, and you—right?"

"More or less. After a while, the girls get to be a duty, a second job."

Hogan shook his bright head. "No wonder Philip Oliver can't keep his zipper shut."

"Is that what Angela told you?"

"That's what everyone tells me. Starting with you."

It took me a second to realize that Hogan had devoted serious thought to Philip's infidelity. Around SoHo, it didn't seem like a particularly notable trait.

"Paul Morse followed Philip and Claudia all the way down with his camera," Hogan reported.

"Paul records everything in the art world."

"Yeah. Everything to do with Amanda and Claudia, anyhow. I asked some people here about him. He's the same guy who was working the camera when Mandy barged into Claudia's group show a few months ago. That kind of thing could make a nice Italian girl angry."

"You don't really suspect Claudia, do you?" I asked.

Hogan half-laughed. "I suspect everybody, until I can prove otherwise."

"Sounds like a swell way to live."

"You have your burdens, Flash. I have mine."

"And what about Angela—does she pass inspection?"

"So far, yeah. A few hundred people saw her at that Katonah Museum shindig on the night of May fourth. The nanny had the day off, coming instead for the evening, but the gardener says Angela was definitely at the house in the afternoon. He's just a little shaky on the exact time he first saw her there. Because of the rain, he was working in the barn. That bothers me some, since the murder was around one, and you can get from SoHo to Westchester, door to door, in about an hour—less, if you push it. Or maybe a little more in bad weather or traffic. Either way, there was plenty of time. But, honestly, if Angela wanted to do Mandy in, I think you're right, she would have offed the lady a long time ago."

"Probably so, when the hurt was raw. Not, what?—nine or ten years later."

"Right," Hogan said. "Though sometimes hate festers. There are people who enjoy their jealousy, in a perverse way, you know. It pumps adrenaline through them like nothing else—

makes them hyper-alert, hyper-vigilant. Believe me, that cheap thrill accounts for half the murders I deal with."

"Which leaves the other half," I said. "Have you considered that there's no love lost between Angela and Claudia?"

Hogan looked at me like I had suddenly become a bit less of a dolt. "What are you saying?"

"Just that Angela might want to frame Phil's new girlfriend."

"What would she gain?"

"Satisfaction. Claudia is the second woman, after Mandy, that Angela has good reason to despise. And Angela doesn't suffer offenses lightly."

"I thought Angela was a friend of yours."

"She is. So why did she let me think the nanny was working on the day of the murder? It's one thing to have friends, Hogan; it's another thing to have illusions."

He nodded, his gaze going off somewhere away from me. We both know something about the hidden costs of friendship.

"So what's up with Angela?" Hogan said. "Showing up here. Is she still carrying a torch for her lost husband or something?"

"Maybe. She wouldn't give up on him back then, even when Philip wasn't keeping his end of the bargain. 'These days, I think I'm married for both of us,' she used to say."

"Some women never wise up."

Hogan paused to exchange a quick wave with the departing intern.

"Working in Homicide gives you the big picture," he said, turning back. "I've seen marriages for money, marriages for social position, marriages for a green card or working papers. Then there are the love matches, the catastrophes."

"Spoken like a true husband."

"Well, at least Philip and Amanda were companions to the end—in a way."

"How's that?"

"For all their spats and jealousy, they went down the same path. They both took it in the head. One fast, the other one slow."

I couldn't laugh. "We've got to find the shooter," I said.

"My guess, this killer was no off-the-street intruder. It hardly ever is."

"Where do we start then?"

"By keeping a careful eye on Claudia and Angela. I've had worse duty."

"And Paul Morse?"

"You bet. Think close, Jack. It's usually someone very close to the victim."

"Probably someone with easy access to the apartment?"

"That's right." He gave me a quick slap on the back. "Someone like you, for instance."

That was Hogan. Always joking around.

19

On Saturday, Angela came by to look at the rental space in my building. She had Melissa in tow, and the three of us walked the length of the apartment from the tall windows on Wooster Street, back through the broad living area, past the kitchen island, to the three rear bedrooms and the expansive utility space, where I thought Angela could keep a few pieces on hand to show visitors.

"Perfect," she said as we made our way toward the entrance again. "Melissa, what do you say? Could you have fun here and do your studies?"

"I could if Uncle Jack would help me."

"I haven't studied for a very long time, Missy."

"It would be good for you, then. And you already know how to have fun. Mom told me so."

With a couple of casual signatures, Angela and I finalized the agreement, and I suggested that we all go to lunch at Félix.

"Lovely idea," Angela said. "But would the two of you mind going without me? I have to dash off to the Bradford School to finish the paperwork. You can take care of Melissa for a little while, can't you, Jack?"

"I'm afraid I don't have much practice."

"Well, don't be afraid. The little devils can smell fear in a second. Right, pumpkin? Just keep her amused for a couple of hours."

"What does she like to do?"

"Oh, just feed her and take her shopping. You certainly know how to do that."

Angela bent down to peer directly into Melissa's eyes. "Don't be difficult," she said. "I'll be back shortly, and I don't want to find Uncle Jack tied up and locked in a trunk."

"Can't I play any games?"

"Yes, you can play at being a lady."

"Ugh."

Angela disappeared into the elevator, tossing a quick "you're a dear, Jack" over her shoulder, and then quite suddenly I was alone with the child. Melissa turned and sized me up. Without Angela's moderating presence, I felt like a calf with two heads.

"Where do you live?" the girl asked.

"Just one floor higher. On the top."

"That doesn't make you any better than us."

"No, it just means I'm your landlord. Most people would say that makes me worse."

The girl and I rode down to the street in silence, cautiously eyeing each other. Melissa was wearing sandals, a pair of white Capri pants, and a striped red-and-white pullover. Her hair was radiantly blond, as only a youngster's can be.

When we emerged into the open air, the street throbbed with colors from the midday crowd, most of them day-trippers. I tried to get Missy to go somewhere sedate for a salad and quiche, but all she wanted was hot dogs from a vendor's cart at the corner of West Broadway and Spring.

"I'm not sure your mother would approve."

"I don't care. You're the boss now. Please, please, Uncle Jack."

Three schoolboys crowded up to the serving window ahead of us.

"Dorks," Melissa said aloud. "Boys are so creepy."

They all glanced at her, and one looked back a second time. "Hi," he said.

Missy—half-turning, granting the kid no response—took my hand.

Once the boys got their food and clomped away, laughing in

honks, we ordered four hot dogs and two cans of Coke. There was nowhere to sit. Gently, as we walked along, Melissa helped me handle the lunch items, sometimes taking the elbow of my bad arm while we checked out the windows of the boutiques on West Broadway and the smaller side streets. The girl had very definite opinions about the clothes and shoes displayed at Dolce & Gabbana, Vivienne Westwood, Giorgio Armani, and the other fashion outposts that were steadily transforming SoHo from an art neighborhood into a high-end shopping mart. Allowing for gradations, the major ranks in Melissa's critical hierarchy seemed to be "yucko," "cool," and "totally salsa."

"You have a good eye for these rags," I told her. It was not an empty compliment.

"I know. I'm going to be a model when I grow up."

"That's a noble aspiration."

"My mom doesn't think so. She says it's a horrid idea."

"Does she?"

" 'Horrid'—that's her word. Why can't she talk like regular people?"

"Well, she's British, you know. English is her second language."

Melissa giggled.

"But if you become a model you'll have creepy boys looking at you all the time."

"That's OK. When you're really beautiful, you can make them do whatever you want."

"Who told you that?"

"Nobody had to tell me. I watch TV."

"Do you have your whole career planned out?"

"No, first I have to get really beautiful. I'm very pretty now, so that's a good start. In about five years, I'll be like a major babe. I'm already way cuter than my mom."

"You shouldn't say things like that."

"Why not? It's true. Anybody can see it."

"Sometimes, Missy, being kind is more important than telling the truth."

"That's the way old people think."

"Apparently so."

"Anyway, I just have to get a little bit hotter each year. It won't be too hard."

"Then what?"

"Then whatever I want."

Our walk took us past the corner building where the Olivers had lived. I tried to distract Melissa by pointing out several gold and silver necklaces and a Gucci handbag in a shop window on the ground floor across the street, a choice boutique with about six dresses on a rack and a jewelry counter to one side near the door. But my efforts were to no avail. The girl had her own agenda.

"Let's go up," she said. "There must be a really humongous blood stain and stuff."

"It wouldn't be good for your digestion."

I steered Melissa quickly past the Prince Street entrance. "Besides, I don't have the keys with me now."

"I do."

"Don't be silly."

"I'm not silly; you're silly. Daddy gave me a whole set for when I came to visit on weekends."

I swore to myself with annoyance. My tenants are prone to dispensing extra keys like party favors—to friends, drivers, relatives, lovers. Luxury renters all want to be secure, as long as it doesn't inconvenience them in the least. Some have even been known to make spare copies for delivery boys from Gourmet Garage. It drives Don crazy. He saw to it that the elevator keys for the Prince Street building are hard to match and that each is clearly stamped "Do Not Duplicate." You can imagine how long that slowed up someone like Philip Oliver.

Forgoing a lecture, I took Melissa away from the murder scene to my gallery, where she was happy to surf the Internet while I made a few calls.

"Did you hear what Tom Cruise did last night?" she asked. "How do you spell Rwanda?"

When Laura returned from lunch, she stuck her head in the back office to say hello. The young visitor made her scowl quickly, until Laura remembered to be patronizing and nice.

"Whose little girl are you?" she asked.

"My daddy's. Two days a week."

"Her mother is Angela Oliver," I explained. "I'm her god-father."

"You've got to be kidding."

Melissa seemed suddenly puzzled.

"Do you know what that word means?" I asked her.

"It has 'god' in it. So I guess it means you're like a daddy, only you won't ever go away."

"Don't be too hard on your father. He's doing his best. Have you seen what's happening to him now?"

"Uh-huh, he's crazy. Everybody knows that. Mom says he has a degenerate brain."

Laura bit her lip.

"It's called a degenerative brain disease," I told Melissa.

"I know, but Mom likes to say it the other way."

Moving near the girl, I bent down to have a better look at her face. "When you're alone together, just the two of you, does your daddy ever act, you know, not crazy anymore? Is he ever just himself? Normal?"

Melissa sighed. "Who can tell? My friends and I talk about our flaky parents all the time. My one friend, Julie, her folks aren't even divorced, but her dad is stranger than anybody. Sometimes, he tries on Julie's mom's clothes, but they're way too small."

Shaking her head, Melissa looked at me with a serious, knit-brow expression. "Grown-ups are all kind of messed up in one way or another, don't you think?"

Laura smiled broadly, guiltily, and excused herself to get back to work.

Sitting down on the black leather couch, I asked Missy if she knew what had happened between her parents long ago.

"Daddy loved Mandy more than he did Mom and me. So he left."

"It's not that simple. Your daddy loves you very much. He told me."

"He told me, too. But he still went away. When you really love somebody you don't go away. You want to be with them all the time. Nobody makes you. You just want to."

"Sometimes it's more complicated than that. Sometimes you love two people at once."

"Then you have to choose."

I got up and went to the coffee maker and poured myself half a cup. Steam rose off the dark surface, and I watched the wisps twist and dissipate before I turned back to Missy.

"You're right," I said. "It took me a few extra years to figure that one out."

"Why? I thought you were supposed to be smart."

"It's a common mistake about me. Stick around and you'll get over it fast."

Melissa wiggled herself off the chair and traipsed over to stand near my side.

"You're funny," she said.

"I'm glad you think so, sweetheart. Funny is much harder than smart."

"That's because you have to be smart first to be funny."

"How did you get so clever?" I said.

"Practice. My mom asks loads of questions, too."

"Like what?"

"Like if daddy ever talks about other ladies, besides Aunt Mandy and Claudia."

"We're all curious about that."

She scowled at me.

"Sorry." I sipped the hot coffee. "It's terrible for you to be in the middle of all this at your age."

"I'm not so young. I'm almost a teenager."

"Really?"

"In five and a half weeks, I'll be twelve. It's practically the same thing."

"I see. Guess times have changed since I was in the sixth grade."

"Seventh, next fall."

A steady click of heels announced Laura's return. She carried some loan forms for me and a paper cup of hot chocolate for Melissa.

"How quaint," I smiled. "Here we are, just like a little family."

"In your dreams," Laura said. "I just figured you were probably being a bad host." She looked around disapprovingly. "I'm going to need this room in about fifteen minutes. Our favorite German client is coming in."

I winked at Melissa. "Let's go, sweets, money rules. We don't want to impede the forward march of art history, do we?"

Laura strode away down the hall, each step sounding like the clink of gold coins dropping into a sack. She was wearing four-inch spike heels and a cropped black skirt. I knew she must be about to close a deal. Laura's legs have sold more art than half the galleries in SoHo.

I went back to the desk and called Angela on her cell phone

to let her know where to find us. Her taxi pulled up to the gallery a few minutes later. I walked Melissa to the Greene Street entrance and watched her cross the few steps of sidewalk toward the open door of the cab, the sun bright on her red-and-white togs.

From inside the yellow sedan, Angela waved and called, "Thanks so much, Jack."

As I headed toward the back of the gallery again, I saw Laura peering at me from behind the reception counter. She shook her head slowly.

"Very touching," she said.

"You're not exactly the maternal type, are you, Laura?"

"Me? No. I've always thought of children as nature's way of telling you to stop having sex." She held up a sheet of slides and picked two. "I'm not ready for that yet. How about you?"

"I've never known what I'm ready for."

Turning, I glanced out again through the glass door and saw Melissa, safely strapped in, gaze back at me for a lingering moment. When our eyes met, she stuck out her tongue. Then abruptly, as the sunlight flared once on her blond hair, the taxi lurched forward and was gone.

20

"Come on, Jack," Hogan said the next day over a drink at MercBar. "Help me out."

We were sitting in a corner near the room divider made of woven deer antlers. The dark space, lit by a glowing kayak suspended over the bar, was packed with lounge cruisers having their first drinks and plotting their night. I remembered the place fondly, from my own predatory times.

"Use your annual junket, just this once," Hogan prodded, "for something other than just harvesting money and getting laid."

"Why," I asked, "should I take financial advice from a guy whose annual income wouldn't pay my dry cleaning bills?"

"Yeah, laugh. But if I were you, buddy, if I had no scruples detectable to the naked eye, I'd take this chance to do some good."

"Like how?"

"Like finding out all you can about this dreamboat Paul Morse. What do you know?"

"Not much," I admitted. "He performs once in a while in rathole galleries and warehouse spaces—in Dumbo or wherever. He shoots video constantly. Some of the footage he airs on late-night cable TV. No one really likes him. Girls think he's hot."

"And not liking him doesn't put them off?"

"Not in the short run, which is probably all Morse cares about."

"That's a break for him. Especially given the local consensus. Everyone I talked to at Amanda's memorial said he's a slimeball."

"You can't please everyone."

"Seems like you'd have to go some, though, to earn a sleazy reputation in this SoHo crowd of yours. You'd have to work pretty hard."

"Unless it comes naturally."

"Anyway, it's your call. Just ask around on your travels this summer. Or would you rather see Philip go down for murder?"

Hogan knew the answer to that. We finished our drinks and wished each other luck.

Little did I guess that the key to the case, the whole fatal charade, would come to me in Switzerland—from my own dear gallery director. I might have known. Nothing happens in the art world that Laura doesn't hear about quickly. Women trust her, and men just want to keep talking to stay in her presence.

The second week of June, we went to do the Basel art fair. Laura, arriving first, oversaw the installation of our booth—a double space in a premium center-aisle spot—while I trailed by a couple days. My first night in town, we attended a reception and then had dinner with some dismal European collectors. Afterwards, Laura and I adjourned, alone, to a cocktail lounge.

I looked around at the plush seating groups and the knee-high little tables, each with a candle encased in red glass. Behind the bar was a mirrored wall lined with shelves holding a hier-archy of bottles. The barman was washing glasses, wiping each slowly with a white cotton cloth. I felt oddly at home. It was one of those nameless lounges in one of those placeless hotels. A Michael Bolton tune played on the sound system, mercifully subdued. I had to remind myself what country we were in—not that it mattered much really.

"What do you know about Amanda's boyfriend?" I asked.

"Paul Morse? Just enough to be disgusted."

"Why's that?"

"He wears those awful three-quarters-length pants. And a baseball cap, backwards."

"Anything more serious?"

"Ask your Icelandic artist friend, the one with the cute little daughter."

"The Viking? Don't tell me Paul acted funny with his little girl."

"All I saw was a grown man flirting with a child." Laura paused. "Nauseating."

"Maybe they were just kidding around."

"Your Viking didn't think so. Paul was making a video of his Madison Square Park project. Little Anna got a big part in it."

"Anything wrong with that?"

"It's the way Paul treated her. Like the whole thing was a date. Fortunately, the Viking is a good father—in his big awkward way. He stayed close. If things had gone any further, I don't think Paul Morse would still be so pretty."

As I listened, something stirred in me like a sickness taking hold. I thought of a day years ago, when I went with Philip to pick up his daughter from a play date in Washington Square Park. Melissa was with a schoolmate, watching some Jamaican acrobats perform in the dry circular basin of the fountain, when she spied Philip and came tearing toward him.

"Daddy, Daddy, can my friend Cindy stay over tonight? She's like really cool and she'll bring some Disney tapes with her and it'd be super fun. I promise I'll do my homework first."

"Oh, all right, princess," her father said. "If you promise."

The girl was in his arms before the reply was half finished, kissing his neck—and peeking over his shoulder to say a polite "Hi, Uncle Jack."

Philip had no choice, of course. Melissa owned him more certainly, more completely, than he owned Oliver Technologies.

"Go, kumquat," he said. "Go get Cindy and Emmanuelle."

The girl squealed and ran back toward the fountain, swerving around skateboarders and NYU kids with guitars, goths in chain-draped black jeans, and gay hunks with single earrings and bright pocket handkerchiefs advertising their preferences—top or bottom, water sports or S&M.

"Adorable girl," I said. "You breed well."

"She's my great hope."

When Melissa started in our direction again, she and Cindy were holding Emmanuelle's hands. The French nanny, about nineteen and dressed in sultry disarray, made a small sensation as she passed through the crowd.

"Isn't it amazing?" Philip said.

"What, Emmanuelle's wardrobe?"

"No, what girls do to your head. Until they're a certain age, all you can think about is how you want to protect them, save them from everything bad in the world. But suddenly they change, they start to grow into women, and then all you can think about—if you're not related by blood—is how you want to screw them stupid."

"Is that why you hired Emmanuelle?"

"No," he said, "I hired her because she's extremely good at her work and speaks wonderful French, which Melissa desperately wants to learn. The two are crazy about each other."

"Very conscientious of you."

"Isn't it, though? I'm quite a devoted father, Jack. The wild nanny sex is just a bonus."

I watched the au pair leading the two girls back toward us through the park. Emmanuelle held their hands tightly, making a straight path through the crowd. The girls—one blond, one dark-haired—jumped and dodged and chattered away, at elbow height. As the threesome came closer, Emmanuelle smiled. She was still some way off, but even at this distance her ripe lips could stir an instinctual response. It was the kind of smile you might encounter on a corner of the Boulevard de Clichy at nightfall.

"And after you sleep with them," I said to Philip, "all you want to do is get rid of them."

"Of course. To make room for the next. It's a biological thing."

"Renewing the species, I suppose. Like looking for breakout artists at an MFA show."

"Sure. We all do our best."

21

So it was that, out of old friendship and brand-new empathy for Philip's loss, I was pulled relentlessly deeper into the Oliver affair. It's what I had to do, for the sweet vulnerable Melissa, for my own peace of mind, for some vague but insistent sense of propriety.

Or so I told myself anyhow.

Maybe a guilty conscience was the real reason I drank too much that night in Switzerland. I don't know.

Back in my room, already a little tight, I downed a couple glasses of minibar scotch before I called Hogan, and another as we talked. I filled him in about Paul Morse—what Laura had told me, little though it was. He thanked me grudgingly, as though he'd rather have heard something more directly tied to Amanda or nothing at all.

"How are you doing?" he asked. "Partied out?"

"It's duller than you think."

"You're breaking my heart."

I let it go. It'd be hard to convince Hogan that evenings of champagne and canapés with German industrialists who collect works by Roni Horn or Wolfgang Laib—polished metal tubes, piles of yellow pollen—are not as madly debauched as he might imagine.

"Any news about Philip?" I asked.

"Nothing solid, but I'm getting a fix on life inside Oliver Technologies. The place is run like a cult."

"That doesn't sound like Phil."

"It's not him, it's Andrews. He directs the show these days, and that's how he directs it. They have regional managers competing

for jewel-studded money clips in the shape of different coun-
tries, the ones with new high-tech markets they want to crack.
The salesmen all memorize long passages from a couple of books
ghost-written under Philip's name a few years ago. *Sell To Be
Rich: Winning the Microchip Revolution* and *The O-Tech Way
to Lifetime Success*. I have copies here. Each chapter lays out
some bullshit promotional strategy: 'The Future Is Cybernetic,'
'One World, One Market, One Winner,' 'Netting Profits from
the Internet.' "

"I get the idea."

"You don't know the half of it. They have these guys standing
on chairs together in team spirit sessions, chanting O-Tech
slogans and singing company songs."

"Makes the gallery business sound tame. Who's your source
for all this?"

"Margaret."

"Who?"

"Remember the tight-assed business lady, the junior exec who
showed us around the offices that day?"

"Do you ever miss one?"

"What? Is it my fault she's unhappy with her boss's scheme?"

"There's a scheme?"

"I don't know for sure yet, but Margaret describes a pretty
vicious scenario. Andrews and his cronies associate the company
as closely as possible with Philip Oliver. He's the genius, their
very own Howard Hughes, and all that. When he gets arrested
on the murder charge, the news stories come out about his
confession and his messed-up brain. The company stock tanks.
Andrews and the boys, as a gesture of faith in the underlying
strength of O-Tech, buy big and buy cheap—knowing all the
while that Philip will get off because they put him up to the
bogus confession in the first place."

"But even if Philip walks, his credibility is shot."

"By then, given the pace of our justice system, Andrews will have been running things for a good year and a half. Six quarters of steady growth, even without the boy wonder. Andrews becomes chairman, the stock returns to its true value, and he and his crew cash in big."

"Why is Margaret letting you in on this? What did Andrews ever do to her?"

"Nothing unusual, for a place like O-Tech. Let's just say he's a pig."

"That makes Margaret an awfully biased source."

"You know anybody who isn't? Believe me, she'll be a great witness."

"But is she telling the truth?"

"Who knows? The D.A. will be able to build a solid case around her, I can guarantee that. And that's all Bernstein asks."

"How's Philip's condition?"

"Worse. He's almost totally out of it these days."

"So what do you think? Is he faking?"

"I don't know. Those slick folks back at the Whitney service didn't know. His doctors don't know. Only Philip knows. And he may be fooling himself."

Once I hung up the phone, everything in the room was off kilter. Downing that third scotch didn't help, I suppose, but it was something to do. Of all the varieties of solitude, none is worse than the void you inhabit, the void you are, at midnight in a foreign hotel room alone. Stunned by booze, trying not to feel or think, you sit on the edge of the bed with the lights out, seeing the vague shapes of furniture in the glow from the window, and then you are gone.

That had been Philip's life for many years. When I first met him, he was convinced that he would die before thirty, and in a sense he was right. The young man he had been—inventive, whip-smart, tireless—gave way in time to a calmer, slower self, still hungry to win but more calculating in his maneuvers. Marrying Amanda was his single best career move. Then that Philip, too, gradually vanished, leaving only the skilled CEO, haunted by his casualties—damages inflicted, losses sustained—alone and restless in luxury hotel suites late at night. There, over the years, he grew ever more exacting in his requirements for call girls and casual pickups, as though the women were subcontracted microprocessor parts—until luckily, at last, Claudia materialized out of the pages of a magazine and restored his lost eager youth.

The spirited artist sustained him for a couple of years, pumping him full of false vigor. But now, with Mandy's murder, the fight seemed to have gone out of Philip once and for all. The person he argued with most often, most vociferously, had ended up suddenly and violently dead. In his psyche, corrupted by disease and liquor and God knows what else, a causal link had been forged between their old bitter words and Mandy's gory demise—a judgmental voodoo that his heart endorsed over the futile protests of his rational mind, whatever was left of it.

He was always susceptible that way.

Once, on a visit to the Sistine Chapel years ago, Philip stopped and stood transfixed in front of the *Last Judgment*, Michelangelo's soaring depiction of the saved on the right hand of Christ being swept up gloriously into Heaven and the damned on the left being cast ignominiously into Hell.

"Stunning," he said. "Terrifying." Other visitors pressed around him, and the guards tried to move him along. He turned expectantly to his wife.

"Oh, what nonsense," Mandy opined. "It's just art, Philip. Pictures selling some tiresome old religion. No one takes these things seriously anymore."

"Don't be such a heathen, my love."

"Oh, I'm not. Faith in rituals is exactly what we need." Mandy gestured with her sunglasses. "Right now, I'm all in favor of the four-course lunch ritual. Then, at six, I'd like to partake of the evening cocktail ritual. By all means, yes. Ceremonies and rituals. What else can preserve us in this barbaric age?"

What indeed?

Once the four of us had paid to visit a young matador as he prepared for the corrida in Madrid. His attendant wrapped him tightly about the middle with a strip of white cotton and encased him in his dazzling jacket. Hardly a word passed between them. To us, the rich *turistas*, the young man said nothing at all —merely nodded once at Nathalie before the door was swung open in front of him. He was already his role.

Well, isn't that what we do for each other time and again, in marriages and the arts, in jobs and professions? Each day we get up and put on the suit of lights—striding out to defy death in a ritualized sport, until the day death inevitably wins.

Death had certainly beaten Nathalie, in the nastiest way, taking its long painful time. At first, after I lost her, everything seemed lighter and cleaner. A weight had been lifted, and I felt joyously free. Only months afterwards did I realize that the lightness came from being empty, and the emptiness would go on forever.

I woke up in the dark, and took off my clothes. The alcohol was still coursing through me like poison. I could feel it in my capillaries and joints, trying to kill me—which might have been all right, if it weren't for the nagging discomfort required. I threw myself back on the bed and wondered what it would feel like to pray.

When I woke again, the room was painfully bright. I stood unsteadily before the bathroom's vicious mirror, glancing furtively at the wreck of my body. If you have ever once been athletic, you get up each morning feeling, knowing, that today you are weaker than yesterday, and that there is no reversing course now, no winning back the force that has gone. There is no hiding the insidious, sad facts from yourself. You drop your eyes. You try not to think about what you have been, try not to see yourself in the glass. Above all, you do not stare at the shriveled thing that dangles, crooked and thin, from your mangled left shoulder. You focus on coffee, a newspaper, and the morning light. For as long as possible, you forget the splendid things you did once with Nathalie, using two good arms and your fit body and the strength that pulsed through them.

Somehow, I made myself presentable in a white shirt and fitted gray suit (Italian but not too Italian for Switzerland) and got down to the dining room for my croissant and café au lait, resolutely silent in my seat near a window. Outside, the good citizens of Basel went about their late-morning business, strolling between stores and offices with enviable, seemingly untroubled precision.

After breakfast, I wandered through some nearby shops, killing time before the fair opened to the first rank of VIP buyers. On a side street, in a Milanese boutique, I came across several racks of dresses for preteens. Pulling one out, I held it at arm's length on the hanger.

"May I help you, sir?" a young woman said in English.

"Yes, thanks, I'm looking for a birthday present."

"For your daughter?"

"No, for a friend."

She regarded me for a long moment.

"For the daughter of a friend."

"Of course." She laid a well-manicured hand on one of the racks. "What is the size of the girl?"

"I'm not sure exactly." I raised my good arm to the level of my sternum. "About this tall. Slender."

"Very good, sir."

She showed me several choices, each more brightly elegant than the last. I settled on a solid-color jumper, pale green, with a plain bodice and thin shoulder straps.

"It's very fetching," the sales girl said.

I wondered where she had learned that mildly arcane English word.

"Your friend will be quite happy, I'm sure." She handed back my credit card. "And her mother as well."

22

For dealers, Art Basel is a work pit. I met Laura at the fair, and for the next five days all we did was sit in the booth and pitch deals to collectors and chat up magazine editors and case other dealers' wares and stay out much too late in restaurants currying favor with curators and museum board members. We sold well—about three and a half million dollars worth over the course of the four-day event—but our plane tickets, shipping, space rental, installation fees, hotel bills, meal checks and bar tabs were higher than ever before. Once the artist cuts were deducted (I have a quirk of always paying my artists promptly and in full), I felt I could have done as well working for a week in a stamping plant.

After the fair, Laura departed immediately for New York. Left on my own, I couldn't get the image of Paul Morse out of my head. In my tainted and restless dreams, he was talking again and again to the Viking's blond, open-faced young Anna, who was also somehow Melissa, while the figure of Amanda Wingate hovered in the background, watching and listening. What did Mandy know? What did she say to Paul once the girl vanished from my dream and the two adults drifted toward the hulking Prince Street building together?

"This Morse punk," Hogan said when I checked in by phone again. "Can you get close to him?"

"I can pretend to be interested in his work. That usually does the trick."

"Good. I need something. Bernstein is all over my ass."

"He's a lawyer," I said. "It's his favorite position."

"Yeah, tell me. So when do you get back?"

"Around the end of August."

"That's over two months from now."

"I need a vacation."

"Your whole life is a vacation, isn't it?"

"Compared to yours, I suppose."

Later, I spent a few days in Lisbon, arranging a museum show for a Portuguese artist, and a couple weeks with friends at a broken-down villa near Siena. Every evening we sat out at a long wooden table with a view down the hills to the darkened valley. We ate and drank wine and talked endlessly. None of the Italians had any firsthand knowledge of Philip and Mandy, though some of them had heard of Claudia. When I asked them about her father's family, their expressions grew defensive. She had an uncle whose name was known with respect, especially farther south.

"And he has friends and relatives in New York?" I asked.

"Certainly, many," someone answered.

"Dangerous friends?"

My host lifted his hands, palms up. "All friends are dangerous," he said, "if you offend them."

That night, after one of the local village's erratic mail deliveries, I retired early to watch a tape that the Viking had sent me—the documentary short that Paul Morse had made for him the year before in New York.

It began with a row of steel beams lying in a gravel pit in New Jersey: a long anticipatory silence punctuated by insect sounds and the distant passing of planes, then dust and a tremendous walloping explosion and the bent, puckered beams raining down. Later, after the pieces had been trucked to Madison Square Park, about a hundred people gathered under the tall, aged trees to watch four "movement artists" slink and sway through the tangle of fractured metal.

Near the end of the tape was a brief party segment with the

ten-year-old Anna, ice-eyed and blond, looking straight into the lens and singing "I Will Survive."

I gave the Viking a call in Reykjavík.

"Laura says you know Paul Morse pretty well."

"Ah, Laura, the great American beauty. How do you keep from falling in love with her, Jack?"

"She makes it easy."

"For you, not for me. Unfortunately, I have no great riches."

"I know, it's a tragedy. Have you heard from Morse lately?"

"Me, no. Only Anna. She used to get e-mails from him now and then."

"About what?"

"Coming back to New York for a visit. He offered to pay her way, to be her private guide."

"How'd she feel about that?"

"Anna loves New York, but Paul Morse gives her the creeps."

"And you?"

"I told him what I'd do if he didn't back off. Anna hasn't heard from him since."

"What was Paul like?"

"A cool guy. Too good-looking for his own good. My girlfriend dug him, though. A little too much."

"Did you talk with him?"

"Only technical things about the shoot. He was excellent."

"Any problems dealing with him?"

"No, not after I got him to take the camera off Anna."

It was odd. The Viking's young daughter was very telegenic, but I couldn't guess what she had to do with the Madison Square Park project.

"Anna felt a little left out," the Viking explained. "Paul made it a point to treat her like someone special, a little star. He even let her sing a song at the end."

"That's not exactly a little girl's tune."

"My Anna is very grown-up in her head."

"I know the type."

"Ha, yes. You know all the female types, don't you, Jack?"

"I don't suppose Paul ever mentioned his love life?"

"You'd have to ask my ex-girlfriend about that."

"Did he come on to her?"

"More likely Svava made some play for him, the foolish girl. That Morse fellow is a babe magnet, Jack—but dodgy."

"How so?"

"Sometimes, when he talked to Anna—too softly, too long, leaning in too close—I just wanted to strap him to one of my I-beams and light the fuse."

"Did he try anything?"

"No, not that I know." The Viking was silent for a moment. "The guy's still alive, isn't he?"

23

At summer's end, I came back to a torrent, a cascade, of New York show announcements and dinner invitations. The Lower Manhattan Arts Festival was starting the second week of September with sixty-five simultaneous gallery openings, and the major museums were not far behind with their fall exhibition debuts. After our new intern had sorted the mailings and printed out the e-mail notices, I spent an hour and a half entering the chosen events into my calendar and sending back the appropriate RSVPs.

Meanwhile, Laura plied me with questions about our own September show—her way, no doubt, of making me feel that I was still in charge. We were opening with Jorge Garcia Ramirez, an installation artist known for his over-the-top recreations of Puerto Rican domestic interiors. He had everything a dealer could ask: "authentic" origins in the street culture of Spanish Harlem, low material costs—how expensive could silk flowers and a few polychrome plaster saints be?—and increasing market cachet after his appearances in the most recent Lyon and Gwangju biennials.

"Besides," Laura pointed out, "it never hurts to start the season with a roomful of Latinas in clear plastic heels."

September is also a prime month in New York for residential moves, which had Don scrambling from building to building to inspect damage and oversee apartment cleanups and rehabs. That fall, neither of us worried very much about the maintenance and upgrade outlays, since rents were notching ten percent higher on new leases and commercial ground-floor spaces in

SoHo had tripled in value over the past two years. Don's one complaint was about my loft "giveaway" to Angela Oliver.

I ran into Angela in the building lobby on the day she moved in. The workmen were wheeling padded chairs into the freight elevator while she counted and watched. Her young daughter, all business, was checking items off a list.

"Everything OK upstairs?" I asked.

"The space couldn't be better. Don did a beautiful job."

"And you're all set with the Bradford School?"

"Melissa had her orientation yesterday, and we bought her school uniform. A plaid skirt, blue blazer, knee socks. She starts a week from Monday."

The girl did not look up from her clipboard.

"Missy, the people at Bradford had best teach you some better manners. Say hello to Uncle Jack."

"It's not fair," the girl answered. "Why me first? He's the one who went away for three months." She checked another box on the form. "Hello, Uncle Jack."

"Only two and a half months. And I brought you a present."

"You did?"

"What on earth for, Jack?" There was a note of forced wonder in Angela's voice. "You didn't have to do that."

"For her birthday, of course."

"You see, Missy," Angela teased. "Now don't you feel ashamed for being so rude?"

"No, it's late. My birthday is way past. I'm practically old already."

Angela half-smiled at me and shook her head.

Later that afternoon, when I stopped downstairs with the black Italian store bag (an item faintly out of place amid the scattered furniture and bubble-wrapped maquettes), Melissa was a little more tolerant.

Granted, she did complain, "There's no card, and it's not even wrapped." But she quickly pulled the Valentino box out of its gold-lettered sack and ran to hold the shift up in front of a bedroom mirror, returning with a broad smile despite her petulant act.

"What do you say?" Angela prompted.

"Thank you, Uncle Jack. For not buying me some stupid kid gift."

"You're entirely welcome."

"It's pretty cool, in a grown-up way." She glanced imploringly at Angela. "Mom, can I try it on now?"

"All right, hurry up. And show us, so we can see if it fits."

The girl was already halfway to the rear of the loft by then. Once she started to fuss and primp out of earshot, I asked Angela if she'd seen anything of her ex-husband that summer.

"Quite a lot, sadly. Philip's spending much less time at the office, and starting to drive young Claudia crazy. She has three gallery shows to get ready before spring, and now the man who used to make life easy for her is becoming a terrible burden. It's not what she signed on for, I'm afraid."

"No. But why should you step in—given how Philip treated you?"

"I don't do that much. I take him to the park once in a while. I meet him for coffee at Il Mondo, so that Claudia can get her materials at Pearl Paint or whatever without enduring his endless pestering questions. You can't believe how Philip repeats himself these days, like a child."

"It's kind of you to take an interest in his latest girlfriend. You weren't so keen on her before I left."

"I've seen what she goes through now. She's not made for it, poor thing. What am I going to do—let Philip rot?"

"Some ex-wives would."

"I don't mind helping Claudia. She's a sweet girl, really, and she never did anything vile to me."

"She wasn't so kind to Amanda."

"Amanda didn't deserve much kindness."

Angela looked at me squarely. There was no false sentiment for the dead, no backing down. Mandy was simply the woman who had stolen her life.

"She was a Wingate," Angela said. "She never gave a thought to anyone else."

"And Philip did? He was pretty heartless to you in the end."

"He was, indeed, except for the Westchester property. He couldn't help himself, I suppose. What can you expect from a young man getting rich way too fast? Girls are everywhere, and he didn't know enough to be kind. I probably didn't either, at the time. You remember how it goes with monogamy, Jack. It's not a thing most people are good at."

"No, not anyone I know."

Angela looked away. She seemed to see something there, in the unfocused distance.

"Anyway, it's not as though my own record were spotless, is it?" she said. "After the breakup, I mean. We were all a bit wild back then. You most of all."

I tried not to let my mind go there. Certain nights and places and people are best forgotten, or held apart in the realm one reserves for unhealthy dreams. Over the years, forgetfulness has proven the best policy for my emotional stability and my friendships.

I do recall, however, asking Philip once—after the divorce— how he felt about Angela's sexual revenge.

"Awful," he said, "just sick. Though, oddly, it doesn't cut down my own desire for her." He laughed. "On the contrary, in fact. It stirs my lust."

"And beyond that?"

"I'm not sure there is much beyond that, for people like us."

Melissa interrupted my reverie, zipping out of the bedroom and prancing toward us like a two-week-old colt.

"Look, Mom, I'm ready for the runway."

She imitated a model's sulking, exaggerated walk. The long-waisted shift hung surprisingly well, exposing her high wide shoulders, smoothly aglow.

"Don't you look cute?" Angela said.

"Not cute, Mom." Missy went up on her toes in white socks. "Fabulous."

Angela watched the girl cautiously. Melissa, her cheeks sucked in, gave a quick pout and turned.

"Well," Angela said, "I suppose it will be nice for the school dance at Christmastime."

"Yay!"

Melissa started to run to the changing area. Then, apparently remembering her Ps and Qs, peeled around and charged back to us again.

"Thank you, Uncle Jack. It's a totally wicked birthday present." She pulled on my limp arm until I bent forward. Her lips brushed quickly on each cheek.

"That's how the French do it," she explained.

"Yes, I remember."

She was gone in a flurry of limbs, leaving Angela and myself suddenly alone again, irrelevant and slightly spent. "To think, this is only the beginning," her mother said.

"The beginning of what?"

"All the girly-girl stuff. I just hope I can handle it."

"Well, you've made a lovely start."

"Twelve years and a long way to go." Angela suddenly looked her age, a wisp of dry hair slipping over one ear. "It takes so much to get a child decently civilized. With so much to fret about—school projects, dance lessons, clothes, music classes. Now boys."

"Don't worry. Melissa is gifted, and she has you—like a mother and sister in one. She'll do fine."

"Good is not good enough anymore, Jack. The kids today have to do better than we did, in every way. Otherwise, what's the point?"

Melissa came back out to the living room, wearing old jeans with fringed cuffs. Her T-shirt read "Peaches."

"Uncle Jack was just telling me how special he thinks you are," Angela said.

"He probably says that about all the girls."

"Maybe they all are to him."

"Well, I want to be different."

"You are, dear. You're special to both of us."

Missy rolled her eyes. "Oh please, Mom. That's so fakey." The girl gathered her hair and snapped it into a ponytail with a blue elastic band. "Sometimes I think the only one who isn't a phony around here is Uncle Paul."

"Who's that?" I asked.

"Paul Morse," Angela said. "A young artist friend of Amanda's. He's been very nice to Melissa. The three of them used to pal around together when Missy came in on weekends. They needed a man around. Philip, you know, was always at the office on Saturdays."

I felt something like food poisoning enter my system.

"Do you know this Paul well, Missy?" I asked.

"Pretty well. He takes me to Tower Records sometimes. We both like Rocky Road ice cream, and he's fun to talk to."

"Where do you talk?"

"At the library. A couple of times he was at the computers when I went in with Aunt Mandy. They don't let you talk too much there, though, even if you whisper. So sometimes we hang out at the Internet Cafe on Lafayette. He really knows how to zoom around on the Web."

"I'll bet he does. Did he show you any strange stuff on there?"

"Sure, that's part of the fun."

"Did he ever take you to his house to show you things?"

"Not yet."

"Don't, Melissa. It's not cool."

"We just go to the park sometimes. We talk back and forth online every day. Instant messages, chat rooms, games—he's great at all that. Anyway, what do you care?"

"Uncle Jack is being possessive, Missy," Angela said. They both seemed relieved, even glad. "It means he likes you a lot."

The girl crinkled her face. "Does not."

"Tell her, Jack."

"You're my fairy-tale maiden—the only girl I bought a present for. No one else, not even your mom."

"Well, good. You made the right choice."

"I didn't choose. It just happened."

"Like a proper knight," Melissa said. Her right arm swept the space before her, and she walked back to her room quietly this time, with a regal tilt to her head.

"She's a charmer," I said to Angela. "You should be very proud."

"Thanks. It's been a hard adjustment for her, with the move and my fall show coming up."

"You've been distracted?"

"The preparations are endless, and Michael is no help. He just asks for more checks—for a catalogue, for announcement cards, for magazine ads. Now my publicist is harassing me for an artist's statement."

That was not a happy thought. I had already seen the over-done mailer, a packet containing Angela's bio sheet, with its sporadic exhibition history, along with color laser prints of her sculpture, a windy press release, and a contact card announcing the availability of her work for private viewing before the "highly anticipated" show at Michael Loomis Fine Arts in November. In just a few pages, the packet contained nearly every error a publicist can make in overselling an artist.

"Before your agent-lady starts trooping suburban art mavens through here," I said. "Let me bring in a few people who matter. A critic or two, a curator."

"Would you, Jack? You're a dear." Her expression turned imploring. "I need an informed response," she said. "And a record. Otherwise, it will be as though the show never happened."

"Isn't it enough that you did it?"

"No, not for me. Being ignored is death."

"Michael won't ignore you, if you sell."

"Right, always that." She gave me a disgusted look. "Meanwhile, everything we really care about comes and goes for nothing. Why?"

"I don't know. Maybe to teach us our place."

24

I couldn't expend too much time on Angela's second career start. Thankfully, she had the resourceful Michael Loomis for that considerable problem. My more pressing concern was getting Hogan's take on Paul Morse. According to a Lower Manhattan Arts Festival brochure, Morse was doing documentary footage for Sylvester Williams, the hedge-fund manager behind the event. Williams—who collected art with his eyes closed, by relying on hearsay and his own patented price-appreciation algorithms—had always wanted to be part of the art scene, so he simply bought his way in, creating the annual burst of pseudo-excitement that was the LMAF: artworks paraded along Broome Street, dancers twining in a former taxi garage near Tenth Avenue and 24th, that sort of nonsense.

Since Williams got his celebrity status by climbing on the backs of hard-working dealers like me, I opted out, saving my gallery's fall debut for the following week. So now I was conveniently free to wander. Paul, as the festival's official videographer, might be anywhere during the openings, but he was sure to turn up that night for the launch party at Pete Lemon's Treasure Chest. I arranged to meet Hogan on Broome, at Wilde Initiatives, telling him he'd have to work late afterwards.

The festival was split that year, with half the activities taking place in Chelsea and half in SoHo. It didn't matter where you went first; both neighborhoods were thronged with art world denizens, glad to be back in town, and with young wannabes wearing the wrong shade of black. The outsiders had probably read the breathless write-ups in *New York* magazine, *Flâneur*, and *Time Out*.

It was impossible to see much art, of course. Everywhere I went, the crowds pressed thick with people talking about their summer travels and discussing dinner plans and afterparty leads. I met my compatriots by the score, kissing cheeks and gripping elbows as I wound steadily through the melee.

I toured Chelsea first, hitting maybe a dozen galleries in the first hour, then cabbed back to SoHo to cruise through the Drawing Center, Jack Tilton, David Zwirner, Caren Golden, Spencer Brownstone, Friedrich Petzel and Artists Space before pushing my way into the horde at Wilde Initiatives.

I was still trying to figure out the dealer's new angle. Having made his mark advising big-money art collectors for HSBC, Frank Wilde had recently developed an enthusiasm for street art and young punksters. These days, his openings were jammed not with A-list spenders but with skateboarders, tattoo freaks, a few old duffer artists, and a lot of pierced and flannel-clad young freeloaders from across the East River. Maybe Frank was having a midlife crisis; otherwise, who cares about these losers?

Hogan was so late that I ran out of adults to talk to and actually had to look at the pictures for a while. They were big, slick Lisa Greystone cartoon paintings, guaranteed (despite the boho-carnival atmosphere) to start the gallery's season off with a healthy cash flow.

Hogan, it turned out, had gotten caught in the crush at the bar table near the door. "Bad wine in plastic cups," he said once he squeezed his way to the center of the main gallery. "You people really know how to live."

Wilde Initiatives was clearly was not the former USMC sergeant's kind of scene. We were jostled left and right, and the noise made it necessary to talk just below a shout.

"Things will improve," I said. "Pete Lemon always throws a good party." Prudently, I didn't mention what kind.

25

To brighten the evening for Hogan, I took him over to Café Noir with a couple of young gallery assistants, both brunettes and both newly liberated from home and college. We sat in the back, where the girls could practice their smoking.

"*Très louche*," one of them said.

In fact, the bar area up front was even noisier than the gallery, filled with international club kids, many of them French. However, our partially enclosed retreat in the rear of the restaurant, behind a beaded curtain, was relatively secluded and calm. We could actually converse as we ate our grilled shrimp, falafel, and couscous. Once the girls went off to the bathroom together, Hogan gave me some news.

"This Morse guy is connected with the Olivers in more ways than one."

"You've been talking to Margaret again?"

"I asked her if Philip had a clue about his wife's little dalliance. She said that nothing gets past him, it's more a question of what he can remember."

"In this instance, it might be a blessing to forget."

"So I asked if she'd ever heard Philip mention Paul Morse."

"Did she know the name?"

"Not just the name but the smooth face and the baby-blue eyes. Seems several of the women at O-Tech think Morse is dreamy."

"He's been to the office?"

"To see Andrews."

I was stumped. "About making videos for the company?"

"She wasn't sure. Turns out Andrews is an art collector, too. It's a vice he picked up from the company founder, I guess."

The girls came back, bringing a maelstrom of small talk. I paid the check, and told them we could all go to the Treasure Chest but they'd be on their own. Hogan and I had to meet a friend downstairs in the dressing room.

The girls looked at each other and shrugged. "No problem."

The club was only a few blocks away, in a bleak stretch of oversized buildings beyond the west edge of SoHo. Long and low, this particular structure looked like a displaced bowling alley, with an anxious crowd shifting on the sidewalk outside. The real action would come later, after two AM, but the arts festival party had already drawn a large clot of hopefuls to the velvet rope. I went up to Steve, the doorman, and told him we were four. He nodded and unhooked the rope and fastened it behind us again. Inside, the place was still half deserted.

"What the hell?" Hogan said.

My friend is not a big fan of hip clubs. I guess workaday Bayside has deprived him of an appreciation for the way room leads onto room, through half-hidden passageways, past various levels and checkpoints, each with brass stanchions and taciturn guards—all the refinements of exclusion that give the journey its addictive, masochistic allure. Hogan resents the sense of an infinite regression of privilege, of ultimately not being cool enough for the innermost sanctum. (Unless, of course, you are.) To him, it's all undemocratic, the antithesis of American classlessness, equal opportunity, and fair play.

"Somebody ought to haul the owner's ass into court," he groused.

What can I tell you? The guy actually believes in such things. SoHo, however, wasn't designed for sentimental ex-Marines. Every dealer knows that his product is half object and half mystique. Intimidation sells art. As long as that's the case, I'm happy to let the non-rich and the cultural bumpkins tremble at my gallery door.

Apart from the LMAF contingent, the crowd that night was a typical Penny Lane mix—about one-third straight, one-third gay, and one-third transvestite. Some hot young "women" of indeterminate gender were dancing in go-go cages.

"There's our boy," I told Hogan.

Across the room, near the still empty bandstand, the tall, peach-skinned young man held an expensive video camera on his shoulder, taping a dancer in a neon pink miniskirt.

"Good equipment," Hogan said. "But guys who look like Morse usually end up in front of the lens, not behind it."

"Who *is* he?" the girls wanted to know.

"Jack's boyfriend," Hogan said. "Didn't he tell you?"

They laughed, a little too eagerly. "Introduce us?" the pret-tier one asked.

"Later."

I steered the young pair to a banquette and got them some drinks.

"Practice being beautiful for a while," I advised. "The competition is going to get pretty stiff in here soon."

26

A bouncer I knew opened the backstage door, and Hogan and I went down to visit Penny Lane before her first set. It wasn't really a dressing room at the bottom of the steep stairs, just a corner of the low-ceilinged basement with some folding screens and a vanity table. The band members were standing around having their last cigarettes under the fluorescent lights. The black leather of their pants matched the sheen of the walls. Penny, her TV-commercial legs crossed, sat dusting face powder over the foundation cream that hid a five-o'clock shadow.

"Wolford hose?" I asked.

"You know me, doll. Only the finest. Who's your friend?"

Hogan came forward and extended his hand. "I'm Hogan, a private investigator."

"Wonderful, if it makes you happy, dear." Penny eyed him from head to toe as she proffered her hand. "Exactly whose privates did you want to investigate tonight? Love your outfit."

Hogan glanced down at his striped tie and Haggar slacks.

"*Moi même*," Penny said, "I'm a chanteuse." She dusted one side of her throat, then the other. "Don't cuff me until after the performance. A girl's got to make a living, you know. Oh, where *have* all the sugar daddies gone?" Penny examined her eyebrows in the mirror. "That's very good, don't you think?…Hmmm, hmmm, long time passing…" Half-turning, she called to one of the clustered musicians, "Michael, I might add a new number to the last set tonight."

"Hogan really is a P.I.," I said.

"'Really'…in reality?" Penny said, drawing back. "Hasn't Mama taught you not to use that word in here?"

"Sorry. It's just that he's eager to meet Paul Morse."

"How unusual. We could all go gray waiting in *that* line, sweetheart." She glanced at Hogan. "Well, not you, I see."

"Hilarious," Hogan replied. "Who else would have thought of a bald joke? I'd laugh, only I'm working right now."

"Whatever you say, dear." And to me: "I love it when they're stern."

Hogan let it pass. "I have a few questions about Morse's romantic life."

"Don't we all?"

"Is he working with you at the moment?"

"Yes, we have a professional relationship. He's documenting my genius for posterity."

"Let's hope he has enough tape."

I left them to their repartee and went over to say hello to the fellows in the band, friends of Penny's from the old neighborhood in the Bronx. They still remembered me from the time I hired the group to entertain at my New Year's Eve party a few years back.

"Great champagne that night," one of them said.

"Gift from a client."

"Have you met Rickie?" another asked.

"No."

Standing nearby was a cute number in a transparent top with black bra, a miniskirt, and dark hose. Even on her spike heels, she was no more than five foot five.

"Are you part of the act?" I asked.

"No, I'm not an entertainer. Are you?"

"Not intentionally."

"Being a fan is important, too. What would Penny do without an audience?"

Curl up and die didn't seem like a very nice answer, so I just shrugged my shoulders. An awkward silence fell between the little cross-dresser and me. Finally, she looked earnestly into my face and asked, "Do you have any children?"

"Not that I'm aware of."

"What a shame. You have very fatherly eyes."

"That's odd, my wife said the same thing. She's not around anymore."

"Women are so fickle. My wife's gone, too, for no good reason. But I do have a wonderful son. A star student at Saint Ann's. He wears button-down shirts and Dockers, and wants nothing to do with his father's dress-up hobby."

"Kids need to rebel, I guess."

"Oh, I'm glad he's so white-bread. It gives me stability."

On those heels, I thought, you could use it.

Hogan came over and steered me away by the arm.

"Do you mind?" I said. "We're having a family-values chat here."

"You can finish your PTA meeting later. Morse is on his way down. Your friend gave me the scoop. In addition to his late-night cable access gig, Morse runs a little production company, also called PM Videos. He deals mostly in weird-ass downtown stuff."

"Is there any other kind?"

"We need to get inside."

"Be my guest."

"I can't do it, Jack. It's not my world, and I wouldn't know how to act. Hell, I can't even find these damned clubs and lounges. But you, you're perfect for the job."

I wasn't sure whether to thank him or be deeply offended.

"Paul's on the stairs," I said. "What exactly do you want me to do?"

"Save his ass. I'll confront him, ride him hard. You shut me up. Be the guy's new best friend."

As Paul descended, he switched on a video lamp, although his blond presence alone might have illuminated the cavern. He was wearing tight jeans and an open-neck shirt.

"PM, honey," Penny said, "this very shiny gentleman would like to talk to you."

Paul turned off the light. "What's up, dude?" he asked.

"I'm looking into the Amanda Oliver murder," Hogan said. "I hear you knew her pretty well." He flashed something that Morse probably thought was a badge, though it was just a P.I. license.

"I knew her, sure. Nothing special. I know a lot of women."

"Yeah, well, the others haven't turned up dead. Not yet, anyhow."

The young man blinked. "Mandy was a friend and a financial backer. That's all. I was totally blown away by her murder."

"My condolences. Now I'd like to get a picture of just how generous her patronage was. Like whether it extended to the bedroom."

"And I," Penny interjected, "would love to have an eight-by-ten reprint of that shot, *s'il vous plaît*."

"Don't you have to go wiggle your ass for money upstairs or something, Miss Lane?" Hogan said.

He turned sharply back to Paul. "You also do some work for Philip Oliver's company. What might that be?"

"It might be a lot of things," Paul said. "In fact, it's a batch of corny training videos for overseas O-Tech employees."

"Very high-culture."

"The gig pays," Paul shrugged. "It helps support my art habit."

"What does O-Tech do with your handiwork?"

"They send tapes out every month to the branches in Europe and Asia. *How to Spot Micro-Circuitry Defects* is one of my favorites."

"I see, you're not just pretty; you're funny, too. Was mocking the hubby's business ventures part of your sex banter with Mandy?"

"I don't know what you're talking about."

"I'm talking about you humping Philip Oliver's wife. A lady who was killed by someone who got very close to her."

Paul looked at Hogan coldly for a second. "Haven't you insulted enough people tonight?"

"I'm just warming up, buddy boy. Try this one. You look scrawny enough to be the suspect some neighbors described to me. A skinny stranger who was in and out of the building a lot when Philip was gone."

"You're a real asshole, you know?"

"I can be." Hogan took his measure. "Want to tell me where you were at midday on Wednesday, May fourth?"

"Getting laid, actually—something you ought to try before your joints go arthritic."

"You mean you screwed Mandy Oliver that day?"

"Oh, gag, no. The woman was old enough to be my mother."

"And that would make you a…?"

Paul flushed, and stepped closer to Hogan.

"Don't mind this guy," I said to Paul quietly, sliding between the two. "I've known Hogan forever. He's all bluster when he has no leads." I drew Paul to the side, away from a confrontation. After exchanging a glare with me, one that looked entirely unfeigned, Hogan stalked off.

"You shouldn't be saying anything without a lawyer present anyhow."

"And that would be you?"

"Me, no," I laughed. "I'm just an art dealer. Jackson Wyeth."

I noted, with some satisfaction, that the name registered immediately on Paul.

"Sorry," he said. "Of course. I should have recognized you. I just didn't expect to run into anyone classy down here."

"I beg your pardon," Penny called out, her voice rising.

"No one from the gallery business, I mean." Paul bowed slightly toward his bejeweled client.

"Jackson knows talent when he sees it," Penny replied. "He happens to be one of my most ardent devotees."

We waited for her to turn back to the mirror.

"I remember your pieces from the video survey at P.S. 1 last fall," I told Paul. "Those junior-high girls making popcorn and talking about Krafft-Ebing cases. Very incisive."

He favored me with a look that held a question, a cautious one; I tried to keep my expression blank, or mostly so. In previous decades, gay men might have glanced at each other this way, neither wanting to be the first to speak up. Today, nobody cares much about man-on-man sex. Only certain other practices—both illegal and politically incorrect—entail elaborate codes and secrets.

"You should come around to the gallery sometime," I told him.

"Believe me, I will."

I gave him a card with my direct number. "Call me next week."

Penny broke in with a complaint. "There's far too much commerce going on here. Out, out. The real art, gentlemen, is about to transpire upstairs."

She was right. We followed the group up to the large room, now jammed, where Penny mounted the stage like a prison-camp commandant and launched into several Velvet Underground covers, soulfully channeling Lou Reed in drag.

The gallery girls, on their third round of drinks, had been joined by two male artists from Dumbo. They all waved and nodded across the crowded space. At the end of the first set, Hogan said he'd had enough and would call tomorrow to work out a plan. That meant that I would have to continue getting chummy with Paul—a disquieting prospect.

But right now I needed to pay my tab and pass the girls on to their slacker studs, before I got stuck supporting an entire Brooklyn art commune at the table. As I waited for my credit card to come back, I leaned against a pillar, watching Hogan thread his way to the red-lit exit past a couple of embracing dykes and a bisexual Guggenheim curator.

27

The first time Paul came to the gallery, he brought a sample of his work. They always do. Ordinarily, I wouldn't have looked at anything in front of him, since it's a position you don't want to be in. React to an artist's work too little, or a shade negatively, and you risk crushing a soul; react too positively and you end up with a house pet.

Paul loaded the tape into the VHS player in the back office, an alcove lined with art books. The screen ran blue for a few seconds, then suddenly bloomed into a series of downtown images—shots from clubs, bars, and galleries, with conversational voiceover and occasional spurts of visual narrative. Barbara Gladstone's director talked about a young artist who had just made a tremendous New York debut with Vaseline sculptures and a nude performance in which he worked his way, rock-climber-fashion, across the gallery ceiling. A transvestite hooker from the Chelsea piers enthused about a sex slave at the Vault who crawled from table to table kissing feet, but only those clad in Italian shoes. A writer for *Arts* magazine, leaning on the bar at Boom, riffed on the "posthuman" import of a new-media survey at Cooper Union.

I asked Paul how and when he got into video.

"It was a real fluke," he said. "After I finished NYU undergrad, people I knew started going off to, like, Prague or Berlin to hang out and make a start. Those were supposed to be the cool scenes. I wanted something different. Then I met Cao Fang, and she took me to Shanghai. For two years it was heaven."

"For a guy like you, it had to be."

"You know China, man?"

"That's a long story. A sad one."

"Yeah, so what can I say? Fang's friends liked my style. I liked what they had to offer."

"What was that?"

"Anything I wanted. Cheap."

On the monitor, Wigstock contestants sang Motown tunes from a stage in Tompkins Square Park.

"And that led you to a career in performance art and video?" I asked.

The monitor shifted to shots of police rousting homeless people from their cardboard shelters under the trees.

"I developed some specialized tastes in China."

That sly dance again. Something told me that Paul wasn't talking about a penchant for roasted duck tongues or shrimp plucked live from a bowl of spiced broth.

"The place will do that to you," I said.

"You travel, you learn," Paul smiled. "I discovered that weird things become a lot more respectable when you rename them art."

"More lucrative, too," I said. "It's one of the keys to my success."

"You know Zheng Bao? He's one far-out artist. You could find his performances on pirated tapes on the streets—eating the flesh of a live pig, spending three days locked in a bank vault with a thin breathing tube. I met him at the triennial in Guangzhou. 'An act recorded,' he said, 'becomes strong like a dream.'"

Judging from the work I'd seen at P.S. 1, my guess was that Paul's dreams ran like a foul ditch through Neverland. The Viking's account of his attentiveness to Anna suggested just how treacherous they might be. To test my hunch, I'd laid out a volume on Balthus's paintings before Paul came to the gallery. When the tape ended, I switched on a table lamp, its light falling softly on the cover image of a young girl splayed across the lap of another female, slightly older, who was lifting the child's skirt. I saw Paul's eyes go to the book, and dart away.

"Where did you train?" I asked him.

"Back in the States, at Cal Arts."

"You didn't opt for film school?"

"I thought about it, but they don't really teach my specialty there. So instead I came to New York and slogged around the gallery circuit for three years. Begging for shows, basically. You know the drill. A regular artist—a sculptor—goes into a gallery, they might hold his slides up to the light for thirty seconds before they say, 'Nice work, but not for us.' Those guys are the lucky ones. Just try to get a dealer to look at a twenty-minute performance video on a Tuesday afternoon. No way. Finally, I decided to wise up and start my own production company. Let other people squirm for the camera, I thought. I'll do the editing."

"You could make a hell of a lot more in commercial work. Music videos, TV ads."

"Not my interest. Even a whore doesn't take every john."

"But you clearly have a penchant for—what should I call it?—a certain degree of luxury."

"Sure. We all need a few goodies to get us through the night. Mine are minor."

The pun was like a secret knock, a handshake of brotherhood in the gathering dark.

"In that case," I said, "you might like to meet a few of my friends. We have an informal discussion group—and an occasional boys' night out—with pictures and a bit of amateur philosophizing. We call it the Balthus Club."

"Sounds promising," Paul said, still being cagey. "I like that old perv's work, even though he's just a painter."

"Take a look over here." I led him to the book I knew he'd

been dying to open. We went through the pages slowly, lovingly. A fake count's rapt images of languid and sensuous female adolescents. Girls, half nude, stretching like cats in rooms filled with slant sunlight. Girls in shorts, hiking among the overwhelming rocks of an Alpine pass.

"Righteous," Paul said. "Really well done. But I'm more of a photo guy, myself."

"Who do you like?"

"Let's look at some Bellmer next time."

That was the thought he left me with. Hans Bellmer's life-size female doll, headless, bound and jammed into a staircase or hung inverted from a tree. The work of an artist, spurned by the Nazis, who depicted his human lover, an eventual suicide, bent double and wrapped in flesh-creasing cords like some infernal unopened gift.

28

That Thursday, Hogan and I attended an Anselm Kiefer opening at the Museum of Modern Art. I thought it would be a chance to see Philip in operation again, and maybe Hogan would even enjoy the high seriousness of the show's esoteric Kraut.

I was right, on both counts. Threading among the artist's enormous landscape paintings dappled with straw, his Nazi salute photographs, his pedestals bearing huge books with lead pages, we encountered at least half the people of note on the New York art scene, gathered back then in the older, smaller, better MoMA, before it became an art mall.

"This Kiefer guy seems pretty damn ballsy," Hogan pronounced, confirming my theory that crime-solving sharpens all one's critical faculties, provided the artwork on view is butch enough.

We came out of the galleries just in time to see a strained meeting between Philip and his second ex-mother-in-law. A tall collection of aristocratic bones, Livinia Wingate stood chatting with friends in front of one of the improvised bars manned by a catering staff in white jackets. Her black Dior sheath was set off by swept-back silver hair and a single teardrop diamond at her throat. Somehow Philip had gotten two steps ahead of the bare-shouldered Claudia. Radiant in red taffeta that night, the *bella donna* had paused to return a hello from a fellow artist—a printmaker, clad in faded black jeans and a black linen jacket—who had somehow finagled his way into the museum patrons' preview.

Even without Claudia's cues and guidance, Philip seemed to realize he should know Livinia, though he was no longer sure why or how. He went straight up to her and announced, "Hello, my name is Philip Oliver, and I believe I murdered my wife."

Livinia's friends, embodying gasps that I could well imagine though not hear, drew back half a step. Mrs. Wingate, however, faced Philip unblinkingly, and without recrimination.

"Good for you," she said. "More men should have the courage of their convictions."

Philip seemed pleased with the response, though a little befuddled. "Did you know Amanda?" he asked.

"Yes, Philip, your wife was my daughter."

He considered this for a moment. "Both at once. Isn't that remarkable? People are so complicated."

"That's right, the best people are. And also the worst."

Claudia swooped in at that moment, apologizing profusely.

"Don't worry yourself, Miss Silva," Livinia said brusquely. "I'd rather hear a muddled version of the truth from poor Philip than a string of pointless excuses from his Italian strumpet."

Claudia hesitated, uncertain for a second what the outdated term meant, unsure exactly who was the object of the older woman's scorn. Then, once the point registered, she uttered an Italian phrase that I did not recognize but that made Hogan half snort with surprise.

"I beg your pardon?" Livinia said.

"Now I see where came from the things that made Philip leave your Amanda."

"The things that made him leave," the grand lady answered, "are barely contained by your dress. Philip will abandon you, too, once they start to shrivel and sag."

So it went with the Wingate women. They were knowing and wise, and it made not the slightest difference when it came to keeping a husband at home.

"You can't deceive me, darling," Amanda said to Philip once, "because I never had any illusions about you. It was all too evident the day you walked out on poor Angela. I knew then that you're a pitiful man-whore and I can't possibly change you. But at least I can make you cheat by my rules."

She told him this one afternoon in Cologne, when we were all a little blitzed from the white wine at lunch. During our private tour, Philip had been a bit too forward, in too obvious a way, with the svelte new curator at the Ludwig Museum. Mandy scanned her up and down and turned away.

"Straight out of grad school," she said.

"Yes," I answered. "One of the best."

"My rival is not another woman, Jack. It's an entire way of life."

"So why do you put up with it all?"

"Because I can predict every move, I suppose. Credit Philip with consistency."

"Does that make it easier?"

Philip was trailing after us now, within earshot, but his proximity only sharpened Mandy's tongue.

"Easier to fight about, yes. At least Philip is true to form, especially about age. My husband is an utter lout, Jack. Boringly so. But there's a certain comfort in that—a marital coziness."

"I remember the feeling."

"It's like one long rehearsal—for what I don't know. But the repetition, the scripted arguments, let me refine my threats and ultimatums quite well."

"That's one way to preserve a marriage."

"Oh, who can say really what keeps two people together or tears them apart?"

Now, as I stood drinking with Hogan on the second-floor landing at MoMA, Amanda's mother moved ceremoniously toward us. There was no escape. We were caught in a herd of soigné museum trustee candidates—mostly men who, like

Philip, had risen fast on a single very salable business idea.

"Hello, Jackson," Livinia said. "Let's slip away from this dreadful company and go down to the garden."

I wasn't sure whether she wanted to escape Philip and his déclassé Claudia, or the newer cultural schemers with their designer-label tuxedos and second-place trophy wives.

When I introduced Hogan, Livinia seemed very pleased to learn that Bernstein had a man hard at work on the case.

"Are the police going to arrest Philip soon?" she asked.

"They can't make anything stick," Hogan said. "The Homicide boys are frustrated as hell because they haven't got a good lead on anybody else either."

"Such incompetence," Livinia said. "You'd think any fool could solve something so obvious."

"Any fool," Hogan said, "is exactly what no cop wants to be."

"And no wife," Livinia answered.

I leaned between them to replace Mrs. Wingate's drink. "You don't think Philip's responsible, do you, Liv?"

"Philip is a sneak," she said. "But not a killer. Murder, I believe, requires standing up and looking your victim square in the eye."

"Not the way it was done here."

"No, not literally—but in principle. And principle is just what Philip has always lacked."

We went down the escalator with Livinia and into the starkly beautiful garden. The night air was warm, and waiters went by with trays of hors d'oeuvres and wineglasses. Crossing the arched footbridge, we sat under the small trees, looking at the discretely placed sculpture intermingled with tables bearing white cloths and single short candles. Through the glass wall of the museum we could see people milling near the door, or being lifted and lowered on the moving stairs.

"I can't blame Philip for what he says now, poor man," Livinia sighed. "Shooting your partner must be a common enough desire. God knows I've had it. And I'm sure my dear Harry has, too. Who could blame him?" She looked away. "Occasionally I wish he'd worked up the nerve. Anything is better than being alive to bury your only child."

I was out of my league. We sat quietly for a moment.

"Plenty of real murders begin with a fantasy," Hogan said.

"Yes, I suppose," Livinia replied. "But Philip couldn't do it from three thousand miles away. Not himself, anyway."

"And you're sure he was three thousand miles away?" I asked.

"He called me the afternoon of the murder. He's been doing that quite often lately, ever since his mind went to pot and he took up with that Claudia person. He rings up again and again to apologize for what an ass he's become. Like a naughty boy who doesn't remember his own silly plea from one time to the next. I suppose he wants absolution. As though I could grant such a thing—or would. All I can do is listen to his voice, small and whining and distant."

"You can't be sure how far away he was really," Hogan said.

"I can when I look at my telephone log. He rings me on his new—what do you call it?—mobile phone. There's a record of each call. That police acquaintance of yours, Mr. McGuinn, showed me a list."

"And on the date of May fourth?"

"Definitely from Los Angeles. Something to do with signal beams and tower sites and whatnot."

"McGuinn gave you a copy of the call list?" I asked.

"Please, Jack, don't you think I can get my own account information from a telephone company—especially one that Harry more or less owns?"

Hogan and I left Livinia in the garden with several members

of the exhibitions committee. Due to the size of her contributions and the importance of her private collection, Liv had been the head of that august body for the last decade or so. She was likely to stay in charge till her death, given the family connections and her spouse's legendary financial exploits. Consequently, art people paid court to Livinia as they would to a dowager queen. Chief among her attendees, once, was the ambitious, fast-rising Philip Oliver. Marrying Amanda had guaranteed him a place on the museum board; leaving her for Claudia was a kind of social suicide. The split must have been a product of mad lust or his incipient brain disease—if there's any functional difference.

29

Hogan and I went back upstairs to see how Philip was doing. We found him and Claudia exactly where we had left them, in the midst of a crowd grown denser as the evening progressed.

"Jesus," Hogan said. "How can they stand each other, these rich people?"

"Oh, you get used to their ways," I said. "If you don't expect too much from them."

"Like a conscience?"

"The wealthy have no shame, Hogan, least of all about money. That's why they're all so baffled by Philip and his accounting mania."

I saw Hogan's eyes dart over my shoulder, as if focusing on an approaching threat.

"Well, if it isn't Jack the one-armed pirate," a familiar voice said behind me.

I half-turned to smile at Paulette Mason, swathed tonight in a caftan of maroon silk. Each passing year has been a little bit crueler to the once-glamorous dealer, who now had a considerable quantity of fallen flesh to hide in those expansive, diaphanous folds.

"You two look like jackals waiting for Philip to stumble," Paulette said. "So you can make off with the delicious young Claudia."

At my side, Hogan tensed, no doubt ready to go at her like a mouthy perp.

"Relax. It's nothing," I told him. "An old friend with a bad sense of humor. We go way back."

All the way to my gallery apprenticeship and many mornings,

long ago, when I shared Paulette's bed and her "breakfast of champions"—a blend of champagne and croissants, reefer and coffee.

"Hello, doll," I greeted my former boss. "Sold any good fakes recently?"

She hooted. "Maybe, but I'll never tell which is which."

"You never did."

"That's right. It's one thing to know the truth, quite another to share it promiscuously, don't you agree?"

"Whatever you say, Paulette. I always defer to your expertise on lies and wantonness."

"A wise choice, my dear. Superficiality like mine is underrated; it may be the purest way to live. Shallowness frees one from any silly pretense to meaning."

"So how's business?"

"Don't remind me." Paulette tossed a light, bright scarf over one shoulder. "Art dealing has simply gone to hell, Jack."

"I see. And where was it before?"

She gave a smirk and a roll of her eyes.

"I swear people have no moral sense anymore," she said, "no social finesse. They're liable to blurt out their real thoughts at the most indelicate moments. Like our ridiculous Philip. He has the modern pathology. Just watch him."

Smiling, Philip was moving about like a well-groomed automaton, greeting old friends and strangers alike. Meanwhile, Paulette retailed the gossip that had recently spread through the art world.

As much as Philip's guilt or innocence, it was his idiosyncrasy that now fascinated our crowd. The tycoon had come to dread the very idea of indebtedness, even the momentary lapse between the time an invoice was received at O-Tech and a remittance was made by electronic transfer. This completely exasperated Andrews and his colleagues, Hogan had learned.

Most businessmen—including my own wealthy clients—consider the standard turn-around interval a float period, when they can, in effect, use other people's money as an interest-free loan. But not Philip these days. No matter that his payments were now routinely posted ahead of their due date, or that the company's assets perpetually exceeded its liabilities. Nothing was fast enough or safe enough for Philip's peace of mind.

"Can you imagine?" Paulette said. "Every dealer from here to Istanbul would kill to have him for a client now."

In Philip's personal life, she told us, it had gotten to the point where he insisted on prepaying—in cash—for restaurant meals, receiving his change at evening's end instead of a bill. Otherwise, the minutes that the food sat unpaid-for on his plate, or in his stomach, tormented him like an interlude of theft. The anxiety had once caused him to vomit into a table-side planter at Nobu. Only cash could appease him. He had a vivid horror of checks and credit cards, with their interminable delays between purchase and actual disbursement.

"I could die in the meantime," he said.

Claudia, for her part, was determined to keep anything else untoward from happening. That evening at MoMA, she stood beside her faltering lover, prompting him from time to time with the name of an approaching friend, intervening at critical moments with little potted scenarios that would give him something to go on.

"Hello, John. How have you and Daphne been since we saw you last summer on Taki's boat?" Hints like that.

Such mental aids enabled Philip to muddle his way through a brief, light conversation. Sometimes everything came back to him perfectly, and he would be hilarious or charming or reserved, as the moment warranted.

It must have been an intriguing pastime for him, talking about events that were like episodes in a movie seen decades before, placing himself imaginatively in the narrative and hoping the plot would play out without disaster. Clearly a very sick fellow, Philip missed no opportunity for financial and ethical inquiry.

"Have you made the right investments?" he would say to all and sundry, while Carl Marks hovered wordlessly behind him. "Do you know what you're worth? Is it more today than it was yesterday?"

The oddest aspect of his dementia was that it was not entirely unreasonable. Checks came in the mail—large denominations with no discernible connection to his efforts, or lack thereof. Financial advisers allocated the funds and made him wealthier still. To Philip, this was clear evidence that he was part of a vast criminal enterprise, or that some cosmic error was unfolding around him. Many associates, apparently, had profited from Amanda's death. The money kept pouring in, as the attentive Carl continuously reminded him.

Thus, to his own ravaged way of thinking, Philip was caught up in a bizarre fraud, a vast conspiracy. Either he was a murderer or somehow he had been made a patsy, the Oswald of a domestic assassination—richly rewarded, so long as he maintained his oddball cover. Therefore his private inquiry had to be conducted in secret, obliquely. He sometimes called me, day or night, with stealthy questions. Who had gained from Mandy's murder, and how much? Why did they choose such a conniving method? How had such evil thoughts gotten inside his head?

30

After a couple of hours, with Hogan growing restless, we left the museum and walked over to a new hyper-designed restaurant in the basement of the Seagram Building. You had to enter the place down a long ramp, for the visual delectation of your fellow diners. That was fine when you came in with someone like Laura, swaying atop endless thighs, but less of a joy with Hogan in a checkered sport coat and brown wingtips.

A row of video screens above the bar offered a time-lapse image sequence as customers maneuvered through the revolving door at street level. Each scene passed from one monitor to the next until it finally disappeared. My buddy and I sat on fancy stools at the bar, woefully out of sync with the young midtown pickup set. Hogan ordered our drinks—straight whiskey for him, gin and tonic for me—and leaned forward to study the videos.

"Cameras everywhere," he said. "Here. In SoHo. All over the damn place. Just not in your buildings."

"I told you my marketing strategy, Hogan."

"Yeah, boho chic. What you didn't mention is that your tenants have too much to hide. The daily tapes would look like a soap opera."

"Fortunately you don't need a video to eliminate Philip, not now. The DNA, the calls to Angela and Livinia—they clear him."

"It still might be someone he sent."

"I have to tell you, Hogan, I don't buy that anymore. Philip is—or used to be—a sharp player in business. But, like a lot of smart guys, he's a dunce at romance."

"How bad?"

"He tried to tell me once that all his affairs just made him feel closer to Mandy. 'Straying actually helps me realize how exceptional she is,' he said. 'I come back to her calmer and more appreciative, and ready to do whatever she wants.' "

"Christ. What'd you say to that?"

"I told him not to do her any more favors."

We turned to our glasses. "Maybe you should have told him how calm and appreciative it feels on the receiving end," Hogan said.

"Don't be too hard on him. He's just a regular guy, with excess cash."

"All the more reason to straighten him out."

I stared at my drink, not wanting to meet Hogan's eyes. "You ask a lot, my friend."

"Do I?" Hogan took a long slug of his bourbon. "Infidelity is a kind of murder, Jack. It kills your faith. After that, we're not worth very much—to ourselves or to anyone else. Look what your wife did to you."

Hogan never cared much for Nathalie, or for her French theory of marriage. I couldn't really explain how dealing with that tall, intractable woman, fighting with her, tallying up her betrayals, gave me the illusion that, after all, I was not alone in the world. Or why, for the sake of that feeling, I was willing to pay an exorbitant price.

"Nathalie didn't believe in guilt," I said. "She thought it was a waste of moral energy. She saved up her remorse for more important causes. The refugees in Chad or whatever."

"How convenient for her." Hogan regarded his drink. "So she got you to opt for a wasted marriage instead?"

"It wasn't a waste, not compared to living without her."

Hogan got up. "I need to piss," he said.

As he made his way through the crush of young execs, I thought how Nathalie and I came to our "pragmatic" arrangement back then. Having lovers, my wife argued, was simply a way of embracing the world.

"Do you think that if I sleep with someone else," she asked, "I will love you any less?"

"No," I answered dutifully. "Unless you get swept away. Unless some Parisian jerk steals your soul."

"And what do you suppose? Is that more likely to happen the way we live now, free and sensibly, or if we imprison each other in some petit-bourgeois cottage? I know you, Jack. You didn't marry me to gain a housewife."

"Are you sure?"

"Absolutely. The fact is you wanted me for this—you wanted the cigarettes and the sarcasm, the traveling assignments for *Libération*, the Saint Germain wardrobe, even our little domestic melodramas. All this dark intellectual glamour, *mon amour*, and enough space for a few younger girls on the side. You imagine it's quite sophisticated, don't you?" She blew a slow stream of smoke. "It's a very American view."

Nathalie knew me, knew her stuff—but Hogan didn't seem very impressed, then or now. He had thrown it all in my face once, urging me to toss her smarmy *copains* out of my life and hers.

"Just stand up, Jack," he said. "Kick the goddamn Frogs down the stairs. It's what she wants, too."

I didn't believe him at the time. All I could say was something insipid. "I can't force her."

"The problem isn't Nathalie, Jack. It's you."

The night had been long; I had no fight left in me. "It's not a creed, Hogan. I'm just telling you what I see around me."

"What do you see? What do your smart, lovely friends show you?"

"The way we all are."

"And how's that?"

"Hopeless."

Hogan reared back slightly, like a boxer preparing to counter-punch.

"Crap," he said. "Don't be such a weak-ass son of a bitch. Do something, Jack. Being a cuckold is a sin. A sin of omission—the laziest goddamn kind."

"I've tried," I said. "Look, Hogan, do you understand what it is to love a woman even though you know she's betraying you? To watch her eyes as she lies to you—earnestly, suavely—while you still feel the merciless attraction overriding everything, even the loathing and the shame? Even the knowing?"

I felt like an idiot as soon as the words left my mouth.

"Yeah, I do," Hogan said. "It's one of the few things we still have in common, you and me."

We let it go at that. Of course he knew.

Looking around the bar as I waited, I began to wonder if I was drunk. Probably so, given what I'd already put away at MoMA. My only drinking problem, as I told Hogan once, is that booze makes my mind race furiously until it blacks out altogether. It's an interesting contest. So now I was off, thinking about big issues in a phony-swank midtown watering hole. Let's see, fidelity is impossible to maintain, I decided, and infidelity is impossible to live with. So there we are—mentally crucified. Really, it's enough to drive a guy nuts—or to drink anyhow. Only the more you hit the bottle, the more your own randy desire seems like God's dirty trick. You want continuity, depth, and connectedness; yeah, sure, but you also want freedom, a game of wild chance. You can't cure your disease, you can only manage its symptoms—sometimes well, sometimes badly.

Maybe that's why Hogan turned to the church, why he knelt

before a crucifix, that gory emblem of our psychic divide. You'd think a Marine, a private eye, would have a more realistic solution. Instead, he worshiped Christ on the cross, nailed to the shaft and the T-beam, torn between two conflicting commandments: to raise your eyes heavenward and love a pure, demanding God with all your heart and strength; and yet to open your arms and embrace your earthly neighbors as your muddled, sinful self. Show me a man who isn't torn by that inner struggle and I'll show you a corpse.

I needed another drink. As I leaned on the counter to flag the bartender, a woman sitting on the stool to my left half turned to face me. Her expression was a little brittle but her neckline plunged impressively, and she was reasonably attractive under an enormous mass of waved and curling brown hair. Attractive enough for that place and hour anyhow.

We nodded.

"That's a beautiful suit," she said.

"Thanks." I looked at her gold bracelet and black Bulgari bag. "Beauty can be very expensive."

She smiled, baring teeth so white they were like the flash from a lighthouse. By then, I was feeling pretty at sea.

"You look like you can afford it," she said.

"Do I?" I smiled back. "I should."

Suddenly a guy was between us, a young Wall Street type with his jacket off and his tie thrown back over one shoulder.

"What can I get for you, babe?" he asked.

"Another gimlet, I suppose."

I couldn't be sure whether the stock-jockey, the hulking fashion disaster, was a real date or just a john. Anyway, it wasn't worth finding out. Every year it gets harder to distinguish between high-end hookers and the girls who just want to have fun—you know, some obscenely expensive Manhattan dinners, a few choice pieces of jewelry, and maybe a first-class trip to Europe, if they play their cards right. It's all fine with me. Either way, you get what you pay for. Generally, the hookers are cheaper and less troublesome.

Hogan came back to the bar and rattled the ice in his glass. He looked over at me.

"This Oliver case sucks," he said. "How are you making out with Paul Morse?"

"Just great. We're bonding over high-class porn."

"And that's going to tell us if the prick is our killer?"

"It could. In the art world, everything is connected."

Hogan drank slowly, waiting. I urged him to think how Amanda Oliver might have reacted if she found out her lover-boy was a totally sick bastard, a smooth schoolyard pervert. Then I told him that I had a method, an unorthodox one, for getting closer to Paul.

Hogan heard me out. "You're convinced that's the best way to get to him?"

"It's what I can do."

"I'm sure."

"Sure of what?"

"That you have an instinct for it."

"Thanks a lot."

"Meanwhile, I'm going to check the apartment buildings and shops around the Oliver place. One of them might have a security camera on the street. Maybe I'll get to see the freak parade going in and out of Mandy's door, with our killer in the mix."

"Those are my friends and clients you're talking about."

"Yeah," Hogan said. "Lucky for them, not every sin is a crime."

"But now I have to delve into one that is—with Missy as my lure."

Hogan put down his empty glass. "Just don't tell me more than I need to know. I've got a P.I. license to protect."

"OK, I'll try to keep you at a distance."

"You better. As far as I'm concerned, Jack, this Balthus Club stuff doesn't even exist."

31

For the plan to work, I needed Melissa on my side—even if the girl didn't yet realize that, in the tangled adult world of Amanda, Philip, Claudia, Paul, and Angela, there was any good side to be on.

That Saturday, I left the gallery early in order to take her, as promised, to the Payard salon on the Upper East Side near the Bradford School. My young neighbor loved the luxurious pastry there, and the vanishing old-fashioned ritual of formal tea in the late afternoon.

When I stopped downstairs to pick her up, Melissa seemed somehow a very different creature. A music video was thumping from the TV in her room, and, although she was dressed primly in a black knee-length skirt and matching sweater, the rhythm of the pop song passed visibly through her as she dashed about grabbing her leather jacket and just the right purse.

"Not the soundtrack I imagined for Missy," I said to her mother. Angela paused on her way out to the post office.

"You can't imagine, Jack. It starts with them so young."

"What does?"

"The vamp business. You think you can ease them into womanhood, teach them to be feminine in subtle ways—and instead they simply race ahead and wave back at you. They leave you feeling like a stodgy old maid."

In fact, I had already noticed a small change in Melissa. Three months of summer languor can do things to girls at that age. Her clothes hung differently now, and she had learned how to cross her legs like a woman.

"She's just at the stage where she realizes that she can get grown men's attention," Angela said. "Beyond the goony looks from boys."

"Really? Do you think she knows what she's doing?"

"You should see her with her friends. If I didn't keep tabs on them, they'd be sashaying all over SoHo like bare-midriff streetwalkers."

"They're just kids goofing around."

"Oh, Jack, you are such a male fool. It's one of your more endearing traits."

"It's nothing," I said. "She's going through a phase, that's all."

"Yes, a long one. I think I'm still in it myself."

"It's not the same."

"Isn't it?"

Angela grasped my bad arm and led me back through the loft to Melissa's room. Through the open door, we could see the bed piled messily with clothes and, on a dresser top, the portable TV flashing and blaring. The screen displayed some young female singer, a hootchy-kootchy dancer with one name, shimmying in a different sparse outfit, in a new setting, every three and a half seconds.

"Before you turn it off, Melissa," Angela called, "show Uncle Jack what you learned."

"Oh, Mom, don't be so *English*, OK?"

"Very well, call me what you will. Just show him."

Sighing, the girl dropped her purse and let her hands hang at her sides. "You mean like this?"

She stood straight and stiff, but at the same moment a small movement began in her torso. First one hand then the other touched her pelvis, its sharp contours rocking back and forth as her weight shifted. Melissa's legs seemed to lengthen as one foot slid almost imperceptibly forward. Her hip movement became more pronounced and she began turning lithely, her hands floating upward and slowly twisting, free of any contact.

A smile came to her face, and at the same time something serious entered her eyes. She rotated, swaying before us, lost in the music.

"That's quite enough," her mother said, flicking off the TV. "Now go try to be a lady with your Uncle Jack."

The spell instantly broken, Melissa picked up her handbag with a shrug. "Prude," she said.

We went out into radiant sunshine, making our way to the corner through a thick Saturday crowd of bridge-and-tunnel shoppers.

Once we were in a cab, Melissa told me, "I didn't even get to show you the coolest part."

"What's that?"

She ran her tongue unhurriedly over her lips and sucked in her cheeks until her mouth was a damp pout.

"Irresistible," she said, in the flattened, husky voice of a model. "It's more than a fragrance."

I forced myself to laugh. "That's pretty good. But watch this."

I arched one eyebrow dramatically while keeping the other unmoved—a sinister vampire expression I had taught myself as a kid.

"Yuck, stop, you big creep," Missy said.

Later, seated in the wood-paneled environs of Payard, my companion was much more ladylike. She sat very straight in her chair, addressing the waiter with great clarity, showing off her best prep-school manners. She had taken off the jacket, and her wide shoulders were squared. We had tea and finger sandwiches, and afterwards one large, lustrous pastry each. As the meal neared its end, Melissa grew increasingly serious.

"I thought about you a lot while you were away this summer, Uncle Jack," she said.

"Oh, I'll just bet. For whole minutes."

"No, really, I did. Every day. I wrote things down in my diary."

"What things?"

"Wouldn't you like to know?"

The waiter came to clear our plates and pour the last of the tea.

"I gave you a different name, though. That way Mom won't guess, if she snoops and tries to find out my secrets."

"Do you hide a lot of things from your mother?"

"Only the important stuff. There's not too much now, but pretty soon there will be."

"Why?"

"Because that's just how it is. Don't you ever read books? When people get older, they always have more and more secrets."

"Be careful," I said. "Storybooks are written for all kinds of bad reasons."

"Oh, such as?"

"Usually because some guy wants to make excuses for himself, or to pretend things worked out better than they actually did."

"And people never do that in real life?"

"Actually, they do it all the time. It's sort of the main thing they do." I forced a laugh. "You see how messed up this all gets?"

"Well, I'm not confused."

"You must be reading second-rate stories then."

Melissa made a face. "No," she said. "I'm just really smart."

"Is that so? Tell me something smart you thought of recently."

"All summer I thought about us. I decided you should be my first grown-up boyfriend."

I put down my teacup with a faint clank. "That's not smart, Missy. It's not even funny."

"Is too. It can be real if you let it be, you big dope. But first you have to pretend really hard. That's the first step to anything."

"You don't even understand what it means."

"Yes, I do. I'm very mature for my age."

"You're very mature for any age. That doesn't make it right."

"And you always know what's right?"

"No, hardly ever. That's why I have to go slow and think all the time. Haven't you noticed?"

Melissa gave an exaggerated sigh. "Men are so retarded. So narrow." She looked at me the way a child looks at a recalcitrant doll. "You think you know so much, but you don't."

I pretended to be shot in the chest. "Ow, you got me, kid. At least we agree on that one."

Fortunately, I had to get on to a dinner party later that night. We took a taxi downtown, both of us fallen quiet. When we got to SoHo, I escorted Melissa as far as our building entrance. She pushed the fourth-floor button; Angela answered and buzzed the door open. As Missy slipped into the lobby, she looked back at me quickly.

"Thanks for the date," she said. "It was fun."

32

Things were going very well with the Balthus Club ploy. Paul—
a realist at heart, so he believed—seemed much happier once
we shifted from painting to photography. Every Monday, when
the gallery was closed, he visited me in the back room, and we
looked at pictures together. Week by week, we worked our way
through Mapplethorpe, Jock Sturges, Sally Mann, even some
selected Lewis Carroll. Paul sometimes smoked a joint, while I
imbibed a high-grade cognac and listened to classical music.
Finally, after many pleasurable sessions, Paul felt secure enough
to tell me about his second, more specialized, PM Videos show—
an irregularly scheduled webcast called *Virgin Sacrifice*.

Like a new-media version of a moveable house party, the
live feed appeared whenever the organizers chose. Given the
way one was "invited to watch," I could just picture the audience—computer geeks who liked to punctuate their Dungeons
and Dragons marathons with reality-based cybersex, Japanese
salarymen with a thirst for watching underage cuties being
turned into bondage nymphs. An access code was issued spo-
radically to members via e-mail. Following Paul's suggestion, I
tapped into a *Virgin Sacrifice* episode alone in my bedroom
one night.

On my computer screen, bracketed by glaring porno ads,
appeared a bit of live-action programming, its key concept contained in the show's title. Production quality was not a major
concern. Basically, the scenes looked like someone's basement

dope-and-music party, with the added feature of a rude sexual initiation at the end. Apparently, the ceremony always involved a certified virgin—this time, a slim brown-haired girl of junior-high age.

"You've got to hand it to these art world types," Paul said as we were looking through a museum catalogue a few evenings later. "They're slick. Same subject—I risk jail time; they get retrospectives at the ICP."

"It's different."

"How? Is there some kind of legal exception for good lighting?"

"You push things a lot farther than they do."

"Do I?" He shrugged. "Only because I'm up-front. Only because I don't disguise the fact that I love it."

"Unlike those International Center of Photography darlings?"

Paul nodded. "Some people get tied up in knots over this stuff, for no good reason. Know why? They project their adult hang-ups backwards onto the kids, who in fact don't really give a damn."

"Are you sure?"

"Listen, those little honeys will all be going at it hot and heavy in a few years anyway. I mean, what high-school kid doesn't screw? Name one."

"I can't. I'm out of touch."

"You see? It's just natural. And take my word for it, the younger they start, the more they dig it. Check out Thailand or Cambodia. Sex is a game to the kids there, like skip-rope. They laugh and smile and tell you to come back tomorrow."

"Maybe that's just an act."

"Go there, try it for a while. Then you tell me."

I wanted him to stop saying those things.

"Look at the sulky tweens in these photo books," he said. "Check out their poses, their faces. What are they—ten, twelve?

Do you think they got that way by accident?" He laughed. "No, Jackson. Someone pointed a camera, someone directed. On the Internet, we make it all look a little rough and low-down, because that's what sells."

"Target marketing?"

"Right, cyber-fantasy."

"And in reality?"

"For the most part, it's just kids having fun."

"Why not film it that way then?"

"No art in that, my man. I've got a trademark look to promote. Raunch pays the bills, even if it doesn't get me a MacArthur grant."

"And you don't think there's a difference between your work and this?" I gestured toward the pile of exquisitely produced photography volumes.

"Only if the fools looking at this artsy-fartsy stuff are blind. Technically, the setup is the same: find some beautiful kids, get them half-naked, ask for a hot pose, let the viewer's mind do the rest. It's the same old gimmick—whether the customer is wearing sweat pants in a Times Square peep-booth or a Brioni suit at a Metropolitan Museum preview."

"But you don't leave it to the imagination. You make it all completely explicit."

"Yeah, I do. So now it's a crime to be honest?"

"Depends on the subject."

"What is it with you older guys? You treat sex like some kind of life-and-death thing."

"Isn't it?"

"Not to these kids. They hang out, they play some video games, they get each other off. What's the big sweat?"

It was hopeless. No matter what I said, I couldn't get Paul to grasp, or even consider, the flesh-and-blood damage his video work did. To him, it was all like the coolest virtual reality game ever.

We had other disagreements. In photographs, I favored a soft mise-en-scène: clear-eyed, nubile girls on the beach, children wrapped in bath towels and wearing heavy makeup. Paul went for heavier, rawer arrangements. *Brother and Sister*, a shot of a naked young man with an erection and a pistol, leaning over a bound female nude; *They Found Her in Bryant Park at 8 A.M. and Took Her Home*, the depiction (real or staged, did it matter?) of a teenage gang rape in front of a mirror. Both were by Paul's favorite artist.

"Larry Clark," he said quietly, "is my God."

It was then that I got the nerve to broach the next step of my plan. "Some of the club members have watched the webcasts," I told him, "but the whole process is a little too techno, too geeky, for my clients. All that cyber-coordinates mumbo-jumbo is annoying for men who are accustomed to getting what they want, when they want it."

"They could buy the compilation tapes," Paul suggested.

"The what?"

"Every season we put together VHS highlights of the most recent sessions. They sell through the Internet here, and on the streets all over Asia."

"Sounds like a cash cow."

"Money comes in faster than it can be counted, I hear."

"But the action is still virtual, on video."

"What else would you like?"

I made him wait a second or two, to show that my answer was serious.

"The real thing, live."

Paul drew back. "That's a very far-out idea."

"Also a lucrative one. The Balthus Club members and their

friends would pay top dollar to attend. These are guys—venture capitalists, hedge-fund managers, corporate executives—who buy tables at museum benefits at ten thousand dollars a throw. Your show would be a bit more entertaining."

I could see the greed, and the chance to be a hero with his porn-peddling bosses, start to work on Paul's resistance.

"How big a pool are we talking about?" he asked.

"The club has about twenty members. Each of them has at least two or three interested friends."

"A group small enough to manage but big enough to pay off."

"That's the beauty of it, Paul."

The strange thing was, as always, that Morse found nothing odd about our conversation. All he cared about was having me give him a gallery show and nominate him for membership in the Balthus Club, where he was already working the contacts in his mind. For the rest, it was as if violating underage girls on camera, before a live audience of rich culture buffs, was as ordinary as making a TV commercial for dish soap. He was excited by the revenue prospects, intrigued by the technical challenges, determined to maintain artistic control—preserving the sense of confined intimacy that prompted his victims' best doped responses. Nothing else.

"I'll mention it to the head guys," Paul said finally. "They might like a new angle."

"Especially when there's a pile of loot to be made."

"There better be. We're not in this business for laughs. You'll have to convince my contact, Sammy. He has to green light the idea before it can go any farther."

I slipped the Larry Clark book back on its shelf and turned again to my guest.

"Don't worry, Paul," I said. "Have you seen some of the art in this place? I can sell anything."

"Yeah," he laughed. "So everybody in SoHo has heard."

There was only one more major hurdle to clear. "You know who's a Balthus Club member?" I said. "Someone you just wouldn't believe."

"No idea."

"That crazy guy, Hogan—the P.I. who was in Penny Lane's dressing room the night we met."

"Christ, how can that toad afford it?"

"He gets comped. For shielding us from his old cronies over in the vice squad."

"I knew that bastard was crooked. Why the hell was he dogging my ass so hard?"

"Just to see if you'd panic. He's working the Oliver case and getting nowhere. It was a desperate move."

"That crap ought to be illegal."

"Probably is—like a lot of other techniques he uses."

"Does he have to be in on this?"

"We need him. He keeps us all out of jail."

"You vouch for him?"

"He's one of us, a Balthus Club member in good standing. What more can I say?"

"Say you trust him."

"With my life."

Paul seemed to measure me briefly. "If things go sour with Sammy, that's exactly what it could cost you."

The point was not lost on me. If it weren't for the danger Melissa faced from Paul and the people behind him, and, more distantly, my debt of friendship to Philip and Mandy, I would have stopped then and there—still safe and comfortably self-ignorant.

"Nothing will go wrong," I said. "Hogan has helped me out with any number of, let's say, special transactions."

"So that's why you put up with him?"

"I have to. The more imaginative forms of art dealing require protection."

I wasn't sure if Paul entirely bought my story just yet, but his gaming blood was up.

"OK," he said. "Let's see what this Hogan is made of."

33

The first real payoff from my meetings with Paul came a week later, when I took Melissa to dinner at Balthazar while her mother, back at the studio, finished work for her impending show. The girl changed her outfit three times, settling at last on a simple black shift. She was convinced that we would encounter Christopher Walken at any moment in the pseudo-French bistro, and she wanted to be ready with just the right touch of casual downtown chic.

"How are things with you and Paul Morse these days?" I asked.

We were seated on a banquette that gave Melissa a commanding view of the cavernous room.

"He's really nutty now. All he can talk about is how he needs to borrow Mandy's laptop from me. So he can log tapes or something."

I fought to keep a poker face. "You have Mandy's laptop? The one she used to keep by her bed?"

"Uh-huh." Melissa studied the crowd, occasionally glancing up at one of the big acid-aged wall mirrors to continue her hunt for celebrities. "Is that bad? He's the one who told me to borrow it from her. He's been bugging me about it for a long time now."

"Since when?"

"This summer." She regarded me coolly, vengefully. "While you were off playing in Europe."

"What did Paul want the laptop for?"

"I don't know. At first, it was like he just wanted me to have it. For goofing around online together. Chatting at night."

"Nothing else?"

"Who knows? Jokes, dumb pictures, some mushy stuff."

With great difficulty, I kept my voice even. "But then he said he wanted to use it too? Maybe he was just looking for an excuse to come over to your house."

"Oh, yeah. All the time."

"In Westchester?"

"In Westchester, in SoHo. He even invited me to his loft in Tribeca."

"Did you go?"

"No, I was too busy thinking about you. About us."

"I'm finally good for something then."

"Just barely."

"What did Paul say about the computer when he told you to borrow it?"

"He asked me to get it for him and keep it in my room. He said to tell Aunt Amanda that I needed it for a field trip from school."

"When did you pick it up?"

She looked farther away. "The weekend before she was shot, I think."

"How was Aunt Mandy then?"

"She was fine. Just awfully restless with Daddy gone. She said, 'Men never stay home very long, Missy. It's a phobia they all seem to have. You better get used to it.'"

"Was she upset?"

"No more than usual. She got upset a lot."

Imagining life with Philip, I could understand why.

"And Mandy didn't think it was curious, your borrowing a laptop from her? Don't you have one of your own?"

"No, just a clunky tabletop thing. Besides, Aunt Amanda was always lending me stuff, giving me gifts. So I wouldn't feel gypped and hate her."

"Did her strategy work?"

"Kind of. Now."

"Now that she's dead?"

"Yeah. Is that weird?"

"No. The dead are always easier to love than the living."

Melissa gave me a questioning look.

"Less hassle."

She shook her head disgustedly.

"Once you had the laptop," I said, "did you ever invite Paul over?"

"No. I told you a million times already, no."

"Did he ever tell you you're special?"

She hesitated. "Well, I am special, aren't I?"

"Very much so." My eyes dropped, and I found myself fiddling pointlessly with the menu. "When did you see him last?"

"Sunday. We went to Central Park. He took some photos of me in my new school outfit."

"But nothing at your loft?"

"Oh my God, no. It's bad enough there with that Hogan guy pestering Mom with questions every few days. If that's what they're really up to."

"They didn't tell me about meeting so often."

"No kidding, Sherlock. Did you expect them to?"

"You're awfully suspicious."

"No, I'm just tired of Mom's so-called dates showing up at all hours."

"Are you jealous?"

"Of Mom?" She laughed.

"Maybe jealous enough to take Paul up on his offers?"

"Oh, ick. Stop it. Why are you being so nosy?"

"I just want to be sure you're safe."

Her eyes focused on me precisely, then softened. "OK, be nice then. That's the way it should be."

"Have you told Paul that we talk about him sometimes?"

Her look turned withering again. "You told me not to tell him. I didn't."

"Good."

"I always do what you say."

"Do you really? Why?"

"Because we're a couple now, numbskull."

"Oh right. How could I forget?"

The waiter came, saving me from further reproach. As we made our way through the meal, I kept the conversation on other topics. It was too soon to confront Missy over her lie. In time, Hogan's work would show exactly who was covering for whom. Obviously, Melissa could not have borrowed the laptop on the weekend before the shooting, because my e-mail message from Mandy was sent on the very morning of the murder—a Wednesday. I doubted that Mandy would use one of Philip's precious desktop systems, rigged as they were with elaborate security codes. Too complicated, and sure to tick Philip off. More likely, Melissa had simply been told by Paul to backdate her story, if anyone stumbled across the machine. Meaning that he, not Mandy, had given it to Missy—after, not before, the murder. That, or the girl had taken it upon herself to protect someone else.

After dessert—one of Melissa's favorites, tarte tatin with crème fraîche—she put her hand on my left arm. Automatically, I pulled away, knowing how vivid its defects would be under her inquiring fingers.

"Don't," she said. "I want to feel it."

"Touch the good one. I'll make a really hard muscle for you."

"No, this one. It's part of you, too."

Melissa's hand grasped the flattened remains of my elbow and pulled the dead limb forward until it lay on the table. Then slowly, searchingly, her fingers moved up the useless forearm, darting suddenly to squeeze the flesh between the ruined joint and my shoulder.

"It's just like grandma's arm up there," she said. "I like how it's all spongy."

"You have unusual taste," I said. "No one's ever told me that before."

"They're just ignorant then."

I touched her cheek lightly with my right hand. "You're a screwy kid," I said.

She made a face. "I'm not so screwy. Not like you."

Her hand slipped down to my forearm, lingering. "Was it always like this?"

"No, not always. When I was young I had two regular arms, just like all the other stupid boys."

"What happened?"

"I grew up."

"Don't joke."

"Let's forget it. It's not a very entertaining story."

"I'll decide. I'm your best friend now, don't you know? Tell me, please."

I had no choice. Melissa had the gift of getting whatever she wanted from me, because she asked for it so unabashedly. So I told her the old, boring tale of how, as a young man starting out in the gallery business, I worked for Paulette Mason—one of the first dealers in SoHo. We were doing a show of a soon-to-be-famous Australian sculptor whose work consisted of granite slabs, four inches thick, angled and propped against one another in a stark, cantilevered geometry. Each work required exact place-ment of its elements, in a specified order, at just the right moment. The resulting configurations, though cockeyed and asymmetrical, stood precariously fixed. That was the power and mystery of the work—its apparent danger, tamed and frozen in place. The slabs' hairbreadth balance between stability and instability, order and chaos, was our prime selling point.

That week, an installation crew had worked for three days

with jacks, block-and-tackle, and winches. Finally everything was ready for the Thursday opening. On Wednesday night, after Paulette had gone off to dinner with a client from Los Angeles, I stayed to send faxes and photocopy the shipping orders and insurance forms. As I was about to leave, around nine, I noticed a scrap of packing tape on the floor among the parts of *Stone Assemblage* #6, a seven-foot-high, 1,200-pound stack. Without thinking, I reached in to grab the scrap of rubbish, and slipped.

"Oh, shit," Melissa said.

I didn't dwell on the rest. How the sculpture collapsed on itself and my body, pinning me to the floor. As the stone plates slammed down, they broke both the upper and lower bones in my arm, and reduced my elbow to powder. The only bit of luck I had was that the weight acted as a makeshift tourniquet; my arm was too compressed to bleed lethally.

"Did you scream?" she asked. "Did you cry?"

"Who knows? I passed out for a while. When I came to, I sure as hell yelled. Some of it in words. But no one was around to hear."

In fact it was not until twelve-thirty that the building's night watchman checked the gallery door. I had a lot of time to think as I lay on my back, trapped by the stone. Mostly I thought about the pain, though from time to time I considered how lovely death would be when it put an end to all my thinking and feeling—when I became utterly absent, as though I'd never existed. In a moment of lesser agony, I remembered standing on a street corner in Paris once with Nathalie, waiting for a taxi in the rain. Only that, out of all our years together—not the passion or the fights or the innumerable parties. Just a random incident, on the Quai du Louvre in front of the Samaritaine department store, the two of us wet and laughing.

Alone in the gallery, I made a list of all the banal moments that I hoped to live again, allowing myself to swear aloud after each successive entry. Coffee and morning brioche were part of the tally. So were socks in the dryer, dropping a token in a New York subway turnstile, turning on the lamp by my reading chair, Hogan's bald head, an Air France boarding pass hand-stamped just before liftoff....I don't know where the list might have ended, if the guard hadn't come.

"Do you miss having your arm?" Melissa asked.

"No, not anymore."

"That's good, I guess."

She was a very sharp girl, so maybe she understood that the loss belonged to me naturally now, like my name, because I had lived it all the way through, from beginning to end, without reserve.

"In a way, the accident made my life. Paulette's insurance company gave me a very big payout. I used the stake to start my own gallery, and took a third of her customers with me. She's never forgiven me. Still calls me names, in fact. Jack the Pirate and worse."

"So mean."

"She's right about one thing, though—it changed me. Sometimes I hardly recognize myself anymore."

"Changed you how?"

"In my head."

Missy regarded me thoughtfully, quizzically.

"When you're wounded, you scream," I said. "When you're not screaming, you whimper. Hogan taught me that. It's the whimpering that no one wants to talk about later."

"Well, I like you this new way," Melissa concluded. "Otherwise, you might not be so nice."

"Why's that?"

"Most men aren't. My mom told me." The girl sat back, letting her voice drop to a whisper. "And she really, really should know."

"Don't say those things."

"Lots of times she doesn't come home at night. And there are always these horny guys hanging around."

"She's a single woman, Melissa. She has a right to some good times."

"We used to have our own good times together—when Daddy was with us. Sometimes I get mad at him for that."

"For what?"

"For going away and making my mother a tramp."

34

When we got back to Wooster Street, Angela was still hard at work.

"Hello, my dears," she called. "I'm nearly finished. Do entertain yourselves for a bit."

She was gluing small sculptural fragments together with a syringe, the kind I'd seen her use to attach strands of real hair to the full-size figures. She wore a filtered mask that made her look like a surgery nurse. At least she had installed, at her own expense, a hooded fan to suck the resin fumes upward and disperse them from the rooftop—just one more toxin in the SoHo air.

"Where's the computer now?" I asked Melissa.

"In my goodies box," she said. "Want to see?"

We went into her room, away from the studio smells and glare. Melissa shut the door, and the light diminished by half. She plotzed on the unmade bed, among the tossed girl things, and reached underneath for the laptop.

"Come on, sit down," she said. "I won't bite."

I sat beside her on the mattress, leaning close enough to see the screen as she booted up.

"I guess this is the part you're looking for," she said as she clicked on the "My Letters" icon.

"Exactly right, as usual."

"Don't tease me, Uncle Jack. I learned all about flattery last week. 'When a person is confident, he or she doesn't need to exaggerate.' That's what Mrs. Dorfman says."

"She should know. Bradford pays her to be sure of herself."

I reached over and flicked the keyboard with my fingers, scrolling down. The evidence of Melissa's fib glowed at us both, a long trail of communiqués that ended mid-morning on the day Amanda was killed.

"I see you were wrong about when the laptop left Mandy's place," I said. "Unless you've been imitating her online for fun."

Melissa laughed and began to close down the computer. As she folded the screen, the hem of her dress slid minutely above her knees. The black fabric was a little too light for the weather, slightly out of sync with reality, like the room itself.

"I just did what Paul asked," she said.

"Be careful."

"Of what?"

"Favors for Paul." My hand brushed back a few stray strands of hair from her temple. "I put great faith in you, Missy."

"You should. I'm very trustworthy."

"When's the last time Paul asked to see the laptop?"

"A few days ago. He keeps wanting to come over when Mom's away, but I won't let him."

"Good for you."

"He's cute and mostly nice, but kind of scuzzy somehow."

"More than you know."

She looked at me expectantly.

"We'll talk all about him some other time," I said. "But right now I need the computer."

"All right, just don't tell."

"It will be our little secret. You like secrets, don't you?"

"Sometimes." She lifted her head. "You know, that's what Paul asks me, too."

"Does he?"

Her voice grew softer. "You look kind of funny," she said. "Are you OK?"

"Melissa, if Paul did something really bad, would you help me catch him?"

"Bad how?"

"I can't tell you yet."

"It doesn't matter. I'll do whatever you say, Uncle Jack. Just ask me nice."

Standing, I slipped the laptop into its black cover and told her that I had to go.

"What's wrong?" the girl asked. "Don't you want to hang out?"

"I wish I could."

"So, do. I've got tons of games and stuff here." She put a newly manicured hand on my sleeve.

"I'm not feeling my best."

"That's silly. Why are you worried—because it's a school night?"

"Yes, something like that."

"I did my homework already."

"Good. Now I have to work, too. With the laptop."

"Just stay for an hour. You're grown up; you can do whatever you want."

I looked at her teasing eyes. "No, Missy, that's just why I can't."

"Scaredy cat."

"I am, yes. Sometimes, kiddo, fear is the best thing we've got."

She curled her legs under herself and smiled, refusing to escort me to the door.

"Sometimes, but not always?"

Melissa frightened me in more ways than one, not least with her ease at deception. I was impressed how beautifully she had lied. Her style contained an implicit promise that, with a few well-chosen words, reality could turn into anything you wished.

I went to the door and pushed it open. "This time," I said, "fear wins."

Missy heaved an exaggerated sigh.

Turning, I walked quickly across the loft and let myself out with a small unacknowledged wave to Angela, masked and focused, still bent fastidiously over her handiwork.

35

After I turned the laptop over to Hogan, he began taking a very concentrated interest in Amanda's boyfriend. Luckily, Paul soon invited us to a Ron Athey performance at P.S. 122. The East Village alternative space, a walk-up, had been partially filled with folding chairs facing a makeshift stage. The drama began before the show, as we were forced to wait in a holding area until each audience member had signed a release form, a formally worded slip of paper stating that we understood the "ceremony" we were about to witness involved blood-letting and voluntary pain. No government funds, we were assured, had been used for this production.

"What's this crap about?" Hogan wanted to know.

"This artist had some flap with a city councilman, or some such thing, in Minneapolis. Endangering public health with HIV-tainted blood, wasting tax dollars on sicko, blasphemous art. You know, typical Middle American stuff. I'm sure Athey was deeply thrilled by the fuss. Now the warning is part of the act, the audience tease."

Paul, wearing his reversed baseball cap, passed through the crowd with a video camera, panning the puzzled but determinedly cool faces.

"Glad you could make it," he said without stopping. "Ron's great, and Hogan here will get a taste of what PM Videos can offer."

The next time we saw Paul was as we filed into the auditorium.

He was stationed behind his tripod with the camera trained on the stage.

Once we took our seats, Hogan filled me in on his own latest activities—some of them anyhow.

"I went back to Claudia's building in Williamsburg," he said. "Knocked on every door."

"Learn anything?"

"Enough. I found a young guy who keeps a studio there, two floors down. He's in love with Claudia. From afar."

"Only one in the whole place?"

"This one's a doozy. He had lunch with her in Brooklyn at exactly the time Amanda Oliver was killed in Manhattan."

"You're sure?"

"May fourth. He planned the whole thing for weeks. Wanted to declare his passion."

"Did he?"

"Yeah, and Claudia said, 'Thanks a lot, but I'm taken.' Broke the guy's heart—but he remembered to get a receipt. From some Thai joint with a big pool in the middle of the dining room. The restaurant uses those machine printouts. Dishes for two, itemized, with a date-and-time stamp."

"What did he save it for, his taxes?"

"Nope. He had it taped in a handwritten journal. Surrounded by the whole saga of his unrequited love, in detail. 'May fourth: my long-awaited lunch with Claudia. I reveal my ardor to her, she rebuffs me, she will never be mine. Life is meaningless now. All is darkness.' Crap like that."

"Very moving."

"Tell me," Hogan said. "I had a similar experience with her myself."

Around us, the lights had gone down. Crowd noises crested, then subsided.

"If this neighbor is so crazy for her," I whispered to Hogan, "his story, even the diary, could be a pack of lies."

"Right," he nodded, "so could a lot of things."

The production opened with a solo bit by Athey himself, a stocky type in his early thirties, sporting a shaved head and elaborate tattoos. He stood solemnly at a pulpit, his body swathed in a sheet. To the accompaniment of his own recorded voice delivering a fundamentalist sermon, he slowly inserted four long, hatpin-shaped needles into his calves and thighs, easing another probe through one cheek, over his tongue, and out the other side of his face.

After that little warm-up, additional performers appeared one by one—a fellow who caressed a black leather boot and lamented how his friend's love for this imperious fetish had cost him several beatings and an early death from disease, a woman who hung small bells from her skin by fishhooks and danced around jiggling a tune. But the deepest impression was made by a tall, thin man in a bathrobe, who trundled an IV stand as he shuffled to center stage. There he opened his robe to reveal that the saline solution was tubed directly into his scrotum, which had swollen to the size and firmness of a medium grapefruit. I forget his pathetic story exactly.

Athey, the star, returned several times. Once to methodically incise the back of a large black man, blotting the designs with paper towels and running the sheets out on clotheslines from each side of the stage, bracketing the audience. Then again, at the end, to perform a wedding ceremony for three women, culminating in a dance by the assembled troupe, all wearing skin-dangling bells.

Well, I found myself thinking in avuncular fashion, bless their hearts, bless their young, solemn hearts. You had to admire the performers in a way. They all seemed so earnest and, to their own minds, so daring—even though their ritual ordeal probably produced less blood and injury than an average high-school football scrimmage.

"Really something, huh?" Paul wanted to know afterwards. "Athey has one powerful message."

"Sure," Hogan answered. "Guys who take it up the ass have a tough time in life. You'll get no argument from me."

Paul laughed uncertainly and stepped away, taping crowd reactions and comments.

"And what about detectives who play around with their suspects?" I said to Hogan.

"The way I'm playing with Morse, you mean?"

"No, with Angela."

He was quiet for a second. "Doesn't matter," he said. "I'm not like you. Or this weirdo crew."

"No?"

"I never let sex impair my judgment."

"Is that right? What makes you so sure?"

"I know what I'm doing, Jack. I don't call it art, or group therapy."

"But do you stop?"

"When I can." He paused. "Or when I have to."

"When is that, when you've had enough?"

"Yeah, maybe. Once I've learned enough to crack the case. Murder trumps everything, even screwing." He slipped on his overcoat, plunging his hands deep in the pockets. "We've got our different ways of getting close to a suspect. At least sex with a grown woman is legal."

I lowered my voice. "You don't think I *like* Paul's party games, do you?"

"What the hell do I know about what people like? Me, I wouldn't much care to stick needles in my face or pump salt water into my balls." He looked around at the crowd. "Just be careful, Flash. These people you're hanging out with…It would be easy to lose touch." He glanced back at me, held my eyes.

"When you believe in nothing," he said, "you'll fall for anything."

36

Personally, I was glad to learn that Claudia wasn't our killer. Murder would have been a waste of her talent. Her social talent, I mean.

Not long after the Athey show, she had her latest opening at Patricia Knowles Gallery—a thronged affair with envious artists milling from group to group under the slashingly stroked canvases. Many stopped repeatedly at the open bar, where myriad art world nabobs—museum curators, magazine editors, name critics, and several collectors (the type whose choices bestowed both market value and social election)—mixed with the usual hangers-on and general civilian populace.

Claudia looked ravishing, in an offhand way, her figure subdued in a bohemian uniform of black jeans and black leather jacket. Philip was with her, or at least in the room, muttering to himself after someone had dressed him in a dark sport coat and propped him up in the archway between the atrium and the main gallery space. He spoke to anyone who came near, though very few did and most retreated quickly from the encounter.

"How is he?" I asked Angela.

She had come, unable to resist the pull of witnessing commercial and critical success, even Claudia's, and unable to abandon Philip in his premature dotage to his increasingly negligent young paramour. You couldn't fault her. Angela was slowly becoming the ex-wife we all wish for, a selfless caregiver who would never abandon her beloved, errant man, no matter how deeply he had once wronged her in the mindless exchanges of sex.

"Oh, he's still harping on the bloody 'I think I killed Amanda' theme," she said. "As though wishing made it so."

I had an idea what the poor bastard was going through. There were times when I could almost believe that I had willed my own wife's death, because when I thought of Nathalie thrashing in the arms of another man—and what is an art dealer if not someone who can grasp visual details more readily than holy commandments?—I wished indeed that she were dead to me, a thing that had never mattered or never lived.

I went over to say hello to Philip.

"Are my accounts in order?" he asked me immediately.

Carl Marks had left him recently, galled by the ceaseless repetition of this question and others, but Philip seemed not to notice his absence—or quite to remember that the accountant with the data-streaming laptop had once been his constant companion.

"They're just fine," I said. "You've got nothing to worry about."

"How much am I worth?"

"Plenty, old dog. A thousand times more than the rest of us."

"Is that enough?"

I straightened the handkerchief that he had pulled from his breast pocket and crudely stuffed back. "It has to be," I said. "We're a bit short of options."

"And my daughter, my dear Melissa? Is she all right?"

"Don't worry, Philip, I'm taking care of her."

"She's a good girl, you know. Confused sometimes, but really very good."

"It seems to run in the family."

Claudia came up, flushed and trailing a covey of admirers, two or three of them women.

"*Ciao*, Jack." We kissed cheeks. "You're so kind to come to my opening. And to look out for my poor, lonely loved one."

Philip peered at us with blank contentment, evidently pleased that this strange, beautiful woman was now touching his shoulder.

"He's not so lonely," I said. "He still has some very good friends."

"Ah, yes. But when we're alone, when he visits to me in Williamsburg, it's sadness. Every night he walks through the loft, for searching his Amanda—trying to make goodnight. No matter how many times I tell to him that his wife is gone, dead. He says, 'Yes, I know.' But after he always asks me again. Many times. No, truly, Jack, you hold no idea."

"Maybe I do."

She turned and regarded Philip gently, brushing a bit of lint from his shoulder.

"Some people will never desert him," I said.

"Yes, it's certain." Her tone shifted, soliciting relief. "And tell me, dear friend, what do you think of my show?"

"I think it will sell wonderfully."

She leaned close against my good arm, the one with all sensation intact. "Keep my secret," she whispered. "All is sold already. Before the opening, everything."

"Congratulations."

"*Grazie*. Come to the afterparty."

"Of course. Where?"

"Gilbert Lowe's place. He's on the sixth floor at…"

"I know the address."

Later, at the party, Claudia was surrounded again—swarmed by gay boys, called after by women, eyed hungrily by married men.

As the guest of honor was drawn farther away and deeper into the crowd, Angela edged over toward the befuddled Philip. Soon she was standing beside him, coaching and distracting him, keeping him happily engaged. For a moment, she told me later, it was much like the old days, except that she was in charge now.

He still knew her name and still greeted her as a foggy acquaintance. But the memory of their marriage and his adultery, of their ten years together, of the divorce—all that was gone. Nevertheless, she seemed determined, and pleased, to reinsert herself in his life.

"Aren't you letting yourself in for a world of pain?" I asked her.

"I don't seem to be able to help it. I'm still so absurdly in love with him, despite all I know."

Philip fussed with his shirt cuffs beside her, oblivious to our conversation, smiling.

"It's not so absurd," I said. "Maybe it's the only thing here that isn't."

The party was the kind that made you wonder why you ever left home. All around stood members of the bicoastal success set—celebrity artists, well-known designers, an architect or two who would be recognized by the readers of *Vanity Fair*, several powerful dealers, a few fashion models, a number of curators who were more courted than four-star restaurant maître d's.

Gilbert Lowe, our host, had made a big splash—literally—in the preceding decade. Physically grand, operatic in manner, he had smashed his way overnight to the center of the international art world with a series of geometric steel sculptures drenched, in flaring nighttime performances, with buckets of molten lead. At one time or another, every cultural publication in the U.S. and Europe had referred to him as "a force of nature."

"Jack," he said now, or nearly sang, "how wonderful to see you here. We're all going to the Sydney Biennale next week. You should join us. I'll have Janice send you a ticket. She's found a fabulous hotel with a floor of rooms ordinarily reserved for the Sultan of Brunei. Afterwards, we're going into the outback in a truck caravan. We'll be sleeping in tents and drinking Mumm's."

"Takes me back to my old Boy Scout days."

"Come then. Come, you derelict. Get in touch with the earth again, the environment."

I thanked him and said I'd check my schedule. Taking a canapé from a tray that floated by, I began to wander the immense space, chatting here and there with colleagues, strangers, and friends.

37

When I got home later that night, I made the mistake of turning on the desk lamp beside Nathalie's picture. The image made me remember what Melissa had said the first time she saw the old photograph: "She looks really gorgeous—in a mean kind of way." The young girl had raised her head haughtily. "I want to be like that."

"Don't be too sure," I told her. "In the end, Nathalie's beauty cost her everything."

I sat down at the desk. In a box that Hogan had shipped over were printouts of all the e-mails that Mandy had sent out from her laptop. My job was to check for references that only an art world insider, or a close friend of the Olivers, could interpret. The stack included countless messages to family and friends, to politicians and cultural leaders, to museum trustees and curators. Then there were the memos to credit card companies, caterers, store managers, tailors, housekeepers, cooks, and repairmen. These generally ran:

> *Let's have no more unpleasantness. My accountant tells me that I do approximately X dollars of business with you each year. I believe this entitles me to a modicum of respect, even deference. Surely I'm entitled to—what do you call it?— "preferred customer status." My purchases, in short, pay your rent. Therefore, kindly stop dunning me for payment, which will be forwarded to you in due time and in full, as all my expenses are systematically paid, at the next quarterly disbursement. Four times a year is quite enough for service personnel and shopkeepers.*

This sounded like trouble in paradise. It must have disturbed Philip horribly—especially the new Philip, gripped by Wolfsheim's Syndrome—to find that his domestic accounts were in constant arrears. But was it a motive for murder? An aggressive prosecutor might try to sell it as one. With a little luck, he might even succeed.

I could face the notes (more like field orders than items of correspondence) only a few dozen at a time. Each day, I rifled through several more sheets. The reading procedure had been, on and off for about two weeks now, my new way of filling the vacant hours of the night.

This time, with the sleeping pills taking quick effect, I decided to skip ahead, just for relief, to the message that Mandy had sent me on the day of her death. I thought the complaint about Erich Tennenbaum and his lowball Rauschenberg offer would cheer me up before I started to dream, reminding me of Amanda in full humor, when the old gang was buoyed by her whooping laugh.

Things didn't turn out that way. Instead, as I was skimming chronologically, I came across scores of e-mails to Paul Morse. Some were loving, some nearly obscene, some desperate. Together they left no doubt that Amanda and the artist had been lovers, or sex partners at least, ever since they met at a benefit auction for Art in General the previous December.

The pair's early messages were, by turns, conspiratorial, sentimental, ecstatic. They plotted how and when to meet—most often between six and eight PM at galleries, followed by a "dinner" at Paul's digs in Tribeca.

"Isn't it divine that we're both living downtown?" Mandy wrote. "Even if the distance does seem daunting sometimes, as though an ocean stretched between SoHo and Duane Street. How I long for you at night. And during the day, too, when I should be arranging a party or giving Krystyna her cleaning instructions for the week. The truth is, you haunt me."

She called Paul "my lightning bolt" and other pet names. The two were truly flush with passion for a while.

After six weeks or so, however, laments and reprimands began to creep into the correspondence. Paul didn't call when he should. He sometimes left her apartment abruptly. He wasn't always at home when she slipped into her bedroom to phone him late in the evenings. Near the end, they exchanged little else but reproaches, punctuated by bursts of self-pity, effusive endearments, and profanity.

So Mandy had it, too, I thought, the great sickness. Just as bad as Philip or Angela or myself. Maybe even as bad as Nathalie. A hex was on us all, a disease nearly every soul shares in this city. Not AIDS, not syphilis—these are only its shadows. No, the great curse is our urge, our blind fervor, to seduce and depart, adore and betray. We exhaust ourselves in pursuit of the best lay, or the next, hoping vainly for what? A brief denial of aging and death? A transient escape from dullness, safety, and the staggering hardships of genuine love?

Above all, Mandy came to despise Paul's PM Videos work. It took him away at key lonely hours and yielded only "smut and drivel." It made him, or revealed him to be, another creature—no longer her golden young god but merely a pale voyeur, peeping through his camera lens, and a pimp of sorts, peddling the illicit images. Just when she thought she knew the worst, she caught an episode of *Virgin Sacrifice*. After that, her tone became insistent and shrill, sometimes hysterical. She would not rest until he was free of "those foul tapes, that abominable program, those criminals."

Then, as if composing her own death warrant, Mandy wrote—on the very night before she was killed—"I will stop this at any cost, even if I have to notify the police."

I stood up and went for a drink. Death was in the room with me now, like a lurking thief. I could picture Paul coming to

Mandy that next morning—his arms open, his lips smiling, and his mind on the gun she kept in the bedside drawer.

But at least, while I drank, Mandy remained alive in her messages. Reading her lilting jibes was vastly different from the grim experience I had once of finding an old note from Nathalie, tucked in a volume of Pascal's *Pensées*. It bookmarked one of the philosopher's most famous reflections: "The eternal silence of these infinite spaces frightens me." In the margin, next to the underlined sentence, my wife had written a single word: "Coward." More mundanely, on the slip of medium-weight paper addressed to me, she had recorded certain common sentiments, bits of domestic business, a column of figures—the everyday chatter of marriage, gracefully penned in her elite lycée hand. Then the signature.

I stared at her name, the chain of indecipherable ink traces. A strangeness came over me. I had been inside this woman's body, faced a thousand household chores and crises with her, been nursed by her through fevers and nausea, fought with her in the depth of the night, suffered at the mere thought of losing her brilliance and beauty. And now this same Nathalie's name sat inertly before me like a word from some extinct language. It was then that I knew she was truly gone, beyond any recall. And that is the one thing I have known continuously, with certainty, ever since.

I got up and phoned Hogan.

His response was matter of fact. "Tomorrow I'll look through her received messages for Paul's answer. Now go to sleep. It's almost three."

At ten the next morning, he called me with the result of his search.

"Got it," he said. "The prick's answer reads: 'We need to talk. I'll come to your place tomorrow before noon.'"

38

The following night, my life changed. I wouldn't feel that subtle, irrevocable shift for quite a while yet, but already my once free and elegant existence had begun to alter in small ways. All because I said too much to a child, all because Melissa came to know me too well.

When I got home from the gallery that evening, I sat back in my reading chair and saw a flashing red light that urged me to play my phone messages. One of them was from Angela.

"Jack, if you get this before ten, could you be a dear and come down? Philip's been hospitalized. I need to go, and I don't want to leave Melissa here alone."

By the time I went down to her place, Angela was wearing a light raincoat, ready to head out into the early autumn chill. Melissa, in tights and a T-shirt, perched on a chair in the kitchen area, her long legs drawn up under her chin.

"He fell," Angela said. "They say vertigo is part of the progression—strange word—of Philip's disease. Claudia is there, but she can't handle this on her own. She asked for me. With Amanda gone, I'm practically his next of kin."

"Don't worry, go. Missy and I will be fine here. Say hello to Philip for me."

"He won't understand now."

"Just let him hear the words."

Angela kissed my cheek. "You are a dear," she said. "As soon as this awfulness is over, I want you to have a drawing. Anything you choose." She turned to Melissa. "Be good with Uncle Jack. I'll give Daddy your love."

"I want to tell him myself."

"You will, sweetheart. When the time is right."

The girl walked over and stood helplessly by the door as her mother went out. When she finally came back toward me, her face was blank.

"What shall we do, Missy?" I asked. "Watch a tape?"

"I've seen them all. They're lame."

Without another word, she strode to the rear of the loft, going into Angela's room instead of her own. A few seconds later, she came back out.

"I guess she really is going to the hospital."

"Why do you say that?"

"She didn't take her hot-date bag, the one with her folding toothbrush and her diaphragm."

"You shouldn't snoop in her room, you know."

"Why not? She always snoops in mine."

"She does that to protect you."

"Me too. I snoop to keep my mom safe. I find all kinds of things in there. Things no one is supposed to know about."

"Such as?"

"None of your business. I'll never tell anyone, ever."

"Why, Missy? Are people asking you too many questions?"

"You, my friends, Mom's friends, Paul. Even that dorky Hogan and the policeman McGuinn."

"What do those two want to know?"

"The stuff Mom and I did on the day that Aunt Mandy was killed. Everything we did, all day long. I tell them and tell them."

"What?"

"Mom and I practiced yoga together and baked cookies. Gingerbread. Two dozen. I've never seen grown men so, like, totally obsessed with how long it takes to make cookies."

"They have to get everything in place. On a time line."

"Why?"

"So they can figure out who shot Amanda. You want that, too, don't you? For your dad's sake."

"I guess." Her expression turned dark. "I don't care much who shot Aunt Mandy. She's the reason my mom is such a disaster these days. Always boinking some piggy guy."

"Don't. You just want to take care of your mother, right?"

"She's everything now, with Daddy gone. Just me and Mom against the world. Unless I count you."

"I'm not very reliable."

"Did Nathalie tell you that?"

"Repeatedly."

It took me a while to talk Melissa into watching *Funny Girl*. What else was I supposed to do—pretend that her father was going to be normal again? We both knew the truth was terribly different.

"The movie doesn't have to be good right now," I said, "just simple and bright. You'll see."

She threw herself on the floor, and I leaned back in some sort of ergonomic armchair.

"Sit with me," Melissa said.

"I'm more comfortable here."

"Selfish."

"Am I?"

For the next couple hours, she scowled at me from time to time, especially during the musical numbers. I evidently knew zilch about youthful taste.

"Well, I'm glad that's over," Melissa said when the film finally ended and the VCR started to rewind. "Old-time movies are way too sappy." She moved to a chair near mine.

"So tell me about school," I said.

She shrugged. "It's not totally sucky, I guess."

"What are you studying now?"

"A bunch of junk. You know, algebra and stuff like that."

"I see the Bradford School is a little more advanced than my alma mater."

"It's OK. The students are all rich, except for some of the black kids and some Asians. And they're super brainy. With scholarships."

"What's your favorite subject there?"

"French, I guess."

"Are you good?"

"Of course. Number one in the class. Want to hear?"

"Impress me."

"*Etre*, imperfect subjunctive: *je fusse, tu fusses, il fût…*" She ran through the whole exercise perfectly, at dazzling speed.

"Great," I said. "I feel like I'm back on the Seine."

"What's wrong then?"

"Nothing."

"Does it remind you of Nathalie?"

"Not exactly. It reminds me that we could have had a daughter your age."

"Why didn't you?"

"We never quite got around to it."

"That was dumb." Missy pulled her shirt down over her knees. "If you wanted one, I mean."

"Nathalie did."

"And you?"

"I didn't know what I wanted."

"So you just did nothing?"

"Sometimes things happen that way—or don't happen. You get distracted. Other things come up."

"Like what?"

My voice dropped. "First we were poor, then we were busy, then she was dead."

Melissa stayed quiet. She made a sour face, averting her eyes.

I looked away as well, and noticed a box by the door. Small arms and legs protruded from the half-closed top.

"What's that?" I asked.

"My stupid dolls. I was going to throw them out, but Mom pulled them back from the trash. She says they 'inspire' her or some dumb thing."

I went and stood over the box, looking down into the tangled mass of plastic torsos and limbs.

"You're kind of rough on your toys," I said.

"They wouldn't behave. I got tired of them, anyhow. I'm too big for dolls now."

The heads and arms had been torn from many of the miniature girl bodies.

"Were you angry about something?"

"No, I was just having fun. Making a change. How many times can you sit and dress up those little snits?"

I had no idea, only a certain degree of marvel at her quick, bitter shift of demeanor.

Melissa got off the chair and took my hand, the way she did whenever we crossed a busy avenue.

"Come on," she said. "Let's take a walk."

I let the girl lead me halfway back through the loft to a coffee table surrounded by a cluster of soft chairs and a sofa. She steered me onto the cushions.

"Sit."

I settled in and watched as she went to the liquor cabinet and fixed a vodka tonic and poured a tall glass of sauvignon blanc. She came back and handed me the vodka and sat down on the floor, leaning back against the couch near my feet.

"Cheers," she said. "*À ta santé.*"

"What the hell do you think you're doing?"

"I'm having some wine. A reward for learning all my lessons so well. How about you?"

"I can't let you drink."

"You can't really stop me. I only do it a little bit, when Mom's away."

"You're too young."

Melissa turned to face me.

"Give me a break, Uncle Jack. Kids my age drink wine all the time in Europe. You told me so yourself. Would you rather have me take Ecstasy with my friends in the lunchroom at Bradford?"

"I'd rather have you be a little girl."

"It's too late for that."

She took a small sip of the wine and sucked her lips in.

I felt powerless, outmaneuvered. So I raised my own glass and drank, the ice cubes tinkling. The mixture was sickly sweet with tonic.

Missy smiled at me, a shade too pretty, too knowing, as she sat cross-legged on the floor.

Well, my first drinks were stolen underage pleasures, too, and I turned out just fine, didn't I? OK, so Melissa was a few years younger than I was when I started, but kids grow up faster these days. You had to change with the times. Maybe you could over-adjust, however. Who knew? It was evident that parenting wouldn't have been my forte.

With just one interior lamp adding to the faint street glare from the windows, I was enveloped in shadows.

"What was it like being with Nathalie?" Melissa asked.

"It's hard to remember."

"Big liar, you think about it all the time. Tell me. I want to know."

"It was like being whole."

Melissa tasted the wine again. "Then why didn't you live together more? Or at least on the same continent?"

"We didn't want to spoil it."

That sounded odd, but it was pretty close to the truth—as near as I was ever likely to get.

Melissa nodded. "You did anyhow, though?" she asked. "Spoil it?"

"Together, yes. Or maybe apart."

"Did you cheat on her?"

"That's beside the point."

"Did she think so?"

"It's what she said, so I went along with it. Fooling ourselves is what we did best. Nathalie was determined, absolutely, not to be jealous. She said, 'Let's not be stupid about sex in the naive American way.' So we weren't. We were stupid about it in the clever French way."

It had all been very civilized. My wife and I conversed like characters out of Racine—and behaved like monkeys. There were times when I thought it would kill me. Once I was even hushed into silence when another man called our Paris apartment. For the sake of discretion, Nathalie, one finger to her lips, waved and mimed me into wordless soft movements. While she murmured on the phone with one of her local lovers, I became a ghost in my own flesh, my own home.

Afterwards, Nathalie and I argued ourselves into exhaustion.

"All I can do," I said to my wife finally, "is love you as much as I can for as long as I can."

Sitting on the couch, she merely stared at me, wordless for once.

"And when I can't stand it anymore," I said, "I won't. I'll go, without a fight."

But, of course, I never got quite that brave. I simply found my own *putes* and girlfriends—and so we went on.

In truth, I'd been finding other women all along, so it wasn't such a drastic adjustment. Nathalie had her graduate studies at the Sorbonne, then her job at *Libération*; I was tied up in New York with the gallery business and the SoHo buildings. We led one life together, and two lives apart.

For an American, I was surprisingly good at the game. Adultery and wit, choice Bordeaux wines and fat profits; those were the drugs of choice in my later youth. Now I had a supply of mordant aphorisms ready for the old Marais crowd, if I ever ran into them back in Paris. "Nathalie died of sophistication the way some people die of cirrhosis." Worldly and wry—that's their mode, even in the sickroom.

Who cares if the cause of my wife's lingering death was a blood disease she caught from some bisexual set designer in Saint Germain? He was nothing. The source didn't matter, the treatment didn't matter, the betrayal didn't matter—not once Nathalie was wasted and bald and delirious.

"Do you miss her?" Melissa asked.

"It's not something I talk about."

"Why not?"

"Because people expect you to grieve, and what would be the point of that?"

Missy looked at the glass in her hand, away from my eyes. "You must wish you could talk to her sometimes. The way I wish I could talk to Daddy."

"Talking did help," I said. "Even when I knew it was mostly lies."

"You see."

I did indeed. Like Melissa, Nathalie understood the great value of hypocrisy. She knew that the gentle con she worked on me was a backhanded tribute to the romantic ideal—the pristine and impossible union that we failed to achieve. Her scheme was a way of honoring our marriage and protecting my psyche. Her words never actually deceived me, and were never meant to. No, the lies simply assured me that, whatever else inevitably happened, Nathalie cared first and foremost for me, for our peculiar, imperfect bond.

I looked down now at the blond, glowing Melissa.

"The finality hits you pretty hard the first time you forget," I told her. "You telephone, and suddenly you realize she's not there. The dead never answer. You stand like an idiot with the receiver in your hand. Then you know: she will never speak to you again, here or anywhere."

I drank slowly, several times.

"At least your dad is still with us," I said. "You can hear his voice, even if what he says is a jumble."

"Do you think that's enough?"

"No, it's not enough. But it's something."

My mind worked on in the silence. When I went to visit Nathalie the last time, the head nurse said, "Will you be all right?" and I said, "Of course." Touching my sleeve, the good woman tried to talk to me for a minute first, but I waved her off and went in.

The bed was surrounded by monitors, tanks, and clear plastic bags on high stands. Tubes and wires led from the equipment into the layered sheets. Under the covers was a rickety form, a thing. I thought it must be a joke. Wisps of hair were stuck to the skull. The head was rounded and moist, and the jaw protruded. From time to time, a monitor beeped. The cheeks had collapsed, and the imitation skin was pulled back from the horse's teeth.

"Madame may be able to hear you," the nurse told me.

So what? It wasn't as though I had come to the intensive care ward with some final, transformative message to impart. No, nothing came to me there. I touched the bed rail, the chrome bars that kept Nathalie from rolling into a bony heap on the floor.

"Well, my love," I said finally, "so we've come to this."

There was no sign of response, and I spoke louder and clearer, and louder again—"So we've goddamn fucking come to this." I repeated, "we've come to this, we've come to this" until the head nurse charged in, followed by the doctor, and then an orderly grasped my shoulders, pulling me back from the bedside, saying insistently, *"Du calme, monsieur. Du calme."*

"Relax, stay calm," I told Melissa softly. "That's the ticket. One should always remain cool and composed in these situations. I have it on the best French authority."

The girl shook her head. "You're really a mess, Uncle Jack. But you don't have to be."

"You know a way to fix me?"

"Maybe you just need someone young and nice to take care of you."

"I was thinking more of someone old and rich."

"Oh, stop it. Behave." Missy crinkled her nose. "*Tu me taquines toujours*," she said. "You're always teasing me." She stood up quickly and finished her drink. "Why, Uncle Jack? That's so nasty."

Melissa came to the couch and sat down on my lap. "Let me tell you a story," she said. "Something funny."

The girl leaned against me with her head on my chest, her voice issuing from the vicinity of my suddenly pounding heart. No doubt she was comforting herself by comforting me. I was, however, more disoriented than soothed.

As she talked softly in her lilting Parisian French, I began, ridiculously, to cry without any sound. Or maybe I cried first and then she spoke to me in French—that night is still a little muddled in my mind.

Melissa's long legs were curled against my stomach, the slight declivity between her thighs curving as she shifted to hug me. "*Il était une fois un tout petit garçon....*" It was the tale of a little boy who was *méchant* all the time to his little sister. I didn't get to hear it all, because there was a rattling of keys at the door and Missy's mother came breathlessly in.

39

"Well, aren't you two cozy?" Angela said as she hung her coat in the entryway closet. She seemed at once distracted and relieved.

"Hi, Mom," Melissa answered. "How's Daddy?"

The girl rose smoothly and carried the two empty glasses to the sink and rinsed them quickly in hot water.

"Oh, fine really. The poor dear just wanted some company. He's resting now. He'll be better soon."

I had never heard Angela lie quite so ineptly. The strain and fatigue must have gotten to her at last. The words sounded hollow, and I could see them fail: the truth hit Melissa, entering visibly into her. It was probably the first time she grasped, felt in her stomach and nerve endings, that her father was going to die.

"Why doesn't that awful Claudia do something for him?" she asked.

"She's just a girl, Melissa. With a whole busy, beautiful life ahead of her. Like you. She didn't sign on for this."

"But why couldn't Daddy stay with us, with the people who really care about him, instead of running away to that big snob Amanda? And now this stupid bimbo, this Claudia?"

Angela shook her head. "You explain it to her, Jack. About men."

It was as though I'd been asked to explicate a theorem in quantum physics.

"I don't understand it myself," I said. "I just live it. Pretty badly most of the time."

"That's so bogus," Melissa said. "So male."

"Exactly," Angela replied, moving toward her, trying to

embrace the girl, who stood stiffly with her arms at her sides. "Now you're beginning to see."

Melissa shook herself.

"You guys are all just too dopey," she said at high volume. "I have to go to bed."

As Angela smiled after her, Melissa turned suddenly and half-trotted back through the loft to her bedroom.

"Good night, sweetie," her mother called. "I'll give your love to Uncle Jack."

Then in a low voice, softly, Angela said to me, "She's such a little drama queen. But I do think she's truly upset. Did I give too much away tonight?"

"Angie, we have to talk."

"I know. The poor child has to be told, of course. I'm so afraid that losing her father will completely derail her. The pity is, she's just now doing so well at Bradford, and starting to think about boys."

"That's great," I said, a bit thrown by my own lack of resolve. "But you shouldn't try to fool her. How is Philip, really?"

Angela parted her lips to reply, but they seemed to freeze rigid and soundless. She looked like a woman zapped in mid-sentence by a stroke. As her head wavered from side to side, I moved closer to her.

At last she said, "He's destroyed."

I didn't want it to be true. There ought to be years yet.

"Something's consuming him," Angela said. "Eating his brain at a ghastly rate."

"Does he know you?"

"Not anymore. He doesn't know himself. 'Sorry to trouble you,' he says. 'Can you believe I've momentarily forgotten my name?' "

"Still," I said, "it sounds like his old self in a way." Philip, the last time I saw him, still had his sly humor.

Angela's face was stricken. "No," she said. "It's not Philip anymore. I mean, it's Philip but…not Philip." As she spoke, she began to strike me rhythmically. "Philip, not Philip. Philip, not Philip."

I didn't try to stop her. Before long her blows rained steadily against my body, racing ahead of her words, thudding on my chest and shoulders in an erratic drumbeat.

"Damn it, Jack," Angela said. She stopped pounding and fell against me, limp, without tears. "Sometimes I want to die myself. It would all be better and cleaner, don't you think?"

"Not for Melissa."

"No." Angela paused to gather herself, closing her eyes and saying the words evenly, one by one. "No, not for Melissa. Thank you, Jack."

We stood apart once more. I walked Angela to the couch and sat her down, asking if she wanted some wine.

"There's a white open," I said. "I had a glass earlier."

Angela seemed not to hear. "This is the worst," she said in a flat tone. "When I'm at home and Philip is not, and there's no one else."

"I'm here."

"Yes, you are, Jack. In your way." She spoke without looking at me. "And there are the men, of course. They help, when they're around. But no one stays."

She looked toward the far, dark end of the loft, where Melissa lay sleeping now.

"At times like these," Angela said, "all the reasons that couples find to split up seem to me perfectly inane. Especially the cheating nonsense. What else could we expect from each other really? Just put up with it, for God's sake. Nothing matters very much except not being alone."

"You're talking like a wife again."

"Yes, Jack, I want a real marriage, a real mate. No matter how wretched it makes me. I need it."

"And you want it to be Philip still? Philip again?"

"It's terribly sophomoric of me, I know. But it's what I've been thinking lately, a lot, looking at him in his hospital bed. I don't seem to be able to stop."

I told her there were worse things to think.

"Oh, I know," she said. "I've pretty well thought them all."

40

When I went back upstairs, I had to face the task of viewing Paul's compilation tape. The package he had sent over sat on my dining table like an exquisitely wrapped letter bomb. Disguised, discreet and perverse—exactly the way I was supposed to like things.

I sliced my way through the brown paper and cellophane. Exposed, the black plastic box bore an O-Tech logo and the title *Microcircuit Sequence Systems: The Basics*. Only a small red X in the upper right corner, and its tiny subscript reading "PM Videos," signaled a variation from the usual corporate training fare.

When I took out the video cassette, however, identification got a bit more explicit. The label read *Virgin Sacrifice, Live, Vol. 3*. I could imagine the cardboard slipcase that would be added by enthusiastic graphic designers in the fly-by-night dubbing mills of Shanghai. With the Asian—particularly Japanese—market in mind, they would lift stills of the very youngest girls, adding a block of provocative text in demotic Chinese and bizarrely translated English.

Once the tape started, I saw immediately that Paul had gone for an outlaw effect. Everything was done by available light, and the moving figures had a ghostliness I associate with early video art. The decor was familiar—a U-shaped group of couches set around a low table bearing liquor bottles and dope. Nearby was an open space for dancing, and beyond that a doorway.

A mobile shot eventually took the viewer through the entrance and down a short hallway to a smaller room. In the center was an inflatable children's swimming pool filled with a glutinous muck that looked like a mix of tapioca and mud. It was here, when things got serious, that the girls—mostly naïve party-lovers or early-teen runaways—would sometimes tumble and roll with each other, or be shoved down and mounted from behind by the Donkey.

El Burro, as his stitched monogram read, was a short Hispanic guy, about forty, who usually performed the climactic "sacrifice." At first, when I saw him standing around in a kind of boxing robe, I didn't really get the nickname. Then, with the first girl drugged and caressed, lightly kissed, ready, almost entranced as she was petted by three or four men, El Burro opened the robe like a theater curtain, and I understood.

The excerpts already sped up the seduction process, edited into a series of predictable acts: initial flirtation with soft words and light touches, followed by drinking and doping, group dancing, petting, some erotic roughhousing, more intoxicants. Then, in the back room, to cheers—full-on sex. Sometimes one wrangler took a girl through the entire process, alternating outrageous sweetness with an iron insistence and subliminal threats; at other times, the young mark passed from one guy to the next until she was delivered up to El Burro.

The repeated arcs of the little drama threatened to grow monotonous, but the variety of the girls—their physical types, their innocence or fake cynicism, their responses to booze or hash or the sight of a bare male organ, their reluctance or alacrity in the carnal act—created an insistent forward-surging-and-retreating structure, recalling episodes in some harsh, long-practiced initiation rite.

A remote control, like the one in my hand, made it possible for connoisseurs to pause, freeze frame, go back and repeat a favored passage in slow motion. Volume could be easily adjusted for those who preferred purely visual stimulation or those who got off on the confused, pathetic, occasionally overly eager vocalizations of the virgins. Only a few of them actually cried.

When the show was done, I lay back for a long while on the bed, looking at the blank blue of the screen and listening to the whir and click of the VCR as it rewound the tape. With the machine chattering relentlessly, I viewed the images again in my mind—backwards this time, in quick succession—as though each forlorn girl were being instantaneously restored, at a comic pace, to her original inviolate state, ready to fall again.

I picked up the phone and called Paul.

"Wasn't it great?" he said.

"It had its moments."

"Did you see that one red-haired chick who…"

"I saw it all."

Calmly, but with a hint of urgency, I told Paul I had a business prospect for his producers. Something much more than distribution to the Balthus Club members, much more than their attendance at the tapings for three grand per head. I could double PM Video's international reach and therefore its profits.

"It's not up to me," he said. "I don't get involved in the marketing plan."

"Who runs the show then?"

"I told you, Sammy, my backer. And a Chinese guy he knows."

"Then hook me up with them. You're good at that, right? I'd like to discuss this opportunity, one businessman to another."

"If you ask to meet these guys, they'll check you out first. Everything, you know. I already told them about Hogan."

"What did they say?"

"They said they knew how to handle guys like him. One way or another."

"All right then, let's make some money together."

Once we hung up, I went into the bathroom and waited forever until the water turned hot enough to wash my face and hands. I stood with my head lowered, while the tape distribution proposal formed itself solidly in my mind, tight and graceful as a poem. Opening the medicine cabinet to take out the sleeping pills, I glanced up and saw my face flash by, unreadable in the swinging mirror. I looked away.

41

Paul said there would be no appointment. He would call a few minutes ahead of time on the day Sammy was ready to meet. Fortunately, he caught me on a slow day when Laura was handling second-tier clients in person and I was doing a lot of phoning and paperwork in the back office.

"Hey, you know Cielo Azzurro on Spring Street?" Paul asked without preliminaries.

"Sure. I don't eat there, but I know it."

"It's kind of cool in a retro way."

"Maybe. They don't know they're retro."

Paul didn't seem inclined to discuss the nuances of modern *trattoria* design.

"Sammy likes it," he said. "He wants to meet there at one."

"Well, we certainly want Sammy to be happy."

"I do. You should too. The place makes him mellow."

"By the way, does Sammy have a last name?"

"None that I've ever heard. I think that's good."

"Why's that?"

"You know, the less you know the better."

Cielo Azzurro, a checkered-tablecloth place, was over on Spring Street between Thompson and Sullivan, an easy walk from the gallery. Sunlight flooded the streets, immersing the shoppers in an autumnal glow finer than anything in the luxury-brand store windows. The air was cool, but no one seemed to notice. People came to SoHo for the galleries and boutiques, not the climate.

I saw Paul from a hundred feet away, his spiked blond hair flashing as he jiggled back and forth in front of the restaurant door.

"Sammy's inside," he said, sounding like a schoolboy about to introduce me to a cool older kid. "He doesn't like to wait."

Beyond the threshold was a single room, dim and garlic-scented, pervaded by the sounds of Tony Bennett's "Boulevard of Broken Dreams" seeping from a jukebox next to the old wooden bar.

At one of the little tables, overwhelming it with his broad presence, was a heavyset man in an open-necked pullover shirt and slacks. Except for the Saint Jude metal at his throat, he looked like a typical suburban visitor hunting for an "authentic" Italian lunch in the city.

He rose from his chair by the brick wall as we approached.

"Sammy," Paul said, and I could hear his voice change subtly, taking on a tremor of subservience, "this is Jack—the new prospect I told you about."

"Hey, real happy to meet you." Sammy's grip was firm. "I hope the last-minute call wasn't a problem."

"Not at all."

As we greeted each other, he smiled broadly and slid his left hand quickly down my back and right side. Then he released his grip, put his hand on my shoulder, and, looking me in the eyes, repeated the procedure on the other side.

"A really fine jacket," he said. "My tailor says you can't never go wrong with cashmere. Me, I think you can trust a man who chooses good fabrics, high thread counts. A guy like that, he's more likely to appreciate the finer points of an agreement, even if they aren't labeled for the whole world to see, you know?"

"Smart tailor you have." I stood in silence for a moment, listening. "Did you pick the music?"

"No, that's Carlo's choice. He owns the joint, but he knows what I like. You can't beat our guy Tony, right?"

"He'll never have Sinatra's chops."

Sammy, with his hands at his sides, eyed me like a boxer.

"Sinatra's dead," he said.

I didn't argue. My new acquaintance had made death sound like a moral failing—one that I just might share.

Sammy reached out and squeezed my left arm, letting his hand rest on my elbow.

"What happened to you here?"

"I had an accident."

"Tough break. The rest of you OK? I'd hate to think that anything else got shrunk up like that."

"No, thanks. The rest of me still works all right."

"Good, good. Sit down. Have some wine."

A waiter came over and poured. I had already braced myself for the selection of vintages available.

"Pinot grigio," I said. "The pesto of Italian wines."

Sammy turned to Paul. "Is your guy making a joke, college boy?"

"That's right," I said before Paul could reply. "A joke among friends."

Sammy raised his glass to me. "To your health, then. *Salute.*" He watched me evenly over the rim.

I took a sip. Paul's boss had clearly seen far too many old gangster movies, treating them as behavioral primers. But I wasn't going to be the one to rag him about it. Hogan had told me once that the imitation wise guys are the most dangerous. They have the most to prove.

"What should I call you anyway, Mr.…?"

"Call me Sammy, Jack." He glanced over at Paul. "I don't know why I like first names so much. I just do."

"It's friendly," I said.

He looked back at me quickly. After a second, he smiled. "Hey, right, you got it. I'm a friendly guy."

We drank silently, no doubt thinking warm thoughts all around.

Paul seemed anxious for things to move along. "Jack has some very good connections, Sammy. He thinks we're missing a big market in Europe."

Sammy leaned toward the young man. "Relax, Paulie," he said. "I can see that Jack here is a good businessman. Look at him. See how calm he is? You should learn from him. Right now we're having some wine, then we'll have a little lunch. When we talk, we talk."

"What do you recommend on the menu?" I asked.

"Don't worry about the menu. Carlo will take care of us. For you, some pasta, then maybe a nice veal piccata. Nothing too heavy."

"Good."

"For Paulie here, maybe some chicken." He chuckled a little.

I smiled, being a friendly guy.

"Me, he'll bring the big salad with olives," Sammy said. "Better for my heart."

"What's the problem?"

"Cholesterol, who knows? The doctor says I should take care of my ticker. So Carlo watches out for me."

I could imagine Sammy's heart having quite a number of defects, some of them physical.

We drank amiably for a few minutes. The salad came at the same time as the pasta course for Paul and me.

"I hear," Sammy said, jabbing at his huge bowl of oil-soaked greens, "you've got a buddy who's a P.I."

"We grew up together," I shrugged. "I can't really help it."

Sammy made a noise down in his throat. "I know what you mean. I got old friends like that from the neighborhood—guys who are cops now. Or lawyers, or judges. They're OK. They understand how hard it is—for me, for them, for everybody—to get by in this high-priced town. Some of them ask for a cut. Nothing too big."

"Hogan's a practical guy. He cares about what he's paid to care about—and ignores what it's profitable to ignore. Simple math. Throw him a few bucks and he'll keep his mouth shut."

"I know cheaper ways to keep people quiet."

"Hogan will keep his NYPD buddies off our backs too. If the vice squad ever gets curious, he's a good shield. I've used him for years."

"For this kind of thing?"

"Now and then. Hogan couldn't care less what you and I do for jollies."

"A sensible guy."

"Just give him what you think he's worth. He'll earn it."

"I've used P.I.s before," Sammy said. "I know the type." His empty fork paused in midair. "The thing I don't know is your type, Jack. What are you? You're one of these art guys, aren't you? Paulie says you own a few apartment buildings down here, too? As far as I'm concerned, doing business with an art dealer, a real estate sharpie, it's like making a deal with the devil."

I was at a loss for a moment. It's not every day that my moral character is impugned by a porn merchant in knit leisurewear.

"The only reason we're still having this discussion," Sammy said, "is that Paulie says you're different from most of them."

"Them?"

"Those people—the high rollers and fancy-boys who moved in here and screwed up the neighborhood." Sammy tore a hunk of bread and waved at the surroundings. "You see this place?" His gesture took in the dark wooden bar, the jukebox, the little square tables, the minor-celebrity photos on the brick wall behind him. "This is how the whole neighborhood used to be. Good people, real food. You could come here at night and have a few drinks and not worry about nothing." He placed the bread in his mouth, chewed twice, and took a long drink from his glass.

"The good life," I said.

"There you go. My mother, God rest her, used to live on Sullivan Street. Got her bread at Vesuvio on Prince Street, her cheese at Joe's Dairy. On Saturday afternoon she put out a folding chair on the sidewalk, she'd sit with her friends, talk about their families. Sundays, she went to mass at St. Anthony of Padua. Always lit a candle for me. She used to lean out her window in the evening and talk to Signora Cassano on the left and Signora Frangella on the right. That was all before the art crowd moved in and the young money grubbers followed them. Now what do we have left? The San Gennaro festival for a couple weeks every year."

"I'm sorry," I said.

"The worst part is, it was one of our own who brought it on. That slick little Castelli character, with his art gallery, his over-priced suits, and his European girlfriends. Doing what? Coming to Mezzogiorno every day with his prissy artists—then bringing the clients, so flush it's not enough for them to buy a damn painting or two, they've got to own the whole neighborhood.

"The next thing you know, the restaurants are charging ten bucks for a friggin' bottle of water and some landlord is trying to squeeze my mother out of her apartment so he can jack up the rent about eight hundred percent. I had to have a little talk with that sleazebag about the value of tenant loyalty. He came around pretty quick. But not everybody has a good negotiator like me in the family. Lots of people got shafted. Now, you come to the neighborhood on a weekend, you can't even walk down the street it's so crowded with…what is it you call them, Paulie?"

"YUCs—young urban consumers," Paul said slowly and dis-tinctly.

"Yeah, you got your yuckies paying insane prices for clothes that make them look like stone junkies, shelling out Park Avenue rents for shithole apartments, and yelling their heads off at each other in the bars every night."

"Come on, Sammy," Paul ventured cautiously. "Times change."

"Times change because punks like you make them change," Sammy said. "And not for the better."

42

I was afraid that our meeting might end then and there, in a massive testosterone eruption. But at that moment, a tall man came up to our table and laid a hand on Sammy's shoulder.

"How's everything? Good?"

Sammy looked up, relaxing again in his seat. "Yeah sure, beautiful…Carlo, meet my boy Paulie."

Paul stood three quarters of the way upright, nodding.

"And this is Jack," Sammy said. "He's a landlord, but don't hold that against him. He hustles art, too. And shares our special interest in youth."

I stood and gave Carlo my hand. His grip was friendly and firm. A tanned, professionally handsome man, he was wearing an open-collar shirt and an Italian sweater that retailed for about nine hundred bucks.

"Art?" he said. "Like statues and pictures on the wall?"

"Some of it."

"Maybe we should put some in here," Carlo said with a smile. "I like my customers to get something extra, something nice."

"I'm afraid the art I sell wouldn't match the décor," I replied. "It's an acquired taste."

"You see?" Sammy reached over and patted my bad arm. "This Jack is smooth."

Carlo showed me his bleached teeth again. "Next time you come, Jack, ask for me. I'll make sure you're treated like a prince." He turned back to Sammy. "How is it with the doctors?"

Sammy shook his head. "Who the hell knows? They got me

eating bowls of grass and walking for thirty minutes a day. Walking, what is that? It's for *contadini*."

"My grandfather was a *contadino*," Carlo said. "He could teach you a thing or two, about more than your health."

"Yeah, but your father was no peasant. Your father rode around in Packards and wore a fine suit every day, just like mine did. What a great country, no? Every generation gets a softer life. Now look at me—you'd think I was some dentist from Jersey."

"No, *paesano*, you don't have that much style."

Carlo winked at me, nodded a farewell to Paul, and headed back to the bar.

"Everybody's a goddamned comedian," Sammy said.

I watched Carlo walk away, moving effortlessly through the maze of tables.

The waiter, eyes lowered, cleared the pasta remnants and delivered the thin slices of veal.

"So tell me something, Jack," Sammy said. "What are you after here?"

Apparently the time to talk had arrived.

"Just a fair return. I'm not greedy."

"What sort of return?"

"Girls and money. You know of anything better?"

"No. But I've already got plenty of both. So why should I bother with you?"

"You have some of both. I can get you a whole lot more."

Sammy dropped his voice. "More? Right now I list about two hundred thousand paying members online, ready to pony up twelve dollars a pop whenever we get a party together, every six weeks or so. Then, twice a year, we do a highlights tape that sells a hundred thousand in Asia at ten bucks a throw. You think you can improve on that?"

"I think you're missing out on huge markets in Europe, Latin America, and the Middle East."

"You'd have to talk to Mr. Zhou about that. His people handle the overseas end of things."

"The Chinese don't have the right contacts outside Asia."

"Don't get me started on the goddamn chinks," Sammy said. "They've taken over everything downtown except one stretch of Mulberry Street. Those tricky yellow bastards really know how to do business."

"But they don't go outside their own network."

"And you do?"

"Copenhagen, Paris, Berlin, Istanbul, Riyadh, Buenos Aires. And I can also bring you investors."

"What makes you think we want investors?"

"With their money, your overhead effectively goes down to zero. You pay them back out of the increased sales abroad— just a minor portion of the additional revenue, minus shipping costs and bribes. The rest is pure gravy."

"And what's in it for you?"

"A small percentage. Of the new business only, of course. You tell me how much. I trust a man like you to be fair."

Sammy leaned forward onto his elbows.

"Really?" he said. "Why is that?"

"Experience."

"Doing business with guys like me?" Sammy smiled faintly. "You don't seem like the type."

"Maybe that's why I'm sitting here in a nice SoHo restaurant and not in a cellblock."

Sammy's eyes hardened. "I have no idea what you're talking about." He sat back and stared at me with a practiced blankness.

"Of course not. That's exactly why we should work together. Half my clients are guys like you, Sammy. Except most of them aren't as honest."

He laughed, and looked over at Paul until he laughed too.

"Goddamn right," Sammy said.

"Suppose I bargained for a fifteen percent cut of the new cash flow," I said, "but afterwards you decided to pay me less. What could I do?"

"Not a thing."

"There you have it, Sammy. See how simple this is?"

"OK. But now listen good, Jack. I keep my goddamn word. That's how I keep my friends."

"Of course. And friends are money. I understand that. Just like in the art trade." I took another swallow of my wine. "Anyway, it's not as though I could ask to examine the books."

"You crack me up, Jack."

I smiled. The alcohol—mixed with fear—was making me bold, maybe reckless.

"Who are these investors of yours?" Sammy asked.

"Some collectors I know. They belong to the Balthus Club. Don't worry, they won't ask the wrong questions. Not as long as the numbers are right."

"What makes you so sure?"

"I'm familiar with their purchasing history. Sometimes they buy artworks that aren't exactly for sale."

Sammy arched an eyebrow.

"These gentlemen want premium stuff, whatever the price," I explained. "I make a few inquiries on their behalf. About a month later, I meet with a certain lady broker I know, usually at a hotel in Zurich. She shows me some works and I authenticate them—the same works I asked about earlier. These are rare pieces, new to the market, since a few days before they were still sitting in some provincial museum or an old village church or a run-down palace somewhere."

"They must pay you a nice commission, these collectors."

"I make a decent living."

Sammy put down his glass and smiled.

"I like this guy," he said to Paul. "He's funny."

"I told you. Jack's really OK."

"He's a funny goddamn guy." Sammy reached across the table and cuffed me softly on one cheek, then the other. "He's smart, he dresses good, he don't take things too serious—I like that."

"Thanks," I said. "I'm flattered."

Sammy watched me for a moment, then spoke over his shoulder. "Get these plates out of here. Bring us some espresso." And to me: "You want something *dolce*?"

"Not dessert, if that's what you mean."

Sammy smiled broadly. "All right, Jack. We understand each other. It's good that we shared this meal. I always like things to be social, so you know who you're working with. Deals come out better that way, face to face. Everybody gets friendly, nobody feels cheated."

The waiter, returning with a tray, dipped in, his eyes fixed on the tablecloth. He placed the coffees in front of us and stepped back.

Sammy emptied two packets of artificial sweetener into his cup.

"So what's next?" I asked him.

"That depends."

I waited.

"Thing is, Jack. You got to prove yourself."

"Prove myself how?"

Sammy fixed his eyes on my face. "Paulie tells me you're real friendly with a little hottie he likes."

"Oh? Who's that?"

"Melissa Oliver."

I didn't respond.

"Age twelve," Paul said, "going on thirty."

I didn't respond.

"Kind of young for us," Sammy observed, "but Paulie says she's got great potential. He even tried to turn her out himself."

"Did he?" I said finally. "What happened?"

"No go, dude," Paul replied miserably. "She's a big tease. Besides, I couldn't get her away from her damned mother long enough to make any headway." He bit his lip. "The girl's prime, though. Don't tell me you haven't noticed."

Sammy turned his attention to the bottom of his empty cup, tiny as a thimble in his thick fingers.

"Paulie's our best recruiter," he said. "If he says she's star material, I want her."

"The girls always give off little signals when they're ready," Paul said, more confidently than before. "Glances, little jokes, hair tosses, long stretches, tight clothes." He was sounding like an eager expert now. "Signs as plain as billboards—if you're not afraid to read them."

"So, Jack buddy," Sammy said, watching my eyes, "are you game? Do you want to come to our next taping session?"

"I'd be glad to."

"Good." He kept his gaze on me. "Just bring the kid with you."

My mouth went a little dry. I wished to hell that Hogan were with me.

"Sure," I said.

"You see," Sammy explained quietly, "we have to be sure you're really one of us. A lot of guys dream, a lot of guys talk. But not everybody plays."

I nodded.

"So how about it? Do you play, Jack? Are you in on the action?"

"If the price is right."

Sammy grunted. Without hesitation, he went item by item down a menu of lewd acts, citing the rates. Each item upped my financial take substantially, if Melissa performed well. Double if she did it on camera.

"Seems fair," I said.

"If you come, you come to play."

"That's right."

"Awesome," Paul interjected.

"Just one thing. When it's Melissa's time," I told them, "I don't want her hurt."

"Don't worry about it," Sammy said. "We'll treat her like a peach."

"All right. When do we tape?"

"When we're good and ready. First Paulie will take you to meet Mr. Zhou. If the chink says you're OK, Paulie will tell you when and where to go."

With that, Sammy stood up. Paul and I rose, too, hesitating beside the table. No one brought us a check.

Lagging, we followed Sammy to the bar near the door.

"I'm stopping here," he said. "I got to discuss a few things with Carlo."

Sammy extended his hand to me. He stood very close. I could sense the broad swell of his chest and belly, even guess at the brand of imported cigar he smoked. For one dreadful moment, I imagined what it would be like—for me, for Melissa—to be pinned and mauled under that reeking weight.

"You know, my daughter wanted to go to that fancy Bradford School," he said.

"Can't blame her. It's the best."

"Yeah, well, it didn't work out."

"I'm sorry."

"They asked too many questions."

I tried my best to appear sympathetic.

"Now, look at this, Jack." Sammy slowly took a photograph out of his pocket. When he held it up, I saw that it was not, as I had expected, an image of his daughter. It was Melissa in her Bradford School outfit—the newly purchased blazer, plaid skirt, and knee socks—standing hips cocked in Central Park, giving the V sign. One of Paul's adoring Sunday-outing snapshots, no doubt.

"Do me a favor." Sammy's eyes were slightly red from the wine.

"Sure."

"Let's have some fun."

"Whatever you say."

"An extra grand if the Oliver brat wears her uniform."

43

A moral change is like aging. The alterations are subtle and deep, the damages cumulative. There is no way to perceive them, except by looking away and looking again, as one must to see the passage of time on the face of a clock.

So it had been for Paul Morse. One moment, he was an MFA kid, enraptured by the flowers of evil—in pictures and books, in late-night brag sessions and grad-school seminars. Unlike most middle-class renegades, however, he had begun to follow through on his bad-boy fantasies in a serious way, out-side the rhetorical bubble of academe, beyond art crits, beyond small dope deals in the East Village on weekend nights. Video had given him entrée into a darker world, and he found there a vice he could love. Now, a few years later, here he was—leading me through the streets of SoHo toward the *Virgin Sacrifice* studio and, beyond, to Chinatown and Mr. Zhou.

"Sammy was pretty tough on you last week," I said as we walked south on Crosby Street.

"It's just his way. You can't judge Sammy or Mr. Zhou like regular people. They're way past all that."

Paul paused midblock opposite a dirty white building that stretched the rest of the way to the corner. It had half a dozen floors with rows of large windows, most of them obscured by stacked boxes. Paul nodded toward a graffiti-marked steel door on street level. "That's where you'll go for the taping, fourth floor. Just ring."

We crossed over to Mulberry, its lampposts strung with red and green tinsel, its shops and restaurants oozing recorded at-mosphere music for tourists—the one last stretch of Little Italy not yet engulfed by Chinatown. Our progress slowed once we hit the shopping throngs on Canal Street, jostling for street food and knockoff designer handbags with equal vigor.

At Mott, we turned south again, onto a sidewalk overrun by fish stands, vegetable stalls, jade trinket stores and cheap dim sum restaurants. Paul strode on relentlessly, twisting through eddies of dark-clothed, dark-haired shoppers whose heads bobbed at the height of his shoulders. His own golden hair seemed to float steadily south like a lantern launched on a slow-moving stream. All the eateries were jammed and too brightly lit. We passed the Happy Road novelty emporium with its video games and its sad dancing chicken, whose wandering movements, within the confines of a tabletop vitrine, foretold fates.

Finally, Paul stopped in front of a shop window cluttered with Asian skin magazines and CD posters depicting passionate crooners, male and female—all young and beautiful with black liquid eyes, all famous for singing about lovelorn sorrows in languages I could not understand.

"This is the place," Paul said. "Just look friendly and don't say anything until we actually get to Mr. Zhou."

Inside, two sales clerks in their twenties seemed to be doing not much of anything while a video monitor played a tape of a Hong Kong game show.

"*Ni hao*," Paul said. "Zhou Dong invited us to the game upstairs. Two o'clock."

The clerks looked at each other, and one glanced at his fake Rolex watch.

"OK, mister," he said. "We go up."

I followed Paul around the counter and through a door to a small landing half buried in bundles of magazines. The narrow stairs were as steep as a ladder.

The clerk led us up two flights. Each landing was fenced off with cyclone mesh. As we passed the second level, a door stood open with a large upright fan oscillating at the threshold. The room's interior was ablaze with fluorescent ceiling lights and crowded with women cutting and sewing rapidly at long tables.

The clerk pushed a buzzer at the third landing, and a baggy-eyed man opened for us.

"I make videos," Paul said. "The *Virgin* show. For my friend Big Sammy."

The man jerked his head toward the door, and the clerk led us into a huge room with an ornate chandelier and massive red Chinese characters emblazoned on the walls. About twenty round tables were scattered throughout the space, each with six or eight men playing a game that involved stacks of small tiles and large mounds of cash. They fell silent, staring at us through clouds of cigarette smoke. I became intensely aware that Paul and I were the only white ghosts in the place.

The hubbub resumed when a good-looking guy, maybe forty years old, ambled across the room to greet us. Wearing an oxford Polo shirt and khakis, he stuck out his hand like a post-Mao Rotarian.

"Paul, baby. How's it hanging, man?"

The exotic Mr. Zhou, I later learned, had spent six years at City College.

He led us briskly to a little office set in one corner of the room. A young man brought in a bottle of baijiu and silently retreated. Mr. Zhou poured.

"Sammy, told me to expect you," he said. "Welcome." We drank the shots of the clear pine-tasting liquor in unison. "You're new to the business?" he asked me.

"To the video business, yes. Not to dealing in general, and not to your product."

"Yeah, well, all businesses are about the same really. After my MBA, I went to work on Wall Street. It wasn't so different from my grandfather's noodle shop."

"Why did you leave?"

"I decided to make faster money as an entrepreneur. It's the Cantonese Dream."

He laughed heartily at his own remark, a joke he'd probably made once a week for the last ten years.

"What's your main business now?" I asked.

"Import-export."

"I know what you export," I said. "That's why I'm here." I fingered the shot glass. "But what do you bring into the States?"

"What would you like?" Mr. Zhou stared at me evenly, his mouth tight. Then, suddenly, he broke into a wide smile. His teeth were bad in the usual Mainland way, darkened by tea and nicotine, starting to gap.

"My goal is to merge business with pleasure. Like you," I said.

"Not like me. Pleasure *is* my business, big difference."

"We're not all so fortunate."

"You don't like your work?"

"Compared to what—life on an assembly line?"

Mr. Zhou grinned and poured again, and I toasted him silently with the baijiu.

"Actually," I said, "it's pretty sweet, my racket. And not so different from yours."

"Are you sure?"

"Every spring I go to graduate thesis shows at a handful of top art schools. I pick one or two artists, and buy out their stuff. A year or two later, I give them a show. If it works, I get fifty percent of the take, plus all the increased value on my stockpile when their prices go up."

"If you pick right."

"Choosing well is my profession, and my particular gift. Besides, I only need to be totally right maybe one time in ten."

"Very attractive odds."

"The rate of increase on a single hot artist makes up for all the others—and more. A lot more."

"Double?"

"More like twenty times over in five years. Fifty in ten."

"I see. Better than a casino, I think."

"As long as the artist's run lasts, which is sometimes for decades. And when they flame out—whether it's after two years or twenty—I drop them."

"Like an old whore."

"Exactly."

Mr. Zhou laughed. "OK," he said. "So what's your plan for Paul's tapes?"

I reiterated the proposal I'd made to Sammy at Cielo Azzurro, adding many details in response to Mr. Zhou's pointed questions. The interrogation, and the liquor shots, went on for thirty minutes.

"Tell me what you think," I said at the end.

"I think we need another drink. An official seal."

In unison, we threw back one more baijiu. "If your contacts are good," Mr. Zhou said, "everybody will be happy."

"My contacts know what they like. You deliver, we'll all make a fat profit. Bank on it. In Switzerland, to be safe."

My new business associate turned to Paul. "This is a very fortunate meeting. Thank you, my friend. I won't forget."

"Sure, OK," Paul said. "I guess you'll have to set up a way to make dubs in Europe, though."

"No problem," Mr. Zhou said. "We can send the masters to Belleville."

Paul drew a blank.

"In Paris," I told him, "another Chinatown. A nice central spot on the continent."

As our glasses were filled again, I thought about the last time

I visited a Belleville restaurant with Nathalie. She had just finished writing a news story on the Russians' stalled invasion of Afghanistan. For two weeks, she had traveled in the mountains with the mujahideen, watching them blast Russian tanks in the narrow passes with shoulder-held missile launchers they got from U.S. suppliers. Nathalie was in a wonderful mood, regaling her French friends with details of fatal ambushes. "For once your CIA does something right," she said to me.

I asked Mr. Zhou if he ever spent much time in France.

"Only a few days in Paris, to visit the grave of Chopin."

"Your favorite composer?"

"Me? No. I'm a Beethoven man. But my father loved Chopin. He was a piano teacher—very refined, with hordes of pupils. During the Cultural Revolution, he was sent to the countryside, to the far end of Xinjiang Province, to build some useless road between two villages. For three and a half years, he spent every day with a shovel. No music, no books. While he worked, not to go crazy, he repeated all the Chopin scores in his head. Every note at first. But after a few months, he began to forget little by little. Later, when I was leaving China, he made me promise to go one day to the maestro's grave and apologize."

Next to me, Paul was turning restless.

"I have to get to the studio soon," he said. "I've got editing to do before the new shipment." He looked half beseechingly at Mr. Zhou. "Are we set here? Once Jack antes up with the Oliver girl, I mean?"

"We'll see," Mr. Zhou replied. "In China, before making a deal, we drink first, like this. We make big idiots of ourselves, we sing karaoke. Then we all go and get laid together."

"I'm familiar with the ritual," I said.

"When you know my drunk face and I know yours," Mr. Zhou continued, "when we have seen each other behave very badly with music and girls, and afterwards said nothing and forgotten the night as though it never happened—then we can start to trust, to do business."

"It's not so different here. But I don't think we have time for the full program today."

"Right, no singing now," Mr. Zhou said. "Next time. Today we just drink and screw."

Paul looked alarmed, but I knew that trying to refuse Mr. Zhou now would only queer the deal. Half rising, he poured one more round, and we clinked glasses again. The baijiu no longer burned.

44

The door opened, and two boys in multicolored sneakers slipped in, maybe eighteen or nineteen years old. Speaking in Cantonese, Mr. Zhou gave them quick instructions that brought fleeting smirks to their faces. We all piled down the stairs.

One level below the ground-floor music shop, we confronted a labyrinth of boxes. The boys wove us though the piles until we came to a metal shelving unit against the street-side wall. They swung the shelves aside unexpectedly to reveal a locked wooden door. Mr. Zhou keyed us in, and we followed him through a dim, damp-smelling tunnel under Mott Street and into a large basement lobby where an old woman sat at a desk.

Behind her were two corridors lined with wood-veneer paneling and punctuated every few feet by doors—some open, some closed. Young Chinese girls, all pretty, looked out at us here and there; others got up from the chairs they had been lounging in, momentarily abandoning their fashion magazines and celebrity gossip.

Opposite the desk, a set of stairs ran up to what I calculated had to be the back room of a beauty parlor. You could hear the nonstop lady chatter up there, and the sound of hair dryers running.

"Just tell Auntie Pearl what you like," Mr. Zhou said, nodding toward the old woman. "You are my guests."

Paul was getting very fidgety. "I really don't feel so well, thanks. Maybe just Jack should go."

"Paul, relax," Mr. Zhou smiled. "It won't take long. I know you."

He spoke rapidly to Auntie Pearl, who produced a key attached to a large numbered rectangle of plastic. It was a little
like getting a locker at the health club.

Two girls—in their early twenties, I would guess—moved
forward from the chairs to take Paul's arms.

"Hi, friend. What's your name?" one asked sweetly. They
were both very cute, both wearing bright tube tops, faded hip-
hugger jeans, and high heels. Their fingers and tiny toes were
painted.

"You call me Ling."

With a girl on each arm, Paul began to move down the left
corridor, seemingly without will, like a man being led to his
execution.

"I'm Hui," the second girl said as they went along. "Maybe
you think I'm pretty, yes?"

Paul gave me a last desperate look over his shoulder before
he disappeared into one of the cubicles.

"You see something you like?" Mr. Zhou asked me.

I shrugged. "All very nice, thanks."

"Ah, I know." With a few syllables, he sent one of the boys
down the right-hand corridor. The kid returned with his arm
draped on the shoulder of a large-eyed teenager perhaps two
years his junior.

"More like this?" asked Zhou.

"Not today."

It was a mistake to refuse. Now Mr. Zhou was in danger of
losing face. He signaled, and the old woman came from behind
the counter.

"You wait here five minutes," she said. "We bring pretty girl.
More young. Fresh, not like these old fish. You be happy."

"I'm happy now," I said quickly, looking around. "I like that
slim girl over there by the stairs. She reminds me of a friend in
Shanghai."

"Ha! Who, your old landlady?" Auntie Pearl laughed. "Her, she's very old girl. Not for you. Almost thirty maybe. Why you want a grannie?"

"I like to learn," I said.

The idea seemed to impress Mr. Zhou. "OK, sure. She's got loads of experience, that girl. I like her, too. She can teach you some tricks."

The man knew his merchandise. Once we got into the tight windowless chamber, the girl, who called herself Xin, proved to be swift and adept with her hands. She hesitated only once, when she saw my bare arm.

"War?" she asked, her voice slightly awed and caressing.

"No," I said. "Business."

That seemed to satisfy her. She probably thought I had run afoul of my own Mr. Zhou somewhere, in a deal gone awry. It was a scene she could easily picture.

After that, I lay back on the hard, narrow mattress and let her do the things she believed would please me. In truth, she was not entirely wrong. Xin was very skilled, not least as an actress. In the near-dark, I could almost believe in her passion. For a while, she loomed over me with her hair down and swaying, her breath coming in half-moaning spurts. She called me *"laowai* baby" and gave a little series of yips. Her repertoire of positions, her rhythms, her cries and groans all flowed expertly; her hand on my cheek afterwards was gentle and lingering. What more could I ask? She seemed to care for me as deeply as anyone ever had, and about as long. In gratitude, I gave her a fifty dollar tip.

When I came out, Paul was already sitting in one of the chairs, his face pale and miserable. The two girls were back to their magazines. Xin came down the dim hall and joined them, and they spoke quickly and softly to each other in a mix of Mandarin and Cantonese, flipping pages and darting their hands to their mouths to stifle the laughter.

"Damn," Paul said from his slump, not bothering to lower his voice. "I've been trying to stay away from the chinks."

"They're hard to give up," I said.

I was a little annoyed with myself for not feeling worse. Supposedly, I had sworn off this sort of thing—for the betterment of my soul or whatever. Yet from time to time, business still had its social demands.

"Take it easy," I told Paul. "Your secret's safe with me."

In fact, I didn't care what anyone did in Chinatown—myself included. Everything gets swiftly mixed up south of Canal Street; they speak a different language there. Besides, what did this brief Chinese excursion amount to? By any normal SoHo measure, my personal life these days was practically sainthood.

Mr. Zhou emerged, finally, trailing two girls of his own. One had dyed red hair, and the other was the high-school kid. As they passed, the teenager shot me a teasing look. She was breathing heavily and trembling, but her half-smile worked all the same.

"Life is good?" Mr. Zhou asked, grinning.

Paul got up nervously. "Yeah," he said. "Now I've got to get back."

Mr. Zhou leaned close to my ear. "Paul is afraid he'll catch yellow fever," he said. "Very sad for the boy."

"He's young," I said. "He hasn't learned how to live with himself yet."

"Yes, yes. You understand. I'm going to tell Sammy you are a good man to work with."

"I look forward to it, Mr. Zhou."

"Call me Zhou Bob. That's my friendly name."

"Like Joe Bob in English. Makes you sound like a redneck."

"I know. Like a Memphis-mafia cracker…from Guangdong."
He had a good laugh. "I'm Zhou Dong in business, but Joe Bob when I play."

"Seems like a swell idea. Living as just one person would be such a bore."

We said our goodbyes and a bowing thank you to Auntie Pearl at the desk. She squawked something at the girls, who rose from their chairs, smiling and saying, "Bye-bye, thank you, bye-bye, hurry back, come again," as we filed through the tunnel door.

45

Paul and I emerged into the shock of the late afternoon sun, glancing at each other awkwardly. "You've got some charming associates," I said.

"Mr. Zhou's all right. He just needs to be in control of everything, you know?"

"It's a common urge."

I looked at my watch. It was three thirty-five, almost time to pick up Melissa at school. Angela, who needed to prepare more work for her show, had asked me to take the girl to her weekly piano lesson.

When I exited the subway on 77th Street, the cool air washed over me—a new man in black cashmere, at ease among the townhouses and prewar apartment buildings. Respectful doormen nodded as I passed, making my way toward Madison Avenue. As I approached the neo-gothic facade of the Bradford School, I saw Melissa across the courtyard with a group of friends.

She smiled and said something to the other girls that made them all laugh. Their monitor—Mrs. Dorfman, in a brown herringbone coat—signaled to the guard to let me in.

"Sorry for the delay," I said. "I was trapped in a business meeting."

"We were beginning to worry," Mrs. Dorfman replied. "Girls, say hello to Melissa's uncle, Mr. Wyeth."

The eight little misses, all wearing uniforms of deeply pleated plaid skirts and white blouses with crested blazers, said in ragged unison, "Hello, Mr. Wyeth. How do you do? Very nice to meet you, sir." Then they bent together in giggles, a random pair of eyes flashing up occasionally from the mass of blue jackets and neatly combed hair. The students suddenly had a great deal to say that neither Mrs. Dorfman nor I could quite hear. I saw blushes on several cheeks.

"Girls," Mrs. Dorfman chided them, "show some manners."

Melissa looked at me beseechingly.

"It's all right," I said. "We really should be off. Missy's piano teacher is waiting. Then we're going to work on her French lessons tonight."

This induced gales of titters. Finally, one of the classmates stepped forward. "Missy said you might come and talk to us about really weird art sometime."

"Weird like what?"

"Animal parts, wrecked cars. Right now we don't get anything past de Kooning." She sliced the air in a series of Zorro-style slashes. "You know, all those hacked-up women with ugly faces."

"That's quite enough, Jessica," said Mrs. Dorfman. "Very generously, Mr. Wyeth has in fact consented to address the class on postwar art. You may discuss New York School painting with him after his lecture, in February."

The girls found this prospect hilarious. Melissa separated herself from their laughter and whispers, taking my hand.

"Come on, Uncle Jack," she said. "Let's go where we can have an adult conversation."

We caught a cab that took us across the park to the Upper West Side.

"Your friends seem to think I'm pretty funny," I said.

"They're just dorks."

"High maintenance dorks, I bet."

"Actually, they all think you're dreamy, if you want to know the truth."

"I always want to know the truth. It's a curse."

Even in the dimness of the cab, punctuated by occasional bursts of reflected light, I could see Melissa's eyes roll.

"You're such a child sometimes," she said.

Her piano teacher turned out to be a Juilliard student in need of pocket cash, an earnest young man with wire-rim glasses and an ostentatious way of counting in German to keep his pupil on beat. The neat minuscule apartment was lined with books. At least Melissa played fluently, with the kind of feeling that Zhou Dong's father would have approved.

Back in SoHo, we stopped for dinner at Marc Sans on Sullivan Street. Lights were just coming on in the cloudy fall twilight. The owner gave us a table along the east wall, "where mademoiselle can see and be seen."

"*Merci bien,*" Melissa said. "*On est toujours à l'aise dans ce bel endroit.*"

Marc, exaggeratedly impressed as always, immediately switched into French, and the two of them bantered away for several minutes about the evening's menu. At Melissa's suggestion, I ordered the duck confit.

"You've made a new conquest," I said when the young owner, slim and curly-haired, went back to the kitchen. "I'm very impressed."

"No, I don't want more than one *copain*," Melissa answered gravely.

"That's not very French of you."

"I don't care. I've decided to be completely faithful to you. It's more daring these days, don't you think?"

"It's hard for me to say."

"You'll see once you get used to it."

"Get used to what?"

"My devotion."

"Very cute. No wonder your friends are so entertained all the time."

"They were laughing because I told them about us."

"Told them what?"

"That you're my boyfriend now."

"Stop it. That's very silly."

"Is not."

"It's a fun game, Missy, but you have to be careful."

"Why?"

"Because some very obtuse people might think you're serious."

"I am serious."

"Stop it."

"It's not up to you. I get to decide."

"Not by yourself. Both people have to agree."

"You do agree, Uncle Jack. You just won't admit it."

Melissa was interrupted by the arrival of two mesclun salads and a basket of bread. She looked at the food very carefully. Raising her eyes to me, she said with great deliberation, "I've decided to be true to you because I see how the other way just massacres everything."

"Like what?"

"Like your marriage to Nathalie, like my daddy's life." She did not blink or look away.

"Your father made some mistakes, like everybody."

"And now he's ended up half crazy, because some sex germ is eating his brain. That's what Mom says, anyway. She ought to know. She's kind of slutty herself."

"Don't insult your mother, Missy."

"What do you know about her?"

"That she's a terrific woman, a good mother. I also know you're her whole life."

"Except when she's off with some guy and forgets all about me. I'm never sure when she leaves the house if it's really, really for an opening or a studio visit or whatever, or just a hook-up with some horny creep."

"You're not being fair to her, Missy."

"Maybe not. But it's what I feel. That's why I want to start fresh with you."

"I might be the worst choice of all."

"You might, but that doesn't matter. I don't care what you do, honey. I just care what I feel. So I'm going to be true to you until you're like really old, maybe fifty or something. Then I'll marry a rich doctor and make him take care of you when you're all twisted up and can't walk and stuff."

"How sweet. Why would you do that?"

"Because you take good care of me now, and no one else does."

"How can you say that? Lots of people take care of you. Especially your mother."

"Sometimes. But I take care of her, too."

"How so?"

"In a special daughter way. You don't get to know."

"Not ever?"

"Only when we get married."

I had a long drink of wine and tried to laugh Melissa's fantasy away.

"Don't kid yourself, Missy," I said. "Once you're grown up, you won't even remember my name."

"Won't I?"

"Guaranteed. The first love is never the last. You'll understand that someday."

"Do you understand it?"

"No, not really."

It was too much. I began to look desperately, vainly for a waiter.

"Why are you being so difficult?" Melissa asked.

"Look, you're a wonderful girl, Missy, but I can't be a boyfriend for you."

"Why not?"

"I'm too ancient."

"You are not. You're too scared, that's all."

"It's more or less the same thing."

She pondered for a moment, her right index finger working the edge of the table. "Why do you always talk to me about being old?"

"Because anything else would be a lie."

"You don't seem old to me. You seem my age."

"It's a trick I learned once."

"I like it. It's magic."

"With you, yes. Not with everyone."

"See how good I am for you?"

46

Word about the next *Virgin Sacrifice* taping came directly from Paul, when we ran into each other at Bob Flanagan's birthday performance at the New Museum.

For several weeks the California artist, who suffered from cystic fibrosis, had been ensconced in a hospital bed in the main gallery. Covers drawn to his chest, he greeted visitors and chatted quietly until the time came to stand up and strip himself naked. Every few hours, completely exposed, he would wrap a rope around his ankles and be winched upside down toward the ceiling. There he hung with arms outstretched in an inverted crucifix position meant to incarnate his art and help clear his lungs of accumulated mucus. But for tonight's landmark occasion—he had attained the odds-defying age of 42—Flanagan promised something unprecedented.

A large crowd was on hand, milling about among the displays that accompanied the artist's live-in project. Near the front was an installation duplicating the look of a pediatrician's waiting room: low tables and chairs, children's magazines and books, a few toys, a low wall of building blocks. Only on second look did one notice that the toy box was salted with rough-sex implements and the blocks were arranged to obsessively repeat the letters "S" and "M." Nearby was a black stool crowned with a tapering butt plug. A long text, Flanagan's memoir and credo, filled one wall, culminating in a catchphrase that, reiterated, encircled the entire exhibition space: "Fight sickness with sickness."

In the rear gallery stood a scaffold holding half a dozen

video monitors suspended in the form of a cross. One showed Bob's head, others his hands, his feet, and his crotch. The last featured scenes of self-mortification—his penis being bound tightly with black leather thongs, his foreskin probed with needles, a nail driven through his scrotum and into a board. To one side of the scaffold lay an open, flower-bedecked casket with a video clip of the artist's living face displayed on a monitor propped against a white satin pillow.

Bob himself, wearing a black T-shirt and jeans with a slim oxygen tank strapped to his hip, circulated among the guests. Joking and gesticulating, he breathed with the aid of a clear plastic tube taped just under his nose. He was an excellent host, doing his best to make everyone feel comfortable and entertained.

Behind him, moving when he moved, was Paul Morse. The familiar shoulder-held camera covered the younger man's pretty face as he shadowed Flanagan. The event was being recorded, in a glare of artificial light, for *PM Videos*.

Once the crowd had filled the room, Bob disappeared behind a curtain. Soon a huge cake in the shape of male genitalia was wheeled out by assistants. Pieces were cut and distributed along with plastic glasses of wine. Finally, Bob reappeared—lying nude on a bed of nails atop a hospital gurney. The overhead track lights revealed a small bead of perspiration on his upper lip, his only sign of discomfort. After a few minutes, he sat up and spoke into a handheld mike, thanking us all for making this birthday such a memorable treat.

An artist I knew vaguely—one of the youth set, with shaved head and Dr. Martens boots—caught my eye and edged closer. He seemed to be screwing up his courage to speak to me, and I hoped it wouldn't be a come-see-my-work pitch.

"How have you been, sir?" the young man asked.

"Fine. Just back from the Hamptons. It was all very chic. Guests arriving by helicopter on the front lawn—that sort of thing."

I enjoyed the little white lie. Bohemian types always assume that SoHo dealers lead gilded lives, and the illusion is good for my brand.

"So," he said wearily, "are you going anywhere interesting after the show?"

"No," I replied. "I'm tired of interesting places, aren't you?"

"Oh, for sure." His eyes brightened. "Dull stuff is actually much more refined. Like, you know, this new French theorist says that blandness is the essence of Chinese culture."

"Does he?" I finished my wine. "I wonder if he's ever had a meal in Sichuan. Or a girlfriend in Shanghai."

Just then Paul—heaven sent at that moment—eased between us, moving in for a final shot over my shoulder.

"Perfect," he said as he switched off the camera and lights. "I never get tired of watching Bob."

Suddenly, with the intense lamps extinguished, everything seemed less important. Paul spoke to me quietly, under the general murmur of resumed chatter.

"We're taping a new *Sacrifice* in a few days. Are you game?"

"Sure, as long as Sammy makes it worth my while."

"He will. Is Melissa ready? Does she trust you?"

"Better than that. She's sweet on me."

"Righteous, man." Paul said it firmly, though he looked a bit hurt. "And her mother?"

"Not a clue."

"They can be real hellcats, you know. Some moms."

"Angela is busy playing Florence Nightingale to her ex-husband, who's marooned in Sloan-Kettering."

"That should keep her distracted." Paul told me to expect a

small group at the Crosby Street building. "What are you going to tell Missy?"

"That we're off to a fun dance party with Uncle Paul and his friends."

"Good, I like the way it sets her up."

"I thought you might."

47

Once I agreed to go to the taping session, everything else started to feel slightly irrelevant, a waste of my time. Certainly Angela's opening proved—to put it kindly—an underwhelming affair. Yet her failure enabled me to put the next part of my plan into motion.

Even though Michael Loomis Fine Arts was not large, too much space separated the few unimportant visitors, most of them Angela's personal friends. Each looked as lonely as her isolated sculptural figures, and only a little less contorted. No drinks were served. For once, information would be my only intoxicant until the afterparty.

"What should I say to Angela?" I asked Laura, who was sleek and deadly looking that evening in a new Gemma Kahng skirt.

"Tell her the show will be well received critically."

"She knows what that means."

"Then make up a smooth story about how recognition builds over time, how Michael will sell things out of the back room for months to come."

"I'm supposed to be her friend."

"So be one." She scowled at my plodding reaction. "Why tell nice people the truth, Jack? Isn't there enough grief in the world already?"

I looked around the room. "I half expect to see Phil here," I said, feeling foolish. I was still a long way from accepting my friend's bleak condition, even though I'd seen some of the devastation for myself. Laura gave me a reality check, reminding me that our former client never left the hospital anymore, could not care for his own daily needs or engage in more than the simplest verbal exchange.

"It's too strange," she said.

"What's that?"

"How they work the same way basically—sex, age, disease." Laura fingered her glass. "Beyond a certain point, your body just does what it's going to do."

I still couldn't quite grasp it. Philip had been fully cogent at the time I lost Nathalie. Yet the breakdown that began only two and a half years ago with negligibly small slips—writing "soon see you" at the end of his e-mails instead of "see you soon"— worsened at a vicious rate, until now it had ravaged him totally, leaving the former magnate only nominally human. In the past few months, with increasing rapidity, memory loss had invaded his brain like an alien cell-killing substance, spreading wildly until his troubled, once-agile mind was obliterated. His thinking had suddenly passed over into a simpler, more blissful dimension, like Dante stepping through the wall of flame to embrace his lost Beatrice.

No one could say exactly when the last trace of guilt left Philip, when the final synapse gave way—the one that formerly con-nected the image of a dead woman, his wife, with the emotional oddity we call remorse. At last, irreversibly, he had entered into a pathological beatitude. Philip was far past crime and punish-ment now, beyond good and evil.

I could have used a little of his oblivion that evening, as the scene grew even more painfully subdued at the loft gathering after Angela's show.

She had invited a bevy of old acquaintances, mostly third-rate artists, and a few junior-level museum people. Two catering tables were overloaded with wineglasses, liquor bottles, smoked salmon, and cheese—enough for a crowd twice the size. The few attendees passed each other at awkward distances, like mutually distrustful scavengers at an accident scene. Only when the drinks took effect did the conversations start to rise in frequency and tone.

I poured myself a vodka tonic and went to see how Angela was doing.

Pretty rotten, it turned out. She was standing alone in the kitchen, scooping unneeded ice cubes into a silver bucket. "This isn't working," she said.

"What isn't?"

"This bloody party, the show, my so-called career."

"Give Michael a chance. You've been away for a while."

"Too long, I know." She stared down at the mound of ice. "There are times when I just hate art," she said.

"You don't mean that, Angela. It's about all we have—the likes of us."

"That's the worst of it. My work was supposed to make life just dandy again after Philip left. Well, it didn't. And now what? I can't pray like your friend Hogan, and all I have to show for my efforts are those damned fiberglass witches."

"That's quite a lot, actually."

Angela shook her head. "A dozen wretched, oversized dolls—do you know what they tell me, Jack?"

"No."

"Art is no match for flesh and blood. Only love is love; only Philip is Philip."

Suddenly, I wanted to touch her, to put my good arm around her waist as we stood by the softly humming refrigerator. But I didn't dare.

"He wasn't exactly sweet to you after he took up with Mandy," I reminded her. "And he's not exactly Philip now."

"No, he wasn't sweet. Not at the end."

"Was he ever?"

"Wonderfully, in the first years. I can't begin to tell you. But he's a man like any other. He threw away the best thing he had. Sometimes I think that's how we all keep ourselves going."

"Why not just move on yourself, then? You certainly don't lack for options."

Her head shifted minutely, slowly, from side to side. "After Philip left, I tried to cut him out of my soul like a cancer. Later I realized the cells had metastasized."

"Are you really that far gone, Angela?"

"All the way. What I felt for him—what I feel—is not a thing I can control."

"I just hate to see you go through this misery for a second time," I said.

She looked straight ahead, past me, past everything. "It's hell to live without hope, Jack."

"I know."

Angela's voice dropped to a whisper. "I wouldn't wish that on Philip. So don't wish it on me."

"All right, whatever you say."

Her eyes returned, powerfully. "I want the right, real thing, that's all. Nothing less. I'm tired of everything else, and I'm too damaged to fight anymore—damaged nearly to death."

"You deserve whatever you want."

"I'm no fool, Jack. I know that someday—not so very long from now—this ridiculous pain, these crazed thoughts and feelings, will slowly end. I'll be myself again, calm and reasonable and rather dull. But in the meantime, I have to think them and feel them. There's no shortcut, no exemption for being smart."

"No, I don't suppose." I finished my drink, placing the glass on the countertop. "At least you have Melissa."

"Yes, I have my daughter." Angela seemed to find herself again. "We have each other. The two of us, no matter what."

Angela picked up the ice bucket and forced her thin lips into a party smile.

"Missy's been looking for you, by the way," she said. "She's in back by the stereo, waiting with something quite important to ask you."

"That's funny. She never likes my answers very much."

At the rear of the loft, I found Melissa cross-legged on the floor, flipping through her mother's old albums.

"What are these things?" she asked. "Like clay tablets or something?"

"Nothing you recognize?"

"It's all super-ancient."

"Angela said that you wanted to see me."

"I was waiting for you."

"Waiting for what?"

"Just good practice. For our future."

"Oh, right. I forgot."

"Did you think about me at all today?"

"Every moment."

"No, you didn't. Phony talker. Pretender."

"Am I?"

"Fake, fake, full of cake."

"It'd be better for us both if I were." I sat on the edge of an ottoman near her. "Actually, I was thinking today about an adventure we could go on together. A secret party. Would you like that?"

"Can I wear my birthday present dress?"

"No, they want to see you in your school uniform."

"They who?"

"Paul and his friends. They want you to dance."

"You told them? It was just for you that day."

"I know. But if you make Paul like it too, maybe we can find out who hurt Aunt Mandy. Then your dad won't be in trouble anymore."

"And the police will stop bugging Mom with so many questions?"

"That's right."

"Why doesn't Paul just help us, without any dancing?"

"He's a little bit selfish."

"I know."

"Was he ever selfish with you?"

"In a way. He told me about that other kind of kissing. The one men really, really like."

"He just talked or he showed you?"

"We looked at pictures on the Internet. I thought they were pretty rank."

"Paul makes video shows like that. That's why he wants you to dance for his friends. I want to bust them, so the cops can get them to tell us what really happened to Mandy."

"Will Paul go to jail?"

"He might. If we learn enough."

She seemed to contemplate the prospect at length while a Roy Orbison song played.

"How do you know his friends will even like me?" she asked.

"They're men. They won't be able to help it."

48

I was glad to get home that night, away from the gallery opening, away from the lingering party chatter that I could still hear below me—down in Angela's loft—where Melissa, too, was shut away in her room for the night. I stretched out, but sleep eluded me. This was the same bed, I thought, where I had made love to Nathalie countless mad times, and where I used to lie awake after she was gone, wishing I could make my body shut down, my heart stop its beating. I wanted to die there, quickly, with no pain or fuss. Unfortunately, you can't erase yourself from the world without violence. Even the strongest human will is not enough to paralyze your lungs, to reduce your vital processes to zero. You can fight sickness with sickness but not life with life. No, it takes a stronger poison than that.

A joke came into my head in the dark. What if Hogan's God Almighty had gone slightly nuts like Angela's ex? It was a funny thought. The result might be the world as we know it. I don't care what Hogan says, there's a flaw in the universe, and its name is death. How's that for profundity—or was it blasphemy? Great, I said to myself, now I'm doing theology on sleep meds and vodka. No wonder that Jehovah, like Hogan, comes into my mind at the oddest times. Often they arrive together.

Nathalie once had everything but innocence, I thought, and now I had everything but faith. Hogan says I lack the daring. You have to be willing to fight—and maybe die—for an innocence that you've already lost and no longer believe in. He calls it thinking like a soldier—a Christian soldier no less. According to him, it's the very absurdity of faith, its evasion of logic and evidence, that makes it the only sane response to an irrational world. Or was it the other way around? Anyway Christ, to Hogan, is like a criminal whose dossier can never be closed. God is a crime against reason—the only one he condones. His theory makes no sense, but I understand it completely. Sometimes I think about Missy that way.

49

I awoke far too early the next morning. To soothe myself in the first quiet hours of the day, I spread some of Mandy's e-mails around me on the bed, reading them randomly, for nostalgia and amusement and for their welcome soporific effect. That changed when I came across a message to Angela dated April 28, six days before the murder. Somehow, in my preoccupation with the exchanges between Amanda and Paul, I'd overlooked two sentences buried in a long tedious thread. The Oliver wives, past and current, were sparring about Melissa's school schedule, taxes on the Westchester house, insurance.

"You're right, my dear," Amanda wrote near the end. "It's pointless to try to settle anything through Philip. That Italian hussy has turned him upside down and inside out, the old fool. We should talk. Call me, and we'll set a time to meet next week while he's away."

I waited until Melissa left for school, then dropped in on Angela with the pretext of morning coffee.

"Thanks for helping out last night," she said.

"I didn't do much."

"You listened. It's a rare courtesy."

"Seems like the least I can do, what with you being the angel of mercy to Philip these days and all."

She shook her head. "Sometimes, when I look at him now, I think death is the only real kindness."

We sat together amid the post-party clutter, in the same ensemble of sofas and chairs where Missy and I, weeks before, had sipped drinks and grown strangely intimate.

"Now I have to be impolite," I said.

"Really, how?"

"I have to ask you if you came to see Amanda the week she was killed."

Angela tested the temperature of her coffee with a fingertip. She lifted a droplet to her lips and tasted it thoughtfully.

"No," she said. "I'm not big on self-abuse." She took a first cautious sip. "What on earth would make you think that?"

"I've been reading Mandy's e-mails."

"Not very tactful of you."

It was my turn to make her wait.

"Do I have to check the files again to see what exactly you wrote back?" I asked finally.

"Don't bother. I didn't reply by e-mail; I phoned. We had business to settle about Missy's new school. And some details of her inheritance."

"Was Mandy happy about that?"

"Probably not. She wasn't exactly thrilled to talk to me for any reason, let alone money."

"What did she say when you met?"

"We didn't. She invited me, but I was far too busy getting ready for my show and the Katonah benefit."

"And you wouldn't want to leave Missy alone in the house in Westchester."

"Of course not."

"Not even with the nanny?"

"The one I had then, no. She wasn't nearly as reliable as Emmanuelle. You remember her—the French au pair Philip hired years ago? A lovely girl. Good for language lessons, but not the best role model for Missy. Still, so far, I haven't found anyone more trustworthy."

I nodded, watching her over my coffee mug. "You have to be very careful these days."

"Yes, it's terrible."

"Some days," I said, "and some people, are worse than others."

"Anybody special in mind?"

"Paul Morse."

"That scum." Angela caught herself, seeming to realize that she'd tipped her hand.

"What's wrong with Paul?" I asked.

"You tell me, Jack. You're a man."

"I thought you were fond of the guy."

"I was until Missy and her friends caught onto him. The girls call his kind 'grody dudes.' They're everywhere. The bastard even tried to use Philip to get to Missy. 'Come on, sit closer. Let's type in your dad's name on Google. I'll bet we get a thousand hits.' She didn't fall for it, thank God."

"Not the way you fell for Hogan's protection?"

Angela looked at me sharply, surprised. "Well, what can you expect?"

It was a pretty good question. Impatient with my silence, Angela went on.

"Just look at us in this city," she said, "The way we run around. We're all killing each other in the name of a good time."

"Is that what you call it?"

"Occasionally. A good time, sure. Or lack of knowing how to do anything better."

"There's emotional killing," I said, "and then there's the real thing."

"You should know—about death by heartbreak, I mean. Once upon a time you were the master. Remember?"

"I have a vague recollection."

"Tell me, then. Tell me one good thing that came out of all your affairs and fake romances, Jack." She waited for me to meet her eyes. "You can't."

I searched my memory. Unfortunately, the findings didn't do much for my self-defense.

"Entertainment," I offered finally. "That's something. For years, I got and gave harmless laughs. What more would you like?"

"Something beyond ourselves."

"Talk to Hogan," I said. "That's his specialty."

Angela regarded me across her coffee mug, savoring its contents. Her voice turned softer. "Why didn't you ever have a child, Jack?"

"I wasn't in the mood."

"You see? Don't be flip. I know Nathalie desperately wanted one."

"Nathalie wanted a lot of things. Unfortunately, they didn't all fit together."

"It's not too late. Not for you, a man. Of course, you have to want the whole chaos of it."

"Want it for what?"

"Oh, making up for our mistakes, I suppose. Going on is what saves us, and children force us to slog ahead no matter what. With a smile, too. Even though they disrupt everything, the little savages."

"Thanks, I'll give it some thought tonight before I sleep."

That afternoon, I called Hogan. We didn't discuss fatherhood issues. Instead, I told him about Amanda's "let's meet" message to Angela, and he gave me the lowdown on the *Virgin Sacrifice* distribution ring.

"The master tape goes out of a warehouse in New Jersey, packed in with a gross of O-Tech instructional videos. Like you said, the only thing that distinguishes it from the others is that red X on the upper-right corner of the label."

"Where does it go?"

"To the Oliver Industries headquarters in Shanghai, and out the back door to a pirate video mill behind the counterfeit goods market."

"Xiang Yang."

"Whatever. The Chinese can dupe anything overnight."

"Yes, I've seen their work."

"How is it?"

"Good enough for porn."

"That figures. From Shanghai the dubs go all over Asia in O-Tech shipments."

"Did you get all this from Margaret?"

"The young lady has grown very fond of me, and extremely pissed off at Andrews. She gave him up."

"Andrews is the deal-maker?"

"Once Paul Morse came up with the idea and the material."

"What about Philip?"

"Innocent as a jaybird—at least of this. Seems he's too good a daddy to be a smut peddler."

"Or a consumer?"

"Nice way to talk about your friends, Jack."

"My mind goes a little bit funny when I don't get enough sleep—it's a hazard in my profession."

"Which one?"

"Both. Art dealing, real estate—neither one is very conducive to mental health."

Hogan wasn't exactly brimming with compassion. "You'd sleep better with a wife beside you," he said.

"Out of boredom?"

"Yeah, right, just laugh. You never gave marriage—your own or anyone else's—much of a chance."

"Shows how much you know, Hogan. I tried hard to understand monogamy once."

"Really? I didn't notice."

"It was an internal process."

50

After we hung up, I tried to keep my dark speculations about Angela from interfering with my work at the gallery. Why had she never previously complained about Paul Morse? When did she get enlightened, and did the key information really come from Melissa? What was Angela's response? Remembering how she dealt with that nurse in Bronxville, I wondered if she had ever paid a visit to Paul, just to straighten him out.

Well, let Hogan do his work, I told myself—if he can tear himself away from Angela's bed long enough to think straight. Meanwhile, I've got a gallery to run.

Laura had scheduled Mick Tarkower for our second show of the season. I set my mind on selecting the best three suites of photographs for our space. The shot of rows upon rows of fluorescent-lit grocery store shelves, in or out? The chained vulture? The Japanese teens with fuchsia hair and pacifiers in their mouths?

In the midst of my deliberations, Angela called to give me an update on Philip. She didn't want to talk about anything else—not the opening, the party, her work, or Paul Morse. Patient care was her whole concern now.

"They're moving him to a hospice," she said.

"He's that bad?"

"There's nothing much left of him. The doctors can't do any more, and he only annoys the nursing staff. The same question over and over again. He wants to know that everything has been paid in advance."

I thought for a moment about the way Philip had lived, and the way he was dying.

"Tell him yes," I said. "He's paid up in full."

How peculiar it must be for him now, I thought. Before Mandy's murder, the accelerating loss of his brain cells had presented Philip, subjectively, with a faultless and loving spouse, a thriving business, innumerable friends, a magical influx of unceasing wealth. In a sense, he had pulled off a great coup: he had solved the problem of happiness. Wolfsheim's Syndrome was a form of intoxication with no sobering up, a drug without any impending crash. Except death, of course.

But after Amanda was killed, cruel mysteries began to plague my friend. His beloved wife was missing, the business was out of his hands, most friends seemed to pity him, his money was as abstract as a calculus formula. Unable to remember the source of his distress, he was forced to ask about it again and again— like a boy who begs his father repeatedly to explain the loss of a favorite puppy.

"Oh, and Jack," Angela said, "I enjoyed our chat today. Do feel free to come down for coffee with me in the mornings."

"I don't want to bother you."

"Not a bother at all. In fact, it'd be nice to have someone I can really talk to. Kids, you know—all demands and silliness. I need a transition, an adult voice, to get into my work after Melissa leaves for school."

"Glad to be of service."

"And there's no sense you prowling around upstairs all alone."

"No sense at all. That's very kind of you, Angela."

"Is it?" She smiled. "I don't know what's come over me lately."

Waiting for Paul's signal about the next *Virgin Sacrifice* taping was beginning to wear on my nerves. One afternoon, to relieve the anxiety and give my young neighbor a treat, I took Melissa to see a Henry Darger exhibition at the American Folk Art Museum. It would also be a chance to find out if she was covering for Angela.

On a pedestal, under a pin-spot, sat enshrined the old manual typewriter on which the mentally defective janitor had composed *The Realms of the Unreal*, his fifteen-volume epic about a stupendous war over child slavery and the fate of seven young princesses known as the Vivian Girls. Many of the long, fold-out illustrations he made—drawn, traced and enchantingly hand-colored—were displayed on the walls or in freestanding glass slipcases that showed both sides of the complex narrative scenes.

"It looks kind of like the Civil War," Melissa said. "Only with little blond girls and huge flowers and storms and flying creatures all added."

"Anything is possible because the war takes place on another planet."

"Who's fighting?"

"The Abbieannians—they're pretty much like Christians—are trying to fend off the Glandelinians, who want to capture lots of young boys and girls for slaves."

"Kids wouldn't make very good workers."

"No? Why not? They're pure energy, like you."

"Work is for grown-ups. Grown-up losers."

Together, we studied the vignettes as they alternated from bucolic gardens to battles and executions, and back again.

"Do you like the way he draws the kids?" I asked.

"Yeah, bunches of them get killed. Choked, hacked up, hung. Shot through the head."

"But not the Vivian Girls. They always escape."

"Like me."

"Really? Are you in danger?"

"Naturally, from men. Mom tells me so."

"Men like your Uncle Jack?"

"Oh, you wish."

We walked on, letting the vivid pictures unscroll as we passed. I said nothing—one of my favorite tactics. Long ago I realized that the thing I had to fear most in the world was the ferocity of my own dark thoughts. So I learned to hide them deep and well—in silence, in work, in banter, in sly stories. And, oh yes, especially in liquor and sex.

"Why do the girls have penises sometimes?" Melissa asked.

"Nobody knows. Darger lived alone in one room and dreamed up these things after work. In Chicago. No one even knew the books existed until after he died."

"Uncle Paul says penises are just for fun, but I don't think so. Girls can have fun without those yucky things."

"Don't be too sure."

Melissa grimaced. "Ha, ha, ha. You're so funny.…Don't you ever get tired of jokes?"

"So be serious with me now."

"All right, darling."

We sat on a bench, with what Darger called the Glandeco-Angelinnian War Storm playing out all around us. Missy's dress was simple and black, with a white collar. She was wearing adult perfume. Being with her, hearing her clear voice, I understood why there had to be fantasy realms we can turn to—a brighter

one like Hogan's heaven or a darker one like Paul's video hell.
Or both, if you were Darger.

"Tell me the truth about Aunt Mandy's laptop," I said.

"What do you mean?"

"You saw the date on her last e-mail. Whoever took the computer must have made off with it on the day she was killed. I
don't think that was you."

"No, I was just pretending. Like Uncle Paul asked me to."

"You were very convincing."

"Sure, I can pretend almost anything."

"But now you're telling the truth?"

"Yes, honey, of course."

"And you're sure Paul took it from Aunt Amanda? If someone
else did, you should tell me now."

The girl's expression grew troubled. "Well." She stroked the
hair away from each side of her face. "What happens to people
in jail, Uncle Jack?"

"Nothing good."

Melissa thought her answer over for a long moment, her hands
folding and unfolding absently in her lap. When she spoke, her
words were firm. "It was definitely Paul. He asked me to take
care of it for him."

"When?"

"A few days after that awful thing happened, you know."

"You didn't think it was strange?"

"Everything is strange about him, a little bit."

"What did he say?"

"Just to keep the laptop so we could be in touch. And don't
tell my mom or anyone. He said Aunt Mandy had gotten a new
one, so she asked him to pass this one along to me. She was all
fine and happy when he left her place."

"And Paul gave it to you several days later, after the murder?"

"Yes."

I spoke slowly, softly, without any emphasis. "You're positive?" I peered into her face. "It's not, just maybe, something you found in your mother's room?"

Melissa reddened. "No, I already told you. Don't be stupid. No."

"Promise me, Missy?"

"I wouldn't lie to you. We're practically married."

"You lied to me already—about the right day."

"That was different."

"How?"

"I didn't want to get anybody in trouble."

52

A few days later, I made a call—more urgent this time—to my morals coach, Hogan. I had gotten a coded e-mail from Paul Morse, saying that the next *Virgin Sacrifice* party was set for six PM the coming Friday.

"Should I go?" I asked.

"Is the girl ready?"

"I think so. More than ready, in some ways."

"You have to follow your instincts on this one, Jack. I can't help you there."

"Thanks a lot. Look where my instincts have gotten me so far."

"I'm talking about your higher instincts this time, Flash."

"Oh, right. You better pray that I have some."

"I do, daily."

That Tuesday, I stopped by Angela's place and offered to take Melissa around to the openings at the end of the week.

"Perfect," Angela said. "I do need to spend time with Philip, poor thing." She called out in the direction of Melissa's bedroom, "Sweetheart, you'd like to see some art with Uncle Jack on Friday, wouldn't you? He's awfully kind to offer."

After a moment, the girl appeared at the end of the hallway, half in shadow. She was uncommonly subdued, staring at me over a white turtleneck that hung halfway to her knees.

"All right," she said. "Can I watch movies at his house afterwards?"

"Of course, dear. That will be lovely, won't it?"

When I arrived on Friday evening, Angela was ready to make a quick departure, lugging a bag of books she planned to read aloud to Philip. As soon as she left, Melissa came out of her room in her plaid skirt and knee socks. There was a great deal of space between the top of her socks and the hem of her skirt. As I talked, awkwardly, she slipped on the blue Bradford blazer over a sweater and a white blouse with a sharply creased V-neck. I explained to her where we were going and what she would have to do there. She nodded; her face did not flinch.

"Only if you want to," I said. "Are you up for it?"

"Don't worry, I'm good at acting," she answered. "I'm practically a star."

"I can believe it. Let's go then. They're expecting us."

"Wait."

She went into the rear of the loft and came back, minutes later, wearing a dark purple coat and a miniature candy-red backpack. The shining patent leather pouch was an alluring touch, a strap-on heart shape bulging outward between her shoulder blades.

"What are you bringing?" I said.

"Just girl stuff. Don't ask."

When we stepped out onto the sidewalk, Melissa shivered once.

"Are you cold?"

"I'll be fine."

We walked east, passing boutique windows until we crossed Broadway and encountered a couple of French restaurants followed suddenly by a bleak intersection. I took Melissa by the hand and led her slowly down Crosby Street. The evening was coming on early, a cool grayness engulfing the garbage bags and bundles of papers stacked in front of the old five- and six-story buildings.

"This street needs some shops," Melissa said.

"You're right, honey. But they'll be here soon enough. Probably a Starbucks, too, before your junior-high days are over."

"I wish there was something here *now*."

I glanced ahead as we passed several darkened doorways. "There's a little tapas joint. They have music there sometimes. Guitars, people clapping. Dancers stamping flamenco on a tiny square of linoleum by the bar."

"It's too cold for Spanish music today."

"That's when you need it most."

"I don't feel like it. I won't have to dance like a Spanish girl, will I?"

"No, not like that."

"What then?"

"You choose."

After another block, the bulk of the designated old building seemed to rise up suddenly. We arrived at a doorway festooned with improvised buzzers.

"Ready?" I asked.

"If you are, Uncle Jack."

I pressed button number four, hand-labeled "China Luck Trading," and a moment later Sammy's voice came out of the squawk box. "Yeah?"

"It's Jack," I said. "With Melissa."

Almost immediately, someone very large and unknown to me opened the door. He was wearing dark slacks and a black T-shirt with a gold chain at his neck.

"You the art dealer?"

"That's right."

"Come in." As we crossed the threshold, he smiled at Melissa and did his best to sound kind. "Hello, young lady. We've been looking forward to meeting you."

"Thank you very much," Melissa answered.

As we squeezed past the doorman, his hands went over me in the same way Sammy's once had. He glanced at Melissa under the fluorescent light in the hallway but said nothing. He knew what was coming, so there was no need to pat her down. Instead, he led us into the ancient elevator, slamming the accordion gate. As he pushed the wooden handle of a drum lever, we rose slowly past several locked floors.

At the fourth level, he stopped and jockeyed the cab up and down a few times to make the match-up even for Melissa.

"Mind the gap, sugar," he said as she stepped out. He closed the elevator and came and stood near us.

Paul and Sammy were waiting to greet the girl. Despite the chilly weather, Paul was in designer jeans and a crisp pale blue shirt with two buttons open at the top. Sammy, eschewing his suburbanite togs, wore a dark gray Canali suit. It fit his bulk well, even though its cut was a year out of date.

Paul kissed Melissa on both cheeks. "Welcome, finally."

As Missy slipped out of her coat, I saw Sammy's eyes go over her with a horse trainer's glance.

"Melissa," Paul said, "this is my friend Uncle Sammy."

Missy extended her hand, and Sammy raised it as he bent forward slightly to kiss the back of her wrist.

"Honored to meet you, miss."

"So polite," Melissa smiled. "You should learn from him, Uncle Jack."

"A very nice uniform," Sammy added. He nodded slightly to me.

"It's so hokey. I don't see why grown-ups like it so much."

"My daughter was crazy about going to the Bradford School."

"What year? Maybe I know her."

"No, she didn't get in."

"Why's that?"

"Some office foul-up. I'm getting it fixed."

Paul led Missy into the larger room. There, clutching her backpack, she was greeted warmly by two teenage girls and a young man who looked as though he had just won an L.A. boy band audition.

"Wow," he said. "Paul was right. You are a real doll."

Unfazed, Missy took her place on the divan between Paul and this other attentive heartthrob.

"I'm David." He reached out to shake her hand.

"What's all this stuff?" she inquired.

Near the coffee table were several microphones, a rack of extinguished lights, and two dormant video cameras. I noticed— farther back, halfway across the room—the telltale red glow of an "on" signal from a camera perched unobtrusively on a shelf. Beyond the tiered wall unit lay the entrance to a dim hallway, the one I remembered well from Paul's compilation tape. I knew where it led.

"We've been working on a video," Paul said casually. "An MTV kind of thing."

"Cool," Melissa answered.

"But we're having a problem," David said. "The dancers need help with their backup routine."

The "dancers" turned out to be two women in their twenties with bathrobes wrapped over skimpy costumes. They came in carrying platters—one supporting a bottle of champagne on ice, the other bearing a huge plate of cookies. The two per-formers smiled, and I could see they were pros who were there to set an example and coax the girls into the activities ahead.

The one with the champagne came up to me, close.

"You must be Mr. Smith," she said.

"I suppose I must."

"I'm Cheryl. Such a pleasure to meet you, I hope." She looked steadily into my eyes. There were small broken veins in her otherwise attractive face. "Could you be a dear and help me open this? I always get scared by the boom."

The cookie girl put down her tray and went to fetch champagne flutes, while I worked the wire off the bottle. Cheryl stood close beside me, her augmented breasts hovering near—without ever quite touching—my wavering right elbow.

"I have a problem," I said. "You'll have to hold it for me."

"Whatever you want, Mr. Smith."

"Call me Ed."

Her two-handed grip was strong. I twisted the cork out with a small, delicious pop.

Cheryl laughed, and I grabbed the bottle to pour the foaming Taittinger into one glass after another.

"Let's drink to a good dance tonight," Paul proposed.

"And to the dancers," his young sidekick said.

We clinked glasses and drank.

The handlers had not yet offered anything to the underage girls. You could see the envy begin to glimmer in the excluded kids' eyes. This was a very practiced crew, a slick operation.

"Sit with me, Ed honey," Cheryl said. We found a place directly across from Melissa, where I could witness every chummy development with Paul.

Rock music began to swell from the sound system.

"Tell me what happened to your arm, baby. Did you lose it in an accident?"

"An art accident."

"Oh." Cheryl smiled warmly and touched my knee. "You're having fun with me, aren't you?"

"Yes, I am."

She leaned away and put her arm around one of the girls, a fake blonde of maybe fourteen with the sad look of a runaway.

"Ed is a really funny guy," she said. "I'll bet he'd give you some champagne, if you asked him real nice."

"Sure," I said. "Let's all have a party."

Cheryl poured for the kid, who drank a half-glass quickly, like so much ginger ale.

Paul had already opened a second bottle and was pouring for Melissa. She took the champagne flute in one hand and a cookie in the other, glancing rather unpleasantly at Cheryl.

Paul began to tell funny stories.

"Do you think I'm pretty, honey?" Cheryl asked me.

"Sure. You're a babe."

"No, really." The schoolgirls were laughing at Paul's nonsense tales. "Sammy says I dance good but I'm getting too old."

"What does he know?"

"He's a big producer; he knows a lot." She touched the runaway kid on the shoulder. "How about you? Do you like to dance?"

"Maybe."

"Come on," Cheryl said. "Show me."

She pulled the girl up by the wrist. Slowly at first, the two of them began to sway and twist to the soundtrack.

The runaway, still in her street jeans and a sweatshirt, had a surprising grace. Raising her hands over her head, she answered Cheryl's movements, adding slight variations, improvising in counterpoint to Cheryl's swaying.

Someone dimmed the lights, and all the girls began to look beautiful. The guys called out encouragement from time to time.

Cheryl's sidekick got the other teenager up—the two older women modulating into a series of stage moves now, while the street girls echoed.

"We should get this on tape," David said. He rose and turned on one of the handheld cameras, weaving in close among the girls and backing away again.

"Get this," the second girl said, and gave him a small shimmy.

"Not like that, honey," Cheryl's friend said. "Lay it on him." Laughing, she went into an old go-go dancer's routine.

A joint started making the rounds, and I saw that when Paul passed it to Melissa his hand lingered needlessly, tenderly, on her exposed thigh, just below the edge of her plaid Bradford School skirt.

All at once, Melissa stood up and drained the last of the champagne from her glass. As Paul bent to refill it, she began to sway in front of him, making the skirt swing while she turned, her weight shifting subtly from one hip to the other and back again.

Cheryl leaned over, touching my face and giving me a full, lingering view of her breasts.

"How are you, baby?" she asked.

"I'm very good."

"Having fun?"

"Loads."

In fact, the enjoyment was beginning to disorient me a little. When I stood, my head was as light as my racing heart.

"Save my seat," I said. "I don't want to miss the finale."

53

I walked to the bank of windows, slumping on the wide sill until I caught Sammy's eye.

"Can I see you for a second?" I asked.

Sammy excused himself from the group, patting one of the girls on the shoulder, and lumbered over to me. "What's up?"

"It's about the money."

"Yeah, what about it?"

"Tell me again how much I get."

"You know the deal. Don't try to Jew around with me now."

"You've started the Internet feed already, and taping for the compilation edit?"

"That's right, it's all running. Leave the show biz to me, Jack. I know what sells."

"I'm sure you do."

"This Melissa is hot, I can feel it."

"That's right. She's a damn minx," I said. "Just like her mother."

Sammy looked puzzled, but pleased.

"Now what about the money?"

"You want to see the color of it?" Sammy grunted. "Is that your damned problem?"

He took out a wad of bills and slapped it on the table next to me.

"Good," I said. "I'm in."

"Damn right you are."

Sammy turned away from me and started walking back toward the party enclave.

"I'm in," I said again, louder this time.

Sammy stopped, and after an instant his face twitched with a mean and suddenly knowing expression.

That's when the door exploded. The metal slab flew back on its hinges, banging against the wall; the nose of a battering ram thrust suddenly through the opening and dropped to the floor.

"Cocksucker," Sammy said.

Melissa was fiddling with the little red knapsack. Beside her, Paul tried to stand. Halfway up, he was knocked to the floor by two cops from the assault squad now swarming the loft.

McGuinn, looming and red-cheeked, pushed Sammy flat against a wall with his gun leveled at the porn boss's head.

"Give me an excuse," he said. "Give me just half an excuse, and I'll blow your face across the room." He jammed his hand tightly against Sammy's throat.

Everywhere cops were pinning and cuffing the stunned *Virgin Sacrifice* crew.

All the girls, except Melissa, were crying. When I went to her and hugged her, she clung to me fiercely.

Two cops pulled Paul to his feet. Hogan, a .45 automatic in his hand, came up to him, talking sharp and low.

"Welcome to the Balthus Club, brother," he said.

"Fuck you."

One of the uniforms leaned Paul sideways and muttered into his ear.

"Bullshit," Paul said. "It's not mine."

"What's not yours?" Hogan asked.

The cop held up a plastic evidence bag by one corner. Inside was the dead weight of a nasty sex toy.

"We found this stuffed between the sofa cushions beside him."

"Not yours, huh," Hogan said to Paul. "Whose then?"

"I don't know. The girl—Melissa—handed it to me."

"Guess we'll find your prints on it then."

"She jammed it at me. I took it before I knew what I was doing."

"Really? She tricked you?" Hogan scoffed. "Sure it wasn't the other way around? Like you showing off and asking her to touch it. Or you giving it to her to stash when you saw us come in?"

"No, I swear."

Hogan looked closely at the sleek, twisted object.

"What were you going to do," he asked, "ram it in her after the Donkey finished his work?"

"I swear to you, I never saw that thing before in my life."

Hogan stretched to meet his gaze, eye to eye. His voice grew tense.

"Listen to me, Morse," he said. "Where you're going, the bull cons know how to deal with a boy like you. Guys who hurt kids tend to get messed up themselves. Real often and real bad. In ways you don't even want to think about."

Paul wavered on his feet.

"God," he said. "You don't understand."

"Just shut up." Hogan holstered his gun and took Paul's chin in one hand. "Let me give you some advice. If you want a nice welcome from the homeboys in Attica, you damn well better cooperate with McGuinn when you get down to the station."

"But I haven't…"

"Shut up, I said. Don't even try."

"She, Melissa…"

"I said don't." Hogan let go of his chin. "Just listen. Right now, buddy boy, the Amanda Oliver murder rap is the best thing you've got going for you. Own up to it. A conviction might get you respect in the prison yard."

"I swear to you. I didn't kill Mandy."

"Sure, sure. You hardly knew her, right?"

"We had sex, that's all."

"Including the day she was shot?"

"What? Sure, I went over for a quickie that morning, before Mandy went shopping. I was just an item on her to-do list."

"Save your bullshit, Morse." Hogan nodded to the waiting officer. "I wouldn't want anything, you know, *unfortunate* to happen to you in the back of a police wagon on your way to get booked."

As Paul was jerked away, he cast a long disbelieving glance at Melissa. She turned her face, leaning on my shoulder. I stared wordlessly back at Paul, without expression.

"You all right?" Hogan asked.

Melissa shivered. "I feel OK now," she said. "Now that you're finally here."

Tightening my good arm around her, I asked Hogan what the hell had taken so long. Had something gone wrong with the rifle mike the cops were using from a window across the street?

"Nothing," he said. "McGuinn just had to check that we had it all down on tape."

The rest was routine.

Once the loft was cleared, Melissa and I rode over to the precinct house in a squad car to make our detailed statements.

The debriefing room was small. Fortunately, since this was such an eventful day, McGuinn's breath didn't stink too badly of booze. He got right down to recording my account of the night. Letting Hogan join the Crosby Street bust had probably violated a dozen NYPD regulations, but it was the only way the burned-out cop could get what he needed: seven solid arrests without a lot of investigative work that would have interfered with his drinking schedule.

I gave McGuinn all the information I had gleaned from Paul Morse, Sammy, and Mr. Zhou. He smiled at me, suddenly a happy and generous man.

"That took some balls," he said.

"Did it? That's not how it felt."

"How did it feel?"

"Necessary."

When I came out of the room, Melissa was waiting for me, wrapped in a police overcoat on a bench under the station's sickly overhead light. A lady cop sat beside her.

"I told them about Paul," Missy said as I approached. She stood up unsteadily and hugged me. "About what he wanted."

"Good."

"And the laptop."

"You did fine."

"She was amazing," the policewoman said. "So clear and precise—every detail. Even the dates."

She lifted the coat from the girl's shoulders, and I replaced it with Melissa's own purple jacket and helped her sling the red heart-shaped backpack into place. Together, we said goodbye to Hogan and left the precinct house, walking silently to the Wooster Street loft in the cold night air.

54

As soon as we entered the apartment, Melissa turned on me in a dramatic huff. It was almost like being married again.

"I didn't even get to see the good stuff at the party," she said. "Do you treat all your girlfriends this way?"

"I don't have any girlfriends lately."

"Well, it's no wonder."

"In fact, Missy, you're my only sweetheart now."

"Maybe." She plopped herself on the sofa and crossed her arms. "And maybe I changed my mind."

"What can I do to make it up to you?"

"You can give me a drink."

"Grapefruit juice, Sprite?"

"You know what I want."

"We're not in Europe here."

"You are. In your head, half the time."

"Have you started reading my mind now?"

"Oh, long ago." Draping herself on the cushions, Melissa gave me a beseeching look. "Don't be such a drag, Uncle Jack. I'm not a child, you know. Not after tonight."

"Maybe not. All right, one drink."

It had been a hard day for us both. I went to the kitchen and poured a scotch for myself and a small glass of white wine for Melissa.

I intended to deposit her at home and make my difficult explanations to her mother softly, in the gathering dark. But my phone had a voicemail from Angela, saying she'd be late at the hospice with Philip—"he's so agitated, poor darling"—and could I please keep Missy at my place and let her sleep in the guestroom if she got tired.

When I returned to the front, Missy was standing in the middle of the living area, crying silently. Her body shook in waves. I put down the drinks and grasped her shoulders, pulling her close against my chest. Her tears quickly wet the front of my shirt.

"Is Paul going to die now?" she asked.

"Maybe. More likely, he'll sit in prison for a very long time. Hogan thinks that, with the laptop and sex tapes, we can prove he killed Amanda."

"Good. And now they'll leave Daddy alone?"

"Completely."

"And no one will bother my mom anymore?"

"No, why should they?"

I calmed Melissa and got her to sit down once more on the couch. Another burst of tears came out of her, like an exorcised demon. Once she was breathing easily again, I sat in the Corbu chair facing her and handed over the wineglass.

She took a long, deliberate sip.

"It's too bad Paul can only die once," she said.

It was much the same way I felt about Nathalie's last, diseased lover. "Once will do nicely," I said, "if it's awful enough."

We talked for a long time that evening. After an hour or so, I started feeling a little out of myself from two or three scotches. Melissa pulled her legs onto the black leather of the couch and half reclined. I saw her stare at the framed photograph on the table beside me. As always, she wanted to know more about Nathalie.

"Were you happy together?" she asked.

"Happy? That's a very big word."

"Were you?"

"I've seen happiness, Missy, but only from a distance."

That's about right, I thought. The way a man astray in the desert sees gushing springs and green shade, an exquisite mirage. I tried to believe in contentment the way Hogan believed in God, but I didn't have the same knack.

"OK, so you weren't happy really. Then why did you stay married?"

"Nathalie wanted it that way."

"What did you want?"

"Whatever she wanted. Or just about."

"You weren't the boss?"

"I was the small-town boy from upstate New York, and she was my chic Parisian wife. I never stood a chance."

The night was deepening. I got up to turn on the floor lamp by the couch. As I leaned across her, Melissa idly took my right hand and kissed the fingers.

"Hey, that tickles," I said.

"You're no fun. It's supposed to drive you mad with desire. I read about it in *Seventeen*."

"Maybe it only works on teenagers."

"It worked on Paul."

"Don't."

"What?"

"Don't make bad jokes."

"Maybe I'm joking, and maybe I'm not."

I couldn't think about that. I couldn't, but I did. For a long time back in my chair, I thought repeatedly about Paul and Missy, playing out all the potential scenarios.

The hour was getting late. As the night continued to darken, Melissa's head began to nod. Finally, still partially sitting up with her legs curled on the couch, she fell into a fitful sleep.

I sat motionless in the leather chair, watching her just five feet away. In the lamplight, her face—though blessed with the smoothness of her brief twelve years—was not entirely untroubled. She seemed to be dreaming of something real, something less than perfect. Her hair was tousled, and her head had fallen to one side against the cushion, offering the line of her neck to the faint mellow light, the flesh sleek as a dagger to the point where her blouse buttoned at the point of its V.

Shifting in the chair, I tried my best to look away. But as my eyes swept down from her throat, they traversed—quickly at first, then more deliberately—Missy's long torso and short skirt and the crook of her legs.

I took another drink of scotch and forced myself to concentrate on the tinkle of the melting cubes, on the tart, smoldered fragrance of the liquor. It was not fair. It was not fair or right to be left alone like this, in the deep night with my memories of Nathalie and the young, supple Melissa lying like a gift on my couch.

When I couldn't stand it anymore, I got up and bent to her and gathered her up with my good right arm. She shifted her weight against me, snuggling.

"You need to go to bed now," I said.

Her answer was faint but distinct: "All right."

There were no stairs to climb, just the sparse sweep of the loft space to stumble across. When we got to the bedroom door, the interior was black as a cave and I could not reach the light switch with my bad arm.

"Help me," I said.

Melissa only leaned against me more firmly. "No," she mumbled. "I like the dark. It's OK."

I steered her to the bed, and we sat down heavily side by side. She took her arms from my neck, and a moment later I felt her hand slide over one side of my face, then the other.

"You're awfully scratchy, Uncle Jack," she said.

I kissed her once on the cheek, not wanting to smell the sweetness of her hair but smelling it anyhow—breathing it in. I stood up.

"You scared me at the dance party tonight," Melissa said.

"I was scared, too."

"You acted funny. For a while, I couldn't see you. Only Paul."

My hand moved forward in the dark until my fingers touched and tangled in her hair.

"And now," I said, "I have to go and do my penance while you sleep."

"Not yet."

I waited, my hand still on her head, as if in benediction.

"Be good and undress me," she said.

I took my hand away. "Don't be silly. Go to sleep now."

"I can't sleep in these cruddy clothes, honey. Think where they've been tonight. Please."

"You're too big to be undressed by a man."

It sounded absurd, backwards, even as I said it.

"It's not 'a man'; it's you, Uncle Jack."

"No, that's a job for your mother."

"She's not here. Neither is Daddy. Please. I really need to sleep."

The darkness was thick and protective, and I reached down and found the bottom edge of her sweater and lifted it over her head. Her arms fell to her sides again. Around the edges of the room's blackout shades a hint of lesser darkness entered, and my eyes began to adjust enough to distinguish Melissa's lank figure from the surrounding gloom. I stroked her head again, and undid the buttons of her blouse. As I pushed the fabric back off her shoulders, my hand slipped inadvertently over her training bra and its tiny breasts.

"What are you doing?" she asked sleepily.

"I'm undressing you for bed."

"Oh, all right."

When I unfastened her belt, she lay back and raised her hips so that I could slide the little plaid skirt down her legs. Her exposed skin, cool to my returning touch, was sleeker than I could have imagined, beyond any memory.

One by one, I rolled off her stockings, the last of her uniform.

"I'm cold," Missy said.

"Get under the covers then."

I lifted the blanket for her, hearing the swish of her legs entering the cotton sheets.

"Where are you going to sleep?" she asked.

"I don't sleep very much anymore."

"Poor baby, that's so unhealthy."

"I'm going to have another drink and wait up for your mother."

As I stood by the bed, I could hear Missy shifting under the blankets. "Kiss me good night, Uncle Jack."

"No, I'd better not."

"Why?"

"I'm not sure exactly. Just take my word for it."

"I can't sleep without a good-night kiss."

It was a trick, and I knew it. The moment I bent to her lips I would feel her arms around my neck, sense her flowing beneath me, pulling me down. I would have nowhere else to go.

"Where are you?" Melissa said.

My answer came as a whisper, "I'm next to you, sweetheart."

"Where?"

I bent toward her, and as I moved something changed. For some unknown reason, stupidly, I thought of Hogan. I saw him sitting in his armchair at home in Bayside, talking to Dorothy.

Somehow, the image of the domestic pair, and of Hogan's bald pate, spoiled everything.

"I'm going now," I told Melissa. "You'll be fine."

"You don't want to kiss me?"

"No."

She sighed exaggeratedly. "Silly man."

55

I left the bedroom and went back to my chair by the windows. In the faint lamplight, the paintings on the surrounding walls seemed alive. Like ancestor spirits, they crowded around me—works that I could have sold to enable Nathalie to be treated in New York. Here they remained, however, because she preferred her French medical team and because I so resented the nature of her illness and its miserable source.

Nathalie had great regard for France's system of health care, and maybe she knew best for herself. She had contracted the disease in Paris; she had heard the curt diagnosis months later in a seventh arrondissement clinic. It seemed only right to deal with the infection there. She and her doctor could smoke their unfiltered cigarettes as they discussed her prognosis; they could quote literature back and forth to ennoble the long, gruesome course of her treatment. She seemed to feel, if not well, at least resigned to the illness in her native environs.

So, after two years of IVs and bedpans, of catheters and MRIs, Nathalie died there in her precious homeland, with a Gallic disdain. Near the end, she spoke of death as an obnoxious intruder, a foreigner—one who would drag her off to some alien uncultured country.

After the burial, where her French friends dropped single roses onto the casket, I returned to New York to live among our early Rymans and Scullys, those stylish abstractions looming with silent reproach now on the white walls around me.

Back then, Philip thought I should simply forget about Nathalie, let loose, and run a little wild for a while. He didn't much lament the end of my marriage, or see why I should either.

How could he? Nathalie was a bad case, the bitch. But she was my bad case, and I loved her. Maybe I loved her because she was such a bad case. Maybe the anguish she gave me was what I wanted most in the world. At least it made me feel alive, and now, for a long time, I had scarcely known if I was living or dead.

I drank one more scotch and listened to the wind in the cornices of the buildings next door, while I carefully catalogued the night sounds along Wooster Street—the rustling of a homeless man going through garbage bags, the slurred voices of late drinkers looking for cabs.

All the time I sat there, I concentrated—at the deepest level—on the blond sleeping girl, telling myself that I must not cross the loft again, must not approach the narrow, flimsy door that stood between myself and Melissa.

And, remarkably, I did not.

Instead, I sat by the dark windows and very methodically drank. I don't remember how much or how long. At one hazy point, I thought that I heard Missy's voice, far and muffled, speaking my name. But it was probably just some terrible longing or fear. Finally, as my eyes were beginning to droop, Angela telephoned.

"Everything all right there, Jack?"

"Fine. Melissa is sleeping."

"It's been a god-awful day. Philip won't let anyone else feed him now. I do nothing for hours but read aloud and wait for him to feel hungry again."

"I'm sorry."

"Don't be. It's rather lovely, in an exhausting way. I need a couple more hours here. Will you just look in on Melissa to see she's not having one of her nightmares?"

"Does that happen often?"

"From time to time, ever since the Amanda thing."

"Kids imagine too much."

"It's gotten even worse since we moved back to the city."

"What should I do if she's awake?"

"Just talk to her. Speak softly and rock her."

"Like a baby?"

"Yes."

"Are you sure?"

"Positive. Melissa won't admit it, but she likes to be held when she's scared."

"You think it's what she wants?"

"I know it. I'm her mother, Jack. I know what's best for my child."

"Yes, you must."

"She'll fall asleep in your arms."

"All right, then. I'll go check on her now."

"You're a dear."

Once I hung up the phone, I stood in the middle of the empty room for a couple minutes, feeling the scotch gather at my temples and begin to seep deeper into my brain. Then I walked for an eternity across the loft.

At the door of the guestroom, I tried to listen for Melissa's breathing, but the wood was too dense.

I pushed the door open, letting the faint hallway light spill in. On the lower half of the bed, one bare leg, sleek and gleaming, lay fully extended on top of the covers. The girl's chest rose and fell regularly. She needed to be tucked in, to be covered.

When I approached, Melissa's respiration changed.

I stood over her—watching and guarding, I told myself. But I was a little too drunk to be entirely sure. Across a great abyss, I reached down and touched Missy's forehead, sweeping back a wave of fine hair that draped across her left eye and cheek. She gave a subdued moan in response. Then a single word came out of her slumber.

"Daddy?"

"No." I answered her under my breath: "No, honey. It's Uncle Jack."

"Oh good, I'm not dreaming. It's you."

"Your mother asked me to check."

"She did? You didn't want to see me yourself?"

"More than you know." Groping in the dark, I found the tangled blanket and sheet. I straightened them with my good hand, guiding her leg underneath.

"That feels so nice," she said.

"The covers?"

"Your hand, Uncle Jack."

"I'm going now."

"No one ever stays with me. Why?"

"Maybe someday, Missy."

"Someday you'll stay, or someday I'll know why you don't?"

"Yes, one of those." I took a step back and paused, listening as her breathing deepened.

"Night, night, love," she said. "Kiss me."

My own breathing slowed.

"I did once," I lied. "You've forgotten already."

"Oh? I'm sorry. One more."

She was not really awake, and I did not bother to explain. What could I say, anyhow?

"Please, Uncle Jack."

It was her last plea, arising out of a dream. As she sank into sleep again, I turned and closed the door of the bedroom behind me and walked back to the dim living room.

Settling, depleted, into the chair, I poured another scotch and watched the liquor turn the melting ice cubes to amber. I breathed in the fumes with each sip.

In this world, I thought, the world where Melissa sleeps, there has to be limit, a boundary you don't cross.

Well, obviously, I had done as well with that resolution as

with all the rest. Face it, Jack, the crossing begins the moment you first imagine, too vividly, just how the encounter would unfold, what you would see, how forbidden and good it would feel. The beauty, the excitement. That was sin. Even if you're an artist—or, like me, an artists' pimp.

And I'm not even the worst. I thought of the *Virgin Sacrifice* audience, those eager perverts watching expectantly for the climactic moment, fast-forwarding to El Burro's clinch. At least I had never rooted for someone with Paul's disease to succeed, never waited with delirious longing for the violation to occur. Which is more than some people can say, including those who might presume to judge me.

I was losing count of my drinks.

Oddly, intoxication was my small moral victory that evening. It distracted me. In my hour of greatest temptation, I did not yield to the worst urgings of my impure heart.

Are there virtues of inaction, I wondered, just as there are sins of omission? I would have to ask Hogan.

One thing was certain, no one will ever know the pain it cost me—that simple act of forbearance on a cold night at the end of November years ago. Was it a great accomplishment? Was it even worth mentioning? Probably not. But it has enabled me to look back at my life without utter revulsion.

I got up and paced the room, touching small random objects, forbidding my feet to turn toward the guestroom and Melissa.

I ended up by the high windows, looking out, seeing nothing. *The heart is deceitful above all things, and desperately wicked: who can know it?* That was one of the verses Hogan had e-mailed me from that damned bible he reads too much, the black leather-bound volume that almost falls apart in his hands. Now the words were stuck in my head.

Well, I had an answer: I can know it—my desperately wicked heart. After so many nights lying alone in the dark, sleepless, I have gotten thoroughly familiar with its every weakness and quirk. I know my deceitful heart very well.

Better make a list of all your little moral victories, Jack. No, not later. Right now.

Surely there had to be some.

Let's see, I may have failed my wife, terribly, but at least I had acted—or failed to act—out of emotional injury, not out of malice. Over the years, I had even managed to do a proper thing or two with Hogan, for people like Mandy, Angela, and Melissa. I felt I could meet Philip's criterion: my accounts were square.

That was all. Still, it seemed like a reasonable tally for a guy in the world I inhabited—a flawed man adrift among faithless lovers and hustlers, in a vast city, alone....Or so I thought as I stood by the windows and watched the wet snowfall and waited for Angela.

Just as I turned and started to walk back across that enormous dark room, I heard a knock at my door.

56

Angela swept into the loft, late and ashen, glancing around quickly.

"Melissa's quiet tonight, is she? Thank goodness."

She took the girl's vacant spot on the couch.

"I'm doing everything for Philip now," she said. "Claudia has nearly abandoned him, and his old mother is useless. The damn biddy can't grasp that her son is dying before her, just like her husband."

"It's a lot to take in."

"Tell me. But blanking out is just a cheat."

Angela joined me in a last drink, rehearsing her woes.

Few visitors relieved her these days, even momentarily. Claudia appeared less and less often, standing helplessly among the IV stanchions and monitors, holding Philip's hand sometimes but unable to speak to him, crying. She watched, tight-lipped, as his ex-wife lifted his bony hips onto a bedpan. Angela comforted the girl. She told Claudia what few coherent phrases her wasted lover, *their* dear one, had uttered in the course of the day. She said not to worry, that Philip would want her to go on with her life and career.

Much later, I would learn that Claudia was granted nothing from the estate—possibly because Philip's dementia had set in before he could get around to making a codicil, possibly because he actually wanted things that way, to square his accounts. Nevertheless, his lover did all right for herself. Claudia's family had a little money of its own, and after the publicity of the Oliver case her career soared for a few years. Her work was featured in international surveys from Germany to Japan to

Australia, before she faded from the art press and the galleries, from critical consciousness altogether, after becoming the wife of a famous auto manufacturer in Turin.

But that was still the unknowable future, as Angela and I sat—fatigued and drinking—in the Wooster Street loft that cold night.

"How's Melissa?" she asked. "Did the two of you have a good time tonight?"

"Yes."

"What a relief. I was hoping you might."

I couldn't make sense of her facial expression. Resolved to tell her what had happened, I began by explaining that Paul was even worse than she had suspected. I filled her in on his relationship with Amanda, on the Balthus Club, on *Virgin Sacrifice*—and on his plan for Melissa. Finally, I described the Crosby Street party.

"How could you, Jack?" Angela said. "I can't believe you used Missy that way."

"It's not like that."

"No? Wheedling Mandy's laptop away from her. Dangling her in front of Paul like fresh bait."

"I know how it sounds. But I didn't really use Melissa. If anything, I kept her from being used."

Angela was too spent, too deeply outraged, to argue. The weight of it all—the failure of her show, Philip's dismal condition, my recklessness with her daughter—all of it seemed to crush her now. She fixed me with her weary, red-rimmed eyes.

"You've never been a father, Jack. You'll never understand."

"No, I won't."

"This is no lark for me, this damn SoHo life. I'm not a gypsy like you. I have a child to raise. It's what I live for now."

She must have felt utterly abandoned in that moment. I had deceived her, Melissa was growing smugly independent, and her beloved Philip was about to fade out of her life for a second and final time.

Over the months that followed, Philip's slipping away from Angela, from life itself—through a protracted round of vomiting, spinal pain, hallucinations, and morphine—was neither fast nor decorous, though it was faster than the doctors predicted. The disease took over his being, and he was spared no bodily humiliation: dribbling oatmeal on his chest, spilling cups of pills, staining himself repeatedly with excrement.

Nevertheless, my friend would eventually manage to accomplish his dying rather bravely—for Angela's sake, I think. Although he did not know who she was, Philip intuited that this woman would remain by his side to the end. Someone would be there to watch his face, to hold his thin hand as he died. Occasionally he called her, weakly, "dear child." When others turned away, in sadness or disgust, his ex-wife stuck with him—stubbornly, unquestioningly—through the last fetid days.

For that loyalty, for those tortuous hours, I was ready to forgive Angela almost anything.

57

On Christmas Eve, Hogan called at about ten o'clock. He had gotten stuck late at his office and, sure that I wouldn't be doing much that night, invited me out for a drink. We had steaks and beers at Fanelli's, amid the old boxing pictures, and when the waitress laid our bill on the checkerboard cloth, Hogan picked it up.

"I owe you one," he said.

"Thanks, I'm not sure for what."

"For serving up Paul Morse."

"It doesn't seem like so much."

Hogan grinned at me, an unusual sight. "A Christmas present came today. The porno bust gave the cops probable cause to search the creep's loft. You know, confirming residence, looking for additional evidence. McGuinn's vice squad pals found plenty, too. Rows and rows of *Virgin Sacrifice* tapes lined up on the hallway bookshelves. And behind them, a gun."

"Amanda Oliver's?"

"Same serial number."

"With Paul's prints on it?"

"No, it was wiped clean."

"But why the hell would Paul keep it?"

"Another half-ass job," Hogan sniffed. "That's how it is with amateurs. They figure out how to kill—or they just lose their cool and do it, blow somebody away in a frenzy—but then they suck at the cover-up."

I thought I understood. "That's where the real art lies, right? In disguising your crime."

"It's not so easy, Jack. Murder is a big, scary thing. Most

people, their heart starts pounding, their mind rushes. Adrenaline kind of short-circuits the brain. They screw up like Morse —take the incriminating laptop away, but stash it with a friend. Muster enough sense to buff down the gun, but not enough to deep-six it somewhere far away."

"Sounds like you've thought it out."

"That's my job."

I nodded. "Still, I wish we had a clearer idea of why Mandy was shot. Sure, she threatened to turn Paul in for the *Virgin Sacrifice* scheme. But he could have sweet-talked her out of that. He didn't have to murder her—not when a little more sex would have kept her quiet."

Hogan looked away across the sparsely populated room. "Why does anyone kill?" he said. "For that matter, why does anyone die?" He paused for a second, as if waiting, not for the first time, for an answer that did not come. "I'm still working on that one. For now, let's have another beer."

Once the two bottles of Rolling Rock came, I asked him if Philip was in the clear once and for all.

"The cops won't give him a second thought anymore," Hogan said. "They've got Morse in the crosshairs now. I ran into McGuinn in here the other night, fairly gone. He blurted."

"Anything you didn't expect?"

"Just the tidiness of it. The Homicide boys don't usually get so lucky."

"Such as?"

"Ballistics did a test. The gun is a perfect match. Same barrel grooves as on the slugs that killed Mandy. The DNA inside the lady was Morse's, too, like he'd already admitted."

"No more surprises then."

"There better not be."

Glancing around at the bar's hardcore loners, I avoided Hogan's eyes.

"What does Paul have to say?" I asked.

"The usual. That he never saw the gun before. He has no idea how it got there. What else would you expect him to say?"

"He could confess, like Philip."

"He's not that crazy."

"No," I admitted. "Not that honest, either."

Hogan raised his bottle. "Anyway, the cops have pulled him off the streets, away from Melissa Oliver and other young girls." He drank deeply. "Once they get the porno and prostitution convictions, he'll be on ice for a long, long time. They'll have years, if they need them, to build a solid murder case against him."

"Makes the prosecutor's job easy."

"That's right."

He sat in silence for a few moments while I poured half my beer into a glass.

"You know," I said, "there's just one thing that bothers me."

The news did not make Hogan look happy.

"We never completely accounted for Angela's time on the day of the murder."

I expected a quick response but instead got nothing. Not even a blink.

"Suppose little Melissa fibbed to us," I said. "Either because she was forced to or because she just wanted to protect her mother."

"What if she did?"

"Angela would have had plenty of time to get back and forth between Westchester and SoHo. Then the girl might have covered for her afterwards—that whole yoga and cookies bit—until the heat from you and McGuinn got too intense. Or until she found the computer in Angela's room."

"Yeah, go on."

"Then Melissa—with or without her mother—might have

decided to shift the blame to Paul Morse, after he came on to her, wanting her cherry."

As Hogan leaned forward slowly, his jacket gapped open and I saw the butt of his gun appear and disappear.

"Forget it," he said. "They've got no case against Angela. No evidence to compare to the stolen nine millimeter or to Paul's misplaced semen and his big urge to get his hands on Mandy's laptop. No e-mail link."

I said nothing for a while. Finally, when the other conversations around us picked up in volume, I reminded Hogan of an awkward fact.

"That's not exactly true, you know. Mandy wrote Angela to ask for a meeting."

"That's right, Flash. But Angela explained everything. To you, to me. And eventually to McGuinn."

"Most times, you're not so easily sold."

"What are you trying to say?"

"Just that Angela is quite a persuasive person, once you get to know her the way you did."

"And?"

"Charm tends to get its way in this world, especially with men. Even fake tough guys like you."

Hogan stopped the bottle halfway to his lips and lowered it again without drinking. "It's Christmas, pal. So I'm not going to break your face for that."

I waited for him to laugh, but he didn't.

Hogan took the long delayed swig, a deep one. "Look, just forget the cockamamie what-ifs here. I know what's eating you." He stared me square in the face. "Me sleeping with Angela means nothing."

"No, not to me." I studied the last of my beer. "But what about you?"

He smiled. "Since when do you worry about me, Jack?"

The waitress came back with Hogan's change, and he handed her a fat tip. She looked very happy. "Merry Christmas, guys," she said.

Hogan waited, eyeing my nearly empty glass.

"And if you're wrong about Paul?" I asked.

"Tough break."

"You don't mean that."

Hogan regarded me evenly, without blinking. "Don't go pussy-boy on me now. I was afraid you might be in over your head."

I tried to muster some evidence to the contrary, but my mind was numb.

"Why? Because I want to be sure?" I asked finally. "Really certain, before the cell door closes on Paul?"

"Sure, certain—that's schoolteacher talk, Jack. I live in the real world."

"Do you?" I said. "Are you sure?"

Hogan, scratching at the label of his empty bottle, made me wait.

"Look," he said, "how wrong could we be really? Nobody's innocent here. The way I see it, there's enough crap in any-body's file to justify a capital charge. In mine, for sure; in yours. And we're choirboys compared to Paul Morse."

"I suppose. But I don't feel very virtuous."

"That's what saves you."

"Does it?"

"Someday maybe."

I drained the last of my beer, preparing to leave. In a few hours, Missy would be opening her presents.

"You know," I said, "Paul really thought I was his friend."

"Same old Jack. A fine chum to all, even murderers and sickos."

Hogan stood and pulled on his topcoat. We nodded good night to the bartender, his ex-fighter's body a dark bulk against the white Christmas lights strung over the shelves of bottles behind him. I put some extra bills on the table for the waitress.

"You're always trying to be some kind of badass, Jack, but you always end up pretty square."

"Do I?"

"If you didn't I'd deck you."

I buttoned my coat and drew my leather gloves out of the pockets.

"Maybe that's just what I need, Hogan."

"To bring you to your senses?"

"No, to help me sleep at night."

58

Outside, in the light snow, Hogan told me that he wanted to attend midnight mass.

"You gave me some things to think about," he said. "Church is good for that."

We walked east along Prince Street, past the old brick hulk that housed the downtown branch of the Guggenheim Museum. On the upper floors, all the lights were out. No one was working late that holiday night. We crossed Broadway and then the poorly lit Crosby Street, passing beyond Lafayette into what were once the upper reaches of the Italian section.

Lately, some real estate agents had taken to calling the district Nolita, for "north of Little Italy." True to Sammy's description, the immigrant enclave had receded, and the narrow streets were now dotted with hipster lounges and hole-in-the-wall storefronts selling one-off items by designers fresh out of Parsons and FIT.

"At least some things never change," Hogan said, lifting his chin sharply.

Glancing up, I saw a plain stone cross on the roof of Old St. Patrick's Cathedral, the emblem hovering stark above the street signs and building tops. We skirted the slush at Mulberry Street and came to an undulating brick wall and the high, wide-spreading trees of the churchyard. It was quiet on the sidewalk under the branches, and we were sheltered briefly from the snow twisting down in large flakes past the streetlights. Across the street at Mekong, a few drinkers clustered at the darkened bar. Next door, plastic buckets of cut flowers shone brightly in a fluorescent glow under the canopy of a Korean deli that never closed. Hogan and I, like two workmen after a double shift, walked on without speaking.

When a car passed, splashing slush onto the bottom of my black cashmere coat, I cursed.

"Hey, life is rough," Hogan said. "Take that rag to your Park Avenue cleaners."

I looked down at the spatter. "One thing after another. Don't you ever get fed up?"

"What did you expect, Flash, peace on earth for your efforts?"

"Maybe. For one night anyhow."

"Good friggin' luck with that, brother."

We walked on.

"Somehow," I said, "I thought I'd feel a lot better about the idea of Paul in a prison upstate."

"Don't worry. You did your part, now the State of New York will do its."

"Which is what?"

"Punishment. A few decades' worth."

"Is that what they teach you in church?"

Hogan stopped, his hands deep in his pockets.

"Maybe that perv will straighten out, but I doubt it. You think you're going to improve a Paul Morse?"

"Maybe he'll improve me." I shook a few flakes from my collar. "Just the sickening thought of him."

We trudged through the snow again, swaying slightly. Our heads were lowered, and I couldn't see Hogan's face when he spoke.

"Get real," he said. "Cops don't make people honest, any more than priests make them holy or doctors make them immortal."

"What's that leave?"

"Duty."

He must have known I was lost.

"The whole idea," Hogan said, "is just to keep everybody alive long enough to die of natural causes, and straight enough to stop screwing each other over."

"Great. I'm deeply inspired."

"That's the deal."

"Anyhow, I did what I could. For Missy's sake."

Hogan hunched his shoulders against the night's cold.

"Sure, big guy," he said. "We're like the last knights of Christendom, you and me."

The snow fell lightly on us, around us, between us.

At Mott Street, we turned left and walked half a block to the church's black iron gate. We stopped, and I said goodbye to Hogan as a few last-minute supplicants passed through the gate to the forecourt.

"Sure you don't want to come in?" he asked.

"It wouldn't do me any good."

"It's not about you, Jack. I'm going to pray for the soul of Paul Morse."

My silence must have communicated all the bewilderment I felt.

"Forgive us our trespasses, as we forgive those who trespass against us," Hogan recited, his delivery impersonal. "That's the beginning and end of the story. Ever heard it?"

"A long time ago."

"Well, don't try to figure it out now," he said. "You won't."

"No, I suppose that's what makes it divine."

"What else would you like?"

"Just something decent out of all this."

It was close to midnight. The bells would start soon, and I wanted to get home to my muffling Wooster Street walls.

"Listen." Hogan spoke quietly. "God's grace flows to anyone who sincerely asks. Even Morse." He laughed. "Maybe even you."

I shook my head. "Then your God is a fool."

Hogan was silent for a moment.

"Think so?" He laid his hand ever so lightly on my good arm. "Just come."

I looked at the gray stone pile under the trees. The central doors gapped repeatedly as silent figures entered, and I could glimpse, through the transparent vestibule partition, a candle-lit interior where statues flickered, their faces seeming alive. I heard the brief plaintive swell of an organ playing "Oh, Holy Night." Outside, the announcement board gave the theme of the evening's service in white letters on black: "For unto us a child is born, and unto us a son is given."

I pushed my good hand deeper into my coat pocket. "No thanks," I said. "Not me. Not tonight."

Hogan jabbed my shoulder. "All right, you dope. It's your bet."

With the snowfall thickening, he turned and walked into the iron-gray church, his silhouette sharpening as the doors opened onto the candlelight, and melting into shadows as they closed.

59

For me, the reward came six months after the Crosby Street bust, when Paul Morse went on trial. At the time, I thought of it as his "first" proceeding, with the murder indictment to follow shortly—once the police cleared up what Hogan referred to vaguely as "a few complications."

On the third day, the Donkey, appearing live on the stand, detailed the *Virgin Sacrifice* production methods. (In private, the D.A. had explained the undocumented alien's legal options. He could cooperate and get a reduced sentence, or he could play dumb and see his family sent back to their fly-blown village in Mexico, while he did hard time for multiple counts of statutory rape.) In the docket, the man was asked if he had ever witnessed Paul Morse engage in any sexual acts with minors.

He replied, "Well, one day Mr. Sammy, he say to Paul, 'Look, pal, you got to play like the rest of us. I want to know I can trust you.' "

"And did Mr. Morse tell you what he took that to mean?"

"He said, 'I got to do this, man, for sure. Otherwise, they gonna stomp me.' Then he did it, OK. To a couple girls. He did it real good."

"And then?"

"And, after that, he did it a lot more. He liked it. At the parties, he was the first after me."

Paul's assistant, having cut a deal that spared him prosecution on some two-bit drug charges, was equally helpful. Staring straight ahead, he detailed, in a flat voice, the editing and distribution procedures. He even talked about the aesthetics of teen porn, the combination of realism and fantasy that he and Paul strove for.

This "J.D. Scratch," real name Joseph Dempsey, was no longer as cagey and noncommittal as he had been on the day, a few weeks earlier, when Hogan and I went to see him at Paul's loft in Tribeca. At the time, he was still logging tapes and doing preliminary edits of art-performance footage, as though he expected Paul to return any day. The tattoos on his thin arms made their own little show as he worked. Staying at his task, he refused to focus on my questions about Paul's activities on the day of the murder.

"I don't know, guy," was all he would say, peering steadily down at the editing panel as if the knobs and levers had just been revealed to him in a vision.

Before long, Hogan grew impatient. "Let me talk to this jerk alone."

I nodded, and he looked down at J.D. "Don't go away, sweetheart."

Hogan walked me over to the door, across a vast stretch of hardwood floor—a square-footage index of the income generated by Paul's rape-on-tape business, as the *Post* had dubbed it in their screaming headlines.

"Twenty minutes," Hogan said. "Twenty minutes of boot camp."

I went out and strolled a couple of blocks to the Odeon and had a gin and tonic, sitting alone at the dim end of the bar, away from the afternoon sunlight leaking through the Venetian blinds. It was a slow lunch day, so the bartender chatted with me about the Jeff Koons show at Sonnabend—huge color photos of the artist joyfully screwing his Italian porn-star wife. "A cathartic celebration of pure sexuality," as one critic wrote.

"Fun smut" was the bartender's more succinct formulation. "Big bucks."

When I got back to the loft, Mr. Scratch did not mind talking anymore. With his arms wrapped across his abdomen, he seemed almost eager to share his recollections. He told us, for instance, how upset his boss had been after reading an e-mail from Amanda one evening.

"Paul looked really worried," the young man explained. "'That crazy bitch is messing with me,' he said. 'She's all flipped out because she saw one of our videos, stuff she doesn't get at all. Stuff she hates. If I know her, she'll blab all over town.'"

With a little prompting, J.D. went on to tell us that he had been sent out for supplies all morning on May fourth, dragging himself from one specialty shop to the next. He was pale, and he would not look at Hogan.

"There's something else," I said. From my breast pocket I drew out a picture of Melissa, a birthday-party shot that Angela had e-mailed to me the previous summer in Venice. "Did you ever meet this girl?"

"Oh, her," J.D. said.

"She was here?"

"No." He dropped his eyes. "But Paul talked about her all the time. Used her picture as his screensaver. You know how he is."

"All too well."

"Her mother did turn up once, though."

"Angela? When?"

"Back before Thanksgiving sometime. She was yelling at Paul, saying he was trying to whore out her daughter."

"What did Paul do?"

"Grabbed her wrists when she clawed at him. Kept telling her nothing had happened, nothing at all. Then she got real icy, man, after he let go. I was scared. When she asked to use the bathroom, I thought maybe she'd come back with a knife she'd picked up along the way."

"Where's the bathroom?"

"Back there, down the hall past the kitchen. Paul has a big knife set in a wooden block right there on the counter. I mean, if you'd seen the look in her eyes…"

Hogan peered down the hall. "Past those bookshelves?"

"Yeah, man," Scratch said. "But I wasn't worried she'd hit him with a book."

"So what did she do?"

"Pissed and left, like a cat marking her territory. Shouted goodbye, you prick, and screw you."

At Paul's trial, I had a similar aim, rather more discreetly expressed.

When I gave my testimony, a few days after Mr. Scratch, I was acutely aware of the bank of faces in the jury box to my left. The eyes of the seven women and five men seemed to reach out in unison. They were looking to me for answers, poor souls. Like clients waiting to be persuaded to buy a piece of art that initially appalls them.

The prosecutor led me, step by step, from my first acquaintance with Paul to the Crosby Street sting I had executed with Hogan. Near the end, he held up an image by a very famous Japanese photographer. It showed a schoolgirl in a short white dress. Barefoot, leaning back on a bank of earth, she pressed her knees together with her feet braced wide apart. The look she directed at the viewer from under her thick bangs seemed at once vulnerable and coy. Between her thighs gleamed a tiny triangle of white panties.

"Is this one of the pictures you discussed in your so-called Balthus Club sessions with Mr. Morse?"

"Yes, it is."

"Would you, in your professional judgment, say that it fairly represents the type of material you perused in those meetings?"

"I would."

"And how many such images do you estimate that you and Paul Morse examined together?"

"Probably a thousand."

He walked to the prosecution table and picked up another photograph that had previously been entered into evidence, out of sight of the jury. He held up a shot of a girl, an American woman photographer's own young daughter, beautifully naked and sprawled in the mud.

"Was this photo also discussed?"

"We didn't say much. We just looked."

The prosecutor had both photographs passed from hand to hand among the jurors for closer inspection. By the time he got to the *Virgin Sacrifice* videotapes, his point had long since been established. Nonetheless, several party episodes were played for the jury in a closed, tightly guarded side room.

God only knows what those twelve good fellow citizens thought of me by the time court returned to open session, but I didn't much care, as long as they convicted Paul Morse.

"This, ladies and gentlemen, is what Amanda Oliver made the mistake of discovering," the prosecutor said. "This is what she objected to before her untimely demise."

The jurors looked at him stoically, unblinkingly, like medical students at a dissection. From time to time, a face turned quickly away, then turned back.

But all this artistry—the photographers', the Donkey's, Hogan's, the D.A.'s, my own—was nothing compared to the skill displayed by Melissa.

On the stand, not quite thirteen yet, she was utterly collected and dispassionate. The prosecutor had instructed Angela to dress her in a simple black jumper and white blouse. Looking demure and child-serious, with her crossed legs invisible behind the oak skirt-guard, Melissa told the jurors how Paul had befriended her, sharing her interest in new clothing styles and asking almost immediately to be introduced to her mother. He easily won that harried woman's confidence, Missy insinuated, with his admiration for Anegla's sculpture project and his kind attentiveness to her daughter.

As she spoke, Melissa was a perfect young lady, the epitome of Bradford School poise. Only her hair, long and luxuriant, caressing her shoulders like tireless fingers, gave a hint of what might have enticed a pervert.

But, as much as all the evidence combined, it was Paul's reaction to Missy's testimony that sank his case. Confronted with her account, needled by the D.A., he flared up in the witness box.

"The lying little witch," he said. "Don't you see? She's using me to hide how she made off with Amanda's computer." His eyes seemed to change color as he spoke. "She's covering for someone else. Maybe for herself, for all I know."

"Just what *do* you know, I wonder," the D.A. said. He picked up a clear plastic bag, holding a corner with two fingers. "Could you tell us, for example, what this peculiar item might be?" He turned slowly, so that each juror could see the oddly shaped metal object dangling from his fingers in a zip-top bag.

"A vibrator," Paul said, in a strangled whisper.

"Speak up, please," the judge instructed.

"A sex toy," Paul said more distinctly. "An electric vibrator."

"I see," the prosecutor said in a measured tone. "A rather unusually shaped implement, isn't it, Mr. Morse? Much more bulbous, here and there, than one would expect?"

Paul lowered his head. "It has a special use."

"And what is that?"

"It's an anal vibrator."

"I see." The D.A. stepped back from the stand. "'Anal' meaning to be inserted in the *rectum*. Is that correct?"

"Yes."

"And during the police raid on Crosby Street, this charming

device was found resting on a couch between you and the twelve-year-old Miss Melissa Oliver? Bearing your fingerprints?"

"She jammed it into my hands," Paul shouted. "She said, 'Take this. Hide it.' She wanted my prints on it. She suckered me."

The prosecutor, unfazed, returned to the table and, with his back to Paul, asked almost casually, "And can you deny that a gun belonging to Amanda Oliver, the girl's stepmother, was later found in your residence?"

"No, but I had no idea. Maybe Melissa's mother brought it there. Who knows? Maybe she was going to shoot me."

"Really, Mr. Morse?" the prosecutor intoned, wheeling slowly, his sharp profile displayed to the jury as he addressed the defendant. "Why on earth would she want to do that?"

Paul recoiled from the question, as if from a whip.

"She's pure evil," he exploded. "So is her daughter. The two of them, torturing men for sick fun."

If the jury had harbored any doubt about Paul's instability, his cruelty, his capacity to inflict harm on innocents, their uncertainty vanished in that instant—with that one imprudent outburst against Angela and her calm, blank-faced daughter. The two sat side-by-side in the visitors' section, prim and unblinking.

Who would want to harbor any terrible thoughts about Melissa? The jurors looked at her furtively. From their reactions, it was clear that she gave them, gave us all, mental respite. And why not? I, for one, had already had enough terrible thoughts for one lifetime.

The prosecutor's summary was sober and compelling.

"You and I are everyday people," he told the jury members near the end. "We work hard, we do our jobs, we raise our families and protect them. But there are other people—self-styled 'artists' like Mr. Morse—who pride themselves on being different from us. On being exceptional. And they think, some of them, that this frees them from the rules you and I and our families all live by."

His tone was mild, in deliberate contrast to Paul's.

"Now, don't misunderstand me, respected jurors—art is very important. Artists *are* different from us, in many positive, constructive ways. When these 'free spirits' display the products of their dreams, showing us things we've never seen before, we all benefit. And the freedom to make art, even unpopular art, even art that shocks us, is one of the most important rights our society provides. Surely, as they so wisely argue, tired and outdated social norms must occasionally be challenged.

"So I would never ask you to condemn Paul Morse because he chooses to look at 'sophisticated' pictures, filthy as they may be."

He paused.

"Not even because he himself *makes* lewd photographs or revolting videos, would I ask you to convict this man. No, that is an artist's privilege, however distasteful."

He stepped close to the rail of the jury box.

"But there are limits. Sometimes in their desire to 'critique,' to 'subvert,' to 'transgress'—terms you have heard from certain scholars and critics called by the defense—artists go too far. They lose all ethical restraint. Then, one day, reality intervenes like a hammer—like a judge's gavel."

An old-school Columbia Law man, the prosecutor was fond of his literary flourishes and grace notes. They probably played well to the curators and art writers in the galley, some of whom had been called to give expert testimony, and all of whom would tie themselves in knots trying to preserve Paul's artistic liberty without condoning his crimes.

Fortunately, the D.A.—seasoned and cunning—also knew how to bring his message home to the folks who really mattered, the jurors.

"But blood is not a fiction, my friends," he told them. "This case—first, last, and exclusively—is about *how* Paul Morse makes his *Virgin Sacrifice* tapes. You can't murder a woman and call it art. You can't assault a man on the street and say, 'It's art.' And to state what I hope is obvious to each and every one of you, you can't lure underage girls into having sex on videotape in the name of 'artistic freedom.' You can't walk away from the terrible pain and suffering you've caused. Forget what Mr. Morse thinks and feels and imagines. What he *does* is heinous. It is not art—and not harmless. It is rape. It is abuse. It is deviant and violent assault. And therefore, ladies and gentlemen, your job today, your solemn *duty*, is to say, loud and clear, that there are some things a civilized society does not tolerate."

Thereafter, the prosecutor spoke with a savvy tinge of regret, mixing tones of pity and fairness. Methodically, he went through the list of charges that the state had amassed against "the self-aggrandizing Mr. Morse." At last, he put aside his notes and addressed the jurors face to face, eye to eye.

"What is Mr. Morse's defense," he asked, "his version of the events? That he was manipulated by a child—a schoolgirl—and by her mother."

He shook his head.

"You have met this girl. You have heard from her mother. Mr. Morse's tale is ludicrous on its face, the last desperate ploy of a sociopath. Whether he believes it or not, I don't know. Frankly, I don't care—and neither should you. His beliefs are not at issue here.

"But what Paul Morse has *done* is clear. He is absolutely and indisputably guilty of the revolting charges against him. The judge will instruct you that the law and common sense are to be your guides in determining a verdict. I ask only, on behalf of the state of New York and the innocents each of us has the moral and legal obligation to defend, that you apply them both fairly—consistent with what you know in your hearts to be right."

From that point on, everything seemed preordained.

Following two days of deliberation, the jury delivered a verdict of guilty on all seventeen counts of sexual congress with a minor, production and distribution of obscene materials, and interstate human trafficking. Weeks later, the judge put the sentence at twenty-five years, with the possibility of parole in fifteen. The outcome, the district attorney later told Hogan and me, seemed about right.

"Good work," Hogan said to Melissa, when we encountered her in the hallway after the sentencing. "Morse is rotten as sin, and you nailed him."

The star witness looked a bit surprised, briefly, as she pulled on her coat.

"Whatever," she said. There was something diffident, almost apologetic, in her manner. "I had to say something up there."

And then, with a few quick, long-legged steps, Melissa was on her way down the green corridor, back to the Bradford School, back to her Wooster Street loft—that stylish SoHo refuge from which Angela was now increasingly absent, tending Philip regularly as he submitted to a hospice routine of clean bed linens and morning sponge baths.

60

The medical staff was surprised at how quickly, how completely, my friend faded after that. The flesh of Philip's arms and legs collapsed against the bone, leaving his limbs like long depleted tubes; his impossibly thin neck protruded from a chest sunken above a popped belly. By then, he probably had no idea where—or who—he might be anymore. At least he was spared the small horror of knowing his fate, or outliving his money.

The last time I saw Philip alive, he looked at me wonderingly, his whole face a plea. His expensive flannels and gabardines had been hung pointlessly in a closet; he was dressed in cotton pajamas, striped pale blue and white. I stared into his eyes for a while—or, rather, let him stare wildly into mine. I had come aching for one last glimpse of the old Philip, dreaming that we might somehow joke about the old days, like the night Claudia danced on the bar at the Stockyard.

Instead, he rasped and mumbled to me repeatedly, "What am I worth?" as though I were Carl Marks with laptop in hand.

Each time I responded, "All your accounts are in order, Philip. Everything paid in advance."

He nodded vigorously, clutching my arm with more force than his shrunken limbs should have permitted.

Yet a few minutes later, he started drifting into sleep, surrounded by a chorus of impersonal beeping machines. I thought about the financial data that used to pour constantly into my friend via his computer screens. Now everything was flowing out: heart rate, temperature, brain activity, breathing. Philip himself had become little more than a stream of information, a sad message.

There was no more for me to say or do. Rising from the bedside chair, I touched his fragile shoulder, spoke his name once—a last time—and left.

Later, I found myself, to my great surprise, prominently named in Philip's will—not as a beneficiary but as Melissa's legal guardian in the event of Angela's death or "permanent maternal incapacity." I wondered how such a phrase, and such a peculiar thought, had come into Philip's head. But, of course, quite a number of bizarre ideas passed through his mind as his dementia grew.

By the time the trial ended, Philip, skeletal and hairless, had forgotten Claudia as though she never existed: it was his last gift to his mistress. She was free to go. The girl, making her farewell visit, wept in Angela's arms. To comfort her, the older woman used a word in Italian that she heard from Philip's lips during one of his feverish monologues. It was his favorite teasing endearment when he and Claudia were first together, passionately and in secret, while Mandy was still alive. The girl wailed once and fled.

From then on, only the two former spouses remained in the room. Philip's mutterings were mostly nonsense by that point, or reduced to sharp howls of fear. The nurses stopped by briefly for linen changes, morphine shots, and thrice-daily vital signs. Otherwise, Angela kept her vigil alone, at all hours, for five desolate months. It was then, I suppose, that my feelings for her deepened beyond the bounds of reason or law.

At the end, like many a dying man, Philip tried to strip himself naked, convulsing in the bed and tugging at his pajama bottoms as though he wished, in the final instant, to lay bare the now shriveled source of his grief. The sounds he made, for the most part no longer human, occasionally coalesced into a word or phrase. Most were banal or incomprehensible: "snow cold," a monotonous "night, night, night." Only one outburst stayed with Angela afterwards, chiming in her mind and letters for years to come.

"Mercy," he shouted, with the striped fabric bunched at his knees. Then, his legs thrashing, his breath rasping and failing, as pink saliva bubbled at the corners of his mouth, he barked a final unappealable judgment: "Not true."

61

A week later, they came to arrest Angela around ten in the morning—not for Amanda's murder alone but for Philip's as well.

She and I were having coffee together in her apartment, as had been our habit ever since Angela so kindly extended her daily invitation. She had a Braun grinder and a sleek Italian coffee machine with twin spouts. As I sat on the couch, I would hear the whir of the grinder once, twice, and then the sound of pressurized drips. Soon Angela—my nurse, as I called her when she delivered the caffeine—would glide carefully from the kitchen island to the seating area, holding her big mug and my small double espresso cup. The little red machine produced a brew that was dark, hot, and bitter. What more could one ask? Laced with sugar, the coffee tasted better than anything I could make for myself or find in the nearby SoHo cafes.

"It's Hogan," the voice said when Angela answered the intercom.

"How nice. I didn't expect you. Jack's here."

When Hogan entered through the loft door, McGuinn was right behind him, looking sober and a bit stunned by the experience of morning sunlight.

"This seems very official," Angela said when the two of them came in and sat down.

"It is," McGuinn said. "It's official as hell."

I looked blankly at Hogan. The two men had not bothered to take off their coats. Underneath, I could see, they were both wearing their best polyester ties.

"You might want to go easy on that coffee," McGuinn advised.

"Something wrong with it?"

Hogan looked first at Angela, then at me. "Do you know how Wolfsheim's Syndrome works?"

"Vaguely."

"Basically, Jack, it rewires your brain. It blocks some of your neural pathways and overloads others." He spoke a bit like a schoolboy reciting his lessons. "The circuits start making totally random connections, crazy hook-ups that come and go in a second."

"Sounds like my old dating life."

I waited for the joke to land, but Hogan remained stone-faced.

"Actually," I said, "I have no idea what you mean."

"No, you wouldn't. That's the point. Your brain gets starved and overwhelmed at the same time. Flooded like an old carburetor. You're not aware of the damage until it affects your behavior and your own actions start to seem strange to you. You gradually lose control. In the end, your body forgets how to function."

"Hideous," Angela said, her voice tense and brittle. "The way it happened to Philip."

"Except it didn't just happen," Hogan said.

My eyes went to Angela, to McGuinn, to Hogan.

"Someone *made* it happen," McGuinn stated. "Or at least sped it along once it started."

We all sat in silence. Slowly, the loft seemed to tilt around me. Still no one spoke.

"Is that what you were doing, Angela?" Hogan asked finally. "Helping nature take its course?"

She stared at him in wonder.

"You see, Jack, some kinds of toxic resin can do pretty much the same thing to your nerves as the disease. Resins like the ones Angela uses back there to patch up her dolls and statues."

"Especially when administered in small doses over time," McGuinn added. "We had a long chat with some doctors about it."

The empty espresso cup was still warm in my hand.

"How have you been doing lately, Jack?" Hogan asked. "Ever feel that your judgment is slightly impaired?"

"Not until now."

"Not until you started having coffee down here every morning, you mean?"

"What are you saying? That Angela has been poisoning me with this?" I extended the white demitasse, its interior streaked with coffee residue.

At that, Angela laughed—sharply.

"Ed, dear, you shouldn't confuse Jack," she said. "He has a lot of important things on his mind."

"More important than murder? What would that be—his painting inventory?"

"He has Melissa to think about."

"So do you, Angela. In fact, you need to think about her very carefully right now."

"I have no idea what you mean."

"She's going to be sort of motherless soon."

"You see," McGuinn said, "we got a report. From Philip's autopsy."

"It documents how the resin compound built up in his brain," Hogan explained. "From the shots you gave him, between his toes, once a week or so at the hospice."

Angela, her face drained of color, glanced from one man to the other.

"Once Philip was diagnosed," McGuinn said, "no one ever questioned his breakdown. No one thought to look for an external cause. Not until Hogan started to question the speed of it. A process that would normally take years playing out in just months."

"Then I remembered your work here," Hogan said to Angela, "all the things you showed me—including the syringes."

"You bastard," Angela snapped. "You can't use anything you took from this loft as evidence."

"That's right."

"You had no search warrant. You're not even a policeman."

"No," Hogan replied evenly. "But the garbage you put out on the sidewalk is fair game. It sits right there in the public domain. Including your old syringes with their toxic residue."

I could see the thought register on Angela's face.

"Not the most considerate means of disposal, sweetheart," Hogan said.

In response, Angela's voice fell—to a tone at once affectionate and pleading.

"Ed, dear, do you remember what you said, what you promised? That first time you came home with me?"

"No. Not the exact words, just the tune of it."

"You said you'd always be kind to me, Edward. In the way Philip should have been but wasn't."

Hogan leaned forward, peering coldly into Angela's face. "Oh, I'm being kind. You'll see exactly how kind."

It felt like I was watching an argument in a dream, except that the confrontation was taking place in real life, unfolding there in front of me on the fourth floor of my Wooster Street building, my home, and not just in a chamber of my own poisoned mind.

"I'm curious," Hogan said. "Did you think screwing me was a free pass for murder?"

"Don't ask me that. You can't, darling."

"All right, try a different one. Which made you feel better—poisoning Philip or shooting Amanda?"

"What are you talking about? I didn't kill Amanda."

"Don't fight me, Angela. Everything will be easier, once you confess."

"Confess to Amanda's murder? Are you mad? Why on earth would I do that?"

"You better think carefully before you answer. You better calculate very, very well. Because you're only going to get one chance."

"This is utterly vicious, a lie."

"Is it, Angela? I have a videotape that shows who entered the Prince Street building that day, and who left it shortly afterwards, clutching Amanda's laptop."

Angela rose up. "Don't bluff me, Edward. There's no security camera over there."

We were all on our feet now, three men standing in a half-circle around one frantic woman—ensuring that she wouldn't bolt for a door, a window, a gun.

"No, there's no security camera in the building. You can thank Jack for that," Hogan said. "But there is a camera across the street, on the back wall of a very fancy little boutique. The lens points toward the jewelry counter." He paused a moment to let Angela picture the scene. "And do you remember what's next to the counter?"

"A display window."

"That's right. With a nice clear view across the street to the Olivers' building."

Angela's expression fell, and darkened.

"The tape was long gone by the time I got there. The cops had impounded it, along with half a dozen others from the area, on the day after the murder. Of course, it takes friggin' forever to watch those things, and McGuinn had no idea who or what he was looking for back then—except Philip, who didn't appear. He put the tapes aside and didn't touch them again until I asked him for a look. Then it was my turn to sit through the boring damn things. Boring until I spotted someone familiar, in the wrong place at a very wrong time."

"I see."

"We can all see now, Angela. That's why you better play ball."

"Or…?"

"Or I can give the tapes back to McGuinn, and he can do a big messy police investigation of the new evidence—freeze frame, image enhancement, that sort of thing. Followed, in a few months, by a trial where everybody, including Melissa, goes up on the stand. She'll have a long time, between now and then, to decide whether to turn on you. Whether to testify against her own mother."

To my amazement, Angela said no more.

"Take a little walk with me, Angela. We can go to Melissa's room. Nice and quiet."

She stared at him desperately, sadly.

"Stop, can't you?" Her command had become a throaty plea.

"Not yet. There's something I want to show you. A couple things."

62

McGuinn and I, left cooling our heels, slumped back in the chairs and made small talk. We were both used to Hogan's private colloquies with suspects and witnesses. I had seen him apply the technique with J.D. Scratch in Paul Morse's loft. McGuinn had witnessed—and benefited from—many such encounters over the years.

"They won't be long," he assured me. "Hogan knows how to make a point."

He must have been playing the security tape for Angela. I was curious to see it myself. It couldn't have been easy for Angela to watch the grainy black-and-white proof of her guilt, infinitely repeatable. How many times in the years ahead would it replay in her memory, the way the *Virgin Sacrifice* images ran persistently in mine?

After about fifteen minutes, the pair returned—Angela, silent now, looking pale and stricken when they stopped in front of us. We got to our feet again.

"Now listen good," Hogan said, watching her. "If you were to confess, Angie, here's how I think it might go."

She didn't move or speak.

"I imagine you must have driven into Manhattan, to SoHo, knowing that Philip was off in L.A. You were supposed to have a serious talk with Amanda. The two of you had already arranged it, by e-mail and phone. I imagine that you got there early, on purpose, and when Amanda didn't answer, you let yourself in with Missy's keys. You knew from your daughter all about the night table with the gun in the drawer."

Angela looked at him pleadingly. But Hogan went on.

"When Amanda got home from shopping, she would have put her things in a closet and gone to sit in her favorite chair, listening to music as you came down the hall."

"I don't want to listen to this."

"No, but you will."

"Please stop."

"Listen to it, Angie. All of it. Then repeat it for McGuinn." Hogan's voice softened. "Somebody is going to pay for killing Amanda Oliver. And it won't be Paul Morse."

"But I…"

"Just do it, Angela, and let all the craziness end here. Do it for Melissa's sake. For Philip's. For your own."

Angela crossed her arms, wrapping herself. She closed her eyes for a few seconds. When she opened them again, they were dull and fixed like the eyes of a corpse.

"What do you want me to say?"

"Tell us how you used your daughter to cover your tracks. How you got her to lie."

For a moment, Angela seemed to be considering her options. All the ones she didn't have.

"It wasn't hard," she said finally. "They were just lies to men."

"That's right," Hogan said. "Melissa is a bright girl—a curious girl, full of questions. But she does what she's told. So when you told her to lie about your time at home on that day, she lied. The two of you dreamed up yoga and gingerbread cookies."

"It was easy enough, like child's play. After all, you were quite ga-ga over me. Jack was totally obsessed with Melissa and that Paul Morse business. And McGuinn, even sober, couldn't think his way out of a corner."

"Watch your mouth, lady," the big cop said. "I'm not in a goddamn corner here. You are."

"Forget it, McGuinn," Hogan said. He addressed Angela carefully. "What matters is that once Melissa found Mandy's laptop in your room, once she gave it to Jack, you panicked."

Angela lowered her arms. As her fingers spread at her sides, I could see that the nails were chipped. A working sculptor's hands.

"You knew what we'd find on the computer, with enough time and reading," Hogan pressed. "Is that when you decided to frame Morse for the murder?"

"That beast. He deserves his cage."

For some reason, I couldn't stay out of it. "You liked him well enough once," I reminded her.

Angela wheeled on me. "And what about you, Jack? Didn't you like him, too—some filthy little part of you? Isn't that why it was so easy for you to entrap him? Easy to draw him in with your dirty pictures and your stories about all the rich pedophiles you know? Let's not forget you're the one who got him arrested. You're the one who told me about the porn tapes and the party on Crosby Street. About his plans for Melissa."

"Yes, but after."

"After what?"

"After you'd already seen through him," Hogan interjected. "After you'd gone to his loft, maybe planning to kill him the way you killed Amanda. But his assistant was there with him, and you ended up planting the gun on his bookshelf instead. After asking to use the bathroom. Probably wiped the pistol down with Paul's own hand towel. So your fingerprints wouldn't be on the murder weapon anymore."

Angela didn't flinch. "Don't push me, Ed. I know how to deal with people who push me."

"Listen to yourself, Angela," I said. "Is that the sort of lesson you want to teach Melissa?"

Angela's chin quivered. She turned to face me and replied very quietly. "Don't speak that name to me, Jack. Now that this is over, I want you to stay away from my daughter."

"Why?"

"Don't be coy. Just stop."

"I'm sorry, Angela, but Melissa needs me. I'm the only person you can name who hasn't hurt her."

"Oh, please." Angela regarded me closely. Something came into her voice that I had not heard before. "This is New York, not Shanghai, Jack. Melissa isn't your little sing-song girl. Leave her alone."

"You're not in such a great position to be giving me orders, Angela. I know too damned much about you now."

"Know? You know bloody nothing." Angela smiled crookedly, ruefully. "You suspect."

"That's right, I do. I told Hogan so."

"And then you depended on our dim, brave detective here— always wrestling with his demons. Even when he's out on the streets, battling the angel of death."

"Is that you, Angela?" I asked.

"Why do you care?"

"Because I loved Mandy. And Philip as well. They saved me once."

"You loved Nathalie, too," Angela said. "How well did that turn out?"

I felt the rush of blood to my face. "Better than you think," I protested quietly. "Better than anyone thinks."

"You do have a corrupt mind, Jackson Wyeth. Everyone knows you did Nathalie in out of spite."

"I didn't kill my wife."

"Not with a gun, no. You just let her die slowly, in shame, for doing the very same things that you did every bloody chance you got, with every slut from here to Rangoon."

"It's not the same."

"No two killings are," Angela said. "Isn't that what your P.I. friend here would say?"

In fact, Hogan said nothing. He simply waited for Angela to wear herself down.

"Just don't plead clean hands with me, Jack," Angela hissed. "I know where your stinking fingers have been."

She was like a hunted animal now, baring her fangs at each circling pack dog in turn.

"Let's just try to make this right for Melissa," I said. "Give her a chance for a normal life."

"Normal, Jack? With you?"

"Maybe. Without you whispering hate in her ear."

"Jack, please," Angela said. "You can't let them do this to me. I'm her mother. She's already lost her father. If I go to prison, it will destroy her."

"You think she can't live without you?" I said. "She can live very well, with my help. It's what Philip wanted, isn't it? What he wrote in his will. I'll give her a beautiful life."

"Will you, Jack? With your dirty art money and your blank moral slate?" Angela spoke softly. "Do you really think one more betrayal will wipe out all the rest?"

"For Christ's sake, Angela, why did you ever make Missy part of this?"

"I had no choice."

"You have one now," Hogan said, stepping between us. "You can tell it all, the whole story, your own way. No one will blame Melissa for lying to cover for you."

"Stop it, Hogan. Please."

"Just keep it simple and clear. You know McGuinn. He doesn't like extra complications, extra work. So just give him a short, plain statement, confessing both crimes. You can rehearse it in the squad car, then deliver it in a cozy little interrogation room with a video camera running. You can pretend it's an art project, if you want."

"Don't make me do this."

"It's my way or McGuinn's. You decide."

I could see Angela break. Physically, mentally, she was done. "All right," she said, soft as an old woman fading. "All right."

"That's better," he said. "Now you're finally getting smart."

Angela turned to me. "You have to see, Jack," she murmured. "You have to see how much I loved Philip. How much I love Melissa now."

"I'm trying, Angela. It's not always easy."

Her eyes widened. "The glue worked on other broken things. It was worth a try."

"You thought death would fix Philip?"

"I couldn't let him suffer for years like a dog."

"So you killed him out of mercy?"

"You watched Nathalie die," Angela said quietly. "Would you wish that on Philip?"

"No, not on anyone."

"He was sick and dying. I couldn't stop it, Jack, but I could make it go faster."

"You think Melissa will see it that way?"

"Yes. Yes, I do. She always listens to me," Angela said with a note of pride. "Someday, if you get to truly know her, you'll understand. You'll see that I did the right thing. Not for anyone else, maybe, but for Melissa. The rest of us don't really matter. We've all screwed ourselves and each other. We deserve whatever we get."

McGuinn, no longer so hostile, came up to Angela and grasped her left wrist—almost gently, it seemed to me, even with a hint of regret. He cuffed it and moved her left arm behind her back and, as she turned, cuffed the right wrist to the left.

"Jack, you've got to tell Melissa what I did today."

"That you confessed to both murders?"

"Yes, exactly. Promise me."

"All right, Angela. I promise. Every word."

"You have to make it real to her. At last. Please, or else she's lost forever."

"I won't let that happen."

"No, don't. She could be so fine for the world. Thank you, Jack."

McGuinn took Angela's elbow and led her toward the door. Hogan, hanging back slightly, leaned close to me.

"This is payback for the Crosby Street bust, Jack. Now we're even."

"We've been even for years. You didn't owe me anything."

"Yeah, well, I owed McGuinn, I owed Bernstein. All the pieces fit now. They need to stay that way."

"Why would anything change?"

"Just see that it doesn't." Hogan glanced around at the couches and chairs, the paintings. "I don't ever want to come to this damn place again."

I grasped his arm, making him pause. "Thanks for not arresting Angela in front of her daughter. Who knows what it would have done to the girl?"

Hogan looked at me as though I were a man condemned.

"Melissa is yours now," he said. "Try to make something decent of her, will you? That's what you asked for once."

"Yes, of course. She's my new chance. My last."

"Yeah, Jack. And you're hers." Hogan's eyes swept the loft one last time. He nodded. "Just don't blow it."

63

I waited for Missy after school that day and brought her home—to my home, on the fifth floor. I feared that the emptiness downstairs, the mute sculptural figures, the faint lingering smell of resin, might profoundly spook her.

Without delay, I sat the girl down on a chair in the front room and told her everything, from beginning to end.

Oddly, nothing seemed to surprise Melissa very much. She had a fixed exasperation that came naturally with her approaching teen years. Whatever adults did seemed equally inconsequential, equally stupid. She sat there in her Bradford School uniform, with her long legs crossed, saying nothing.

"Angela wanted me to tell you exactly what she did today. How she confessed."

"What, Uncle Jack? That she did the right thing? OK, fine. You told me."

"Are you angry at her?"

"Not really."

"She's worried about how all this will affect you."

"Why?"

"She put you in the middle of something grisly, something insane."

"No big deal. We helped each other out, that's all. It's what mothers and daughters do."

I couldn't tell if Melissa was incredibly brave or simply in shock.

"You and your mom against the world—is that it? Like you told me once?"

"Yeah, sisterhood." Melissa sighed deeply, looking down. Her blond hair covered her face.

"Sometimes I feel like just myself," she said, "and sometimes I don't know where Mom leaves off and I begin."

"What did Angela say to you afterwards?" I asked. "After the murder?"

Melissa looked up. "A lot of junk. Kind of loud, because the windshield wipers were on. She just kept saying how horrible it was, what had happened, but that it just had to be. It was kind of monotonous."

"You were in the car with her? She took you along? How awful for you, Missy. What did you say?"

"I said, 'OK, Mandy is dead now. Calm down.'" The girl shrugged. "I said it a couple of times. It wasn't a major issue really. Mandy was half dead anyhow from the cancer."

"Half dead? No, no. Amanda was halfway well. She'd been successfully treated."

"Oh, you don't know anything." The girl shifted in her seat, keeping her eyes on me. "Mom gave me the 411 before we drove into SoHo."

"If Mandy was sick again, she never told me."

"Why would she? You're not real family. Not one of us. You're not in anybody's family, are you?"

"No, not for a long time now."

Melissa gazed at me with a look that resembled pity.

"But Amanda was getting better," I said. "Her hair was growing out."

"Don't you get it?" the girl demanded. "It was just one of those dumb stories that adults tell each other when they're scared. They told Aunt Mandy the cancer wouldn't come back, but it did. Bad things always do, don't they—sooner or later?"

"No, not always. They're not going to come back to you. I'll see to that."

"Will you, Uncle Jack? That's so sweet."

Her hair fell forward in waves on both sides of her face.

"Your father's lawyer will make sure I'm confirmed as your legal guardian," I told her. "It's in Philip's will."

"Then everything's fine, isn't it?"

"But you must be terribly afraid for your mother now."

"Not really. Mom can handle herself. She's a killer, right?"

Melissa kicked off her shoes and rolled down her knee socks, crossing and recrossing her legs to pull the white stockings off one after the other.

"That's better," she said. "My legs were so itchy, you know."

She bent forward, looking steadily up at me, rubbing her calves slowly as she spoke. "And Uncle Bernie will see that I get my money?"

I must have shown my puzzlement.

"Daddy's money. My inheritance."

"Yes, of course."

"Good." She sat straight again. "But we might have to fight with Amanda's family first."

"Who told you that?"

"Mom did."

I watched as Missy rummaged through her purse, searching for a mint. Once she retrieved the little plastic box, she offered me a round white candy before taking one for herself. Always the polite Bradford girl.

"I didn't know you cared about money so much," I said.

"I don't care about it at all—not the dirty paper, the numbers in columns. I just care about being free. That, I care about really a lot."

"How much?"

"Gobs. I'll do just about anything for it." She looked at me defiantly yet earnestly, making sure I had heard. "As long as I can choose whatever I want afterwards. Whenever I want."

I had heard her, all right.

"You shouldn't think that way," I said. "No one is free completely, Missy. To be that free you have to stop caring if anyone loves you."

"But I'm pretty, Uncle Jack. People will always love me. Until I'm really old anyhow, and then who cares?"

"You can't live that way. It's too sad."

"But you do. I mean, the way I want to live. Free." She straightened her skirt, without taking her eyes from me. "I need to be the boss of my own life. No one else."

"Well, a fortune will certainly help, once you're old enough."

"Of course, in eight years. When I'm twenty-one."

There was a glint in her eye for a moment, or I thought there was.

"It will be about time, after all the waiting and stuff I've had to do for it." She put a white lozenge on her tongue. "I've had like eons of waiting already."

"When did you start thinking about all this?"

"When Daddy got sick."

"He told you his plan?"

"No, I had to ask him. I made him promise."

"All by yourself?"

"No, Mom said I should."

"And was making me your guardian also your mother's idea?"

"No, dummy, she totally hates it. It was mine."

"Why?"

"At first daddy wanted to put in my grandparents or some nice couple he knew. I said, 'Oh please, no. They'll just try to make me ordinary.' I mean, bleh, gag, how boring. 'But Uncle Jack won't.' "

"Right. Uncle Jack couldn't."

"It's the best part, don't you think—me and you? Besides the money, I mean."

"You should be very grateful to your father, Missy. Philip was wonderfully generous."

"Well, what did you expect me to do when I grow up? Get a stupid job or something?"

I had never thought of Melissa's life in quite those stark terms. She gave me a long unreadable glance. As I watched, her tongue worked the mint around methodically inside her mouth.

"Luckily," I said, "you don't have to worry about that now. Not ever."

"Good."

"While you're in school, you can keep your place here. With a live-in nanny and housekeeper. With tutors. And I'll be here, right up above."

"Like a guardian angel."

"Of sorts."

"Will you really take care of me, Uncle Jack? Always?"

"If that's what you want."

"You know what I want."

"Do I? Tell me."

"I want us to be together. Just us."

"All right, we'll put all this horror behind us."

"You're the best. It will be our secret now, honey."

"Will it?"

"You always wanted that, didn't you?"

"What?"

"To have a secret with me. I wanted it, for sure."

"Well, you've gotten your wish then, Melissa."

"Of course. I always do."

For some reason, my right hand had begun to tremble.

"Don't worry," Melissa said, noticing. "I'll be good."

"I can only hope."

"You'll see." Smiling, she shifted restlessly again in the chair.

"But why are you so far away, Uncle Jack? Let's sit on the couch together."

She moved swiftly to the sofa. Drawing a deep breath, I followed in my own slow way. We sat side by side. It was not a cure for my trembling.

"And what do you wish for now?" I asked

"For you to come see me every day."

"All right, then, I will."

"Anytime, Uncle Jack. I'm right downstairs."

"Yes, I'll come down every day."

"Or sometimes I'll come up."

"Whatever you want, Missy."

"I know."

64

That is nearly all I can remember now about the Oliver affair. I am surprised, really, how completely the scenes have come back to me, how effortlessly the words have flowed. Call it a feat of reclamation. The SoHo we knew in those days has now vanished like a dead civilization, like the towers that once presided, ablaze with light, over our restive journeys through the downtown streets. To record this minor episode, to write it out with clarity and ease, in a sustained delirium, has required merely the shattering of my life, the death of several friends, the loss of my last tender illusions. Apparently that's the price art commands, if it is more than a joke. But I'm not complaining. Fine merchandise, as any dealer will tell you, is always a bargain in the long run.

Under my watchful eye, Melissa flourished. Once Angela's arrest was reported, my art world friends, appalled by the travesty of motherhood, grew immediately sympathetic to Missy, holding the girl in a kind of sacred awe. The fact that she was "brilliant"—the term her tutors invariably used—certainly helped, but it wasn't the only winning factor.

My ward was utterly gracious. Even Missy's nannies adored her. Unfailingly polite and obedient to them, she was like a model prisoner currying favor with her indulgent guards. (The same could not be said of Angela, who regarded her life sentence as a license to make each day hell for everyone else—especially her penitentiary mates and her low-wage, undereducated keepers.) The fortunate Melissa, unlike her mother, knew exactly when her freedom would come.

Being the child of a murderer might have caused Missy some problems at the Bradford School. Instead, her familial calamity impressed her classmates and cowed the trustees. After a single emergency meeting, Mrs. Dorfman announced the board's unanimous decision: "Surely this poor girl cannot be held in any way responsible for the crimes of her mother. The Bradford School will continue to welcome her."

It was all very uptown and enlightened. Hogan's much-thumbed Bible may have something rather different to say on that score—the phrase "unto the third and fourth generation" sticks in my mind—but I concede that Old Testament interpretation is not my strong suit. Making large donations to educational institutions, however, is.

New York University concurred with Bradford's judgment. After Melissa earned her undergraduate degree—attending classes that were never more than a short walk away from the Wooster Street loft—she was swiftly admitted to the school's Institute of Fine Arts up on 78th and Fifth. I was touched that she chose to study art history at my alma mater. Missy wanted, she said, "to find out how we got where we are culturally."

"And where are we, anyhow?" I prodded her.

"You should know, Uncle Jack. You live it every day."

"That's not the same as understanding it."

"But you do understand. And so do I."

"Do you? You know what art is for these days and what it means?"

"Of course. It's for the rich, and it doesn't mean anything." She laughed. "All my teachers are impressed by my insights now. Because you taught me so well when I was young."

As you can see, my position as godfather and legal guardian is something I take very seriously. Over the years, it has made me attentive, in ways I had never dreamed possible, as Missy slowly evolved from a surrogate daughter to my regular "plus one" at openings and receptions to the indispensable hostess at my Wooster Street parties.

There were a few difficulties along the way, of course. The cyber-economy went bust and the value of O-Tech stock plummeted, costing Andrews and his top executives—the ones who hadn't already been booted due to the porn distribution scheme —their plush jobs in a shareholders' coup. But over the years before Melissa turned twenty-one, the company recovered and the Oliver fortune grew again.

Amanda's family, as Angela had anticipated, did indeed put up a fierce fight to keep the bulk of Philip's wealth from going to Missy—the daughter of the woman who had murdered their loved one. The Wingates had a superb team of lawyers and a rather compelling case, but not one that could stand up to Bernstein and his associates. The transfer of assets took place on schedule, the same year my lovely ward completed her undergraduate studies.

Melissa hardly seemed to notice. Apparently, it had never occurred to the girl—a sleekly curved young woman by then— that she might not get what she wanted.

I, on the other hand, made quite a fuss over Melissa's landmark birthday. The two of us had a long, elaborate celebration that evening. Afterwards, I took her to dinner at Daniel and later for drinks—completely legal at last—at a sedate ninth-floor lounge with a glass wall overlooking Columbus Circle and Central Park. As we sipped our Armagnac and tried to identify the spot, near the Sherman Monument, where Paul Morse had once photographed her in a school uniform, I asked Melissa how it felt to be a woman finally, and a rich one. She looked at me, then out over the streams of red taillights, the vast rolling park, the tall sentinel buildings lining its edges, guarding the city's dark heart.

"It feels like justice," she said.

I suppose we might have feared for Paul's eventual return, but by then he had already been killed in prison, as Hogan half-foretold. Grown pudgy and considerably less handsome, he bled out in a laundry room corner, still protesting (according to the guards who arrived a few foot-dragging steps too late to aid him) that he had never forced or harmed anyone, child or adult. Meanwhile, Sammy—never the made man he wished to be—resigned himself to serving one long prison sentence after another, without hope of parole.

And just as quietly, for years, I have watched the young men come and go downstairs, even while continuing to visit Missy from time to time myself—the good landlord, the kind uncle. That is the role that has fallen to me, or that I have fallen to. During her college days, when Melissa shared the space with friends—she was always "the girl with the awesome loft, the tech heiress"—we remained regular dinner partners and traveling companions.

Angela, resentful, raged at me in letters from a succession of prisons, each one more high-security than the last. My life with Missy, in this vigilant mother's view, was an offense against nature. She harangued her daughter, but the girl, even after becoming financially free, ignored the frantic protests and stayed on.

Yet I have paid a price for my minor triumph. Melissa still lives downstairs, but with a young husband these days—a nice, sandy-haired Wall Street junior analyst who has not yet learned how to wear his Brooks Brothers suits. The young couple has been married for two banal years.

When she introduced us, I felt as though I might have seen her spouse somewhere once long ago, in a dark after-hours bar, with his tie flipped back over his shoulder—a young Goldman Sachs bull.

Ever the proper guardian, I gave Missy away at their wedding, leading her down the aisle on my good arm one furiously bright May afternoon at a Presbyterian church on Park Avenue. What else could I do? Marriage is a mistake nearly everyone makes at some point in life. Melissa, too, must take her grueling turn and grow wise.

The ceremony was the kind of civilized ritual that her Aunt Mandy would have approved. As the organ played, Howard received his dream girl like an untarnished prize. Still, he never seems quite comfortable around me—perhaps because, as Melissa said when we first met in the elevator, he feels embarrassed by my needless rent-charity and prefers "to work for a so-called living."

This prideful Howard, for some reason, seems to distrust me and the whole Wooster Street arrangement. Probably he is wary of any deal that is out of line with the market, and he is prudent to be. SoHo has pitfalls that even the boardrooms of Wall Street can't match.

Soon enough, I'm sure, this stalwart fellow will haul his bride off to a safe little town on the Metro North line. Yes, the day is inevitably coming for Melissa to think about good schools and top soccer leagues, not for herself this time.

Last fall I noticed a swelling of her midriff, and she said, with a blush, that things would be changing around here very soon. In a few months, I could expect to find a stroller on the landing; maybe I would even learn to change diapers.

When she told me, she pressed against my torso for a kiss, her body momentarily brushing my left arm. Her husband, shifting his weight, stood by with his eyes averted toward the doorjamb.

"The child is quite a surprise," Howard said. "We hadn't been planning this yet."

"I know," I replied.

Why do we do these things to each other? For all my time spent with Hogan, I still wonder where crime begins. Does it creep upon us through circumstance? Is it purely our own doing? Or does it spring from some inborn evil for which we are, though roundly punished, paradoxically blameless?

No, forget that. The idea of original sin lets us off the hook too easily—as I once let Melissa off.

65

"I didn't know how to tell you," she said to me a few days after the joyful announcement, once her Howard had gone off to work one bright September morning.

"It's fine," I replied. "Wonderful."

Missy touched her belly. "Did you hear what I said?"

"Yes." I looked around at my paintings, my closets, my loft, my elegant home. "I'm very happy. And your mother will be thrilled."

"I can't stand this."

I remained still, devoid of words.

"Can't you say something, Jack? Can't you hold me?"

"You've got your husband for that now."

"That's right, thank God." She drew back slightly. "And the baby? You don't even want to know?"

"Would it make any difference?"

"I suppose not," she said. Then, after a moment, shaking her head: "No, it definitely wouldn't."

"So there we are, Missy. All of us where we belong."

"It's too sad, really. You know there were times when I truly cared for you over the years. A lot of times."

"I do know. You mentioned it once or twice, although I was a bit distracted, back in your college days, by the blow jobs."

"Please, Jack. Don't. Please." She drew a long breath. "Not everything is a joke."

"What is it, then?"

"Can't you please be real—just this once?"

"I tried reality, Missy. It didn't work out."

"Stop, please."

"Nathalie in her hospital bed was as real as anything gets. How's that for you?"

Melissa was crying quietly, her face lowered. I wanted to feel something, the way I did a long time ago. Just about anything would have done, I think. Love or jealousy or rage. Anything. But wishes don't always come true.

When Missy looked up, her face seemed to have broken into a thousand pieces, like a shattered doll's head.

"I have to leave here," she said. "All of it—you, SoHo, this sickness."

"Why?"

Her eyes flashed at me. I had not seen such an expression since that distant day at the Darger show, when I asked her once more about Amanda's laptop. She said now, standing pregnant in the Wooster Street loft, what she must have thought then: "For Christ's sake, Jack, don't be entirely dense."

But I was. I couldn't help but be. Then one day, weeks later, when Melissa was in her second trimester, yet another letter came from her mother.

I kept the unopened envelope on my table for a day or two, glancing at the return address when I passed. Melissa, too, ignored it, uninterested. Finally, one night after she left to go downstairs for the evening, I slit the letter open. The message was in black ink on three plain white sheets of paper, scrawled at great speed.

Dear Jack,

I know you hate me. That scarcely matters now, since I rather hate myself, too—for what I did to Philip and you. What matters is the truth.

Beware of Melissa. This newest game with her—the marriage, the three of you housed together, the duplicity—it just can't go on. I forbid it. You have to put an end to all this genteel depravity, Jack. If you know what's bloody good for you.

Some things are just too vile. You can see that, can't you? Or you will when I tell you.

Melissa is a killer. A murderer—even though she'll never admit what she's done. Yes, your dear, sweet little girl.

That day riding home in the car, with the rain falling, she was simply blank. "Mandy is dead now" is all she would say. "Mandy is dead now. I killed her." It had no meaning to her. It was a statement, not a reality. I couldn't get her to tell me why. I had to beg the details out of her, over weeks, just to be able to cover up properly.

You probably don't believe me even now. You heard me confess to everything after the police came. But you knew, you should have known, what was really happening: I was saving my child. I did what I had to do—I lied, I accused myself— to give her a free life. I did it without a second thought, as mothers do. She never thanked me, and she never will. Not Melissa. So much for your "one true and loving heart."

Can you imagine my own life since then? I've had to think of you—the pair of you—all these years. Living in SoHo, steeped in sin and arrogance, while I pace here and scream.

Fortunately there were compensations over the years: Melissa's progress at school, her boyfriends, her inheritance, her husband.

But now this. This abomination. It's too much.

That's why I'm telling you, Jack. Go and look. Missy pried a floorboard loose in her bedroom. She told me once, when she came for one of her rare visits—in a whisper, so the guards couldn't hear. You know what she hid there? A gift from your friend Hogan: a copy of the security tape, the one from the boutique. The one that shows her leaving the car, going in, coming out with Mandy's laptop.

I had no idea. I thought she was just picking up the computer for some school project. I sat in the car, double parked, clueless, while she shot her stepmother twice in the head.

Hogan described the whole sequence to me, frame by frame. It was the first thing he did when he took me into Melissa's room that morning. He had me picture Paul Morse arriving at eleven in the morning and leaving an hour later. Amanda coming out for a brief shopping trip afterwards, returning with a Morgane Le Fay bag.

Then he made me sit on the bed, where I could see all the clutter. He told me to look carefully at every item—Melissa's clothes, her CDs, her jewelry, her shoes, her brushes and combs, her books. He asked me to imagine her life without them, locked in a prison cell one third the size of her bedroom, my beautiful young daughter with no one to talk to or meet, except dyke thieves and arsonists and killers, all of them strung out on smuggled-in drugs. What would years of that do to my baby?

There was no doubt, he said. With the premeditation, then the attempt to pin the murder on Paul—the prosecutor would be sure to try her as an adult. "If Melissa is not a mental adult, then we're all minors," he said. "All lost and dangerous children, every one of us."

Either way, she was doomed, unless I took her crime on myself, unless I sacrificed myself.

Years later, before she graduated from Bradford, Hogan gave a copy of the tape to Melissa. He told her, "This is to keep you honest. Jack is my best friend. I have another copy. Don't ever make me use it."

That's when Missy stowed the tape under her bedroom floor. She's half forgotten it, I'm sure. The same way she's half forgotten me.

But I won't be forgotten, Jack. I exist. I demand to be

recognized. You have to hear and see me; you have to re-member Angela Oliver—as a woman, an artist, a mother. Yes, and a murderer—of poor Philip. But not of Amanda! No, I won't make it easy for you, and I won't go away. You can keep me in prison, but you can't keep me out of your mind. I'm too much a part of your life. I gave birth to the woman you love.

Oh, don't deny it. Not to me. I watched the pair of you for too many years. I saw. You can't hide any longer behind that suave disguise, that good uncle mask. Not now. You've gone too far.

Damn you, can't you see who Melissa really is?

You can watch the tape, Jack. Anytime. Black and white— as plain as words on paper. All you have to do is go downstairs and look.

But you won't, will you? No, you don't want to wreck your fairy-tale Wooster Street setup, your playhouse. You don't want to botch the little make-believe life you've constructed for yourself. For yourself and your precious Melissa.

Well, I'm botching it for you. Because I can't stand it. Because it can't go on anymore. I've told Melissa that you know everything. What she's done, what she is. I wrote to her yesterday. It's over now.

You don't want to read this any more than you want to see the surveillance tape. You don't want the truth, Jack. Not the whole of it.

That's why you'll never be Hogan.

God knows if you'll ever be a man at all.

Yours righteously,
Angela

After I read the letter a couple times, I set it aside and walked to the liquor cabinet for a scotch. I wanted to sit for a few minutes to decide exactly what to think. Holding my drink, I settled into the armchair—the same one I sat in the night of the Crosby Street bust, the night that Melissa lay sleeping behind a narrow door on the far side of the loft.

The rantings of a madwoman, a confessed killer, locked up for years in a cell. That's what I thought. Angela could not give up control, or the attempt at control, even as she sat in her orange jumpsuit in a maximum security prison. Unable to strike out at us any other way, she would try to poison us with her words. We didn't have to let her. We could go on. Other things were pressing on me. I was preoccupied with the new art season and the preparations for Melissa's childbirth—a baby present to buy, the electrical sockets to childproof. I had exhibitions to mount and bills to pay.

"You stupid bloody fool, Jack." I could just hear Angela saying it. Well, if she thought I was obtuse, she had only herself to blame. The damage she did to my brain, the legacy of her resin-laced morning espresso, is slight but irreversible. My doctors are quite clear, quite ruthlessly honest, in their prognosis. They say the deterioration could soon accelerate, leaving me at first a single beat—one mental half-step—behind my former self, behind all less afflicted thinkers. How will I know if it happens? My unnamable feelings for Melissa—whatever they are, if I've ever known what they are—may have a similar effect. Just as a man's failing eyesight makes all young women lovelier.

It may be, in fact, that a gentle forgetfulness, a slight vagueness about what is happening now, is the best state in which to begin the journey of advancing age. I've only just stepped out onto that long avenue, in the first dim hour of evening, but I already know where it leads. Where all streets lead.

"I opened the letter from your mother," I told Melissa the next day. "She accuses you, rather graphically, of killing Aunt Amanda."

"So, what's new? Mom accuses everyone, blames everyone. Except herself."

"That's true; she always did."

"Every time I visit, she has a new conspiracy, a new culprit. You might be next."

"What reason would I have to kill Mandy?"

"If she knew half as much about your art dealing as I do, you'd have lots."

"Maybe." I stepped closer to Missy. "Then you've given up on Angela, have you? Whatever happened to 'me and Mom against the world'?"

"That was a long time ago. My mother is so over, Jack."

Melissa was wearing a maternity dress from one of the best SoHo shops, its long swoop disguising her distended stomach. When she turned her eyes to me, her blond hair shone radiantly around her face—almost blindingly.

"Did you try to cover for her back then?" I asked. "Is that why you played Paul Morse for a fool?"

"I don't know. Maybe."

"Or did Angela actually put you up to it? Did she teach you to shoot so that you could be her living weapon, her revenge?"

Melissa shrugged. "Could be. Or maybe I thought it all up myself. Maybe it was my idea from the first, and she was just the good mom trying to save me. Who knows? Who even cares anymore?"

"I do, Missy. Tell me."

"Tell you what?"

"Did you play me, too?"

"Oh, you mean did I make you have dirty thoughts, Uncle Jack?"

I couldn't answer.

"Well, maybe those naughty ideas were there in your head all along. Maybe you just got lucky and found me."

"You call that luck?"

"Most men would kill for it."

"Or die rather, like Paul."

"Oh? Was it really so bad, what we had? I never heard you complain."

"How could I? You worked together, you and your mother. To trap me, to make me helpless against you."

"Did we? You poor little man."

"All that girlish flirtation."

"Do you think I was kidding?"

"Or the night I undressed you. Did you call Angela from the bedroom after that? Did you tell her to phone me, so I'd come to you a second time?"

"Stop. You're losing it, Jack. What's wrong with you? With your mind?"

"You, Melissa."

She half-smiled, holding my eyes. "Really?" Her voice lowered. "Me now, love, or me back then?"

"You always."

Slowly, her face took on a distant cast. "It was all so, so long ago, darling. When I was just little. It seems like a dream, doesn't it? Let's not blame each other for dreaming."

"Your mother says there's a way I can know for sure."

Melissa paused, regarding me evenly.

"There's a way to know everything, Jack. If you want to search for it hard enough." She reached out and took my right hand, holding it warmly. "But do you?"

Without waiting for an answer, Missy placed my hand on the swell of her belly. She held it down, pressing lightly, until I detected a faint stirring beneath my palm, deep inside her.

"Can you feel it?"

"Yes."

"Say you can feel it, Jack."

"I can feel it."

"You can feel my babies?"

My glance betrayed my surprise.

"Twins, Jack, a boy and a girl. If they don't kill each other inside me first. I feel so nauseous, like a hungover drunk every morning."

"Don't say that."

"Should I lie for you—the way I did in the old days?"

"No."

"Say you can feel them, then."

"I can, yes. I do."

"Now tell me. Exactly how much do you want to know?"

Melissa put her other hand on top of the first, pressing my palm more firmly to her swollen womb.

"How much truth can you live with?"

I peered at her desperately, still my beautiful Missy.

"How much, Jack?"

I had no answer, then or now.

Epilogue

The new child, I suppose, is what we have to compensate us for failures and losses, for the early deaths of Mandy and Philip, for the slow demise of my Nathalie. Always and only the coming on and coming on and coming on of new life. Not as a corrective—since nothing in the past can be redeemed, least of all the unchanging dead—but as a fresh start, a perpetual beginning. Melissa is not living out the balance of her parents' lives; she is living her own. So, too, will her daughter. That is the terrible beauty of it.

One evening when Hogan and I were drinking at Pravda, I asked him about the security tape. He turned his head away and shrugged.

"Forget it," he said. "I made that up to see what Angela would say. She said plenty."

"And you wouldn't be saying that now just to protect me— the way you protected Melissa back then?"

"Come on, Jack. Do I seem like that kind of guy?"

Even now, those questions—Missy's, Hogan's—still come to me sometimes at night, when I hear the baby's cry below me, as piercing as a car alarm.

Don tells me we could soundproof the intervening floor and make the money back on tax deductions and an improved rental rate, once I decide to stop underwriting the increasingly affluent, ungrateful young family downstairs.

Not so large a family as expected, however. Melissa returned from the hospital with only one child. The male twin, she told me, vanished in the womb.

I didn't quite understand.

"He died and was absorbed," she said. "It's fairly common." Reclining on the cushions of my couch, Missy was having her first cup of chamomile at home after a painful delivery. "The pediatrician said not to feel bad at all. It just happens."

"Absorbed by what?" I asked

Missy sipped her tea. "By his sister, naturally."

No doubt Don is right. I might be happier without the sounds from below. But it is not a matter of reason. Melissa's daughter has spoken, long before words have been granted her—a message less of fear or discomfort than of sharp impatience. Or accusation. This child, this Jacqueline, is like ourselves reborn, fierce in her innocence, demanding the world at any price. Each night, her shrill voice rouses me from my imperfect sleep, and I lie patiently while the room composes itself around me in the dark.

So be it. Someday, soon perhaps, I will go down and retrieve the buried tape. Someday, if it exists, I will sit in my chair near the window and watch the grainy footage. And someday I will live alone, with only strangers in my building, steeped in full and awful certitude.

But for now, in these last nights together, I choose to lie awake and listen, attuned to the slightest change in the infant's wail down below, as Melissa, ever the attentive mother, rises and shuffles across the floorboards to her antique crib, my costly gift. With those few steps, I know, she delivers soothing words— mixed with the comfort of her ample breasts, her tepid milk—to the little monster howling for our SoHo sins.